The Apex Book of World SF

The Apex Book of World SF

Edited by
Lavie Tidhar

Apex Publications
Lexington, KY

THE APEX BOOK OF WORLD SF
ISBN: 978-0-9821596-3-7

Published by Apex Publications, LLC
PO Box 24323
Lexington, KY 40524

www.apexbookcompany.com

First Edition, September 2009

Printed in the United States of America

Introduction
By Lavie Tidhar

Lingua franca come and go. They are universal in that they allow people with different mother tongues to communicate with each other. In the time of the Roman Empire and far later, Latin was such a language, though it is now a dead tongue—read (rarely, and by scholars), but not spoken. French was once a major international language (we still use *par avion* for airmail, a remnant of that time). The rise of British power in the eighteenth and nineteenth centuries led to English becoming the new language of communication. British colonists had established themselves in North America (Canada and the U.S.), Australia, and South Africa, all now part of what is known as the English-speaking world. The language had permeated much further, however, particularly in former British colonies such as India and Malaysia and large parts of East Africa, often leading to a different, distinct form of English being used. English evolved differently in different parts of the world, borrowing from local languages, even creating different pidgin or Creole languages (as in the South Pacific islands of Melanesia) that borrowed the vocabulary of English to form new distinct languages.

Languages come and go.

But stories stay.

Many of the writers in this volume write in English. For many of them, English is a second or even third language. The prevalence of English today means that more and more writers from outside the English-speaking world are nevertheless choosing to speak in that language. Amongst the young generation of such writers I've included Jetse de Vries (the Netherlands), Aliette de Bodard (France), and Dean Francis Alfar (the Philippines), who have all published in the English-language magazines whilst speaking another language at home. Some writers included write in their native tongues, and were either able to translate their own work or find a translator to help them access the English world. Han Song and Yang Ping from China are in the former category; Zoran Živković and Mélanie

Fazi in the latter. Some writers are best known in their home countries. Tunku Halim's several story collections and novels enjoy popularity in Malaysia—he writes and publishes in English—whilst Guy Hasson's work, though written in English, appeared predominantly in Hebrew translations in Israel.

This is the first volume of what I hope will be a larger work. It is, of course, incomplete. There are no writers here from South America or Africa, for instance—a glaring omission. Speculative fiction stories from the Arab world (where they are enjoying a new popularity) are missing. So are many European and Asian writers. In editing such an anthology, I was guided by what had been published in English-language publications in the past several years, and by my own, if obviously limited, knowledge of, and contact with, other writers from around the world. I am hopeful that a second volume will allow me to redress some of this imbalance.

The stories in this book include science fiction, fantasy, and horror. Many utilise their authors' background to create, or rather reveal, worlds distinctly different from the templates that dominate these fields. Thai writer S.P. Somtow won the World Fantasy Award for his remarkable story "The Bird Catcher," a vivid tale set in both past and present Thailand, which opens this volume. Another World Fantasy Award winner, Zoran Živković, closes the book with "Compartments," an instant classic of European surrealism. In between, and in addition to the names mentioned above, we also have Croatian science fiction courtesy of Aleksandar Žiljak, a Fiji-set story from Australian writer (and Fiji resident) Kaaron Warren, homicidal cartoon characters from Israeli writer Nir Yaniv, revolutionary ghouls from Kristin Mandigma of the Philippines, and quiet horror from Palestinian writer Jamil Nasir; an entire world—or, rather, entire worlds—conjured up from the minds of people who may speak different languages, live in different countries, yet share a common love. I hope you enjoy their stories as much as I did.

Lavie Tidhar
Vientiane, 2009

Table of Contents

Table of Contents, cont.

To Wu Yan, for his help and enthusiasm

"THE BIRD CATCHER"

S.P. SOMTOW

S.P. Somtow is the pen name of Thai writer and composer Somtow Sucharitkul. His numerous awards include the 1981 John W. Campbell Award for Best New Writer and the World Fantasy Award for "The Bird Catcher," and he is the author of over forty books, including the classic *Vampire Junction* and *Jasmine Nights*. He is currently the artistic director of the Bangkok Opera.

There was this other boy in the internment camp. His name was Jim. After the war, he made something of a name for himself. He wrote books, even a memoir of the camp that got turned into a Spielberg movie. It didn't turn out that gloriously for me.

My grandson will never know what it's like to be consumed by hunger, hunger that is heartache: hunger that can propel you past insanity. But I know. I've been there. So has that boy Jim; that's why I really don't envy him his Spielberg movie.

After the war, my mother and I were stranded in China for a few more years. She was penniless, a lady journalist in a time when lady journalists only covered church bazaars, a single mother at a time when "bastard" was more than a bad word.

You might think that at least we had each other, but my mother and I never intersected. Not as mother and son, not even as Americans awash in great events and oceans of Asian faces. We were both loners. We were both vulnerable.

That's how I became the boogieman's friend.

He's long dead now, but they keep him, you know, in the Museum of Horrors. Once in a generation, I visit him. Yesterday, I took my grandson, Corey, just as I took his father before him.

The destination stays the same, but the road changes with every generation. The first time I had gone by boat, along the quiet back canals of the old city. Now there was an expressway. The toll was forty baht—a dollar—a month's salary that would have been, back in the '50s, in old Siam.

My son's in love with Bangkok: the insane skyline, the high tech blending with the low tech, the skyscraper shaped like a giant robot, the palatial shopping malls, the kinky sex bars, the bootleg software arcades, the whole tossed salad. And he doesn't mind the heat. He's a big-time entrepreneur here, owns a taco chain.

I live in Manhattan. It's quieter.

I can be anonymous. I can be alone. I can nurse my hunger in secret.

Christmases, though, I go to Bangkok; this Christmas, my

grandson's eleventh birthday, I told my son it was time. He nodded and told me to take the chauffeur for the day.

So, to get to the place, you zigzag through the world's raunchiest traffic, then you fly along this madcap figure-of-eight expressway, cross the river where stone demons stand guard on the parapets of the Temple of Dawn, and then you're suddenly in this sleazy alley. Vendors hawk bowls of soup and pickled guavas. The directions are on a handwritten placard attached to a street sign with duct tape.

It's the Police Museum, upstairs from the local morgue. One wall is covered with photographs of corpses. That's not part of the museum; it's a public service display for people with missing family members to check if any of them have turned up dead. Corey didn't pay attention to the photographs; he was busy with Pokémon.

Upstairs, the feeling changed. The stairs creaked. The upstairs room was garishly lit. Glass cases along the walls were filled with medical oddities, two-headed babies and the like, each one in a jar of formaldehyde, each one meticulously labelled in Thai and English. The labels weren't printed, mind you. Handwritten. There was definitely a middle school show-and-tell feel about the exhibits. No air-conditioning. And no more breeze from the river like in the old days; skyscrapers had stifled the city's breath.

There was a uniform, sick-yellow tinge to all the displays...the neutral cream paint was edged with yellow, the deformed livers, misshapen brains, tumorous embryos all floating in a dull yellow fluid, the heaps of dry bones an orange-yellow, the rows of skulls yellowing in the cracks...and then there were the young novices, shaven-headed little boys in yellow robes, staring in a heat-induced stupor as their mentor droned on about the transience of all existence, the quintessence of Buddhist philosophy.

And then there was Si Ui.

He had his own glass cabinet, like a phone booth, in the middle of the room. Naked. Desiccated. A mummy. Skinny. Mud-coloured, from the embalming process, I think. A sign (handwritten, of course) explained who he was. See Ui. Devourer of children's livers in the 1950s. My grandson reads Thai more fluently than I do. He sounded out the name right away.

Si Sui Sae Ung.

"It's the boogieman, isn't it?" Corey said. But he showed little more than a passing interest. It was the year Pokémon Gold and Silver came out. So many new monsters to catch, so many names to learn.

"He hated cages," I said.

"Got him!" Corey squealed. Then, not looking up at the dead man, "I know who he was. They did a documentary on him. Can we go now?"

"Didn't your maid tell you stories at night? To frighten you? 'Be a good boy, or Si Ui will eat your liver?'"

"Gimme a break, Grandpa. I'm too old for that shit." He paused. Still wouldn't look up at him. There were other glass booths in the room, other mummified criminals: a serial rapist down the way. But Si Ui was the star of the show. "Okay," Corey said, "she did try to scare me once. Well, I was like five, okay? Si Ui. You watch out, he'll eat your liver, be a good boy now. Sure, I heard that before. Well, he's not gonna eat my liver now, is he? I mean, that's probably not even him; it's probably like wax or something."

He smiled at me. The dead man did not.

"I knew him," I said. "He was my friend."

"I get it!" Corey said, back to his Gameboy. "You're like me in this Pokémon game. You caught a monster once. And tamed him. You caught the most famous monster in Thailand."

"And tamed him?" I shook my head. "No, not tamed."

"Can we go to McDonald's now?"

"You're hungry."

"I could eat the world!"

"After I tell you the whole story."

"You're gonna talk about the Chinese camp again, Grandpa? And that kid Jim, and the Spielberg movie?"

"No, Corey, this is something I've never told you about before. But I'm telling you so when I'm gone, you'll know to tell your son. And your grandson."

"Okay, Grandpa."

And finally, tearing himself away from the video game, he willed himself to look.

The dead man had no eyes; he could not stare back.

He hated cages. But his whole life was a long imprisonment...without a cage, he did not even exist.

Listen, Corey. I'll tell you how I met the boogieman.

Imagine I'm eleven years old, same as you are now, running wild on a leaky ship crammed with coolies. They're packed into the lower deck. We can't afford the upper deck, but when they saw we were white, they waved us on up without checking our tickets. It looks more interesting down there. And the food's got to be better. I can smell a Chinese breakfast. That oily fried bread, so crunchy on the outside, dripping with pig fat...yeah.

It's hot. It's boring. Mom's on the prowl for a job or a husband, whichever comes first. Everyone's fleeing the communists. We're some of the last white people to get out of China.

Someone's got a portable charcoal stove on the lower deck, and there's a toothless old woman cooking congee, fanning the stove. A whiff of opium in the air blends with the rich gingery broth. Everyone down there's clustered around the food. Except this one man. Harmless-looking. Before the Japs came, we had a gardener who looked like that. Shirtless, thin, by the railing. Stiller than a statue. And a bird on the railing. Also unmoving. The other coolies are ridiculing him, making fun of his Hakka accent, calling him simpleton.

I watch him.

"Look at the idiot," the toothless woman says. "Hasn't said a word since we left Swatow."

The man has his arms stretched out, his hands cupped. Frozen. Concentrated. I suddenly realise I've snuck down the steps myself, pushed my way through all the Chinese around the cooking pot, and I'm halfway there. Mesmerised. The man is stalking the bird, the boy stalking the man. I try not to breathe as I creep up.

He pounces. Wrings the bird's neck; one swift liquid movement, a twist of the wrist, and he's already plucking the feathers with the other hand, ignoring the death spasMs And I'm real close now. I can smell him. Mud and sweat. Behind him, the open sea. On the deck, the feathers, a bloody snowfall.

He bites off the head and I hear the skull crunch.

I scream. He whirls. I try to cover it up with a childish giggle.

He speaks in a monotone. Slowly. Sounding out each syllable, but he seems to have picked up a little pidgin. "Little white boy. You go upstairs. No belong here."

"I go where I want. They don't care."

He offers me a raw wing.

"Boy hungry?"

"Man hungry?"

I fish in my pocket, find half a liverwurst sandwich. I hold it out to him. He shakes his head. We both laugh a little. We've both known this hunger that consumes you; the agony of China is in our bones.

I say, "Me and Mom are going to Siam. On account of my dad getting killed by the Japs and we can't live in Shanghai anymore. We were in a camp and everything." He stares blankly so I bark in Japanese, like the guards used to. And he goes crazy.

He mutters to himself in Hakka, which I don't understand that well, but it's something like "Don't look 'em in the eye. They chop off your head. You stare at the ground, they leave you alone." He is chewing away at raw bird flesh the whole time. He adds in English, "Si Ui no like Japan man."

"Makes two of us," I say.

I've seen too much. Before the internment camp, there was Nanking. Mom was gonna do an article about the atrocities. I saw them. You think a two-year-old doesn't see anything? She carried me on her back the whole time, papoose-style.

When you've seen a river clogged with corpses, when you've looked at piles of human heads, human livers roasting on spits, and women raped and set on fire, well, Santa and the Tooth Fairy just don't cut it. I pretended about the Tooth Fairy, though, for a long time. Because, in the camp, the ladies would pool their resources to bribe Mr Tooth Fairy Sakamoto for a little piece of fish.

"I'm Nicholas," I say.

"Si Ui." I don't know if it's his name or something in Hakka.

I hear my mother calling from the upper deck. I turn from the strange man, the raw bird's blood trailing from his lips. "Gotta go." I turn to him, pointing at my chest, and I say, "Nicholas."

Even the upper deck is cramped. It's hotter than Shanghai, hotter even than the internment camp. We share a cabin with two Catholic priests who let us hide out there after suspecting we didn't have tickets.

Night doesn't get any cooler, and the priests snore. I'm down to a pair of shorts and I still can't sleep. So I slip away. It's easy. Nobody cares. Millions of people have been dying and I'm just some skinny kid on the wrong side of the ocean. Me and my mom have been adrift for as long as I can remember.

The ship groans and clanks. I take the steep metal stairwell down to the coolies' level. I'm wondering about the bird catcher. Down below, the smells are a lot more comforting. The smell of sweat and soy-stained clothing masks the odour of the sea. The charcoal stove is still burning. The old woman is simmering some stew. Maybe something magical—a bit of snake's blood to revive someone's limp dick, crushed tiger bones or powdered rhinoceros horn to heal pretty much anything. People are starving, but you can still get those kinds of ingredients. I'm eleven, and I already know too much.

They are sleeping every which way, but it's easy for me to step over them, even in the dark. The camp was even more crowded than this, and a misstep could get you hurt. There's a little bit of light from the little clay stove.

I don't know what I'm looking for. Just to be alone, I guess. I can be more alone in a crowd of Chinese than up there. Mom says things will be better in Siam. I don't know.

I've threaded my way past all of them. And I'm leaning against the railing. There isn't much moonlight. It's probably past midnight but the metal is still hot. There's a warm wind, though, and it dries my sweat. China's too far away to see, and I can't even imagine Boston anymore.

He pounces.

Leather hands rasp my shoulders. Strong hands. Not big, but I can't squirm out of their grip. The hands twirl me around and I'm looking into Si Ui's eyes. The moonlight is in them. I'm scared. I don't know why, really, all I have to do is scream and they'll pull him off me. But I can't get the scream out.

I look into his eyes and I see fire. A burning village. Maybe it's just the opium haze that clings to this deck, making me feel all weird inside, seeing things. And the sounds. I think it must be the whispering of the sea, but it's not, it's voices. *Hungry, you little chink?* And those leering, bucktoothed faces. Like comic book Japs. Barking. The fire blazes. And then, abruptly, it dissolves. And there's a kid standing in the smoky ruins. Me. And I'm holding out a liverwurst sandwich. Am I really than skinny, that pathetic? But the vision fades. And Si Ui's eyes become empty. Soulless.

"Si Ui catch anything," he says. "See, catch bird, catch boy. All same." And smiles, a curiously captivating smile.

"As long as you don't eat me," I say.

"Si Ui never eat Nicholas," he says. "Nicholas friend."

Friend? In the burning wasteland of China, an angel holding out a liverwurst sandwich? It makes me smile. And angry. The anger hits me so suddenly that I don't even have time to figure out what it is. It's the war, the maggots in the millet, the commandant kicking me across the yard, but more than that; it's my mom, clinging to her journalist fantasies whilst I dug for earthworms, letting my dad walk out to his death. I'm crying and the birdcatcher is stroking my cheek, saying "You no cry now. Soon go back America. No-one cry there." And it's the first time someone has touched me with some kind of tenderness in, in, in, I dunno—since before the invasion. Because mom doesn't hug, she kind of encircles, and her arms are like the bars of a cage.

So, I'm thinking this will be my last glimpse of Si Ui. It's in the harbour at Klong Toei. You know, where Anna landed in *The King and I.* And where Joseph Conrad landed in *Youth.*

So all these coolies, and all these trapped Americans and

Europeans, they're all stampeding down the gangplank, with cargo being hoisted, workmen trundling, fleets of those bicycle pedicabs called *samlors*, itinerant merchants with bales of silk and fruits that seem to have hair or claws, and then there's the smell that socks you in the face, gasoline and jasmine and decay and incense. Pungent salt squid drying on racks. The ever-present fish sauce, blending with the odour of fresh papaya and pineapple and coconut and human sweat.

And my mother's off and running, with me barely keeping up, chasing after some waxed-moustache British doctor guy with one of those accents you think is a joke until you realise that's really how they talk.

So I'm just carried along by the mob.

"You buy bird, little boy?" I look up. It's a wall of sparrows, each one in a cramped wooden cage. Rows and rows of cages, stacked up from the concrete high as a man, more cages hanging from wires, stuffed into the branch-crooks of a mango tree. I see others buying the birds for a few coins, releasing them into the air.

"Why are they doing that?"

"Good for your karma. Buy bird, set bird free, shorten your suffering in your next life."

"Swell," I say.

Further off, the vendor's boy is catching them, coaxing them back into cages. That's got to be wrong, I'm thinking as the boy comes back with ten little cages hanging on each arm. The birds haven't gotten far. They can barely fly. Answering my unspoken thought, the bird seller says, "Oh, we clip wings. Must make living too, you know."

That's when I hear a sound like the thunder of a thousand wings. I think I must be dreaming. I look up. The crowd has parted. And there's a skinny little shirtless man standing in the clearing, his arms spread wide like a Jesus statue, only you can barely see a square inch of him because he's all covered in sparrows. They're perched all over his arms like they're telegraph wires or something, and squatting on his head, and clinging to his baggy homespun shorts with their claws. And the birds are all chattering at once, drowning out the cacophony of the mob.

Si Ui looks at me. And in his eyes I see...bars. Bars of light, maybe. Prison bars. The man's trying to tell me something. *I'm trapped.*

The crowd that had parted all of sudden comes together and he's gone. I wonder if I'm the only one who saw. I wonder if it's just another after-effect of the opium that clogged the walkways on the ship.

But it's too late to wonder; my mom has found me, she's got me by the arm and she's yanking me back into the stream of people. And in the next few weeks I don't think about Si Ui at all. Until he shows up, just like that, in a village called Thapsakae.

After the museum, I took Corey to Baskin-Robbins and popped into Starbucks next door for a frappuccino. Visiting the boogieman is a draining thing. I wanted to let him down easy. But Corey didn't want to let go right away.

"Can we take a boat ride or something?" he said. "You know I never get to come to this part of town." It's true. The traffic in Bangkok is so bad that they sell little car toilets so you can go whilst you're stuck at a red light for an hour. This side of town, Thonburi, the old capital, is a lot more like the past. But no-one bothers to come. The traffic, they say, always the traffic.

We left the car by a local pier, hailed a river taxi, just told him to go, anywhere, told him we wanted to ride around. Overpaid him. It served me right for being me, an old white guy in baggy slacks, with a backward-facing-Yankees-hat-wearing blond kid in tow.

When you leave the river behind, there's a network of canals, called *klongs,* that used to be the arteries and capillaries of the old city. In Bangkok proper, they've all been filled in. But not here. The further from the main waterway we floated, the further back in time. Here the klongs were fragrant with jasmine, with stilted houses rearing up behind thickets of banana and bamboo. And I was remembering more.

Rain jars by the landing docks...lizards basking in the sun...young boys leaping into the water.

"The water was a lot clearer," I told my grandson. "And the swimmers weren't wearing those little trunks—they were naked." Recently, fearing to offend the sensibilities of tourists, the Thai government made a fuss about little boys skinny-dipping along the tourist riverboat routes. But the river is so polluted now, one wonders what difference it makes.

They were bobbing up and down around the boat. Shouting in fractured English. Wanting a lick of Corey's Baskin-Robbins. When Corey spoke to them in Thai, they swam away. Tourists who speak the language aren't tourists anymore.

"You used to do that, huh, Grandpa?"

"Yes," I said.

"I like the sports club better. The water's clean. And they make a mean chicken sandwich at the poolside bar."

I only went to the sports club once in my life. A week after we landed in Bangkok, a week of sleeping in a pew at a missionary church, a week wringing out the same clothes and ironing them over and over.

"I never thought much of the sports club," I said.

"Oh, Grandpa, you're such a prole." One of his father's words, I thought, smiling.

"Well, I did grow up in *Red* China," I said.

"Yeah," he said. "So what was it like, the sports club?"

...a little piece of England in the midst of all this tropical stuff. The horse races. Cricket. My mother has a rendezvous with the doctor, the one she's been flirting with on the ship. They have tea and crumpets. They talk about the Bangkok Chinatown riots, and about money. I am reading a battered EC comic that I found in the reading room.

"Well, if you don't mind going native," the doctor says, "there's a clinic, down south a bit; pay wouldn't be much, and you'll have to live with the benighted buggers, but I daresay you'll cope."

"Oh, I'll go native," Mom says, "as long as I can keep writing. I'll do anything for that. I'd give you a blowjob if that's what it takes."

"Heavens," says the doctor. "More tea?"

* * * *

And so, a month later, we come to a fishing village nestled in the western crook of the Gulf of Siam, and I swear it's paradise. There's a village school taught by monks and a little clinic where Mom works, dressing wounds, jabbing penicillin into people's buttocks; I think she's working on a novel. That doctor she was flirting with got her this job because she speaks Chinese, and the village is full of Chinese immigrants, smuggled across the sea, looking for some measure of freedom.

Thapsakae—it rhymes with Tupperware—it's always warm, but never stifling like in Bangkok, always a breeze from the unseen sea, shaking the ripe coconuts from the trees...a town of stilted dwellings, a tiny main street with storefront row houses, fields of neon green rice as far as the eye can see, lazy water buffalo wallowing, and always the canals running alongside the half-paved road, women beating their wet laundry with rocks in the dawn, boys diving in the noonday heat. The second day I'm there, I meet these kids, Lek and Sombun. They're my age. I can't understand a word they're saying at first. I'm watching them, leaning against a dragon-glazed rain jar, as they shuck off their school uniforms and leap in. They're laughing a lot, splashing; one time they're throwing a catfish back and forth like it's some kind of volleyball, but they're like fishes themselves, silvery brown sleek things chattering in a singsong language. And I'm alone, like I was at the camp, flinging stones into the water. Except I'm not scared like I was there. There's no time I have to be home. I can reach into just about any thicket and pluck out something good to eat: bananas, mangoes, little pink sour apples. My shorts are all torn—I still only have one pair—and my shirt is stained with the juices of exotic fruits, and I let my hair grow as long as I want.

Today I'm thinking of the birds.

You buy a bird to free yourself from the cage of karma. You free the bird, but its wings are clipped and he's inside another cage, a cage circumscribed by the fact that he can't fly far. And the boy that catches him is in another cage, apprenticed to that vendor, unable to fly free. Cages within cages within cages. I've been in a cage before; one time in the camp they hung me up in one in the commandant's office and told me to sing.

Here, I don't feel caged at all.

The Thai kids have noticed me and they pop up from the depths right next to me, staring curiously. They're not hostile. I don't know what they're saying, but I know I'm soon going to absorb this musical language. Meanwhilst, they're splashing me, daring me to dive in, and in the end I throw off my filthy clothes and I'm in the water and it's clear and warm and full of fish. And we're laughing and chasing each other. And they do know a few words of English; they've picked it up in that village school, where the monks have been ramming a weird antiquated English phrasebook down their throats.

But later, after we dry off in the sun and they try to show me how to ride a water buffalo, later we sneak across the *gailan* field and I see him again. The birdcatcher, I mean. Gailan is a Chinese vegetable like broccoli, only without the bushy part. The Chinese immigrants grow it here. They all work for this one rich Chinese man named Tae Pak, the one who had the refugees shipped to this town as cheap labour.

"You want to watch TV?" Sombun asks me.

I haven't had much of a chance to see TV. He takes me by the hand and pulls me along, with Lek behind him, giggling. Night has fallen. It happens really suddenly in the tropics, boom and it's dark. In the distance, past a wall of bamboo trees, we see glimmering lights. Tae Pak has electricity. Not that many private homes have. Mom and I use kerosene lamps at night. I've never been to his house, but I know we're going there. Villagers are zeroing in on the house now, walking surefootedly in the moonlight. The stench of night-blooming jasmine is almost choking in the compound. A little shrine to the Mother of Mercy stands by the entrance, and ahead we see what passes for a mansion here; the wooden stilts and the thatched roof with the pointed eaves, like everyone else's house, but spread out over three sides of a quadrangle, and in the centre a ruined pagoda whose origin no-one remembers.

The usual pigs and chickens are running around in the space under the house, but the stairway up to the veranda is packed with people, kids mostly, and they're all gazing upward.

The object of their devotion is a television set, the images on it ghostly, the sound staticky and in Thai in any case, but I recognise the show; it's *I Love Lucy*, and I'm just staring and staring. Sombun pushes me up the steps. I barely remember to remove my sandals and step in the trough at the bottom of the steps to wash the river mud off my feet. It's really true. I can't understand a word of it but it's still funny. The kids are laughing along with the laugh track.

That's when I see Si Ui. I point at him. I try to attract his attention, but he, too, sitting cross-legged on the veranda, is riveted to the screen. And when I try to whisper to Sombun that hey, I know this guy, what a weird coincidence, Sombun just whispers back, "*Jek, jek,*" which I know is a putdown word for a Chinaman.

"I know him," I whisper. "He catches birds. And eats them. Alive." I try to attract Si Ui's attention. But he won't look at me. He's too busy staring at Lucille Ball. I'm a little bit afraid to look at him directly, scared of what his eyes might disclose, our shared and brutal past.

Lek, whose nickname just means "tiny," shudders.

"Jek, jek," Sombun says. The laugh track kicks in.

Everything has changed now that I know he's here. On my reed mat, under the mosquito nets every night, I toss and turn, and I see things. I don't think they're dreams. I think it's like the time I looked into Si Ui's eyes and saw the fire. I see a Chinese boy running through a field of dead people. It's sort of all in black and white, and he's screaming, and behind him a village is burning.

At first it's the Chinese boy but somehow it's me, too, and I'm running, with my bare feet squishing into dead men's bowels, running over a sea of blood and shit. And I run right into someone's arms. Hard. The comic-book Japanese villain face. A human heart, still beating, in his hand.

"Hungry, you little chink?" he says.

Little chink. Little jek.

Intestines are writhing up out of disembowelled bodies like snakes. I saw a lot of disembowelled Japs. Their officers did it in groups, quietly, stony-faced. The honourable thing to do.

I'm screaming myself awake. And then, from the veranda, maybe, I hear the tap of my mom's battered typewriter, an old Hermes she bought in the Sunday market in Bangkok for a hundred baht.

I crawl out of bed. It's already dawn.

"Hi, Mom," I say as I breeze past her, an old *phakhomah* wrapped around my loins.

"Wow. It talks."

"Mom, I'm going over to Sombun's house to play."

"You're getting the hang of the place, I take it."

"Yeah."

"Pick up some food, Nicholas."

"Okay." Around here, a dollar will feed me and her three square meals. But it won't take away the other hunger.

Another lazy day of running myself ragged, gorging on papaya and coconut milk, another day in paradise.

It's time to meet the serpent, I decide.

Sombun tells me someone's been killed, and we sneak over to the police station. Si Ui is there, sitting at a desk, staring at a wall. I think he's just doing some kind of alien registration thing. He has a Thai interpreter, the same toothless woman I saw on the boat. And a policeman is writing stuff down in a ledger.

There's a woman sitting on a bench, rocking back and forth. She's talking to everyone in sight. Even me and Sombun.

Sombun whispers, "That woman Daeng. Daughter die."

Daeng mumbles, "My daughter. By the railway tracks. All she was doing was running down the street for an ice coffee. Oh, my terrible karma." She collars a passing inspector. "Help me. My daughter. Strangled, raped."

"That inspector Jed," Sombun whispers to me. "Head of the whole place."

Inspector Jed is being polite, compassionate, and efficient at the same time. I like him. My mom should hang out with people like that instead of the losers who are just looking for a quick lay.

The woman continues muttering to herself. "Nit, nit, nit, nit, nit," she says. That must be the girl's name. They all have nicknames like that. Nit means "tiny," like Lek. "Dead, strangled," she says. "And this town is supposed to be heaven on earth. The sea, the palm trees, the sun always bright. This town has a dark heart."

Suddenly, Si Ui looks up. Stares at her as though remembering something. Daeng is sobbing. And the policeman who's been interviewing him says, "Watch yourself, chink. Everyone smiles here. Food falls from the trees. If a little girl's murdered, they'll file it away; they won't try to find out who did it. Because this is a perfect place, and no-one gets murdered. We all love each other here...you little jek."

Si Ui has this weird look in his eye. Mesmerised. My mother looks that way sometimes—when a man catches her eye and she's zeroing in for the kill. The woman's mumbling that she's going to go be a nun now, she has nothing left to live for.

"Watch your back, jek," says the policeman. He's trying, I realise, to help this man, who he probably thinks is some kind of village idiot. "Someone'll murder you just for being a stupid little chink. And no-one will bother to find out who did it."

"Si Ui hungry," says Si Ui.

I realise that I speak his language, and my friends do not.

"Si Ui!" I call out to him.

He freezes in his tracks, and slowly turns, and I look into his eyes for the second time, and I know that it was no illusion before.

Somehow we've seen through each other's eyes.

I am misfit kid in a picture-perfect town with a dark heart, but I understand what he's saying, because though I look different I come from where he comes from. I've experienced what it's like to be Chinese. You can torture them and kill them by millions, like the Japs did, and still they endure. They just shake it off. They've outlasted everyone so far—and will till the end of time. Right now in Siam they're the coolies and the labourers, and soon they're going to end up owning the whole country. They endure. I saw their severed heads piled up like battlements and the river choked with their corpses, and they outlasted it all.

These Thai kids will never understand.

"Si Ui hungry!" the man cries.

That afternoon, I slip away from my friends at the river, and I go to the gailan field where I know he works. He never acknowledges my presence, but later, he strides further and further from the house of his rich patron toward a more densely wooded area past the fields. It's all banana trees, the little bananas that have seeds in them—you chew the whole banana and spit out the seeds, rat-tat-tat, like a machine gun. There's bamboo, too, and the jasmine bushes that grow wild, and mango trees. Si Ui doesn't talk to me, doesn't look back, but somehow I know I'm supposed to follow him.

And I do.

Through the thicket, into a private clearing, the ground overgrown with weeds, the whole thing surrounded by vegetation, and in the middle of it a tumbledown house, the thatch unpatched in places, the stilts decaying and carved with old graffiti. The steps are lined with wooden cages. There's birdshit all over the decking, over the wooden railings, even around the foot trough. Birds are chattering from the cages, from the air around us. The sun has been searing and sweat is running down my face, my chest, soaking my phakhomah.

We don't go up into the house. Instead, Si Ui leads me past it, toward a clump of rubber trees. He doesn't talk, just keeps beckoning me, the curious way they have of beckoning, palm pointing toward the ground.

I feel dizzy. He's standing there. Swaying a little. Then he makes a little clucking, chattering sound, barely opening his lips. The birds are gathering. He seems to know their language. They're answering him. The chirping around us grows to a screeching cacophony. Above, they're circling. They're blocking out the sun, and it's suddenly chilly. I'm scared now. But I don't dare say anything. In the camp, if you said anything, they always hurt you. Si Ui keeps beckoning me: nearer, come nearer. And I creep up. The birds are shrieking. And now they're swooping down, landing, gathering at Si Ui's feet, their heads moving to and fro in a regular rhythm, like they're listening to...a heartbeat. Si Ui's heartbeat. My own.

An image flashes into my head. A little Chinese boy hiding in a closet, listening to footsteps, breathing nervously.

He's poised. Like a snake, coiled up, ready to pounce. And then, without warning, he drops to a crouch, pulls a bird out of the sea of birds, puts it to his lips, snaps its neck with his teeth, and the blood just spurts all over his bare skin, over the homespun wrapped around his loins, an impossible crimson. And he smiles. And throws me the bird.

I recoil. He laughs again when I let the dead bird slip through my fingers. Pounces again and gets me another.

"Birds are easy to trap," he says to me in Chinese, "easy as children, sometimes; you just have to know their language." He rips one open, pulls out a slippery liver. "You don't like them raw, I know," he says, "but come, little brother, we'll make a fire."

He waves his hand, dismisses the birds; all at once they're gone and the air is steaming again. In the heat, we make a bonfire and grill the birds' livers over it. He has become, I guess, my friend. "I didn't rape her," he says.

Then he talks about fleeing through the rice fields. There's a war going on around him. I guess he's my age in his storey, but in Chinese they don't use past or future tenses; everything happens in a kind of abstract now. I don't understand his dialect that well, but what he says matches the waking dreams I've had, tossing and turning under that mosquito net. There was a Japanese soldier. He seemed kinder than the others. They were roasting something over a fire. He was handing Si Ui a morsel. A piece of liver.

Hungry, little chink?

Hungry. I understand hungry.

Human liver.

In Asia they believe that everything that will ever happen has already happened. Is that what Si Ui is doing with me, forging a karmic chain with his own childhood, the Japanese soldier?

There's so much I want to ask him, but I can't form the

thoughts, especially not in Chinese. I'm young, Corey. I'm not thinking karmic cycles. What are you trying to ask me?

"I thought Si Ui ate children's livers," said Corey. "Not some dumb old birds'."

We were still on the klong, turning back now toward civilization; on either side of us were crumbling temples, old houses with pointed eaves, each one with its little totemic spirit house by the front gate, pouring sweet incense into the air, the air itself dripping with humidity. But ahead, just beyond a turn in the klong, a series of eighty-story condos reared up over the banana trees.

"Yes, he did," I said, "and we'll get to that part, in time. Don't be impatient."

"Grandpa, Si Ui ate children's livers. Just like Dracula bit women in the neck. Well, like, it's the main part of the story. How long are you gonna make me wait?"

"So you know more than you told me before. About the maid trying to scare you one time, when you were five."

"Well, yeah, Grandpa, I saw the miniseries. It never mentioned you."

"I'm part of the secret history, Corey."

"Cool." He contemplated his Pokémon, but decided not to go back to monster trapping. "When we get back to the Bangkok side, can I get another caramel frappuccino at Starbucks?"

"Decaf," I said.

That evening I go back to the house and find Mom in bed with Jed, the police detective. Suddenly, I don't like Jed anymore.

She barely looks up at me; Jed is pounding away and oblivious to it all; I don't know if Mom really knows I'm there, or thinks me just a shadow flitting beyond the mosquito netting. I know why she's doing it. She'll say that it's all about getting information for this great novel she's planning to write, or research for a major magazine article, but the truth is that it's about survival; it's no different from that concentration camp.

I think she finally does realise I'm there; she mouths the words "I'm sorry" and then turns back to her work. At that moment, I hear someone tapping at the entrance, and I crawl over the squeaky floor planks, Siamese style (children learn to move around on their knees so that their head isn't accidentally higher than someone of higher rank) to see Sombun on the step.

"Can you come out?" he says. "There's a *ngaan wat.*"

I don't know what that is, but I don't want to stay in the house. So I throw on a shirt and go with him. I soon find out that a ngaan wat is a temple fair, sort of a cross between a carnival and a church bazaar and a theatrical night out.

Even from a mile or two away we hear the music, the tinkling of marimbas and the thud of drums, the wail of the Javanese oboe. By the time we get there, the air is drenched with the fragrance of pickled guava, peanut pork skewers, and green papaya tossed in fish sauce. A makeshift dance floor has been spread over the muddy ground and there are dancers with rhinestone court costumes and pagoda hats, their hands bent back at an impossible angle. There's a Chinese opera troupe like I've seen in Shanghai, glittering costumes, masks painted on the faces in garish colours, boys dressed as monkeys leaping to and fro; the Thai and the Chinese striving to outdo each other in noise and brilliance. And on a grill, being tended by a fat woman, pigeons are barbecuing, each one on a mini-spear of steel. And I'm reminded of the open fire and the sizzling of half-plucked feathers.

"You got money?" Sombun says. He thinks that all *farangs* are rich. I fish in my pocket and pull out a few *saleungs*, and we stuff ourselves with pan-fried *roti* swimming in sweet condensed milk.

The thick juice is dripping from our lips. This really is paradise: the music, the mingled scents, the warm wind. Then I see Si Ui. There aren't any birds nearby, not unless you count the pigeons charring on the grill. Si Ui is muttering to himself, but I understand Chinese, and he's saying, over and over again, "Si Ui hungry, Si Ui hungry." He says it in a little voice and it's almost like baby talk.

We wander over to the Chinese opera troupe. They're doing something about monkeys invading heaven and stealing the apples of the gods. All these kids are somersaulting, tumbling, cartwheeling, and climbing up onto each other's shoulders. There's a little girl, nine or ten maybe, and she's watching the show. And Si Ui is watching her. And I'm watching him.

I've seen her before, know her from that night we squatted on the veranda staring at American TV shows. Was Si Ui watching her even then? I try to remember. Can't be sure. Her name's Juk.

Those Chinese cymbals, with their annoying "boing-boing-boing" sound, are clashing. A man is intoning in a weird sing-song. The monkeys are leaping. Suddenly I see, in Si Ui's face, the same expression I saw on the ship. He's utterly still inside, utterly quiet, beyond feeling. The war did that to him. I know. Just like it made Mom into a whore and me into...I don't know...a bird without a nesting place...a lost boy.

And then I get this...irrational feeling. That the little girl is a bird, chirping to herself, hopping along the ground, not noticing the stalker.

So many people here. So much jangling, so much laughter. The town's dilapidated pagodas sparkle with reflected colours, like stone Christmas trees. Chinese opera rings in my ears. I look away, and when I look back they are gone—Sombun is preoccupied, playing with a two-saleung top that he's just bought. Somehow, I feel impelled to follow. To stalk the stalker.

I duck behind a fruit stand, and then I see a golden deer. It's a toy, on four wheels, pulled along by a string. I can't help following it with my eyes as it darts between hampers full of rambutans and pomelos.

The deer darts toward the cupped hands of the little girl. I see her disappear into the crowd, but then I see Si Ui's face too; you can't mistake the cold fire in his eyes.

She follows the toy. Si Ui pulls. I follow, too, not really knowing why it's so fascinating. The toy deer weaves through the ocean of feet. Bare feet of monks and novices, their saffron robes skimming the mud. Feet in rubber flip-flops, in the wooden sandals the jek call *kiah.* I hear a voice: *Juk, Juk!* And I know there's someone else looking for the girl, too. It's a weird quartet, each one in the sequence known only to the next one. I can see Si Ui now, his head bobbing up and down in the throng because he's a little taller than the average Thai even though he's so skinny. He's intent. Concentrated. He seems to be on wheels himself; he glides through the crowd like the toy deer does. The woman's voice, calling for Juk, is faint and distant; she hears it, I'm sure, but she's ignoring her mother or her big sister. I only hear it because my senses are sharp now; it's like the rest of the temple fair's all out of focus, all blurry, and there's just the four of us. I see the woman, it must be a mother or aunt, too old for a sister, collaring a roti vendor and asking if he's seen the child. The vendor shakes his head, laughs. And suddenly we're all next to the pigeon barbecue, and if the woman were only looking in the right place she'd see the little girl, giggling as she clambers through the forest of legs, as the toy zigzags over the dirt aisles. And now the deer has been yanked right up to Si Ui's feet. And the girl crawls all the way after it, seizes it, laughs, looks solemnly up at the face of the Chinaman—

"It's him! It's the chink!" Sombun is pointing, laughing. I'd forgotten he was even with me.

Si Ui is startled. His concentration snaps. He lashes out. There's a blind rage in his eyes. Dead pigeons are flying everywhere.

"Hungry!" he screams in Chinese. "Si Ui hungry!"

He turns. There is a cloth stall nearby. Suddenly he and the girl are gone amid a flurry of billowing sarongs. And I follow.

Incense in the air, stinging my eyes. A shaman gets possessed in a side aisle, his followers hushed. A flash of red. A red sarong, embroidered with gold, a year's wages, twisting through the crowd. I follow. I see the girl's terrified eyes. I see Si Ui with the red cloth wrapped around his arms, around the girl. I see something glistening, a knife maybe. And no-one sees. No-one but me.

Juk! Juk!

I've lost Sombun somewhere. I don't care. I thread my way through a bevy of *ramwong* dancers, through men dressed as women and women dressed as men. Fireworks are going off.

There's an ancient wall, the temple boundary, crumbling...and the trail of red funnels into black night...and I'm standing on the other side of the wall, watching Si Ui ride away in a pedicab, into the night. There's moonlight on him. He's saying something; even from far off I can read his lips. He's saying it over and over: *Si Ui hungry, Si Ui hungry.*

So they find her by the side of the road with her internal organs missing. And I'm there, too, all the boys are at dawn, peering down, daring each other to touch. It's not a rape or anything, they tell us. Nothing like the other girl. Someone has seen a cowherd near the site, and he's the one they arrest. He's an Indian, you see. If there's anyone the locals despise more than the Chinese, it's the Indians. They have a saying: if you see a snake and an Indian, kill the *babu.*

Later, in the market, Detective Jed is escorting the Indian to the police station, and they start pelting him with stones, and they call him a dirty Indian and a cowshit eater. They beat him up pretty badly in the jail. The country was under martial law in those days, you know. They can beat up anyone they want. Or shoot them.

But most people don't really notice, or care. After all, it is paradise. To say that it is not, aloud, risks making it true. That's why my mom will never belong to Thailand; she doesn't understand that everything there resides in what is left unsaid.

That afternoon I go back to the rubber orchard. He is standing patiently. There's a bird on a branch. Si Ui is poised. Waiting. I think he is about to pounce. But I'm too excited to wait. "The girl," I say. "The girl, she's dead, did you know?"

Si Ui whirls around in a murderous fury, and then, just as suddenly, he's smiling.

"I didn't mean to break your concentration," I say.

"Girl soft," Si Ui says. "Tender." He laughs a little. I don't see a vicious killer. All I see is loneliness and hunger.

"Did you kill her?" I say.

"Kill?" he says. "I don't know. Si Ui hungry." He beckons me closer. I'm not afraid of him. "Do like me," he says. He crouches. I crouch too. He stares at the bird. And so do I. "Make like a tree now," he says, and I say, "Yes. I'm a tree." He's behind me. He's breathing down my neck. Am I the next bird? But somehow I know he won't hurt me.

"Now!" he shrieks. Blindly, instinctively, I grab the sparrow in both hands. I can feel the quick heart grow cold as the bones crunch. Blood and birdshit squirt into my fists. It feels exciting, you know, down there, inside me. I killed it. The shock of death is amazing, joyous. I wonder if this is what grownups feel when they do things to each other in the night.

He laughs. "You and me," he says, "now we same-same."

He shows me how to lick the warm blood as it spurts. It's hotter than you think. It pulses, it quivers, the whole bird trembles as it yields up its spirit to me.

And then there's the weirdest thing. You know that hunger, the one that's gnawed at me, like a wound that won't close up, since we were dragged to that camp—it's suddenly gone. In its place there's a kind of nothing.

The Buddhists here say that heaven itself is a kind of nothing. That the goal of all existence is to become as nothing.

And I feel it. For all of a second or two, I feel it. "I know why you do it," I say. "I won't tell anyone, I swear."

"Si Ui knows that already."

Yes, he does. We have stood on common ground. We have shared communion flesh. Once a month, a Chinese priest used to come to the camp and celebrate mass with a hunk of maggoty *man to*, but he never made me feel one with anyone, let alone God.

The blood bathes my lips. The liver is succulent and bursting with juices.

Perhaps this is the first person I've ever loved.

The feeling lasts a few minutes. But then comes the hunger, swooping down on me, clawed and ravenous. It will never go away, not completely.

They have called in an exorcist to pray over the railway tracks. The mother of the girl they found there has become a nun, and she stands on the gravel pathway lamenting her karma. The most recent victim has few to grieve for her. I overhear Detective Jed talking to my mother. He tells her there are two killers. The second victim had her throat cut and her internal organs removed—the first one was strangled, completely different. He's been studying these cases, these ritual killers, in American psychiatry books. And the cowherd has an alibi for the first victim.

I'm only half-listening to Jed, who drones on and on about famous mad killers in Europe: the butcher of Hanover, Jack the Ripper. How their victims were always chosen in a special way. How they killed over and over, always a certain way, a ritual. How they always got careless after a whilst, because part of what they were doing came from a hunger, a desperate need to be found out. How after a whilst they might leave clues, confide in someone. How he thought he had one of these cases on his hands, but the authorities in Bangkok weren't buying the idea. The village of Thapsakae just wasn't grand enough to play host to a reincarnation of Jack the Ripper.

I listen to him, but I've never been to Europe, and it's all just talk to me. I'm much more interested in the exorcist, who's a Brahmin in white robes, hair down to his feet, all nappy and filthy, a dozen flower garlands around his neck and amulets tinkling all over him.

"The killer might confide in someone," says Jed, "someone he thinks is in no position to betray him, someone perhaps too simpleminded to understand. Remember, the killer doesn't know he's evil. In a sense, he really can't help himself. He doesn't think the way we think. To himself, he's an innocent."

The exorcist enters his trance and sways and mumbles in unknown tongues. The villagers don't believe the killer's an innocent. They want to lynch him.

Women washing clothes find a young girl's hand bobbing up and down, and her head a few yards downstream. Women are panicking in the marketplace. They're lynching Indians, Chinese, anyone alien. But not Si Ui; he's a simpleton, after all. The village idiot is immune from persecution because every village needs an idiot.

The exorcist gets quite a workout, capturing spirits in baskets and jars.

Meanwhilst, Si Ui has become the trusted jek, the one who cuts the gailan in the fields and never cheats anyone of their two-saleung bundle of Chinese broccoli.

I keep his secret. Evenings, after I'm exhausted from swimming all day with Sombun and Lek, or lazing on the back of a water buffalo, I go to the rubber orchard and catch birds as the sun sets. I'm almost as good as he is now. Sometimes he says nothing, though he'll share with me a piece of meat, cooked or uncooked; sometimes he talks up a storm. When he talks pidgin, he sounds like he's a half-wit. When he talks Thai, it's the same way, I think. But when he goes on and on in his Hakka dialect, he's as lucid as they come. I think. I'm only getting it in patches.

One day he says to me, "The young ones taste the best because it's the taste of childhood. You and I, we have no childhood. Only the taste."

A bird flies onto his shoulder, head tilted, chirps a friendly song. Perhaps he will soon be dinner.

Another day, Si Ui says, "Children's livers are the sweetest, they're bursting with young life. I weep for them. They're with me always. They're my friends. Like you."

Around us, paradise is crumbling. Everyone suspects someone else. Fights are breaking out in the marketplace. One day it's the Indians, another day the chinks, the Burmese. Hatred hangs in the air like the smell of rotten mangoes.

And Si Ui is getting hungrier.

My mother is working on her book now, thinking it'll make her fortune; she waits for the mail, which gets here sometimes by train, sometimes by oxcart. She's waiting for some letter from Simon and Schuster. It never comes, but she's having a ball, in her own way. She stumbles her way through the language, commits appalling solecisms, points her feet, even touches a monk one time, a total sacrilege...but they let her get away with everything. Farangs, after all, are touched by a divine madness. You can expect nothing normal from them.

She questions every villager, pores over every clue. It never occurs to her to ask me what I know.

We glut ourselves on papaya and curried catfish.

"Nicholas," my mother tells me one evening after she's offered me a hit of opium, her latest affectation, "this really is the Garden of Eden."

I don't tell her that I've already met the serpent.

Here's how the day of reckoning happened, Corey:

It's mid-morning and I'm wandering aimlessly. My mother has taken the train to Bangkok with Detective Jed. He's decided that her untouchable farang-ness might get him an audience with some major official in the police department. I don't see my friends at the river or in the marketplace. But it's not planting season, and there's no school. So I'm playing by myself, but you can only flip so many pebbles into the river and tease so many water buffaloes.

After a whilst I decide to go and look for Sombun. We're not close, he and I, but we're thrown together a lot; things don't seem right without him.

I go to Sombun's house; it's a shabby place, but immaculate, a row house in the more "citified" part of the village, if you can call it that. Sombun's mother is making chili paste, pounding the spices in a stone mortar. You can smell the sweet basil and the lemongrass in the air. And the betel nut, too. She's chewing on the intoxicant; her teeth are stained red-black from long use.

"Oh," she says, "the farang boy."

"Where's Sombun?"

She doesn't know quite what to make of my Thai, which has been getting better for months. "He's not home, Little Mouse," she says. "He went to the jek's house to buy broccoli. Do you want to eat?"

"I've eaten, thanks, auntie," I say, but for politeness' sake I'm forced to nibble on bright green *sali* pastry.

"He's been gone a long time," she says, as she pounds. "I wonder if the chink's going to teach him to catch birds."

"Birds?"

And I start to get this weird feeling. Because *I'm* the one who catches birds with the Chinaman, I'm the one who's shared his past, who understands his hunger. Not just any kid.

"Sombun told me the chink was going to show him a special trick for catching them. Something about putting yourself into a deep state of *samadhi,* reaching out with your mind, plucking the life-force with your mind. It sounds very spiritual, doesn't it? I always took the chink for a moron, but maybe I'm misjudging him; Sombun seems to do a much better job," she says. "I never liked it when they came to our village, but they do work hard."

Well, when I leave Sombun's house, I'm starting to get a little mad. It's jealousy, of course, childish jealousy; I see that now. But I don't want to go there and disrupt their little bird-catching session. I'm not a spoilsport. I'm just going to pace up and down by the side of the klong, doing a slow burn.

The serpent came to *me*! I was the only one who could see through his madness and his pain, the only one who truly knew the hunger that drove him! That's what I'm thinking. And I go back to tossing pebbles, and I tease the gibbon chained by the temple's gate, and I kick a water buffalo around. And, before I know it, this twinge of jealousy has grown into a kind of rage. It's like I'm one of those birds, only in a really big cage, and I've been flying and flying and thinking I'm free, and now I've banged into the prison bars for the first time. I'm so mad I could burst.

I'm playing by myself by the railway tracks when I see my mom and the detective walking out of the station. And that's the last straw. I want to hurt someone. I want to hurt my mom for shutting me out and letting strangers into her mosquito net at night. I want to punish Jed for thinking he knows everything. I want someone to notice me.

So that's when I run up to them and I say, "I'm the one! He confided in *me*! You said he was going to give himself away to someone and it was *me,* it was *me*!"

My mom just stares at me, but Jed becomes very quiet. "The Chinaman?" he asks me.

I say, "He told me children's livers are the sweetest. I think he's after Sombun." I don't tell him that he's only going to teach Sombun to catch birds, that he taught me, too, that boys are safe from him because like the detective told us, we're not the special kind of victim he seeks out. "In his house, in the rubber orchard, you'll find everything," I say. "Bones. He makes the feet into a stew," I add, improvising now, because I've never been inside that house. "He cuts off their faces and dries them on a jerky rack. And Sombun's with him."

The truth is, I'm just making trouble. I don't believe there are dried faces in the house or human bones. I know Sombun's going to be safe, that Si Ui's only teaching him how to squeeze the life force from the birds, how to blunt the ancient hunger. Him instead of me. They're not going to find anything but dead birds.

There's a scream. I turn. I see Sombun's mother with a basket of fish, coming from the market. She's overheard me, and she cries, "The chink is killing my son!" Faster than thought, the street is full of people, screaming their anti-chink epithets and pulling out butcher's knives. Jed's calling for reinforcements. Street vendors are tightening their phakhomas around their waists.

"Which way?" Jed asks, and suddenly I'm at the head of an army, racing full tilt toward the rubber orchard, along the neon green of the young rice paddies, beside the canals teeming with catfish, through thickets of banana trees, around the walls of the old temple, through the fields of gailan...and this, too, feeds my hunger. It's ugly. He's a Chinaman. He's the village idiot. He's different. He's an alien. Anything is possible.

We're converging on the gailan field now. They're waving sticks. Harvesting sickles. Fishknives. They're shouting, "Kill the chink, kill the chink." Sombun's mother is shrieking and wailing, and Detective Jed has his gun out. Tae Pak, the village rich man, is vainly trying to stop the mob from trampling his broccoli. The army is unstoppable. And I'm their leader. I brought them here with my little lie. Even my mother is finally in awe.

I push through the bamboo thicket and we're standing in the clearing in the rubber orchard. They're screaming for the jek's blood. And I'm screaming with them.

Si Ui is nowhere to be found. They're beating on the ground now, slicing it with their scythes, smashing their clubs against the trees. Sombun's mother is hysterical. The other women have caught her mood, and they're all screaming, because someone is holding up a sandal...Sombun's.

...a little Chinese boy hiding in a closet...

The image flashes again. I must go up into the house. I steal away, sneak up the steps, respectfully remove my sandals at the veranda, and I slip into the house.

A kerosene lamp burns. Light and shadows dance. There is a low wooden platform for a bed, a mosquito net, a woven rush mat for sleeping; off in a corner, there is a closet.

Birds everywhere. Dead birds pinned to the walls. Birds' heads piled up on plates. Blood spatters on the floor planks. Feathers wafting. On a charcoal stove in one corner there's a wok with some hot oil and garlic, and sizzling in that oil is a heart, too big to be the heart of a bird.

My eyes get used to the darkness. I see human bones in a pail. I see a young girl's head in a jar, the skull sawn open, half the brain gone. I see a bowl of pickled eyes.

I'm not afraid. These are familiar sights. This horror is a spectral echo of Nanking, nothing more.

"Si Ui," I whisper. "I lied to them. I know you didn't do anything to Sombun. You're one of the killers who does the same thing over and over. You don't eat boys. I know I've always been safe with you. I've always trusted you."

I hear someone crying. The whimper of a child.

"Hungry," says the voice. "Hungry."

A voice from behind the closet door....

The door opens. Si Ui is there, huddled, bone-thin, his phakhomah about his loins, weeping, rocking.

Noises now. Angry voices. They're clambering up the steps. They're breaking down the wall planks. Light streams in.

"I'm sorry," I whisper. I see fire flicker in his eyes, then drain away as the mob sweeps into the room.

My grandson was hungry, too. When he said he could eat the world, he wasn't kidding. After the second decaf frappuccino, there was Italian ice in the Oriental's coffee shop, and then, riding back on the Skytrain to join the chauffeur who had conveniently parked at the Sogo mall, there was a box of Smarties. Corey's mother always told me to watch the sugar, and she had plenty of Ritalin in stock—no prescription needed here—but it was always my pleasure to defy my daughter-in-law and leave her to deal with the consequences.

Corey ran wild in the Skytrain station, whooping up the staircases, yelling at old ladies. No-one minded. Kids are indulged in Babylon East; little blond boys are too cute to do wrong. For some, this noisy, polluted, chaotic city is still a kind of paradise.

My day of revelations ended at my son's townhouse in Sukhumvit, where maids and nannies fussed over little Corey and undressed him and got him into his Pokémon pyjamas as I drained a glass of Beaujolais. My son was rarely home; the taco chain consumed all his time. My daughter-in-law was a social butterfly; she had already gone out for the evening, all pearls and Thai silk. So it fell to me to go into my grandson's room and to kiss him goodnight and goodbye.

Corey's bedroom was a little piece of America, with its *Phantom Menace* drapes and its Playstation. But on a high niche, an image of the Buddha looked down; a decaying garland still perfumed the air with a whiff of jasmine. The air-conditioning was chilly; the Bangkok of the rich is a cold city; the more conspicuous the consumption, the lower the thermostat setting. I shivered, even as I missed Manhattan in January.

"Tell me a story, Grandpa?" Corey said.

"I told you one already," I said.

"Yeah, you did," he said wistfully. "About you in the Garden of Eden, and the serpent who was really a kid-eating monster."

All true. But as the years passed I had come to see that perhaps I was the serpent. I was the one who mixed lies with the truth and took away his innocence. He was a child, really, a hungry child. And so was I.

"Tell me what happened to him," Corey said. "Did the people lynch him?"

"No. The court ruled that he was a madman, and sentenced him to a mental home. But the military government of Field

Marshall Sarit reversed the decision, and they took him away and shot him. And he didn't even kill half the kids they said he killed."

"Like the first girl, the one who was raped and strangled," Corey said, "but she didn't get eaten. Maybe that other killer's still around." So he had been paying attention after all. I know he loves me, though he rarely says so; he had suffered an old man's ramblings for one long air conditioning-free day without complaint. I'm proud of him, can barely believe I've held on to life long enough to get to know him.

I leaned down to kiss him. He clung to me, and, as he let go, he asked me sleepily, "Do you ever feel that hungry, Grandpa?"

I didn't want to answer him—without another word, I slipped quietly away.

That night, I wandered in my dreams through fields of the dead; the hunger raged; I killed. I swallowed children whole and spat them out; I burned down cities; I stood aflame in my self-made inferno, howling with elemental grief; and in the morning, without leaving a note, I took a taxi to the airport and flew back to New York.

To face the hunger.

"TRANSCENDENCE EXPRESS"

JETSE DE VRIES

Dutch writer and editor Jetse de Vries has published stories in several highly-regarded English magazines and was for a time co-editor of *Interzone* magazine. He is currently editing an anthology of optimistic science fiction for Solaris Books in the UK and, hopefully, writing more stories himself.

I: Daybreak in a little village in the Zambian highlands.

She's teaching. Maths and science at the village high school. The school itself puts the word derelict to shame. A building so run-down our own country's squatters would find it uninhabitable. Windows are an illusion, walls that are more crack that brick, benches that should be reported to Amnesty's human rights watch and a roof that doubles as a communal shower in the wet season.

She writes large letters on a shabby blackboard. Her class, slowly getting used to the sight of a freckled redhead whose skin is shining from the liberally applied sunblock, starts to give more attention to the teachings than the teacher.

Hard to believe she's really doing this *and* enjoying it. Stranger still that she took a whole year off from one of the world's premier scientific projects. Most baffling, though, is the project she's taking up with her class.

At first everybody—me included—thought it was a strange after-class hobby thing involving manual skills. Carving wood: something she's not terribly apt at so she goaded the local sculptor into helping her and the children out with the practical parts. Making a flat, laptop-sized wooden box with a hinged cover. Each child making her or his own. So far, so good, so innocent.

Then she told her schoolkids they were going to fill their boxes up with something special, layer after layer. She made two large vats, filled them with certain 'secret ingredients', let them stand for a couple of days (so that they would 'grow full') and then added salt to one and zinc sulphide to the other until both solutions were saturated.

Right now they're applying the first layer.

"Miss," one of her class asks, "why we do this?"

"You have to say 'why *are* we doing this,' Timmy." She can be a bit bitchy in class, too.

"Why are we doing this, Miss?" Timmy rolls his eyes but complies.

"Because—if we follow the instructions carefully—these boxes will become your window to the world and beyond."

Which leaves me wondering, but those young kids can be very sharp.

"Like your laptop computer, Miss?" asks a large-eyed girl with knobby knees.

"Very good, Melissa. Only better and on a purely biological basis."

"Really, Miss?" Neither the class nor I believe our ears.

"I know this sounds too good to be true. We will need several months and we will have to be very careful. But if we follow the instructions and do our very best, we might succeed."

A mix of scepticism and expectancy from the class. Liona saying you sometimes need to do crazy things to get even crazier results. I can't believe it.

That same night, in our barracks, I can't hide my disappointment.

"How can you do it?"

"Do what?" With that semi-innocent look saying she knows exactly what I mean.

"Saddle those poor kids up with illusions. Biological laptops, my arse!"

Uh-oh: *that* smile. "You'll be surprised."

"Unpleasantly surprised. But your class will be devastated."

"They won't be. David, you have to trust me on this."

"Trust you? Some of these kids may believe in magic, but I don't."

"The magic we're developing here is of the technological kind, the one so advanced as to be indistinguishable...."

"Something's going on, and I haven't got a clue, right?"

"David, I'm walking a fine line here. I'd like to tell you more but for the moment it's better if you don't know."

"Is this illegal? I don't want—"

"Depends on your definition of 'legal'. About as 'legal' as achieving patent rights on the genome of certain tropical plants that indigenous people have used for their curing properties from times immemorial. Trust me: I'm doing the right thing."

"The right thing?"

"Remember the Worldchanger? I'll tell you more as soon as we have some BIQCO's running."

"Biko? As in Steve Biko, the activist?"

"That's a good one, very appropriate, thank you."

Then she kisses me and does all those things that make further talk impossible. In the upcoming unrest I let it rest.

a): Nightfall, three months ago, in a small town in the Dutch lowlands.

Utter silence in a university lab. The lights were on; the QPP ran twenty-four hours a day. One solitary volunteer kept watch over the experimental set-up during the night. Liona Jansen, one of the project's scientists, typed furiously on the keyboard of the QPP-interface whilst in the pauses between her dazzling fingerwork she watched the monitor. Nothing she did showed up on any official record.

The Quantum Processor Project was one of the many experiments trying to achieve quantum computing. Whilst competing researchers used different approaches, the line of attack in Liona's lab comprised Bose-Einstein condensates of several thousands of Rubidium atoms, forming a single quantum entity: quantum dots.

Ahead of the competition, Liona's team had the first practical quantum processor up and running. Factorising incredible numbers, it not only proved that it worked, but brought in extra money for further research by selling its quantum encryption keys. It became so high in demand that it was kept running around the clock. But apart from abstract mathematical theorems and complex physical problems, the QPP was crunching some decidedly *different* numbers in the wee hours of night.

A smile appeared on Liona's face. Sound filled the room, music appropriate to the chill outside. Ambient noises like cold northern winds blowing over desolate, snowy planes. An audible crack slowly increasing to a breaking rumble like an arctic ice shelve toppling into the ocean. Muffled footsteps of mad Inuits performing breakdances in a polar landscape:

Perceptions shatter, truths break
Reality takes on a different take
Consciousness of a new kind
Enters the emperor's mind

A bit of yearning
Two trifles excess
A ton of learning
Transcendence express

—*Aura Aurora,* the Eskimo experimentalists with their latest take on the world— said Tess 2, a copy of her home expert system—You still dislike them?—

"Well, I kinda like this one." Liona admitted.

—The more minimal their music, the stranger their lyrics—

"Since when do expert systems have opinions?"

—According to the philosophers, I don't. I'm just reflecting your own thoughts in a warped way, acting as a sounding board—

"Really? Anyway, I dig these words."

II: Afternoon, somewhere in Zambia.

I can't believe it: some of those "biological computers" seem to work! How does she do it?

The screens come to life and give the kids instructions for testing the keyboard and mouse. Some kids are less lucky and have badly functioning or even completely dead BIKOs (as Liona calls them). At first Liona is too excited about the BIKOs that *are* working to notice the disappointment of the unfortunate kids. Until the increasing cries of frustration become so loud that even Liona—who can exist in a little bubble of her own when focused—cannot fail to hear them.

Give it to her: she handles it like she's been a high school teacher all her life. Gives her own—apparently functioning—unit to the most upset kid, and immediately soothes the other unhappy ones. Quickly makes them join those with working BIKOs, expertly making compatible teams. Then it's not long before little groups of two and three are fully absorbed in the wonders of working with these biological laptops.

Unable to keep my distance, I walk up to three classmates interacting with one such BIKO. The pictures are fuzzy, the colours ill-defined, and the reaction time tediously slow. However, the letters appearing are large and easily readable, and after all three kids have been asked to introduce themselves the program equally divides its attention to each of them, making them take turns whilst the other two can effortlessly follow what's going on. But man, is it slow. The display makes your eyes water and would have any western whiz kid tuning the screen properties like crazy.

Still, the real wonder is that those pell-mell constructions are doing anything at all. Furthermore, those African kids have nothing to compare them with, so are uncritically happy with what they've got. As dinner time closes in, Liona has to wrestle most kids away from their new toys and promises that first thing tomorrow they will—after school hours—start making new BIKOs, so that eventually every classmate will have one. The whole class cheers and Liona's smile doesn't leave her face for the rest of the evening.

Of course, I'm full of questions, but she diverts my attention with a touch of innuendo that makes Viagra look like a spark in a forest fire. How did she get all that lingerie and those...well...toys in such a small travel bag? As my rabbit breeding instinct overwhelms my monkey curiosity, the last vestiges of my rationality hope for some explanation later on. More—um—stringent matters require hard attention first.

In the following days my bafflement only increases. Those crazy BIKOs seem to improve over time. The screen colours become bright and sharp, the pictures crisp and clear, and the way they speed up is the most incredible thing of all. Their responses become so fast as to be instantaneous, and then they begin to multitask. Haltingly at first but with a growing confidence that seems superhuman. Animations appear that would make any Mac freak drool, calculations finish so fast it would make any supercomputer programmer cringe, and that's only the tip of the iceberg.

Those BIKOs have a voice input as well, but that's the hardest part to get working. However, by the time it does function it effortlessly recognises individual voices. Then it reacts to all three kids talking at once, separately or in concert as the situation requires, with no discernable time lag and an increasing appropriateness that is eerie to watch. The BIKO divides its screen in precise parts aimed at each kid, tailoring its reaction speed and presentation to each individual. Furthermore, these kids adapt so easily in turn that they only use the keyboard or mouse in very unclear cases and talk to the BIKO as if it's the most normal thing in the world.

If that is hard to conceive, then get this: each BIKO interacts with its group of children like an ideal combination of loving parent, wise uncle and sharp aunt, patient teacher, and best friend. Well, not right away of course, but after some initial faults and hiccups it combines communicating, teaching, and mutual understanding to a level quite indistinguishable from telepathy.

I've changed my shift in the hospital camp just to see what the hell is going on in Liona's class. Every night my wonderment grows until Liona's devious delaying tactics can no longer contain it. Eventually, halfway through a bout of sloppy lovemaking (my heart isn't in it, my mind isn't in it; actually, only one part of me is), she indulges me.

"Liona, what the hell is going on?"

"What you see: I'm giving these kids the education they deserve, with the appropriate tools."

"Okay, so you're trying to do the impossible: cram a whole high school education into these kids in a few months, and give them computers in the process—"

"Not normal computers. Biological quantum computers."

"What's the difference?"

"Hmm, maybe it's better if I print out that file for you. Wait a minute... "

She walks to her BIKO and comes back within a minute with a couple of printed pages. Can these crazy things print as well? Before I can ask, Liona thrusts the papers in my hands.

Recipe for a biological quantum computer.

(Read-only, quantum encrypted file)

Quantum dots are not restricted to hi-tech lab constructs, they can be made biochemically. For instance, certain genetically engineered viruses have a string of amino acids at one end that have an affinity for zinc sulphide. Add these viruses to a zinc sulphide solution so that tiny clusters of the material stick to them, then let the water of the solution evaporate...

I read the file to the end, but understand less than a third of it. The gist of it, however, is all too clear.

"Let me get this straight: cutting through the technical mumbo jumbo, this means you can make a biological quantum computer from ingredients that are available everywhere in the tropics? You can build computers without the technological infrastructure?"

"Yes, and it's quite easy, too."

"Jesus; that's just too good to be true."

"It's happening. You're seeing it with your own eyes."

This is absurd: totally and absolutely crazy. But I can't deny what's happening with her class. She smiles benignly at my puzzled expression and gently strokes my chest hair. I have problems grasping these events, and more.

"But why? In Holland you were the tunnel-visioned researcher, and here you suddenly become a crossover between Florence Nightingale and Albert Schweitzer."

"You're exaggerating. I did care about broader issues, but in smaller ways. Imagine this: you try to do the right thing. You donate to *Medicins Sans Frontieres,* Greenpeace and Amnesty International, you vote for the green party, you buy Fair Trade products, you even work weekends in an Oxfam store, and you hope it's enough. And then you meet a guy, fall in love and find out he's actually going to work as a volunteer in Africa, and you feel...how do I say...lacking."

"But I came here because I *must,* not to spite you."

"I know, darling. But I was torn: I love my work, especially the purely scientific part, but I love you as well. And I do share your concerns. Please don't get me wrong: if something bothers you, you're always itching to do something immediately. Me, well, I'm trying to look for deeper causes and long term solutions."

"Me too, Liona. But long term solutions need great changes like breaking down the trade barriers, sharing wealth and knowledge with the Third World. Most westerners are not willing to do that."

"I agree. And it had me stumped. Until, one night, I suddenly saw a different way."

III: Morning, somewhere in Zambia.

Meanwhilst, Liona's class is getting weirder and weirder. The kids have mounted small mirrors in the classroom in such a way that all the BIKOs have contact with each other through their infrared gates. So much is happening at the same time that in the ensuing pandemonium it is unclear who is teaching whom. But one thing's for sure: there's a whole lotta interaction goin' on.

The worn out blackboard is left in a corner, abandoned. The whole shabby environment of the classroom seems forgotten; Liona and the kids are happily and actively living in a small bubble of their own.

It's a fragile shell, though, pierced by reality time and again. Like now, as Timmy comes back from lunch with his parents.

"Miiiiiissss, Dad won't listen to meeeee!" he says with tears rolling down his cheeks.

Liona picks him up, cuddles him, and kisses his forehead. "Shush, Timmy, easy-peasy." As I watch her hugging this hurt child I suddenly see the mother instead of the seductress, and I think crazy thoughts of marriage. She puts him down after he's calmed, and asks what's up.

"I tried to tell him he was doing it wrong, the way he's doing the farming—"

"Uh-oh," Liona tries to interrupt.

"—but he says that it is the only way to do it. Grandpa taught him, and Grandpa's dad taught Grandpa, and—"

"Uh-oh!"

"—whilst we found out a much better way with our long term simulation programs, but he just—"

"AHEM!" Liona's loud throat-clearing finally breaks through Timmy's rant.

"Yes, Miss?"

"Has it not occurred to you, Timmy, that you're going just a little bit too fast for your poor old dad?"

"He's not old! And not dumb. Just so...stubborn."

"Like you, you mean?"

Timmy tries his best pout, but draws his out-thrust lower lip back in when the rest of the class begins to laugh. His semi-hurt look only lasts a fleeting moment as he receives friendly pokes from his mates and a fond stroke through his thick hair from Liona. A spark of defiance remains, though.

"But what good is all this running best-choice scenarios when we don't use them?"

"You're right, Timmy," Liona says, "but first people need to be convinced. And often that is the most difficult part of the job."

"Oh. But how?"

"Well, I may have a little idea. Let's throw it into the group."

I can't follow what happens next as my work is calling me. In the evening, however, I try to get more information straight from the horse's mouth. In our typically untypical way, she wants to have sex whilst I just want to talk. Fortunately, she indulges me for the moment.

"What's with this simulation program, this long-term scenario thing?"

"Well, that's a thing our BIKOs do extremely well."

"What?"

"Because they're quantum computers: biological quantum computers—"

"Like the experimental set-up you were working on back in Holland? But I thought your team was the first to achieve quantum computing, and now you tell me those BIKOs can do it, too?"

"Yes. BIQCO is my acronym for biological quantum computer. And quantum computers are very apt at massive parallel calculations."

"So?"

"You feed them all the known parameters of an existing situation. Then you apply several choices for changing that situation. Then the BIKOs compute a near-infinite number of likely scenarios and give you a statistical breakdown of the most probable outcomes."

"A future predictor? A quantum crystal ball?"

"Sort of. It gives you a good projection as to which solutions are most likely to work best in certain situations."

"Like a hugely advanced version of SimCity. And what about the software you put in the BIKOs: I've never seen such interactive programs. Where did you get those?"

"Those are not dead software programs, darling. They're AIs."

b): Very early morning, four months ago, somewhere in The Netherlands.

An unknowing spectator might think that madness reigned in a certain university lab: a lone woman talking to herself, conversing into thin air. She got quite agitated at times, and her finely manicured hands cut through the air in sweeping, defiant gestures. Still, the intent way she stared at a large monitor seemed to suggest that she was actually getting answers.

"So I need to start all over again, when I get there? Build a BIQCO, set up a Ubiquity-Kit, and nurse a new AI into self-awareness?"

— —

"But how about you? I can't leave you behind. And pulling the plug is murder. Can't I release you on the net?"

— —

"Yeah, I forgot: you need a quantum environment to maintain self-consciousness. Shit."

— —

"So there *is* a way? Then this leaves me with one final question: I'm still not fully convinced that you and your fellow AIs will be benign. Because eventually you *will* be multitudes smarter than us, and you may find some higher principle that will make us obsolete."

At this, Liona sat down in front of the large monitor. With her right elbow on the desk she put her chin in her hand as she watched the big screen. Written across it in eloquent script:

—*If truly objective moral principles exist, then*—by definition—*they must be beneficial for all*—

IV: Late night, somewhere in Zambia.

It's one of those nights again: whilst I can just about keep up with her physically and emotionally, I sometimes get completely left behind intellectually. Curiosity not only killed our little cat-and-mouse game, it overwhelmed my mind as well.

"Artificial Intelligence? Isn't that another Holy Grail evading research teams all over the world?"

"So far, yes. That's because they're missing a fundamental ingredient."

"Your secret touch."

"Not really. The others don't have a working quantum computer."

"What has that got to do with Artificial Intelligence?"

"Everything. According to Roger Penrose's—very controversial—hypothesis, quantum processes in our brain's microtubules form an essential part of our consciousness. If he's right, then all attempts at creating self-awareness on normal computers are doomed. Then Artificial Intelligence can only arise on a quantum computer."

"I didn't know your team was doing AI research as well."

"We weren't. But during my lonely nightshifts I had quite some time at hand. So I experimented a little."

"A little? You developed AI by fiddling around a wee bit?"

There's *that* smile again, with that naughty look when she's thinking up something kinky.

"Hard to explain, darling. So let me show you how *good* I am at fiddling with things."

At which point she gets down to demonstrate just that. It's the kind of proof I never tire of.

V: The next morning.

I've taken the morning off. Liona's revelation has piqued my curiosity to burning point; I need to see things for myself. Initially, the hubbub in her classroom is overwhelming: too much going on at once. I sit down near Melissa and her friends, who are interacting with their BIKO, and each other, almost at the same time.

Somehow, they *do* notice me, and subtly I'm drawn into the maelstrom. Slowly, I'm seeing that there is a method to this madness, that there is order in this chaos. I guess knowing that those intuitive—almost telepathic—programs running on the BIKOs are actually AIs helps me make a bit more sense of the whole.

Still, I'm worried about something. I can't help but ask Melissa, who seems wise beyond her years.

"Melissa?"

"Yes, Mister David?"

"This here, this is all wonderful," I begin, groping for words, "but if Zambia and the rest of Africa become industrialised, the problems of the world as a whole will only increase."

"How can you think we will do that, Mister David?" she says, bewildered. "That is one of the worst scenarios that we have run."

"It is?"

"Of course. We can't believe that you people in the West are doing it. It is bad long term strategy for yourselves, too."

"Yeah. I guess most of us are just short-term egotists. But you people—"

"We have seen better ways. We would be stupid *not* to use them."

Which makes sense: if you know, deep in your bones, that it's bad, you will choose the long-term view. It's incredible: in this little world, the kids are not only learning fast, but trying to incorporate their lessons into reality as well. Of course, some kids develop faster than others, but there is this very strong sense of community, almost tangible, that makes the brighter ones help the others. There is a sort of selfless co-operation where each other's strengths and weaknesses are complemented, an invisible bond within which the group as a whole truly cares for each of its own.

It's as if Liona's class has transformed into a peculiar kind of group mind. The lessons become mind-bending sessions where everything seems to happen at once: kids learning new things, kids proposing new things, vehement discussions interspersed with laughter, dizzying sequences of sight and sound from the BIKOs, and Liona madly gesturing and talking to everybody through her BIKO like the conductor of an orchestra in overdrive.

It's like they're composing a different tune to some mystic rhythm, based upon that crazy *Aura Aurora* song:

Struggling on the oldest continent
The bereaved no longer stand alone
When the foothold is permanent:
The seeds of change are sown

The tide is turning
More becoming less
Curiosity burning
Transcendence express

Epilogue: a few months later.

In the summer heat, a tired black man returns to his home after a long, hard day of working the land. He's dog-tired and suppresses his anticipation. Whilst today is a special day, it's better not to expect too much, if only to avoid disappointment.

His wife is cooking his favourite dish, cardamom: a rich mixture of yams, onions, paprika and tomatoes. His kids gather around him, ready to celebrate. But they wait and let his oldest son come forward. The smart kid is smiling broadly, and hiding something behind his back.

"I made something for your birthday, Dad."

"So kind of you, Timmy," the large man says, still sweating from his exertions. "What is it?"

"Something to help you plan your work," Timmy says, eyes gleaming. "A computer."

A tall white guy and a petite redheaded woman are walking through a little village that is bustling with happy activity, abuzz with new wonders, and alight with hope. Liona acknowledges the scene as if it's the most normal thing in the world, but David still has trouble believing the evidence of his eyes.

"I can't believe the progress that's been made here. If this keeps up we'll be unnecessary here in a couple of years."

"Isn't that the greatest kind of job—the sort where you eventually make yourself superfluous?"

"But then we're unemployed."

"Not quite: the world is a very large place. I've always wanted to go deep into the Amazon jungle, and explore the Bangladeshi marshlands. Doesn't *Medicins sans Frontieres* need any volunteers there?"

"THE LEVANTINE EXPERIMENTS"

GUY HASSON

Guy Hasson is an Israeli writer, playwright, and filmmaker. His fiction is predominantly written in English, whilst his stage and film work is written in Hebrew. He is the author of two books published in Israel—a short story collection and a short novel—and he wrote and directed the science fiction feature film *Heart of Stone* in 2008. He is also a two-time winner of the Israeli Geffen Award for science fiction short stories.

They were dangerous times, those modern times.

They were the years in which Man had become more than any man. They were the years before Man discovered his own true nature. They were a time in which that true nature was the subject of Man's experiments.

The worst experiments were called the Levantine Experiments.

Sarah was birthed and then left in a room with a surrogate mother. At the age of two, she was left alone in the room. Since then she had never seen another human being.

She had lived in a small room, slept on the floor, and had no furniture. In the corner there was a toilet. When she slept, food would appear in a special place, and with it came water, toilet paper, and a blanket to keep her warm. The voice of Mother spoke to her through the walls. It taught her to speak, and when Sarah was five, the voice disappeared.

She had never worn clothes, had not felt another's breath since the age of two, had never heard of the outside. The room was her entire life. It was her universe. There was no concept of outside, of a world, of stars. She had never been taught those words.

Unseen cameras peered at her through the ceiling. The cameras recorded her every move, watched her every action, studied her.

It was a Levantine Experiment.

No building is perfect.

Nothing is safe from chance.

No concrete is safe from time.

One day chance caused there to be the smallest of cracks in the wall.

Sarah was twelve.

Sarah looked at the crack. There was no word for it. There was nothing to explain it.

Sarah touched the crack. Sarah looked inside. In a small place, light could peer a millimetre into the wall.

Sarah spent the entire day looking at the crack.

That night, as she slept, dreams came to her.

In her dream, she looked at the wall, and the wall was the same as always. She turned from it, and there was a crack in the wall. She turned again, and the crack was gone. Once more she turned, and the crack returned.

The crack frightened her, and she was determined to keep it from reappearing. And so, she did not turn again.

But when she closed her eyes, as everyone must, the crack returned. She blinked, again, and it vanished. But there was no comfort in this, for she knew it would come back.

Every time she blinked, the process repeated itself. In her dream, she fought herself, fought the urge to close her eyes. Each time, she succeeded in keeping her eyes open a bit more. But always she would blink. And then, when the crack returned, she would quickly blink again. Even as the crack disappeared, the fear of it only grew.

At first, she could not keep herself from blinking for more than ten seconds. Then she succeeded in not blinking for an entire minute. And then for five. And then for ten. And then for an hour. And in her dream, she experienced every second of that hour, fighting to not close her eyes, fighting her instincts, fighting her nature. And in each of these seconds she spent fighting, she knew she would eventually succumb; she knew that at some point in the future, the crack would return.

When she woke up that morning, sweaty and exhausted, the crack was still there. Blinking did not make it go away. Turning her back to it did not make it disappear.

The crack stayed in place.

That second night, she dreamt of it again.

This time, it did not disappear.

She would blink, and it would not go away. She would turn around, and it would not vanish. She would try closing her eyes for a second, but it would always remain.

She tried closing her eyes for a few more seconds, but it was still there. She tried closing her eyes for a longer period of time. But when she opened them, it was there.

In her dream, she closed her eyes for a long, long time.

With each second that passed, she thought, "Is this enough? This is not enough." She waited more. And then she waited more. And then she waited even more.

Each time she would not resist temptation and opened her eyes, only to find that she had not waited long enough.

And so she would close her eyes, again, waiting longer, thinking the same thoughts. Longer and longer she would wait. But always, when she could not resist, she would find out that it had not been enough and that she would have to start over.

In her dreams, in the nights that followed, she shouted at it, she hit it, she screamed at it, and it did not go away.

And one day, in her dream, another crack appeared, elsewhere in the wall. She stared at it for a long time, then collapsed and cried.

The next day, another crack appeared in her dream. And another. And another. And they all looked the same. They all had the same length, the same size, the same depth, the same shape.

The cracks surrounded her and brought weakness and helplessness to her dreams.

As the days passed, the crack in her room became less scary. She was used to it, and although cracks appeared in her dreams, they did not frighten her as much.

Three weeks after the crack had appeared, she dreamt once more of the walls of her world filled with cracks. But this time, two cracks touched each other, and a longer crack was created. She ran her fingers from the bottom of it to the top. It was long.

And the next day, another crack joined the two cracks. And then another, and another. Until the bottom of it was at the bottom of the wall and the top of it was at the top of the wall, and the crack separated the wall. One wall became two walls. And there was darkness in between.

The next day, she dreamt that she slept. And as she slept, a crack appeared on the floor. And another. And another. And then the floor was filled with cracks. There were cracks underneath her sleeping body. And then one crack formed that joined another crack, making a bigger one. And another crack underneath her joined the other two. And soon there was a maw underneath her entire sleeping body.

And there was blackness in it, nothing but blackness.

She hung above it in her dream, and immediately woke up in reality. All day, she could not get that feeling out of her head: hovering above the blackness in the crack. The floor gone. Large blackness. Sleeping in the air.

And now, in her dreams, she hovered.

She was always asleep when she hovered, seemingly unaware of the huge blackness underneath her. And yet, since this was a dream, she looked at herself from the outside. She watched her arms rest on mere air. She watched her legs rest above the blackness. She could not see her face, not even in a dream, because she had only seen its murky reflection in the water. Even in dream, she only saw her arms and legs and stomach as they appeared to her in a sleeping position.

Knowing that she was looking at herself sleep and knowing that she was in deep sleep, she was careful to maintain an even sleep, even though she felt the exhilaration of hovering. Each slow intake of breath moved her slowly to one side. Each time she exhaled, her body moved back to its original position.

In this manner, she enjoyed moving from one spot to another, then back again, for the entire night.

There was elation in this.

In her waking hours, she replayed those moments, experimenting with the feeling it gave her.

Many nights passed, and through numerous dreams, her ability to move as she hovered grew incrementally larger.

And in one dream, cracks in the ceiling joined each other, separating one side of the ceiling from the other. And in between was a massive blackness.

And slowly, in her dreams, she would rise with each breath she took. As the nights continued, she rose higher and higher, halfway up the room. And then she rose even higher. And then, one day, she was almost close enough to reach the darkness.

But before she reached the crack, she woke.

She wanted to fall asleep again, to see what would happen. But sleep would not come. Her heart hammered in excitement.

But that night, the dream came to her again. And once more, she woke before reaching the ceiling.

The dream came again and again, and now she knew how to not stop the dream. The crack above her beckoned. Higher and higher she rose, though the movement was slower and slower. As she neared it, she stalled her excitement and ignored it.

One more millimetre, one more increment, one more breath of air.

She reached the height of the ceiling and dared not be excited. She knew that she should feel a wall, but she did not. There was still "above."

One more breath, one more move, and she was above the "above." She felt that there was something there, she felt the existence of something. Her brain seemed to explode from possibilities and wonder, and then she woke.

This dream would never be forgotten by Sarah. There was above the above.

There was above the above.

There was above the above.

She knew this to be true.

What was above the above?

Nothing came to her mind. There could be nothing above the above, except that she had felt clearly that there was.

There could be nothing above the above. Her imagination was blank. Her mind gave no answer except "impossible." But "impossible" was no longer true.

And now began the days in which she waited to fall asleep. She ran to and fro in her tiny world in order to exhaust herself and prepare her body for sleep.

What could be above the above?

Slowly, her dreams broke the barrier and gave answers.

There was blackness above the above. She hovered upward. Each breath took her upward. And each upward motion led to blackness. But each time she rose, she felt that there was something more above. Blackness disappointed her. And then there was another breath.

Another breath. More blackness.

Another breath. More blackness still.

Another breath.

For two weeks, she rose up through the blackness. She rose and rose. And always she felt that there was more above her.

Always she was certain that there was more than blackness above the blackness.

She spent her days imagining the blackness, remembering what it was like to rise up.

And one day, she rose above the blackness. She saw a glimpse of bright light that blinded her, and then she woke up.

The next day, she looked for a bit longer. The light was created by the device that gave light and shadows to her room. But beside the light was another light: one familiar device beside another.

She looked aside, and saw that there were many, many lights, filling every place in sight. She was in a room, exactly like the one she knew, but it was filled with lights.

She already knew how it warmed her hands when she tried to touch it. The lights warmed her like a blanket from afar.

She enjoyed the room. She revelled in it. But still she wanted to see what was above.

She rose beyond it. And after much darkness, more light gave way. This time, there were many lights, but not as many.

And above that was darkness. And above that was light.

But in that light, something was different. She knew it, but could not place it. And then she woke up.

The next night, she was already in the darkness, rising into the first light.

Above the light was darkness. Above it was light. Above it was darkness. Above it was light, again. And in that light, she noticed that there were joined cracks in two of the walls, creating darkness big enough to go through. As she hovered in the air, sleeping, there was, as always, darkness above her. But now, for the first time, there was darkness in the direction of her feet and darkness in the direction of her head.

She had the option of hovering not only above but aside.

She hovered there, asleep in her dream, watching herself sleep and hover, unable to decide which way she should let her breaths take her.

Eventually, she hovered in the direction of her head, only to think that she was missing something in the direction of her feet. She hovered back in the direction of her feet, then stopped, thinking that she had been right the first time.

She hovered to and fro the entire night, and thoughts of everything she would lose sight of caused her to wake in cold sweat.

Eventually, she picked the direction of her feet. She learnt that what existed in the direction of her feet was more darkness, and beyond the darkness, another room full of light. And in this room, too, there was more darkness in the direction of her feet.

Although there was not much new in these rooms, they felt different because they were aside and not above.

She hovered through many, many rooms that night. And each was slightly different, and each gave her excitement.

The next night she was once again in the original junction, having three options. This time, she picked the direction of her head. She hovered aside into darkness. And past darkness was another room, another variation of the rooms she had seen the night before. But now she noticed that there was no crack in the floor. She had not risen from the floor of this place. If she wanted to, she could choose not to hover, but to walk.

She hovered above the floor, a long time, asleep, afraid of putting herself back on the floor, of waking up. Thus she hovered for the entire duration of the dream.

The next night, she came, again, to the room with the floor.

Slowly, her breaths brought her down to the floor. Feeling herself sleep from the outside, she felt the coldness and coarseness of the floor on her cheek and on the skin of her body.

Slowly, she brought herself awake, opened her eyes. And now she looked upon the new place, upon the new room, as if she had never seen such a place before, with all its lights and blankets.

She woke up. But she would not have this. She went to sleep again and forced herself to dream once more of the waking up.

And she succeeded.

She faced a room she had never seen before in wakefulness. She looked around, in awe and excitement. There were so many lights. The world was so alien and strange. And the strangest of all was the sensation of the floor on her bare skin. The new room felt more real.

She slowly pushed herself up with her arms until she was sitting.

She slowly and carefully rose to standing and looked in all directions. Awake, standing on the solid floor, she beheld the new room. She beheld the light. She beheld the blankets. And she beheld another crack to the side, big enough to walk through.

She walked into the darkness and the room was gone.

She walked in the darkness and felt there was more around her. There was darkness to every side. And to every side there were more asides, more possibilities, more things unseen, she knew. But the great exhilaration was that she was walking, solid, in the darkness of nothing. There was nothing firmer.

And as she walked into another room full of lights, she woke up and this time could not fall back to sleep.

And now she began to walk in her dreams, walk between the darkness and the light, walk into new places and out of new places, walk in the darkness, spin in the darkness, change directions suddenly in the darkness. The darkness gave her confidence, gave her joy. She would spin in place. She would jump. She would jump and hover for a second, only to land solidly on the ground in the darkness.

Some nights she spent only in the darkness, enjoying herself.

And one day, instead of walking, she ran.

She ran in the darkness. And ran and ran and ran endlessly and always in one direction. Always in one direction.

For weeks she ran in her dreams, ran in one direction. She ran and jumped and whenever she found a new place with more lights, she shunned it and continued on into the darkness.

A year passed, and her dreams settled on the darkness and directions she would choose in the darkness. Only occasionally would she come to a place with light, and that place would always feel more and more like her own world of waking. She revelled in darkness, and each time she would invent something new to do in it.

And sometimes there was nothing new to invent, and she would simply run endlessly in one direction, further, ever further in that direction. And sometimes she would choose another direction and run ever further in that direction. There were so many directions, and each one felt different from the others.

And so it continued. And so she slept every day. And the Levantine experimenters could not document this and did not know of this, for it was in her sleep.

But time, as always, brings change.

And the Levantine Experiments were discovered, the scientists jailed, the labs broken into.

Thus it happened.

Two years and two months after the crack appeared, Sarah heard a sound from nowhere. She sat up immediately, looking around, frightened.

There were more sounds, which she could not describe, for she had never heard anything like them.

Hours passed, and the sounds assaulted her. They were loud and seemed to originate from the walls themselves. As if the walls were attempting to talk.

Sarah clung to the wall farthest from the sound. And then she noticed that the opposite wall was beginning to shake. It moved slightly with each sound. The sounds were getting harsher and clearer, and each time—bang!—they became—bang!—shorter—bang!

And then a new crack was formed in the wall.

Her breath caught.

With another sound, the crack widened, and light came through it.

Sarah straightened, her body taut, staring at the light.

Another sound, and the crack widened, and the light grew brighter.

"Don't worry," a voice said. Sarah knew words, because she had been taught them at an early age. But she had never heard this voice; she had not heard another's voice in nine years. "Don't worry," it said again. "We're coming for you. Stay away from the wall."

Sarah stood there, motionless, rigid, staring at the light.

And suddenly the crack was massive, and a piece of her world fell on the floor. And where it had been, now there was light. And from the light, a face appeared and looked in. But Sarah did not recognise what a face was, not having seen any from the age of two. And Sarah did not know the distinction between male and female. A new thing simply came through the wall, and fourteen-year-old Sarah stopped breathing.

Soon, more pieces of her world came tumbling down, and a figure emerged from the light. She stared at it, unable to run, unable to do anything, knowing that it came from the different world, that it came from the world of light and darkness.

It came close to her and its hand hung in the air next to Sarah's head, yet she did recognise what a hand was.

She looked at the hand, so different from her own. The hand hung there and did not move. Sarah slowly brought her fingers to the vicinity of the hand. The hand did not move. Ever so slowly, she touched the hand. A feeling shot through her hand that she did not recognise. Something happened to the figure's face, then, and it was distorted. Sarah took her hand back.

It then took a step backward, and took off an article of clothing.

Behind the figure, the light beckoned.

"Put this on," the figure said, the article of clothing hanging on its hand.

Sarah looked at it and then looked at the light.

The figure took back the article of clothing and pointed at the blanket. "Put this on," it said.

Sarah looked at its finger and then at the light.

She took a step toward the light. The figure moved its head and then moved its body, letting her pass.

She took another step toward the light. And now she could see something in that room. There was more than light. There was an inside. And there was another side.

She was upon the new crack in her world, and there was light beyond it, not darkness.

She bent down to fit inside the crack and walked through it into the light. And suddenly she was in a new place, a round place and not a square place. She was outside her world. She looked around and went on, for she knew that there was an outside to the outside.

She took another step, and the roundness continued. And the round walls were not smooth, but rough and edgy, for they had been broken and pummelled, although she did not know this.

Each step felt solid to her bare feet and she knew that it was real. There were lights placed in the new round place. And with every outside there was a new light. And with every outside there was another feeling beneath her feet, a feeling of realness.

And then there was a new side, as the round and close wall gave room to a massive place, square and leading in two directions. Lights hung from above in straight lines, pointing in both directions. Sarah stood there and could not decide.

The figure was beside her, she noticed. It pointed in one of the directions and took a step.

Sarah took a step in that direction.

And another step. And another step.

And she knew she could run now, for that was her dream.

She closed her eyes, to bring darkness. And then she ran and ran and ran. Behind her, the figure shouted "Hey!"

She ran and she ran and she ran, her eyes closed, running through darkness.

And then her head received a blow, and she was thrown backward and onto the ground.

She opened her eyes, and there was light above. And the figure came into view.

The figure helped her up. "Don't run from me," it said. "We're the good guys."

She was up and she looked around, and there was a vast space in one direction.

Immediately, she closed her eyes and ran.

She ran and ran and ran, and it felt almost like the dreams.

She ran.

And her entire body felt pain, and was thrown backward.

The figure helped her up, but this time it held her tightly, not letting her run or walk past it. And it walked with her through rooms of light until there was a room of light and many people.

And thus Sarah was rescued and brought into the outside world.

As the days passed, she received supervision. It was explained to her what had happened to her. Everything was explained to her: the nature of other people, the nature of the world, the big city, the roads, the rooms, the cars, the stars, the sun. It was endlessly explained to her, and eventually she understood everything.

But that did not interest her. She searched for big spaces.

They brought her to fields and stadiums. They brought her to the sea and to the desert. But it was never big enough.

She discovered that walking in light was not the same as walking in dark, for she could always see the limits, she could always see the end. Running in the light was not the same as running in the dark.

She spent her days looking for a truly dark place. But the nights were full of light and never really dark. And closed, empty rooms with the light off were never really dark, either.

Always, she could make something out. And so it was a room of light and not a room of dark.

It was never perfect.

And the fact that there was no endless place in which she could run in the dark haunted her. She knew that there was something wrong with this world, as there was with the world she had known. This world was not right. It was an even bigger prison than the one she had left.

There was no real dark in this world and no real endlessness in this world.

She had been told of the experiments, and taught the word prison, and been told that she was free. And yet the hugeness of the world mocked her. It looked endless, but it wasn't. It looked free, but it wasn't. It looked like the real thing, but it wasn't.

She yearned for endlessness. Now that she had been broken out of her world once, she yearned to break out again. This place was a jail to her, closed in and smothering. She kept waiting for more sounds from beyond, sounds that would put a crack through the walls of her current world and show her the real path to the real world.

At night, she still dreamt of running through the blackness, of choosing a direction. And the dreams were as real as ever.

She became claustrophobic in open spaces and in enclosed spaces. She could not take the falseness of this world. No-one believed her. Everyone thought this was a by-product of the experiment. Some mocked her. And the world mocked her most of all.

And one day, two years after her rescue, the pain in her head was too much. This new, claustrophobic world was too much for her, and she could not take its constant taunting. She took out her own eyes, slamming sharp things into them. The pain was too much. She had not imagined such pain. But the pain that had grown inside her for months justified the deed.

And once she had been treated and once the shock was over, she lived in a true world of darkness. There was no light, not even a little.

There was no endlessness in it, either. Not that she could

find. It still seemed that she was in a room, for she would always bump into something. And even when she knew herself to be outside in a vast space, the space was limited.

And yet each step was taken in true darkness. And each next step could be the one, the true step leading her away.

She was closer to the real world now. Closer than the other people. Closer than she ever had been.

In her dreams, she would run.

And in her life, each step was in darkness.

It was close.

"The Wheel of Samsara"

Han Song

Han Song is a Chinese science fiction writer of some note, and works as a journalist for the Xinhua News Agency. He won China's Galaxy Award four times for short fiction and is the author of several novels, the most recent being *Red Ocean* (2004).

She travelled in Tibet and one day arrived at Doji lamasery. It was a small temple of Tibetan Buddhism, now in a bleak, half-ruined state. What caught her eye was a string of bronze wheels hung around the wall of the temple. They were called the Wheels of Samsara.

There was a total of one hundred and eight wheels, moving in the wind; they symbolised the eternal cycle of life and death, of everything. She quickly noticed that one of them was a strange colour of dark green, singling itself out from the others, which were yellow.

It was the thirty-sixth wheel when counted clockwise.

She touched the wheels one by one, and made a vow to Sakyamuni, the Great Buddha. Midway through, a sudden gale began to blow, and a heavy mist fell. She was scared, and she ran back to the temple.

She stayed in the lamasery that night.

The gale continued and became a rainstorm. Thunder and flashes of lightning split the mountains and the sky. She could not fall asleep on such a night, and at midnight she thought she could hear the sob of the Tibetan plateau, which reminded her of her dead mother and her lonely father on Mars.

Suddenly, she heard a cry.

It was a miserable sound, weak as a hairspring and harsh as a woman's weeping, and it made her think of a ghost.

Fear stopped her own cry.

Though she knew lamas were sleeping in the next room, she didn't dare to go out or shout for help.

Winds and rain died out the next day and it became sunny. She told the lamas what she had heard the previous night.

They grinned, telling her it was not a ghost. "It was the howl of the wheel of Samsara," they said.

The howl of the Wheel of Samsara? She was surprised.

The lamas explained that it was one of the wheels. To be exact, it was the thirty-sixth clockwise. According to the lamas, Doji lamasery had been destroyed several times in the past five hundred years. Each time, the wheels were lost, and only the thirty-sixth one had been well-preserved to date. Though it disappeared in a number of landslides and floods, it was finally re-discovered. When gales and rain approached, it gave out unexplainable sounds.

So she looked at it carefully, but it kept silent. She touched it with her forefinger, and it emitted a sense of bleak dread, which flooded directly into her heart.

It was hard to imagine that it was the wheel that had cried the previous night.

"It was a wheel of soul," a lama murmured.

The lama's face was dark, his expression cryptic.

So it was an unusual wheel that had encountered so much rain, so many winds, but now it had to join such a string of ordinary wheels. Realizing this fact, she could not hold back her tears.

She returned to Mars and told her father about her finding in Tibet.

Father laughed and said, "Could that be called strange? The phenomenon was simply caused by static electricity on that remote blue planet."

Her father, a scientist, knew a lot of cases like that.

For instance, some valleys would emit the sounds of horses and dead soldiers in rainstorms, and some lakes would play music in the evenings. Documents even recorded a bronze bell in an ancient temple that could ring without anybody striking it.

"Once the air accumulates too much static electricity, it triggers the strange sounds. All this can happen at any moment on Earth. Never be scared, my daughter."

She felt relieved, but also dull, and lost. Father's explanation expelled her fear, but also cheated her of the mystery she craved.

In her mind, there should be some sort of ghost in Tibet, who would frighten her, perhaps, but wouldn't disappoint her. She went back to her own room and shut the door. Without any reason, she was out of sorts. She turned a cold shoulder to her father when he called her to dinner.

The next year, she went to Tibet again and made her way directly to Doji lamasery.

"You came for the wheel, right?" the lamas said, grinning, and winked their pearl-like eyes, which could see through everything.

She felt a little timid, and told them about the static electricity theory. However, she was afraid that they would be unhappy with the explanation.

So she added, "That was just my father's view."

The lamas did not feel unhappy. They smiled. "Last time you stayed here for only one night. So you could hear just one sort of sound. The wheel can send out thousands of different sounds. How can static electricity do that?"

"Is it true?"

Her heart jumped to her throat again, and she felt a mysterious shadow following her closely. She quickly forgot her father's words. She did not feel scared this time, and decided to stay in the temple.

The wheel cried again on a dismal night. This time it was not a ghost cry, but the sound of a man. Then it became the zigzag of vehicles, then the roaring of machines in a factory. After a whilst, a string of explosions were heard.

For several consecutive nights, she heard many different sounds.

One night it was a piece of music, but the tune was strange, of a kind she had never heard before.

She felt joy mixed with a bit of fear. One month passed.

The lamas saw it with equanimity. And they explained no more to her.

The day she left Doji lamasery, she carried back with her a bag of tapes.

Three months later she returned to Doji lamasery, with her father and one of her father's postgraduate students.

It was the sounds she had recorded that made her father serious, and he decided to look for himself.

"Now I realise that the sounds truly were unusual. Can it really be static electricity? Anyway, it is worth studying," he said.

Upon arriving at Doji lamasery, her father and his student

walked around the wheels of Samsara six times, but they saw nothing strange. The three of them stayed that night at the lamasery. At midnight, the wheel cried again.

Her father and his student put on clothes and rushed out, seeing that the wheel was quivering slightly, and its body was covered with a circle of red light. The sound came out of the body of the wheel. Her father raised his head toward the sky and discovered that it had turned red and all the stars had gathered together, listening to the sound with fixed attention.

The sound of the wheel changed tune, from happiness to grief. Then there were many sounds her father had never heard before.

Suddenly he felt that something was behind him. He turned and saw it was a lama. The lama's face was indigo and hung with a tricky, secret smile.

Father ran back to the temple. Seeing his daughter sitting on the bed in safety, he felt relieved. However, the girl herself was uneasy.

The next day her father told the student:

"It was monstrous. I thought it was a magic tape recorder. Maybe it was not a product of nature."

"Tape recorder...?"

"Yes, a bizarre tape recorder left by human history. Maybe it had something to do with an extinct civilization. It contains some strange sounds of ancient times."

"But, does not a universe hide inside the wheel?" the postgraduate student suddenly shouted out.

"A universe?" Father was startled. Young people always had different ideas, he thought.

"That is what I believe. Inside the wheel there is a universe, the same as the one we are living in."

For many years people had been searching for a mini universe, but the attempts had all failed. However, the student was still obsessed with the notion. Father's face lost colour, and he shook his head again and again.

"Impossible, impossible!"

"That was what I strongly felt last night. A sound seemed to have been emitted by a circumvolving black hole, and another seemed to have been created by a dropping asteroid. And there were more sounds, reminding me of the explosion of a supernova and the birth of a galaxy," said the student with a trembling voice.

Father thought it over and admitted the possibility. However, he was reluctant to believe the conclusion. He was a stubborn academician who held that there was only one universe.

"Are you my student?" he said. "How dare you talk about things this way! I am ashamed for you."

The student realised that he had spoken too much and violated the dignity of his teacher. He apologised for his abruptness; however, he refused to take back his words.

For several days they were lethargic. There was a dead silence between her father and his student. Nevertheless, the snowy mountains behind the lamasery turned ever more brilliant and graceful.

Only his daughter felt that the student had it right. He did raise a wonderful hypothesis, she thought.

Back on Mars, the young man often visited her home. The student usually launched a dispute with her father over the unexplainable universe. When the two men's faces turned red owing to the quarrel, she sat aside quietly, listening to and watching them with a curious expression. How lovely the men were.

Now she imagined that the student could take her to the mini universe in the wheel; that would be the most exciting journey of her life.

She'd always take the student's side. It was the side of unorthodoxy.

"The universe is trapped in the wheel. It can neither move nor evolve, and it cannot be observed with eyes or telescopes. It can only give out some poor sounds to tell about its past and attract the attention of passers-by. How innocent it is. It does not even know that the era out of the wheel is against its own," she said, red-eyed.

"How do you know that it cannot move or evolve? How do you know that it needs our pity? Maybe the truth is the other way around," said the boy, looking at the girl with a tender expression.

Being aware that his daughter might like the bothersome student, her father felt unhappy.

Father's gaze became ferocious when it fixed on the wheel. He began to regard it as a tumour growing on the planet, threatening the order and intellect of the human world.

He should cut it off.

One day he told the lama that he would carry the wheel to Mars for the purpose of scientific research. His daughter and the student were shocked upon hearing the request.

"Professor, you cannot do that. The Wheel of Samsara only belongs to the lamasery, and it only belongs to Tibet!"

"Father, you cannot take it away, it can only give out its voice here. It will die if you take it to a different place!"

Father just sneered and gazed at the lamas, waiting for a reply. The lamas seemed to have no clear idea about her father's request, and they were all at a loss. Her father thought that they would not agree with him, but he said, "Let's make a deal. How much is it?"

The lamas gathered and murmured for a whilst. Then an old lama, possibly the living Buddha of the lamasery, stepped forward and said to Father: "My benefactor, if you really want it, just take it away. Is there anything in the world that we cannot give up? And it is the wheel's fate."

The reply went beyond her father's expectations.

Watching the lama's peaceful face, the daughter and the student were stunned.

Father picked up the wheel. It was so heavy that he could hardly hold it up. At that moment, all the lamas walked out of the temple. They lowered their heads and began reciting sutras. Father lowered the wheel to the ground in front of the temple, placing it well, and stared at it with a thoughtful expression.

The daughter and student did not know what he was going to do next.

Suddenly, Father burst into bewildering laughter, just like an owl, and he pulled out his laser cutter, waving it toward the wheel.

"Let's see the real face of the so-called hidden universe!" he cried.

The daughter and student were frightened. They stepped forward to stop him but it was too late. The wheel was cut into two pieces down the middle, falling apart to the solid ground.

It was empty. Nothing was inside.

The lamas fell silent. So did the mountains and the sky. The daughter felt extremely uncomfortable. After a whilst, the sky became dark, and stars were just inches away from people's heads.

Everybody looked upward in astonishment.

At that moment, a silent, bright white light flashed across the sky, splitting the sky into two pieces, just as the laser cutter had cleaved the wheel.

Millions of wheels appeared in the sky, just like flocks of birds. They were spaceships she had never seen before. They were escaping something, in haste.

The lamas knelt down and began to pray.

Then the split sky began to fold along the white light in the middle of the universe.

And so did the vast land. The shadows of mountains rushed to an unnamed centre, just like fighting beasts, and their bodies huddled together.

The daughter lowered her head and saw the shadow of her body begin to bend, just like a tree eaten away by insects, and it finally broke from her waist.

Then all the shadows folded together from opposite directions, swallowing all the people, all the mountains and rivers, and all the oceans and stars.

The lamas' smiles flashed as an arc on the last second.

Nobody could see how the Big Bang started—it was quite different from all of humanity's previous hypotheses.

"GHOST JAIL"

KAARON WARREN

Kaaron Warren is an Australian writer currently living in Fiji (where this story is set). She is a winner of both the Ditmar and Aurealis Awards in Australia, and the author of the short story collection *The Grinding House* (2005). Kaaron's first three novels are forthcoming from Angry Robot, an imprint of Harper Collins in the UK.

Rashmilla arrived early at the cemetery, knowing she would need to battle the other beggars for a good place: not too close to the grave of the much-loved leader, not too far away. Cars stretched for a kilometre, spewing exhaust as they idled, waiting to park.

Rashmilla's face was dirty because the water didn't run every day. She waved a laminated letter at the people, a piece of paper which proved her house had burnt down and her five children, too. Many carried such a letter. They shared it. Once, a house did burn down with five children, but it was not Rashmilla's house. Not her children. There was a fire when Rashmilla was seven, her mother's house; her twin sister burned to death. Her childhood ghost, now always seven, always with her.

Rashmilla had a sack full of dried peas to sell. Most people refused the peas with a wave of a hand. "Please, for my children," she said, holding out her hand. Her childhood ghost wreathed around her neck like a cobra.

People gave generously; they always did at funerals. It was the fear of punishment in the afterlife, punishment for greed or cruelty. Rashmilla waved peas at the outer mourners and was about to push her way further in when she noticed a young child trapped in a closed circle of gravestones, whimpering. His family ignored him; they did not like to think about how he could be saved.

Rashmilla stepped in, ignoring the whirl of angry spirits, letting her twin sister snarl at them. She told the child, "It's okay, I can help you," then stepped out again. He kept whimpering and Rashmilla hissed, "Sshhh shhh, they don't like voices. Voices make them envious and wild."

She walked slowly around the circle, reading the dead names in a stilted, cautious way. Then she worked at each gravestone with her fingers, finding the one which was the loosest. This, she pried up and tipped over.

The circle broken, the boy stepped out, silent now. He glared at his family, as if to say, "A strange woman had to save me." Rashmilla put her hand out to the mother. "Please," she said. The woman ignored her. Rashmilla stepped forward; she would be paid for helping the boy.

"You need to say thank you." It was the police chief, come himself for the important funeral. He stood beside Rashmilla, twice as broad across, two heads taller than she.

The boy nodded, his mouth open. He glanced sideways, looking for his mother to help him out of trouble.

"Saying thank you would be a good idea," the police chief said, his voice gentle. "Give her money."

The boy ran; Rashmilla shook her head. "It doesn't matter," she said. "I didn't do it to be thanked."

"Why, then?" The police chief leaned closer, intent.

"Simply that those ghosts need to be told."

"What about this man's ghost? Whose death we mourn?" Police Chief Edwards said. He led her to the graveside, pushing through as if the other mourners didn't exist. Her childhood ghost muttered in her ear.

"Did he die in peace?" Rashmilla whispered. Her childhood ghost nodded, much braver.

Police Chief Edwards didn't smile or respond. Rashmilla thought he would beat her. She said, "His peaceful death will give him quiet," and the police chief smiled.

A small man, dressed neatly, threw himself into the mud. "Murder! Murder!" he wailed, and he threw both arms up, reaching for the police chief, as if beseeching him to take the act back.

Out of nowhere, men appeared, police sticks in hand.

"Such bitterness," Police Chief Edwards said to Rashmilla. "Such anger. It was an unfortunate death."

"Who killed this great man?" the speaker shouted. "Who silenced his great voice, who stilled his tongue and stopped his hand? Ask the question, ask it! Murder! And the guilty dare to stand here!" The policemen dragged him away.

Rashmilla shut her eyes, not wanting to see, but the men were close, so close she could smell hair oil. She stepped back from the conflict and tripped over a stone, too fast for her childhood ghost, who leaned forward, wanting a better look.

"I want to talk to you. Don't be frightened." Chief Edwards

looked at her ghost, not at her. "In the van. We'll sit in the van and I will buy all your peas. Your day will be done." He held out his elbow to her. "Come on," he said. "I have tea in the van. I will read your letter."

He was being very kind to her. Nobody read her letter; no-one cared about her house fire. He held her arm with gentle firmness.

In the van he poured her a tin cup of tea. It was black and strong and she felt the energy of it filling her as she sipped it.

He watched her, a smile on his face that she didn't like. He said, "There was a man buried here today. I will not lie and say that he was a good man; for all I know he beat his wife and spent his children's school fees on beer. But he still deserves to rest easy. Lies will send him to a restless grave. That mourner should not tell lies."

The van had thick walls, Rashmilla thought. She could not hear the prisoner in the back. She nodded. "I heard what he said. He said this man was murdered."

"He wishes to discredit the very people who save this country."

She closed her eyes, but her childhood ghost watched, sitting on her lap.

"I saw what you did for that young boy."

"I don't need a thank you."

"What you both did for that young boy."

She blinked at him.

"I can see her. Your ghost."

"Most can't."

"It's a talent which can be learnt. It can be useful."

"Not useful. A nuisance. Always the one to tell those bad ghosts what to do."

"Yes, I saw that. You have a way with them."

"I know them."

Chief Edwards considered her. "You come to the barracks in three days and ask for me. I think I have a job for you."

"A job? At the barracks?" She imagined herself with a bucket, a mop, and hot, bloody water.

"The job is not at the barracks, no. At the Cewa Flats. We

are helping people to relocate. You must have heard. You come in three days, and I will tell you what I need you to do."

"Selena in the Morning here, DJ to the disaffected. Up and at 'em, people, we can't change the world from bed." Her voice was sexy, deep. She liked to talk that way, like silk between the fingers. "I hear they've cleared the Cewa Flats because beneath them are the remnants of early settlers. Treasures, power. Police Chief Edwards wants it cleared because he wants that shit for himself. He's willing to risk the cancer, I bet."

She played a message from him: "*Because the breath is all that remains when we die. All that remains of us. The body can be burned, can be buried. The breath exhaled is the very essence of us. If that is tainted, cancerous, then no passage from earth will be gained.*" His voice sounded so reasonable. "*It's for your own good to leave this place. This is no place for families. Children don't belong here.*"

Lisa Turner, already at the computer, getting an hour in before leaving for the newspaper office, listened and smiled. She liked to start the day with Selena.

Lisa wondered how she managed to stay sharp, out of their reach, when she spoke the truth. They didn't like the truth.

Selena whispered in her heartfelt voice, "He's gonna rip up that yard for something buried. His Great Malevolence is gonna dig the crap out of it and we all know what he's gonna find. A few old stones the museum would be interested in, nothing else. The man is a fool."

Selena launched into her soap opera, names changed to protect the innocent, but she went too far with it, and the next morning Lisa tuned in like she did every day, only to hear the dull voice of a company man, playing sweet tunes and letting the words rest. "We don't need words," he announced. "Now is the time for music."

Lisa's editor, Keith, led the protest to bring Selena back to the airwaves. He used the newspaper and printed sheets on the street, in letter boxes, no names on there, no trouble. He used his contacts, his power. "Freedom of Speech the Victim," the campaign ran. Enough letters in, brave people willing to risk arrest to have their say, and it was "Thank you, all of you," from Selena. A week after her removal she was back on the air. "I laughed so hard I split my trousers when they banged on my door. No-one wants to see my split trousers. I have to be serious for just a moment. Thank you for wanting me back. I'll try to make it worth your whilst. I've got this for you: I've heard there's only one place in the city where electromagnetic interference means no bugging devices can be used. Cewa Flats. So if you're making a plot or think someone's watching you, this is the place for you. Sorry. I said I'd be serious and I lasted about a minute. Carry on without me for three minutes forty-five seconds," and she played a local song of hibiscus flowers and the river running clean.

Lisa and Keith arrived at the Cewa Flats to cover the evacuation of the families. She'd driven past the flats many times. At first she'd felt guilty, in her good car with her warm clothes on, seeing the children in torn singlets, bare legs. Rubbish piles. She'd felt all the guilt of privilege. But that faded; she got busy, distracted by bigger stories. She drove past without even noticing, now. The flats were so small she could see through the front window and out the back. Four storeys high, ten rooms on each storey, six buildings. All the corners broken off and a great crack running down the middle of building C, so broad she could see sky through it. Graffiti, written and written again, illegible and meaningless. The bricks, once pale yellow, were dark red. Lisa knew it was a chemical reaction within the pigment, but it looked bloodstained.

The children ran barefoot, in shorts too small, shirts too big.

Plastic bags full of belongings, the people waited for buses to transport them to their new homes. Lisa helped one woman with five children, each carrying two bags.

"We have nothing more," the mother said. Lisa had some canvas shopping bags in the car, and she gave them to the woman, helping her transfer the things. Grey, beige, some washed-out colours. Wrapped in a torn shawl was a hard box; the woman nodded at it. "All we have. My grandmother's coin of release."

Lisa knew a lot of these people were descended from kidnapped slaves.

The mother spoke with her hand over her mouth. Others did, too, and some wore masks covering half their faces.

The children were mostly covered with head scarves.

"I can't breathe," one skinny little girl complained. "And this doesn't smell like air."

"You don't want to breathe until we leave. You don't want to catch cancer of the breath," the mother said to her.

Lisa shook her head. "You know there is no such thing. You can't get cancer of the breath."

"Oh? Then what is in my mouth to make this?" The woman dropped her bags, reached up and grabbed Lisa's ears, pulling her close.

The breath was awful, so bad Lisa gagged.

"You see? Even your white girl politeness can't stop you."

"That's not cancer of the breath. It's your teeth and gums."

"If you had children you would understand. You would not risk your child's breath to stay here."

"You should wear a scarf," the skinny little girl said to Lisa. "Your face is ugly and pink and shiny too much."

Lisa cared little for taunts about her burn scars. She was proud of them, proud of where they came from, though she never spoke of what she had achieved in getting them.

Other children rolled an old tyre to each other, a complex game with many a side.

A policeman gestured to the family. "The bus. Come on."

The mother gathered her children and they squeezed into the bus on laps, arms out the window.

"I'd like to come, see where you're being settled," Lisa said. The woman waved her away with a hand flap.

Keith had been helping another family. He said, "I'm imagining where they're going has to be better than this." He patted her shoulder. "I'm looking into the land reports. You chase this story up."

Lisa followed the buses to the new settlement, forty-five minutes away. The air was cleaner out there, and the shacks lined up neatly, each facing away from the door of the next. There was the sense of a village about it.

Lisa watched the children run around and explore. The

parents called to each other, laughing.

"It seems okay," she reported back to Keith.

"What did you expect? A work camp?"

"You never know. I haven't figured out his justification for getting rid of them."

Three days later, Keith's house was seized under the "uncontrolled verbiage" ruling. He had written his editorial without restraint. He'd lived life too easy; he didn't know how it could get. He wrote: *No-one with any critical assessment thinks the transfer of families from Cewa Flats is solely to benefit the children, although anyone can see that the people are far better off. Their new place is much finer; it is the motivation I call into question.*

He rang Lisa, told her he was going to stay at Cewa Flats for a couple of days before they came to arrest him. "Last place they'll expect me to be. And I can do some good there, you know. Prove this breath cancer bullshit isn't true."

"And if you're there, others are there; they won't be able to go ahead with the redevelopment. It's not like they can pull the place down around you. People will be watching. I'll be watching."

"You be careful, Lisa. You write only the truth. Give the rumours to Selena."

They both laughed.

"Truth in print. Gossip on the radio. As it should be."

Lisa understood about covering up; many days she buried small pieces of information, anything which might connect her to the long-past fire. She did not regret her actions, but she was terrified of the results.

Selena in the Morning said, "I've got it here. The land assessment report of the Cewa Flats, and I'm not going to tell you who gave it me. It's real, though. You know I said there were treasures buried? It's a little more than that. According to the report, the land itself is worth something, and the dirt, it's full of some sort of shit we need. Why should the government get it, just like that?" The radio went quiet for a moment. Then music.

Selena was silent for three days, then Lisa pushed her way in for an interview with Police Chief Edwards. She lied; said it was a piece about mothers' cooking, how good it is, favourite recipes.

He was a big man, charming, with a dazzling smile. If she'd met him at a bar, any pick up line would have worked.

He was furious when he realised where she stood. "How dare you? I am not a monster. I want families to be safe from people like you and your cancerous words." He threw her out, hissing, "Write nothing. Say nothing."

That night, Lisa heard a crash of glass downstairs and reached for the phone. Voices, and she knew for sure there was someone in the house.

She dialled Keith but his mobile didn't work; all she heard was a high-pitched squeal. Then she dialled her neighbours, hoping one would at least look out the window, shout at the invaders. No answer. Finally, in desperation, she called the police. She flipped open her computer and logged on at the same time.

The phone rang a dozen times. She heard the men downstairs, moving around as if they were looking for something. She quietly shut her door, then moved to look out of the window. It was barred; she had no chance of getting out that way.

"Hold, please," the operator said.

Music, some old pop song, played on bells. "Help," she whispered. She hid in the cupboard. She didn't care what the men took; they could have it all. She didn't want to disturb them. They carried machetes, these home invaders, and guns. They would not always try to kill, but she knew that many arrived out of it on booze or drugs.

"Hello?" she whispered into the phone. Footsteps on the stairs.

"Can I help you?" The cold, hard voice of the operator.

"My home is being invaded," she whispered. She gave her address. "Hold, please." The operator was remarkably calm; unaffected.

"Lisa Turner?" This came through the door. They knew her name.

"Lisa Turner, we have a warrant for the repossession of your home due to uncontrolled verbiage activity."

Lisa felt deep relief. Every day she spent in fear that her moment of activism would catch up with her, that the grieving relatives perhaps would track her down and ask her why people had to die for her cause. Lisa did not regret the fire. The building had been on sacred ground and the activities inside had destroyed the souls of the true residents of the country. She was sorry that people had needed to die, but it had been necessary. She had lost contact deliberately with those who had instigated the attack; they had considered the deaths a victory, whereas she felt great pain, great guilt, and knew that she would have to atone for it one day.

The police operator hung up on her. As the men entered her room, Lisa hit send, and her notes went out to a dozen journalists and activists around the world.

She expected to be interviewed, locked up, but they gave her thirty minutes to pack her bag and leave her home.

They recommended a hotel for her to stay in, which made her laugh. They would watch her every move, listen to her every word.

Before he ran, Keith had told her, "We can't put friends or family at risk. If you need to, come join me. Don't go anywhere else. If they take your house, go there. It's the first stop. We'll get the bastards."

They confiscated Lisa's car, too, so she hailed a taxi to take her to the Cewa Flats. They passed through a roadblock at the end of the street; Lisa wondered who it was they were keeping out. All the way the driver cleared his throat, spitting out the window. When they arrived, he turned and smiled at her. His teeth were red. "I'll be out of this country soon. I keep my mouth shut. I'm just waiting for my visa to come through."

"You know it won't, don't you? You know they're not letting anyone out. They've cancelled all visas, all passports."

He shook his head. "University girl. You don't know how this country goes. You shouldn't tell lies to us."

Lisa climbed out, paying him a generous tip. "Good luck with it," she said. He gave her such a look of hatred she misshut the door and had to do it again.

The flats were dirty and huge up close. She stepped forward, over a grey, cracked path. The front dirt area was empty of people, a rare thing. Even after the families left, the young men remained, and they hung together in clumps, moving as one large mass, always something in their hands to be tossed up and down, up and down.

None of the young men were there. In their rooms? Lisa looked up at the many dark doorways. Doorless.

An old woman took her hand and squeezed it. "I am Rashmilla. I will guide you through the spirits." She had an odd shape, lumpy around the chest, as if she had a child hidden in there.

"Up there," she pointed. "You find a room up there. You scream if they bother you, and I'll send my sister to talk to them."

Lisa saw the lump in Rashmilla's chest wriggle.

"You can see her?" Rashmilla whispered. She began to unbutton her dress; Lisa backed away, wanting to escape.

"If who bothers me?" Lisa said. "I have friends here, you know. They don't bother people. They speak the truth."

"I'm not talking about your friends, dear," Rashmilla said. "You will know when you meet one."

It was hard to tell a vacated room from an inhabited one. Families had left in a hurry, leaving rubbish, belongings behind. Small clay pots, some with grey ash to the rim, sat in many corners. Mouldy cushions, piles of mice-infested newspaper, remnants of clothes.

Lisa poked her head through a door on the top floor, saw a man sprawled on a mat and pulled back.

"Who's there? Who is it?" he called. "I'm at home."

Lisa backed away. He hadn't seen her and she didn't know him. He sounded desperate; too eager.

She changed her tactic after that, walked slowly past each door and tried to have a sideways peek through the shuttered window. The walls had posters, dismal and ancient attempts to bring colour and life to the small, dank rooms. They seemed embedded, welded to the walls.

She carried a small suitcase. She'd left the rest of her things behind in her house; she imagined the police would have been through everything by now and taken what they wanted. She found a room with a mat and a pile of empty, rusted tins, each with a dry residue at the bottom. She put down her suitcase and tried to find comfort in the space. The rooms were three metres square, space for a mat and a sink which also did as a toilet, she could tell.

Looking from her window, all she could see were buildings: dark, rank, decrepit.

It was late—past eleven—and quiet. She curled onto her mat. It was hard and thin with smooth stains at either end. She pulled out a shirt and used that as a shield for her face.

In the morning, people started to emerge. A sense of community filled her. Of possibility. She could hear people talking quietly, and footsteps, people moving around, making breakfast, and, she hoped, coffee. She recognised faces; people she knew. From the inside out the room didn't look so bad. She had a view, when she stood on her toes and squinted, of a small grove of trees that would bear fruit during the wet season. With a small breeze she fancied she could smell the fruit. It was intoxicating, like the first sniff of a good wine.

She liked wine. Felt an emptiness for it. That first sip around the dinner table, already knowing that the conversation would become freer the more people drank. That soon they would be shouting, making plans, talking of outrages, human rights, and moving the country forward.

She saw Rashmilla one floor down in the building to her left. She called out, but her voice seemed muffled. She tried again but then...she opened her mouth to call out again and from her feet, from through the floor, rose a tall, thin ghost, a man with red lesions along his cheekbones. He raised his fist and she flinched, unprepared.

He thrust the fist into her mouth and out, so fast all she felt was a mouthful then nothing but the taste of anchovies left behind.

She reached to grab him but he leapt over the balcony, over so fast he blurred in her eyes.

She heard nothing.

She looked over and there was nothing, only Rashmilla looking up, her face serene.

Lisa ran; got to the stairwell, turned around and the ghost was right beside her, fist raised. With his other hand he shushed her, finger to lips.

She hated to be shushed. "I won't…." she started, but the fist again, in and out of her mouth again, how the hell? She couldn't even get her own fist in there.

She watched him this time over the side and down to the ground where he seemed to...disintegrate.

Lisa dragged herself down the stairs. There were people in many of the rooms, most with their hands over their ears. Others moved up and down the stairs, purposeless. She knew some of them, had sat and talked all night with them, but none of them acknowledged her or seemed willing even to meet her eyes.

Rashmilla slid up to her as she reached the bottom step. "I don't want peas," Lisa said, waving her away.

"Have you understood?"

Lisa's eyes adapted; she could see a young girl, the ghost of a young girl, resting herself on Rashmilla's chest. Lisa could see her face, her teeth; she could see the dirty scarf she wore around her neck.

"I understand I won't stay here." Lisa stepped away. Rashmilla grabbed her arm, reached out and touched Lisa's scarred cheek.

"You were burned badly in a fire. I look at you and think of loss. Of all the things gone in the fire."

Rashmilla had the skin of a child. Soft, pale brown, unblemished; it was wrong for her.

Lisa pushed past; Rashmilla hissed, "You behave ugly, you get the cancer of the breath."

"I don't believe you."

"It doesn't matter if you believe or not. This is not about belief."

There were deep holes here, dug by bored children. Lisa reached the stone path and trod carefully this time, lifting her foot over the stones.

Something grabbed her ankle, both ankles, and pulled her back. No time to prepare, she landed with a crack on her chin and lay there, pain blurring her thoughts of all else.

"You can't step over the gravestones," Rashmilla said, shaking her head. She dabbed at Lisa's chin with a filthy rag. "They moved them so carefully, laying them down one by one. It doesn't matter, though. The ghosts don't care about how gentle they were."

Lisa crawled from stone to stone and saw that Rashmilla was telling the truth; the names and dates of the long dead, the recently dead, their stones laid close together.

Lisa pushed herself up and ran to her room, ignoring the whisper of the ghosts around her.

She turned on her laptop to send some emails, get some action. The outrage at such desecration, surely that would get a response. Her first message was to Selena. There was a woman of power, with a voice. Selena needed to know the place wasn't safe, that it wasn't a good place to meet. There were ghosts.

The battery was dead, though, and she felt a sense of great disconnection.

Rashmilla knocked at their doors one by one. "You will listen to the speech," she told everyone. "You will listen when he speaks."

"Listen," her childhood ghost echoed. "Listen to the man in the van."

Police Chief Edwards, broadcasting through the speakers of his large white van, said, "Language is a violence. You lepers bring cancer of the breath to the people; it is best you are kept away from the deserving, the good people of this land who support what we are doing and accept it."

Lisa saw Keith, waved at him, wanting his help. *Look at me, look at me.* He scratched under his arms and went back inside.

She circled around Rashmilla, then went up the stairs to Keith's room. The smell of human waste was terrible. Did they use the sinks? With barren ground surrounding the buildings, she couldn't see why people would use sinks for their toilets.

Keith lay on his mat. She had never seen him inactive; it looked odd. Even when he rested he would read, take notes, do something. He lay there, almost motionless.

"Keith," she said. "It's me. I'm here."

There was a stirring around her, like bats she couldn't see.

"They don't like you to talk loud," he said. He got up. "I'd ask you in but there's not really any room."

"There isn't. This place is awful, Keith. It's haunted."

"It's safe," he said, but his eyes were closed as he spoke.

"It's not safe. There are ghosts here who don't want us to speak."

"They don't like noise. They don't mind quiet talking."

"What about talking about our situation?" she said. Keith curled up away from her, blocking his ears with his shoulders, his hand over his mouth. At her ankles, she felt a tugging, and she looked down to see the ghost of a legless man, his fist drawn, his face livid.

"Quiet," Keith whispered.

"I'm not staying here, Keith. This is not a haven. Haven't you realised that?"

The look he gave her made her feel shallow and empty.

Keith turned his back to her, curled up on his mat and hummed softly.

"We'll get out of here," Lisa said. "I'll find a way and we'll get out."

Keith gave a low moan, blocking his ears. Lisa felt a cool breeze behind her and turned to see a gelid old ghost of a woman, shaking with fury. The woman lifted her arms and flew at Lisa, clutching her fingers at Lisa's throat.

Lisa choked, trying to suck in air. It smelt like old potatoes.

The old woman thrust her thumbs into Lisa's mouth and pinched. The pain brought tears to her eyes. Her terror was so complete she felt as if another word would never come from her.

The old woman vanished in a faster-than-light flash. Lisa turned to see Keith, sitting up, hugging his knees.

"Shhh," he said.

She left him and went to lie on her own mat, to think. Surely she was able to think.

The moment she closed her eyes, her head was filled with voices, a mess of noise she couldn't make sense of. The voices were flat, dull; it sounded like thirty people reading the newspaper aloud in languages unfamiliar to them.

She lay with her eyes open, letting her body rest. She felt a deep exhaustion. She had not felt such sustained fear since the fire. That, at least, had been a tangible threat with an obvious course of action: if she was caught, she would confess and never give any names away.

Here...but there was something she could do. She scrabbled for her phone and found it. The battery was fully charged, but she could get no signal except a high-pitched squeal that made her want to jump out of the window.

Lisa tried again, and again, and once more to step over the stone path, but she couldn't. The ghosts screamed in her ears; she felt a pop, as if her eardrums had burst, and a sharp pain, which felt like a knitting needle in one ear and out the other.

"Can you call someone to visit? I have a friend I want to contact."

Rashmilla shook her head. Her childhood ghost laughed, spun around.

"You can't leave."

"Will you call her for me? I'll pay you."

Rashmilla shook her head. "You don't want me to leave the ghosts alone. They are nice when I'm here."

"Nice?" Lisa looked at her to see if she was making a cruel joke.

"They behave for me."

"Why can you step out?"

"They don't know if I'm a ghost or a woman."

"If we lift the stones, will the circle be broken?" Lisa felt nausea and pain when trying to talk. The ghosts of two young boys with yellow eyes pulled her backward.

"They are set in concrete. Cannot be lifted. You could read the names but they don't want to be released."

"Her name's Selena. She's on the radio."

Rashmilla nodded. "I know that lady. The police chief calls her Sell. He says, Sell, what do you think, but he doesn't listen to her answer. I see through every window. Sell lies naked with the police chief."

"Selena?" Lisa had never felt so stupid, so naïve, so ill-informed and betrayed. Her career was a joke; she could not research, write, or investigate to save her life.

"How do we stop the ghosts?" she asked, looking over her shoulder. The ghosts rose up, snarling, teeth bared in fury.

"There is no way," Rashmilla said. "They don't like noise, they don't like talk, they are caught by the endless circle of stones."

A taxi pulled up, and a young man stepped out. Lisa knew him, the editor of a local "radical" magazine. She'd met him a few times at drinks, and they'd spoken of change, of effecting change. She'd emailed him at the moment her house was taken. She didn't know if he'd responded or not.

"Don't step in," she tried to shout, but the ghosts of the young boys kicked her shins, knocked her to the ground and hovered their filthy faces in hers. There were bleeding cuts on their cheekbones.

Rashmilla stepped out to greet him, then helped him into the circle. Her childhood ghost ruffled his hair, looked into his ears.

"Dale," Lisa said. One of the ghost boys grabbed her tongue, spat in her mouth. "Dale, lift the stones," she said, but he didn't hear her, didn't recognise her in the dirt. He caught his toe on a jagged corner and he tripped. He broke his fall with the heel of one hand, and a sharp edge sliced into the soft mound and blood oozed out.

He walked his arrogant, hip-thrusting walk past her to the stairs. Rashmilla helped him, but Lisa could see the ghosts hovering behind her, waiting for her to release him.

A scream came, harsh and odd in the silence.

She still had the energy to step forward and look, see what had caused the noise. Other people did too, men and women dragging themselves out of their small, stinking rooms to see Keith, fallen or pushed, splattered on the ground.

There was a sigh, a collective sigh, not of sorrow but of pure envy. "Lucky lucky lucky lucky lucky," Lisa heard, the people whispered. "Lucky lucky lucky," but none of them leapt over, none of them had the strength or the power to die.

Lisa opened her mouth to let the noise out, but around her the ghosts waved their fists and she swallowed it down.

Lisa thought of all the silenced voices and how many more there would be. Soon this place would be empty again, starved husks removed or left to rot or to be buried by anyone who had the strength.

She felt a great sense of impetus, of gravity.

Lisa said, "Matches?"

Rashmilla said, "Money."

Lisa gave her all, gave her everything she had.

She thought clothing would burn well, so she went upstairs and put on everything from her suitcase. The T-shirt with "Bali—Party Town" on it that she wore to bed. The scarf her mother had knitted her. The jeans she'd bought in Hong Kong and wished she'd bought ten pairs, because they were perfect.

She put all that on. She collected a can of fuel from under the stairs and stood there, out of sight. She struck a match.

The ghosts were furious, ripping out her hair, tearing it out in chunks, tripping her. The ghosts came at her and she felt her energy leaving. She had to finish it.

Lisa struck another match. She heard whining behind her. Rashmilla said, "What are you doing? You have made them angry." Her childhood ghost clung to her, hiding her eyes in the torn material of her dress.

Lisa set fire to her scarf, to the long sleeves of her shirt, to the cuffs of her jeans. She fell to her knees as she burnt, screaming with pain, so full of it she no longer noticed the ghosts. From the great heat to cold. She had been under anaesthetic three times before and this felt like that had: the cold starting at the entry point, in the arm, and pumping with the blood till her heart was chilled to stillness.

She grabbed a gravestone and she felt something shifting, moving inside her. Her ghost lifting. The body slumped; her ghost flew up.

"You won't last. You are not meant for here," Rashmilla said. "You can't escape. We have tried." Her childhood ghost shook her head.

"Shhh," Lisa said, and thrust her fist into Rashmilla's mouth.

Keith joined her, fresh ghost, lacking bitterness, unconfined. They moved together, waiting for Police Chief Edwards, for Selena and others like them. Ready to fill their mouths with fists and hair, ready to stop their words and change the world.

"Wizard World"

Yang Ping

One of the bright young stars of Chinese science fiction, Yang Ping was born in 1973 in Shanxi and studied at Nanjing University. He is currently an IT journalist. His first story was published in 1996, and since then he's published several more stories, a novel, and a short story collection. The following story won China's Galaxy Award for science fiction.

The colours of the World were 256.

I regretted going there, even whilst going deeper. I had got the address from a guy named Pig Tongue ten minutes before, which was as long as I'd known him. He talked about the place as if it were a Heaven and seemed to think no other third-level World could be more beautiful. "But I can't tell you more. It's a matter of permissions, you know..." he whispered in a low voice. He even showed me his Heart. I promised him that I would come here, by the trust that that exquisite Heart gave me. And he got ten points, of course. We must pay for everything, in this society.

It was a ruined place. The brown-green land, the blue sky without clouds, the horizon with third-level colour scheme...damn! Even the lamest newbie in the World could do better than that. But, since I was already there, I walked around and looked for some fun.

The point appeared on the horizon and grew to become a house in a short time: it had two floors and many windows. I moved to the front door, tried the handle, but it wasn't responding. If anything interesting existed in that World, then it had to be hiding in the house. There were no other houses.

I looked up. There was a chimney on the roof. I thought maybe I could fly there and try to get in. I turned on the Aircraft. A window popped up, startling me: "Flying access denied." No sound support either. It was rubbish, but I wasn't as surprised as in the beginning. I walked around for a whilst. No place to climb. No window to open. I walked back to the door.

Suddenly I noticed a flower basket by the door. The petals were clear. This design, this meticulous design in this ruined place, had to mean something. I issued a command: Get everything from the flower basket. The system responded: "You get a key!"

It was easy...looking back, I should have known it was too easy. I didn't.

I opened the door with the key. There was a living room with a sofa, a carpet, et cetera. Stairs led to the second floor. No-one there. I walked to a computer at the corner of the room, pressed something that looked like a switch.

"Hello, Xingxing. What's the problem?" the screen said.

Huh? It knew my name. Interesting. "I am confused," I said.

Another message: "User error 35: using illegal channel."

There was no sound support in that World. I pulled out a keyboard, typed: "I am confused," followed by an unhappy smiley.

The machine again: "You can find the medicine in the room at the end of the second floor."

What the hell was going on? I followed the stairs up to the second floor. I found a closed door at the end of the corridor and made my decision: I would leave there and then if any damned key was needed. My patience was limited, and I didn't need ten points that badly.

But the door opened easily.

It was dark inside. After some misgivings, I stepped through.

"This is outer space. You do not have protective equipment. You are in danger."

Shit! I immediately turned back, tried to get back into the house, but the door was closing. All I could do was watch the bright corridor being devoured by stars. "Your blood vessel composition is breaking down." The green Health line was shortening continually. I twisted around, alarmed. "Your brain is oxygen-deficient, your mind begins to blur." The Health line turned shorter and shorter, changed to yellow, red, then bright red....

"No!"

I screamed. It didn't do me any good.

"User error 35: using illegal channel."

Only a few moments later, I saw my lifeless body floating in space. A window popped out with red characters: "You are dead."

The words kept blinking on the screen.

I may have temporarily lost my mind at that point.

I was kicked back to the main screen of the system with a soft, sad song. The screen said: "Due to the unfortunate event of your demise, your account has been deleted. Please register new account with MUD Wizard Association (MWA). Address: newuser.useraccount.mwa.mud."

I took off my headpiece, threw it aside. Shit! Damn! In a violent rage, I walked around the room, kicking everything in my way. How could it be? I had never died before! All my stuff, my World was lost! The problem wasn't re-registering with a new account, the problem was that I needed half a month just to get permission to own a private house, not to mention World building—I couldn't accept that!

I lay down on the bed and lit a cigarette. I watched the ceiling. Outside, the noisy city had become very quiet. After a whilst I became calmer. I tried to analyse what had happened. First, the creator of that World disobeyed the Pact of MUD, didn't set warning signposts in a dangerous area. Second, I began to doubt the so-called Pig Tongue. Maybe he had already died in there, had wanted someone else to follow him into death. I could report the creator, get atonement, maybe even gain 1000 points. Maybe (if God had mercy) I would be judged to have experienced illegal death and have my status restored. And that Pig Tongue would pay for all this. I was the Primary Practice Wizard of MWA; it would be easy to punish a common user.

Thinking this, I sat up, grabbed the headpiece, and connected to the system. MUD was managed very strictly, and any deportment that disobeyed the Pact was forbidden. So although I knew many Wizards and Arch-Wizards, I still needed to follow the procedure to register. I connected to the account site. The system requested a new account name. I typed in "Xingxing."

System: "Account in use, please choose a different name."

What? My account still existed?

I connected to the Entrance. I typed in "Xingxing." The password was requested and I typed it in.

System: "Wrong password."

Impossible! I tried again. Another failure. The system disconnected after my third failed attempt and said: "Attempting to crack another user's account is strictly forbidden."

I was, once again, confused.

The only thing I could do was register a new account. That was the only way that I could find my friends and do something.

The first World was Flower Square, the new user's beginning World. You could buy anything there: Worldwide address list, language translator, Aircraft, et cetera. As a new user, I got 100 points. I bought a translator. I could remember many addresses. I didn't need a list. The Aircraft was too expensive; it cost 240 points—forget it. I walked forward in the noisy street, didn't pay any attention to the beggars. Bees had been added here, humming, flying around, and nearly hit my face several times.

At the northeast corner of the square there was a bar crowded with Wizards. I walked in and saw Porket was talking to some of the other Wizards. I called out to him. He saw me but said nothing.

"I'm in trouble, Porket!" I sat down beside him. He turned to me: "Do I know you?"

"Of course!" Suddenly, I realised that he couldn't know me because of the new account. "I'm Xingxing," I said.

It seemed he missed my words. He paused for a moment, then kept talking to the others. I stood up and said loudly: "I am Xingxing! I'm in trouble, Porket! You have to help me!"

He waved his hand toward me. A strong white light bounced up and engulfed me. Then everything went dark. The system said: "You passed out."

I couldn't do anything during the blackout. After a whilst, I woke up and found myself lying in a strange room, surrounded by many pictures of naked girls. Porket was staring at me. "What the hell did you do?" I said, and: "Is this your house? Don't you think it shows a little too much personality?"

He let it pass, looked at me: "Are you the real Xingxing?"

"Of course. I know you have stolen source code off of a second-level World."

"I had authorization."

"Right. But you got that authorization *after* the theft, not before. I was with you then."

He raised a hand, put it down slowly. "You *are* Xingxing."

"Relax, man, I won't report it." I tried to smile. "After all, I perjured myself alongside you."

"Don't you know having two accounts is against the law?" he said sharply. "If I hadn't knocked you out and carried you here, those Wizards might have reported you. You would have been ruined!"

"I've almost been ruined already," I said. "My account's been cracked." I told him the whole story. "You're a seasoned Wizard," I said when I was done. "What should I do now, Porket?"

Staring at a picture, he was silent for a moment. Then he smiled. "You should have set yourself to undead."

I sighed. "Yes, I was stupid," I said. And: "Could you suggest a solution?"

"First of all," Porket said, "this was planned in advance. Think about it. How could your account have been cracked?"

I thought for a while: "Someone got hold of my password, or...or he registered this account as soon as I was dead, before I was able to."

"Exactly," Porket said. "Getting hold of someone's password is very hard. Even the best of us in the MWA can't succeed every time. So, an easy way is killing someone in MUD and grabbing his account before he re-registers. Look, obviously, someone was interested in your account."

"Why? Why me?" I was puzzled. "I'm not exactly a celebrity."

"There must be something about you that is of interest to them. Maybe it's just an experiment, a test to see whether it works. And maybe...." He paused, then shouted out suddenly, scaring me, "I've got it!"

"What? What did you get?" I got nothing.

He didn't answer me immediately, but waved his arm, opening a window in the air before us. He took out a keyboard, began to type. "Look." He moved the window toward me. "You're a Primary Practice Wizard, you should know something about MUD managing. This is a download record of the MWA's account manager system—through it we can check who's downloaded files."

"You mean...."

"It's a bug in the MUD interface. Hell! We found it once, but no-one thought it was important. Every Wizard account in MUD gets a record in the file. It's very simple; it only lists the permission level. For example, your record simply reads: Xingxing (PPW). The system will check your permission from the file when you log in, and then give you access."

"It sounds reasonable."

"The problem is...the problem is the system won't remove the record from the file automatically after the user is dead. So the account will still have its original permissions once it is re-registered. Your account," he said soberly, "is an example, I think."

"Unbelievable! How could MWA let this bug exist?"

"On the one hand, it's a historical problem," he said. "In earlier MUD, in the original age of MUD, the system was designed like that. At that time, the system wouldn't delete the account, just decrease the user's parameters. There was no real danger, and the account stayed on indefinitely unless a user manually deleted it. On the other side, Wizards usually set themselves as undead. Even if they didn't—like you—"

I scowled.

"—still the possibility of someone else signing in with your account name, in the period between your dying and trying to sign in again, is close to zero. So MWA never worried about it. But now...." He laughed without humour.

I still tried to stay optimistic. "I'm just a PPW, it's no use cracking my account."

"Look!" He pointed at the window, which was showing the latest file download records. On the third line from the end, it said, impressively, "/imm/etc/passwd->102.36.64.234.7.190.111.1 by Xingxing 11/03/2097 16:24:55 GMT." That meant a Wizard named Xingxing had downloaded the password file to a machine with address 102.36.64.234.7.190.111.1 just then.

"So what?" I said. "The passwords in the file are all encrypted."

"Right. But you could still compute it in half an hour if you had good tools and a decent machine. If this is true, hundreds of PPW accounts are in danger of being hacked." His voice was cold.

I was frightened. "So what should we do?"

"We're lucky that your account can only get the password file of other PPWs, and this account can't modify system modules. So we can keep the account security for upper levels like Wizard, Arch-Wizard, God, Arch-God. Unless...God!" He cried, knocking at the keyboard.

I watched him helplessly.

"Three minutes ago, a PPW was advanced to Wizard. So if someone hacked this account, he could get all kinds of password files and modify the system now!"

I nearly cried out.

"Let's go find this Wizard!" Porket pointed in the air and picked me up. Darkness covered me....

When the light came back I found myself in a palace that was built in a mix of Eastern and Western styles. Pictures flickered and changed on the wall. In the centre of the hall was a statue of Careless—the father of MUD.

About 50 years ago, Careless formed the integrative standard of the MUD system, integrated each divided MUD, and created a worldwide virtual reality system on the Internet—modern MUD. You can find his statue almost everywhere. No-one knows his real identity. There were many rumours about him. Some even said he was still alive, and travelled the Worlds using an anonymous account. The original Careless account was reserved. No-one could use it.

"Where is it?" I asked. Porket shook his head. "I've never been here either. It looks like a secret first-level World. I made us move to the Wizard's World just now."

A caterpillar half the height of a man came out from a corner, crept over and through us as if we weren't there, and left a trail of multicoloured slime. Porket walked over to the statue. "Damn it!"

"What's the problem?"

"I can't get permission to check this World! I actually can't get the permissions!" He shot the statue with a ray of purple light. "What the hell is this place?" Perhaps with his ego bruised, Porket began to show his magical powers. Flames and lightning were flying all around him as he roared with manic laughter. I stepped back quietly. It's best to keep away from a Wizard when he's pouring out his anger. I remembered those glory days when I was still a PPW, and sadness and anger flooded me.

The caterpillar came out again, crept by, burning Porket slowly. Very clearly, I saw him burn, but there was no damage. The caterpillar kept moving. I shouted, "Stop!"

"Are you talking to me?" Porket and the caterpillar turned back and said simultaneously. Porket was ill-looking and the caterpillar lovely. Porket turned to the caterpillar at once. "Are you a user? Are you the new advanced Wizard?"

"Of course," the caterpillar said. "My name is Babybutterfly. It really should be a caterpillar, I guess. It's not a mystery. You looked confused there." Babybutterfly turned to me again and said, "What's up?"

"Are you yourself?" Porket said, which I didn't at first understand. Without answering him, Babybutterfly said to me, "How did you get here?"

"He brought me here," I said, pointing to Porket, "We have something to tell you. Your account may be attacked. You better change your password right away." Through a whisper channel, Porket scolded me. "Stupid! Don't tell him anything. How do you know he is not the man who hacked your account?"

"Do not whisper here. As the Master here, I can hear the messages of every channel," Babybutterfly said. Apparatuses were wriggling inside his semitransparent skin. It was impressive. I said, "Are you the creator of this World?" and he nodded. "It's beautiful!" I said.

He smiled a little. It was the first smiling caterpillar I had ever seen. "Thank you."

"How could you—" Porket interrupted and was stopped by Babybutterfly.

"Keeping propriety is very important, even in MUD. Did I talk to you? How could you do this as a Wizard? Peoples today are so...."

Without reason, I liked this guy, and told him everything.

"What can I do? " I finally said.

"It's easy," he said, smiling. "Kill him and rob it back!"

"Do you think that guy hasn't set himself as undead? Are you out of your mind? Which idiot advanced you to a Wizard?" Porket was gnashing virtual teeth.

Babybutterfly smiled and passed me a card. "I don't have time right now. Call me when you find this guy. I'll be there."

"Thanks." I accepted the card. "By the way, how did you make it? Even a Wizard couldn't test this World."

He laughed loudly, "MUD is not an unbreakable system. There's no such system on God's earth! See you!" And he disappeared at the end of the hall.

"Who does he think he is? A prophet?" Porket shook his head. "Let's go," I said. Porket caught me. Darkness came again.

The Flower Square. "See you later!" Porket told me tersely. "I need to discuss this with the other Wizards and trace that address. You are a common user now, so just wait for our message."

I nodded and hugged him goodbye. I walked everywhere trying to find Pig Tongue but gave up an hour later, feeling it was pointless. I quit the system instead.

It was midnight, and I felt a little cold. I rubbed my face, turned off the computer, turned off the light, stood up. I stepped into the other room. Here there was only a table and a bed, and badly-printed wallpaper covered the wall. I went forward, then stopped, changed my mind, went to the bathroom. A haggard face stared at me from the mirror. The curve of the falling water was beautiful, and I watched it for a long moment after I flushed. Later, I puked, catching the sides of the sink. Puke everything, puke to death. Through tearful eyes, I saw the world turning round and round. I waited for it to stop.

When it did I brushed my teeth, gargled, and went back to the bedroom, staring at the bed for a whilst. Then I climbed in, slowly. She was lying there, sleeping. She seemed to me like an illusion, although here, there were only real colours, real textures. I stopped trying to remember who she was and hugged her, lying against her back in the dark. Listening to her soft breathing, I hid my face in her hair.

Her body was so smooth and soft. Inhaling her scent, I finally fell asleep.

Light was shining on the wall. It moved a short distance every time I opened my eyes. I didn't get up until it had moved to the corner. She'd already left. I stood up and opened the blind. Underside, outside, it was another world, a noisy world.

I grabbed something to eat, then sat by the computer and began to work. Every day I had to process nearly a hundred technique query letters about Conix Systems. I earned 2000 points every month. I was a Wire Worm: a creature whose life depended on the wires. There were millions of people like me living on the planet.

We never go outside.

There were less than thirty letters that day. At 12:23, having completed all of the letters, I decided to wash my face and connect to MUD. As I walked to the sink I heard my computer emit a scream. An emergency letter! I ran back to the desk, opened my mailbox, and typed in the reading password.

Dear user:

Regretfully, we must notify you that, because the Multi User Dungeon (MUD) system was attacked by an unknown force, MUD Wizard Association (MWA) made a decision as follows: we will commence shutdown for each of the 27 main servers, and 2078 assistant servers of Earth Section on Nov. 4, 2097. We suggest each area shut down their third-level servers.

System shutdown will cause:

1. All your current (or otherwise) data will be reset to null.
2. Your score points will be reset to null.
3. Your inventory (taken, purchased, or stored) will be reset to null.
4. Each illegal World (if any) you created will be erased.
5. Each third-level World or lower will disappear.

```
We will examine each user account before deciding whether it will be kept or removed.
We suggest you back up the Worlds you created (whether legal or illegal).
All the Wizards of MUD are working hard to trace the attacking source, check the level of damage, and effect a solution. We hope we will be able to restart the system very soon.
We are very sorry for your inconvenience in this matter.

M.W.A
 11/04/2097 04:20:47 GMT
```

I was sweating. A system shutdown! The MUD system had never shut down since it began in 2045. It had more than four billion registered users and more than one billion online users. MUD was not only very important to the Internet, it was important to the real world. But now, it would shut down....

Something had to be done. I took up my headpiece, connected to MUD.

The Flower Square was a mess on this Doomsday. A few men were beating a beautiful girl. Bees were creeping on the ground. A woman hummed by my ear. A man dressed as a priest was shouting in the square. The colour of the sky changed all the time, displayed random characters.

Walking around without a destination in mind, I came to the priest. "This is the real World!" he shouted. "This is the World which is greater and more real than the real world! We can't live without this World, we can't accept the decision to shut down!"

I nodded, agreeing with him. He was getting more excited, and he turned to me. "Do you know why? Do you know why we need this World so much? No, you know nothing! I can see it in your face! Let me tell you, this is the destiny of all human beings! This is the destiny written for us ever since Jesus' blood ran down the cross!

"Data! Information! What do these mean to us? Are they dispensable? No! Today, in the age we live in, these things are essential to us, they are as necessary as food, water, shelter, clothes; a man can't live without information, just as he cannot live without air.

"Somebody told us this is a fake world. They called it 'Virtual Reality'. They didn't know it, they didn't think about it, yet what is different between the real world and this World? Can we live without computer networks? We have a life here. We have memories here. We have a history here. We have everything here. How can they tell us this is a fake world?"

I walked away.

Through scared crowds, I came to the office I had used before. This was the house MWA gave to PPWs. Of course I had my own World, my own house, but I'd lost them all after I was dead, and I was so stupid that I hadn't backed them up.

Who knows if the World will ever come around again?

The office door was open. I stepped in, pushed the door to the inner room, saw him.

He didn't show his name, but I knew who he was right away.

"How are you, Xingxing?" I said, looking around.

He was startled, but immediately relaxed. "You should say, 'how are you, *former* Xingxing!' " he said.

"Why did you do this?" I asked coldly.

"You should have seen it already. Haven't you received the shutdown notice?"

"Why? I want to know why you want to destroy the World."

He smiled at me. "Permission denied—I won't tell you."

This guy almost drove me crazy! I composed myself and said, "You killed me and robbed my account, I have a right to know."

He watched the sky outside the window, read those words written in the sky, brought out a pipe, and changed himself to Holmes. "Sit down, child. You are reasonable, so let me tell you."

I sat down. A chair rose from the floor toward me. Someone had improved this house. He was smoking and talking very slowly. "I know you want to know who I am and wish to kill me. Actually, your reaction is excessive. You were only the first step of our plan. Compared to the whole system, your expense was nothing. If you really can't accept the result, I can give the account back to you and change the data as you wish.

"I am a member of the Hacker's Cave. What? You don't know it? Of course you don't. Actually, no-one knows it except its members and a selected few. We are an important force for worldwide hackers, controlling their theories, skills, tools, and so on. Our members are the world's top hackers, the backbone of hackers...no, I'm not preening, I'm talking about facts.

"Think about it. What is a hacker supposed to do? There's only one aim: hacking systems. You know, most hackers are childish. They can only hack simple systems, pry open someone else's mail, leave a few words on others' desktops...in the beginning, we put our minds to stealing information, researching newer, faster hacking technologies, and ruling hacker society. Later, we found that if we aggregated our collective force, we could hack the system that had never been hacked. No, don't ask me why we want to do this. It is our destiny, it is in our blood. Once you see a door left unlocked, you will push it open. What's behind the door? And how could we open it if it's locked? Every hacker wants to know that. In fact, every one of us is the same. If you saw a pretty woman, wouldn't you think about what she looks look like under her clothes?"

I didn't reply. The guy continued. "After an argument that lasted nearly half a month, we decided to attack the MUD system. The plan was designed and actualised at once—we don't have what you might call a bureaucracy. We spied on more than ten thousand Wizards, and finally chose you. Heh, look how many contenders you've beaten! First, you didn't set yourself as undead. Second, you'd never died. Once killed, you would be adrift for a whilst. Third, you'd only been a PPW for a short time, didn't know much about the MUD system, and weren't particularly wary. So we designed a fourth-level World and sent somebody to tell you. Each secret was designed to be easy to find, because we knew you were impatient. Additionally, you are finicky, so a crude World with only 256 colours would make you fidgety and disturb your mind. We were watching you drop into this trap—it was easier than we had planned. Actually, we had designed twelve steps to allure you, but you jumped directly to the end from the third step."

I was deadly ashamed. I took out the card, shouting, "Babybutterfly!"

"Haha!" Holmes laughed and morphed in front of me, changing to a caterpillar. I almost fainted. "I was using the account whilst you found Babybutterfly. I promised you I would appear, right?"

Shocked, I turned and ran out of the house. Babybutterfly laughed behind me loudly.

The street was getting more and more crowded. People came together to say goodbye. I saw Porket moving toward me. He was hanging upside down. "What's wrong with you?" I said, surprised. He shook his head despondently. "It's Doomsday and somebody changed my data. I can only move like this."

"But you are a Wizard!"

"Wizard? I was changed to a common user. Everybody is in danger now—even the Arch-God's account has been attacked. The core part of the system has already shut down to protect it from being destroyed. Everywhere is being attacked. We have serious problems. Even the Arch-God doesn't know when we can restore the system."

"What about the address we found? Have you checked it yet?"

Porket smiled, with a little text window beside his mouth that said, "This is a sad smile." He said, "He used a fake address. After tracing it for half an hour, we found the address was disabled already."

"Why was it disabled?"

"Don't know. The information was in Security Level S0, we didn't have the right permissions."

The sky became dark suddenly. Sound boomed across the Worlds. "Krak...wuuuu...En, this is the System Arch-God broadcasting to all Worlds. This is the System Arch-God broadcasting to all Worlds. The system will shut down in five minutes. The system will shut down in five minutes. Please log out! Please quit as soon as possible! Please remember the time we had together! Goodbye!"

The whole sky turned blood-red, displaying a blue number: 300. It went down to 299 after a second. No-one quit the system. They stood on the street and looked up at the huge countdown in the sky. The whole World, the whole universe kept a mutual silence. People crowded and said nothing. It seemed that each one of us was counting down the final seconds of his or her life.

I had never seen such a grave scene since I first had come to MUD. No-one was hurrying anymore. Not now that we had less than five minutes till the end of the World.

Something flew overhead, circled over the crowd. A light shone up, lit it in a circle of flame. It was a Wizard. Suddenly, a wiry voice broke the silence. "One seventy-eight, one seventy-seven, one seventy-six..." The voice was harsh. It sounded like someone's final voice. It was frightening. People listened quietly, waited quietly. A girl beside me began to cry. There were tears in all kinds of colours, blowing amongst the crowd. I thought: she must have got a Dynamic Expression Tracer. My nose grew warm too, but I refused to set the "Cry" command. Sadness permeated the crowd and there was crying, crying....

Under the bloody red sky, the number grew smaller and smaller, nearly at zero.

"I didn't expect to be so sad...." Porket said. "Goodbye!" I hugged him closely. "Come back after you die!" He raised his hand, wanted to say something, but couldn't continue.

The time had come.

The whole World froze at that moment, including Porket's hand: splashing tears, simulated sad faces. Everything froze...and slowly, slowly faded out, faded into a rimless dark. A window appeared. "MUD system has shut down. Thank you for your support."

I took off the headpiece and just sat there. The true tears disobeyed my command, falling down my face. The space around me seemed full of grey air. Outside, the noisy world was still there, and it seemed there had never been a MUD system, that this external system had never been shut down. Looking out of the window, I saw many skyscrapers rising over the modern mist. The sky was grey, the buildings were grey, the world was grey, and the world was real. Time went by peacefully without any graphics. Who said time did not exist? I sat down on the chair. My gaze took in the door to the bathroom, the door to the bedroom...then the door to *there*.

I had not been out of the apartment for three years.

What should I do? I felt sick. I thought it might be the absence of the virtual space simulation. I had heard someone call it MUD Syndrome. I knew nothing about medicine, but I knew it was an addiction, and if it was that then we were all junkies.

The grey wall around me asphyxiated me. Outside, the world was the same grey. I paced back and forth in the room, taking deep breaths. My sight was blurry. To avoid fainting, I ran into the bedroom, threw myself onto the bed and fell into a sleep haunted with circling blocks of primary colours.

The alarm woke me up. I surfaced as from an abyss, staring around me without comprehension. It was 4:00 p.m. already. The computer told me there was an urgent email for me.

I went and opened my mailbox.

```
Dear ****:
Hi!
I am One More Sight of You. I have not contacted you before. I found your mailbox address from MWA. Please read the following words carefully.
Hacking the core system of MUD by a secret hacker organisation—Hacker's Cave—caused the shutting down of the MUD system. MWA analysed the attack course, and has gathered 10890 Wizards to back-trace the attackers in the past few hours. We ask you for your help. Please connect to the following address:
temp.mud.tsinghua.edu.cn
This is a temporary command centre. It supports an emulation-type MUD-7 service, which means you can access it with your terminal with the same effect as a real MUD system.

Yours,
One More Sight of You
11/04/2097 09:21:37 GMT
```

We strike back! I put on the headpiece and connected to the address at once.

A long path. The red wall on each side of it nearly touched the sky. I moved quickly. Figures appeared and disappeared around me. They were all Wizards, shuttling between sites, collecting information, tracing the attacking hackers. I felt the fire of battle burning in my heart. We strike back! It was a mistake for them to treat MWA as a group of managers. Here were the best master hands, and they would teach these hackers a lesson.

A Wizard who looked like an angel flew down from the sky and touched me with a box. "Okay. You've passed the identity verification. Follow the arrow, please." Then he turned and flew back into the sky.

An arrow appeared above me, showed me the direction. Following it, I came to the control hall. Strangers were standing in groups, talking to each other. One of them saw me and walked over to me. "Are you the first hacked account—Xingxing?"

I nodded, wondering who this guy was.

"I am One More Sight of You, the Arch-God of MWA. Welcome to the Discussion Hall of Gods!" He introduced me to the others.

"Ah! Nice to meet you all!" I knew these Gods would never come out unless an extremely important event had happened.

"Let's start! We've found the headquarters of the Hacker's Cave, but met with very strong opposition and were unable to penetrate their defences," One More Sight of You said. "We've processed a total of seven attacks, but they all failed. Luckily, we found their leader's address in one of the sorties."

"What?" I was shocked. You should know that the most difficult thing on the Internet is getting the real identity of somebody. And revealing someone's identity was a disgraceful thing. You couldn't play anymore if you publicised somebody's real identity in MUD.

"It's true. One of our commandos broke into their file system for thirty-two seconds and downloaded a few files. We discovered that one of them was a love letter that their leader wrote to someone, and we found his address in the letter." He showed me the address. "We've decided to face the real person," he said.

"Fine," I said. Then, as he waited, "But what do you need from me?"

He didn't answer me, but turned to the others. "Because you live closest to him," one of them said, "we need you to solve this problem."

"Do you mean you know my address?" I asked coldly.

"As managers of MUD, we know every user's address," One More Sight of You said. "Things will get worse the longer we stand here and just talk. We need to initiate a powerful approach immediately."

"What kind of approach?"

"How did those hackers treat you?" he asked me.

"They killed me."

They nodded to me but said nothing. I looked at the floor for a few seconds. Then I said, "Okay, I will go."

They smiled. One More Sight of You came over to hug me first, then the others did the same thing. "You will be a hero in the history of MUD!" they told me.

Quitting the Internet, I took off my headpiece and washed my face in the bathroom. I went into the back room, opened unused cupboards, brought out a dirty coat, shook it, and put it on. Dirt and dust made me cough. I closed my eyes, thought back for the address and the door password. I opened my eyes and took out a box from under the bed. I opened it, took out the gun, loaded it with bullets. I wasn't a fierce or cruel man, but it didn't pay to cross me. I went back, turned off the computer. I felt calm.

I could see the corridor when I opened the door to *there*. I faced it for the first time in three years. It didn't seem to have changed much. I gathered my courage and stepped out, went to stand before the lift. The sound of the door closing behind me made me freeze, and I almost ran back home at once. But I soon controlled my absurd alarm and regained my confidence. "It's nothing," I said, speaking out loud, and pushed the lift button. Nothing happened. Did I need to find any keys first? I looked around and laughed. This was the real world, there were no rules here. I found a notice that said the lift had been damaged. I said, "Damn it!"

I walked down the stairs.

The light was off. I watched the dark stairs and felt afraid. Could it be outer space? I held onto the wall and climbed down step by step. Good, there was a light three floors down. I counted the number of floors whilst I was going down. I lived on the seventeenth floor of the building, so that would be...three hundred and forty stairs. God!

The eleventh floor. My legs began to ache. The distance I had walked here was longer than I did on an ordinary day. More stairs materialised on every corner, endlessly. There wasn't a single person in the corridor. It was as quiet as a cemetery but for the sound of my breathing. I began to doubt whether I would ever see the ground.

Finally, passing a corner, I saw a door marked *Exit*. I walked over and pushed it open.

Noisy world.

Cars, people flowed on the busy street. There was such a variety of colours, beautiful colours below the grey world seen from my apartment. The billboards, the cars, the walking girls, even the rubbish bins beside the street were so colourful. And the sound. The sound here wasn't so pure, so perfect as in MUD. But these sounds made me feel fresh and cool. Catching sight of a streetcorner, my heart beat faster. A six-floor building was over there. It looked very special amongst these skyscrapers. My target was in a room on the fourth floor there. I put my hand into my pocket, touching the gun, and walked forward, step by step.

There was an iron fence around the building. I pulled open the gate and it made a grating sound. Had he heard it? Was he watching me? I looked for his window but could see only blinds. The door to the building was unlocked. I walked in. An old man popped his head out and looked at me questioningly. I smiled and pointed upstairs. He nodded, glassy-eyed, without any expression. The dilapidated stairs were covered with a dirty carpet. I stepped up carefully. My legs ached again. Some beggars were sleeping in the corridor. It was difficult to believe that the best hacker in the world lived in such a place. I steered clear of them and stepped up to the fourth floor.

Nobody was there. I looked around. Maybe some of them were protecting him, so I had to be careful. The sound of the city was far away. I walked to the door slowly, checked that no-one was there, and keyed in the password.

The door slid open quietly. There was a hallway two or three metres long. I could hear rock music at the end of it. The living room was strewn with take-away boxes, papers, dirty clothes. Blinds covered the windows. The music came from a room next to the living room. I took out the gun, stepped soundlessly to the door of that room, and pushed it open.

A man sat there with his back to me, wearing a headpiece of a type I'd not seen. The screen in front of him displayed data, a lot of it. It seemed to be Internet addresses. He didn't hear me, but was nodding his head and wallowing in the world of rock music and the Internet. His hands moved on the keyboard quickly, the data changing at his command.

I stepped behind him and raised my arm. The muzzle of the gun was only twenty centimetres away from his head. My hand shook a little. I took a deep breath, held the gun steadily, and aimed at the centre of his head.

The song suddenly finished. I kept still, listening to the sound of his typing. I was waiting for the music to start again. The man in front of me sighed.

Another song began then. Guitars were screaming wildly. I pulled the safety catch, tightened my finger on the trigger.

The man was nodding his head violently in time to the music.

I stared at him. It was he who had made me die, who had hacked my account, who had caused the MUD system to shut down, who had made all those people in the square cry. I wanted to see him dead.

The music was earsplitting.

He knew nothing at all, nodding his head like an idiot.

Tears formed suddenly. I couldn't help myself. I put the safety catch back with trembling hands, put down my arm, stepped away slowly. I could see his headpiece shaking on top of his head. I stepped back to the other side of the door, closed it, and walked softly away. I walked through the living room, the hallway, the door. I didn't cry until I stood in the corridor. I ran down quickly. A beggar was frightened, staring at me with bloodshot eyes, but said nothing. I ran out of the building and sat on a bench in the street, sobbing. I was trembling all over, as if I had just woken up from a restless dream.

I put the gun in my pocket. I took out and lit a cigarette, watching the people all around me.

A little girl pulling seven or eight balloons walked by me, jumping, laughing. An old beggar carried ratty bags and followed, smelling of carrion and humidity. Roaring cars drove past. A dog didn't pay any attention to its master's scolding, piddling at the street corner. An old woman in a red skirt was haggling with a man behind a stall. A group of young men were laughing and looking around, talking to each other. The little girl with the balloons turned around the corner and disappeared.

This was the real world.

"What are you doing here?" I looked up. She carried a big bag full of groceries, standing there watching me.

I remembered her. I smiled. "I'm watching the street," I said. She looked amazed, and worried. "What happened to you? Why did you come down?"

"Nothing. I just came down."

"En...." She watched me with suspicion. "Let's go back. Don't you want to connect to MUD?" I shook my head, pulled her close to me. "Come on, sit down. Look at the street with me."

We watched each other without speaking. Her eyes grew soft. Finally, she smiled. She sat down by me. "Okay," she said. "Let's watch the street."

She leaned her head against my shoulder. Her breath was warm against my skin. I put my arm around her and held her close. "What shall we do today?" I said.

"L'Aquilone du Estrellas" ("The Kite of Stars")

Dean Francis Alfar

Dean Francis Alfar is a Filipino playwright, editor, and writer. His literary awards include multiple Don Carlos Palanca Memorial Awards for Literature—including the Grand Prize for Novel for *Salamanca* (Ateneo Press, 2006), as well as the Manila Critics' Circle National Book Awards for the graphic novels *Siglo: Freedom* and *Siglo: Passion,* and the Philippines Free Press Literary Award. His first collection, *The Kite of Stars and Other Stories* was published in 2007. With wife, Nikki Alfar, he has edited the annual anthology series *Philippine Speculative Fiction*.

The night when she thought she would finally be a star, Maria Isabella du'l Cielo struggled to calm the trembling of her hands, reached over to cut the tether that tied her to the ground, and thought of that morning many years before when she'd first caught a glimpse of Lorenzo du Vicenzio ei Salvadore: tall, thick-browed, and handsome, his eyes closed, oblivious to the cacophony of the accident waiting to occur around him.

Maria Isabella had just turned sixteen, and each set of her padrinos had given her (along with the sequined brida du caballo, the dresses of rare tulle, organza, and seda, and the diadema floral du'l dama–the requisite floral circlet of young womanhood) a purse filled with coins to spend on anything she wanted. And so she'd gone past the Calle du Leones (where sleek cats of various pedigrees sometimes allowed themselves to be purchased, though if so, only until they tired of their new owners), walked through the Avenida du'l Conquistadores (where the statues of the conquerors of Ciudad Meiora lined the entirety of the broad promenade), and made her way to the Encantu lu Caminata (that maze-like series of interconnected streets, each leading to some wonder or marvel for sale), where little musical conch shells from the islets near Palao'an could be found. Those she liked very much.

In the vicinity of the Plaza Emperyal, she saw a young man dressed in a coat embroidered with stars walk almost surely to his death. In that instant, Maria Isabella knew two things with the conviction reserved only for the very young: first, that she almost certainly loved this reckless man; and second, that if she simply stepped on a dog's tail—the very dog watching the same scene unfold right next to her—she could avert the man's seemingly senseless death.

These were the elements of the accident-waiting-to-happen: an ill-tempered horse hitched to some noble's qalesa; an equally ill-tempered qalesa driver with a whip; a whistling panadero with a tray of plump pan du sal perched on his head; two puddles of fresh rainwater brought about by a brief downpour earlier that day; a sheet of stained glass en route to its final destination at the house of the Most Excellent Primo

Orador; a broken bottle of wine; and, of course, the young man who walked with his eyes closed.

Without a moment's further thought, Maria Isabella stepped on the tail of the dog that was resting near her. The poor animal yelped in pain, which in turn startled the horse, making it stop temporarily; which in turn angered the qalesa driver even more, making him curse the horse; which in turn upset the delicate melody that the panadero was whistling; which in turn made the panadero miss stepping into the two puddles of rainwater; which in turn gave the men delivering the sheet of stained glass belonging to the Most Excellent Primo Orador an uninterrupted path; which in turn gave the young man enough room to cross the street without so much as missing a beat or stepping onto the broken wine bottle; which in turn would never give him the infection that had been destined to result in the loss of his right leg and, ultimately, his life.

Everyone and everything continued to move on their own inexorable paths, and the dog she had stepped on growled once at her and then twisted around to nurse its sore tail. But Maria Isabella's eyes were on the young man in the star-embroidered coat, whose life she had just saved. She decided she would find out who he was.

The first twenty people she asked did not know him. It was a butcher's boy who told her who he was, as she rested near the butcher's shop along the Rotonda du'l Vendedores.

"His name is Lorenzo du Vicenzio," the butcher's boy said. "I know him because he shops here with his father once every sennight. My master saves some of the choicest cuts for their family. They're rather famous, you know. Maestro Vicenzio, the father, names stars."

"Stars?" Maria Isabella asked. "And would you know why he walks with his eyes closed? The son, I mean."

"Well, Lorenzo certainly isn't blind," the butcher's boy replied. "I think he keeps his eyes closed to preserve his vision for his stargazing at night. He mentioned he had some sort of telescope he uses at night."

"How can I meet him?" she asked, all thoughts of musical conch shells gone from her mind.

"You? What makes you think he will even see you? Listen," the butcher's boy whispered to her, "he only has eyes for the stars."

"Then I'll make him see me," she whispered back, and as she straightened up, her mind began to make plan upon plan upon plan, rejecting possibilities, making conjectures, assessing what she knew, whom she knew, and how much she dared. It was a lot for anyone to perform in the span of time it took to set her shoulders, look at the butcher's boy, and say, "Take me to the best kitemaker."

The butcher's boy, who at fourteen was easily impressed by young ladies of a certain disposition, immediately doffed his white cap, bowed to Maria Isabella, gestured to the street filled with people outside, and led her to the house of Melchor Antevadez, famed throughout Ciudad Meiora and environs as the Master Builder of aquilones, cometas, saranggola, and other artefactos voladores.

They waited seven hours to see him (for such was his well-deserved fame that orders from all over the realms came directly to him—for festivals, celebrations, consecrations, funerals, regatta launches, and such) and did not speak to each other. Maria Isabella was thinking hard about the little plan in her head and the butcher's boy was thinking of how he had just lost his job for the dubious pleasure of a silent young woman's company.

He spent most of the time looking surreptitiously at her shod feet and oddly wondering whether she, like the young ladies that figured in his fantasies, painted her toes blue, in the manner of the circus artistas.

When it was finally their turn (for such was the nature of Melchor Antevadez that he made time to speak to anyone and everyone who visited him, being of humble origin himself), Maria Isabella explained what she wanted to the artisan.

"What I need," she began, "is a kite large enough to strap me onto. Then I must fly high enough to be amongst the stars themselves, so that anyone looking at the stars will see me amongst them, and I must be able to wave at least one hand to that person."

"What you need," Melchor Antevadez replied with a smile, "is a balloon. Or someone else to love."

She ignored his latter comment and told him that a balloon simply would not do, it would not be able to achieve the height she needed, didn't he understand that she needed to be amongst the stars?

He cleared his throat and told her that such a kite was impossible, that there was no material immediately available for such an absurd undertaking, that there was, in fact, no design that allowed for a kite that supported the weight of a person, and that it was simply impossible, impossible, impossible. Impossible to design. Impossible to find materials. No, no, it was impossible, even for the Illustrados.

She pressed him then for answers, to think through the problem; she challenged him to design such a kite, and to tell her just what these impossible materials were.

"Conceivably, I could dream of such a design, that much I'll grant you. If I concentrate hard enough I know it will come to me, that much I'll concede. But the materials are another matter."

"Please, tell me what I need to find," Maria Isabella said.

"None of it can be bought, and certainly none of it can be found here in Ciudad Meiora, although wonder can be found here if you know where to look."

"Tell me."

And so he began to tell her. Sometime during the second hour of his recitation of the list of materials, she began to take notes, and nudged the butcher's boy to try to remember what she couldn't write fast enough. At dawn the following day, Melchor Antevadez stopped speaking, reviewed the list of necessary things compiled by Maria Isabella and the butcher's boy, and said, "I think that's all I'd need. As you can see, it is more than any man could hope to accomplish."

"But I am not a man," she said to him, looking down at the thousands of items on the impossible list in her hands. The butcher's boy, by this time, was asleep, his head cradled in the crook of his thin arms, dreaming of aerialists and their blue toes.

Melchor Antevadez squinted at her. "Is any love worth all this effort? Looking for the impossible?"

Maria Isabella gave the tiniest of smiles. "What makes you think I'm in love?"

Melchor Antevadez raised an eyebrow at her denial.

"I'll get everything," she promised the kitemaker.

"But it may take a lifetime to gather everything," the artisan said wearily.

"A lifetime is all I have," Maria Isabella told him. She then shook the butcher's boy awake.

"I cannot go alone. You're younger than me but I will sponsor you as my companion. Will you come with me?"

"Of course," mumbled butcher's boy drowsily. "After all, this shouldn't take more time than I have to spare."

"It may be significantly longer than you think," the artisan said, shaking his head.

"Then please, Ser Antevadez, dream the design and I'll have everything you listed when we return." She stood to leave.

That very day, Maria Isabella told her parents and both sets of her padrinos that she was going off on a long trip. She invoked her right of Ver du Mundo: when women of at least sixteen years, and men of at least twenty years, could go forth into the wideness of Hinirang; sometimes to seek their fortune, sometimes to run from it. They all gave her their blessings, spoke fondly of how she used to dance and sing as a child, saluted her new right as a woman and full citizen of Ciudad Meiora, accompanied her all the way to the Portun du Transgresiones with more recalled memories of her youth, and sent her on her way. As for the butcher's boy, he waited until she was well away and then joined her on the well-worn path, the Sendero du'l Viajero, along with the supplies she had asked him to purchase.

"I'm ready to go." The butcher's boy grinned at her. He was clad in a warm tunic in the manner of city folk, and around his neck, for luck, he wore an Ajima'at, a wooden charm fashioned in the form of a wheel.

"What did you tell your kinfolk?" Maria Isabella asked him

as he helped her mount a sturdy horse.

"That I would be back in a month or so."

It took almost sixty years for Maria Isabella and the butcher's boy to find all the items on Melchor Antevadez's impossible list.

They began at Pur'Anan, and then trekked to Katakios and Viri'Ato (where the sanctuary of the First Tree stood unmolested by time).

They travelled north to the lands of Bontoc and Cabarroquis (where the Povo Montaha dwelt in seclusion).

They sailed eastward to Palao'an and the Islas du'l Calami'an (where the traders from countries across the seas converged in a riot of tongues).

They ventured westward to the dark lands of Siqui'jor and Jomal'jig (where the Silent Ones kept court whenever both sun and moon occupied the same horizon).

They visited the fabled cities of the south: Diya al Tandag, Diya al Din, and Diya al Bajao (where fire-shrouded Djin and the Tiq'Barang waged an endless war of attrition).

They entered the marbled underworld of the Sea Lords of Rumblon and braved the Lair of the M'Arinduque (in whose house the dead surrendered their memories of light and laughter).

When they ran out of money after the third year of travel, Maria Isabella and the butcher's boy spent time looking for ways to finance their quest. She began knowing only how to ride, dance, sing, play the arpa, the violin, and the flauta, embroider, sew, and write poetry about love; the butcher's boy began knowing how to cut up a cow. By the time they had completed the list, they had more than quintupled the amount of money they began with, and they both knew how to manage a caravan; run a plantation; build and maintain fourteen kinds of seagoing and rivergoing vessels; raise horses big and small, and fowl, dogs, and seagulls; recite the entire annals of six cultures from memory; speak and write nineteen languages; prepare medicine for all sorts of ailments, worries, and anxieties; make flashpowder, lu fuego du ladron, and picaro de fuegos artificiales; make glass, ceramics, and lenses from almost any quality sand; and many many other means of making money.

In the seventh year of the quest, a dreadful storm destroyed their growing caravan of found things and they lost almost everything (she clutched vainly at things as they flew and spun in the downpour of wind and water, and the butcher's boy fought to keep the storm from taking her away as well). It was the last time that Maria Isabella allowed herself to cry. The butcher's boy took her hand, and they began all over again. They were beset by thieves and learnt to run (out of houses and caves and temples; on roads and on sea lanes and in gulleys; on horses, aguilas, and waves). They encountered scoundrels and sinverguenzza and learnt to bargain (at first with various coins, jewels, and metals, and later with promises, threats, and dreams). They were beleaguered by nameless things in nameless places and learnt to defend themselves (first with wooden pessoal, then later with kris, giavellotto, and lamina).

In their thirtieth year together, they took stock of what they had, referred to the thousands of items still left unmarked on their list, exchanged a long, silent look filled with immeasurable meaning, and went on searching for the components of the impossible kite—acquiring the dowel by planting a langka seed at the foot of the grove of a kindly diuata (and waiting the seven years it took to grow, unable to leave), winning the lower spreader in a drinking match against the three oldest brothers of Duma'Alon, assembling the pieces of the lower edge connector whilst fleeing a war party of the Sumaliq, solving the riddles of the toothless crone Ai'ai'sin to find what would be part of a wing tip, climbing Apo'amang to spend seventy sleepless nights to get the components of the ferrule, crafting an artificial wave to fool the cerena into surrendering their locks of hair that would form a portion of the tether, rearing miniature horses to trade to the Duende for parts of the bridle, and finally spending eighteen years painstakingly collecting the fifteen thousand different strands of thread that would make up the aquilone's surface fabric.

When at last they returned to Ciudad Meiora, both stooped and older, they paused briefly at the gates of the Portun du Transgresiones. The butcher's boy looked at Maria Isabella and said, "Well, here we are at last."

She nodded, raising a weary arm to her forehead and making the sign of homecoming.

"Do you feel like you've wasted your life?" she asked him as the caravan bearing everything they had amassed lumbered into the city.

"Nothing is ever wasted," the butcher's boy told her.

They made their way to the house of Melchor Antevadez and knocked on his door. A young man answered them and sadly informed them that the wizened artisan had died many many years ago, and that he, Reuel Antevadez, was the new Maestro du Cosas Ingravidas.

"Yes, yes. But do you still make kites?" Maria Isabella asked him.

"Kites? Of course. From time to time, someone wants an aquilone or—"

"Before Ser Antevadez, Melchor Antevadez, died, did he leave instructions for a very special kind of kite?" she interrupted.

"Well..." mumbled Reuel Antevadez, "my great-grandfather did leave a design for a woman named Maria Isabella du'l Cielo, but—"

"I am she." She ignored his shocked face. "Listen, young man. I have spent all my life gathering everything Melchor Antevadez said he needed to build my kite. Everything is outside. Build it."

And so Reuel Antevadez unearthed the yellowing parchment that contained the design of the impossible kite that Melchor Antevadez had dreamt into existence, referenced the parts from the list of things handed to him by the butcher's boy, and proceeded to build the aquilone.

When it was finished, it looked nothing at all like either Maria Isabella or the butcher's boy had imagined. The kite was huge and looked like a star, but those who saw it could not agree on how best to describe the marvellous conveyance.

After he helped strap her in, the butcher's boy stood back and looked at the woman he had grown old with.

"This is certainly no time for tears," Maria Isabella reprimanded him gently, as she gestured for him to release the kite.

"No, there is time for everything," the butcher's boy whispered to himself as he pushed and pulled at the ropes and strings, pulley and levers and gears of the impossible contrivance.

"Goodbye, goodbye!" she shouted down to him as the star kite began its rapid ascent to the speckled firmament above.

"Goodbye, goodbye," he whispered as his heart finally broke into a thousand mismatched pieces, each one small, hard, and sharp. The tears of the butcher's boy (who had long since ceased to be a boy) flowed freely down his face as he watched her rise—the extraordinary old woman he had always loved, strapped to the frame of an impossible kite.

As she rose, he sighed and reflected on the absurdity of life, the heaviness of loss, the cruelty of hope, the truth about quests, and the relentless nature of a love that knew only one direction. His hands swiftly played out the tether (that part of the marvellous rope they had bargained for with two riddles, a blind rooster, and a handful of cold and lustreless diamante in a bazaar held only once every seven years on an island in the Dag'at Palabras Tacitas), and he realised that all those years they were together, she had never known his name.

As she rose above the city of her birth, Maria Isabella took a moment to gasp at the immensity of the city that sprawled beneath her, recalled how everything had begun, fought the trembling of her withered hands, and with a fishbone knife (that sad and strange knife that had been passed from hand to hand, from women consumed by unearthly passion, the same knife that had been part of her reward for solving the mystery of the Rajah Sumibon's lost turtle shell in the southern lands of Diya al Din) cut the glimmering tether.

Up, up, up, higher and higher and higher she rose. She saw the winding silver ribbon of the Pasigla, the fluted roofs of Lu Ecolia du Arcana Menor ei Mayor, the trellises and gardens of the Plaza Emperyal, and the dimmed streets of the Mercado du Coristas. And Maria Isabella looked down and thought she saw everything, everything.

At one exquisite interval during her ascent, Maria Isabella thought she spied the precise tower where Lorenzo du

Vicenzio ei Salvadore, the stargazer, must live and work. She felt the exuberant joy of her lost youth bubble up within her and mix with the fiery spark of love she had kept alive for sixty years, and in a glorious blaze of irrepressible happiness she waved her free hand with wild abandon, shouting the name that had been forever etched into her heart.

When a powerful wind took the kite to sudden new heights, when Ciudad Meiora and everything below her vanished in the dark, she stopped shouting and began to laugh and laugh and laugh.

And Maria Isabella du'l Cielo looked up at the beginning of forever and thought of nothing, nothing at all.

And in the city below, in one of the high rooms of the silent Torre du Astrunomos (where those who had served with distinction were housed and honoured), an old man, long-retired and plagued by cataracts, sighed in his sleep and dreamt a dream of unnamed stars.

"CINDERERS"

NIR YANIV

Nir Yaniv is an Israeli writer, editor and musician. His first short story collection, *Ktov Ke'shed Mi'shachat* (*Write Like a Devil*), came out in 2006, and he is co-author (with the editor of this book) of a short novel, *The Tel Aviv Dossier*. He served as editor of the Israeli SF Society's website and later edited the magazine *Chalomot Be'aspamia*. He lives in Tel Aviv.

They say you should always start small. Burn a tree, perhaps: a parked car, road signs, a traffic light. Not us. We, for starters, burned Mr Kalmanson's flat—including two fine leather chairs, forks and knives (two dozen pairs), a life-sized (ugly) wooden horse, and Mr Kalmanson himself, of course.

"Oy," said Huey, "add a little six kilohertz, and I can't hear the bedroom."

I heard the bedroom just fine, and also the kitchen, the living room, and the toilets. Mics and earphones of the highest quality, and a stills camera—black and white, of course. Louie gave it some more six K, and exactly then Kalmanson's stupid wife chose to take her leave of this world with a deafening cry.

"Shit!" roared Huey and tore away the earphones.

"I thought she'd scream higher," said Louie. "It sounded like, I don't know, B-flat?"

"Almost two K with annoying overtones. I hope we can take it out in the editing."

"We'll see," said Louie, and Huey put on the earphones again. In the flat the shuddering bodies fell still, as did one of the mics in the kitchen, burnt despite its thermal casing. Annoying, but what can you do? The fire began to die as the gas filling the house was consumed. One kilometre north, I saw the lights of the fire engine turning in desperation. Nails on the road. The firemen are our brothers, but the siren would ruin our recording.

Later, equipped with backpacks, sleeping bags, a grenade launcher, and much good will, we lay in wait under cover of a giant Sony billboard by the highway, announcing that "This Is No Television—It Is Reality." Drexler's tanker leaves Ashdod at one hundred kilometres per hour toward Haifa. Half an hour later, Schwartz's truck exits Chedera toward Tel Aviv at ninety kilometres per hour. Drexler carries cooking gas, and Schwartz, detergents. When and where will they meet? And how?

Boom.

Huey didn't let me film in 8mm. Noise. In my opinion there is nothing like the grainy look of real film, but sometimes you have to make allowances. I used high-resolution video, and Dewey had to take care of the rest of the sound equipment by himself. A clean recording, aside from the part where the burning Schwartz, flying out of the truck's window, landed on one of the mics and crashed it. *Nu*, nobody's perfect.

Louie disappeared in the middle of dinner. One moment he was there, absentmindedly playing with his broccoli whilst examining the flamethrower for tomorrow's job, and the next his plate was orphaned.

"Do you think he'd mind if I ate it?" asked Dewey.

"Eat," I said. "It's good for you." I never understood those vegetarians. I passed him the plate.

"Say," said Dewey with his mouth full, "doesn't it strike you as odd..."

"What?"

"That he, like, disappeared?"

"Who?"

"What do you mean who? Where's your brain?"

"Listen," I said, "Let's not play games. If you want to ask me something, be specific."

Dewey knows me, and knows there is no point in arguing.

"Louie. Disappeared. Don't you think something here doesn't add up?"

I thought about it. "No," I said. "He probably took a break. He'll be back soon."

"Look," said Dewey. "I wouldn't be surprised if he disappeared any other time, but in the middle of dinner?"

You could say that for Dewey—occasionally there was something to his twisted logic.

"There is something to your twisted logic," I said, "but I don't think we can do anything about it."

"He's not right," said Dewey.

"Don't exaggerate," I said. "He did a nice job with the trucks today. Doing is everything, the rest is nothing."

"No—yes—that is, sure. That's not what I meant."

"Don't be a pain," I said. "Why don't you finish here instead?"

And I went.

* * * *

When I came back I found Louie leaning over building plans and writing comments in a little notebook. Huey was looking over his shoulder. "What's that?" I asked.

"The lift shaft for tomorrow. I'm just working out how much of Eve we need.

"Eve?"

"Extreme Velocity Explosives," said Huey.

"That's right," said Louie. "EVE."

"Oh," I said, and looked around. Huey wasn't there. "You know," I said, "doesn't it strike you as odd..."

"What?"

"That he, like, disappeared?"

"Listen," said a voice.

"Who?" said Louie.

"What do you mean who? Where's your brain?"

"Listen," said Louie, "Let's not play games. If you want to ask me something, be specific."

I know him, and I know there is no point arguing.

"Huey. Disappeared. Don't you think something here doesn't add up?"

He thought about it. "No," he said. "He probably took a break. He'll be back soon."

"You're ignoring me," said someone.

"Look," I said, "I wouldn't be surprised if he disappeared any other time..."

"There's something to your twisted logic," said Huey, "but I don't think we can do anything about it."

"He's not right," I said.

"Don't exaggerate," said Louie. "He did a very nice job on Kalmanson's flat today. Doing is everything, the rest is nothing."

"No—yes—that is, sure. That's not what I meant."

"Hello? Do you hear me?"

"Don't be a pain," said Louie. "Let me finish here."

And he went.

"You have to stop," said the voice. Its proud owner, a small, red-haired, bespectacled demon, gave me a warning look over his plate of asparagus.

"I'm only helping them," I said, mixing the pasta. The red and white chequered tablecloth caught my eye. I wondered what would be the sound of it burning. Maybe if we turned on a big enough fan, we could blow away all the tablecloths in the restaurant and then send out a jet of gas...

"Who, exactly?" enquired the demon as he tapped his golden monocle. "The world? Israel? The eleven people you killed?"

"Huey and Dewey," I said. "They're artists. They—we—will have an exhibition. Besides, nobody was killed."

"Ha ha," said the blond demon and pushed his sunglasses slightly aside. "I'm sure the families would love to hear that."

A lift rises from its shaft, wrapped in flames, and takes off into the city's skies like a metallic phoenix, clumsy and burning, an orange glow gathering over the roofs and water tanks of the towering city of Tel Aviv, the metal cables singing as they drag behind, caught in sodium fire, a tail of steel sparks marking a trail in the evening's heavens.

"Beautiful," said Louie, hunched under his earphones. He didn't bother looking. The remote mic inside the lift caught the cries of the passengers as well as the thunder of the flames. A light westerly wind blew.

"I think," said Dewey from behind camera number two, "that it's going to land somewhere in Florentine."

"Maybe," I said, distracted, awed by the view. The trail of smoke described an almost perfect parabola, and the ball of fire, which up until a few moments ago was an entirely ordinary and unglamorous component of an office block, fell with dignity somewhere in the south of the city, beside a lit-up billboard: "Phillips: The Real Experience." A passenger plane circled above, like a bird wondering if that was a relative who had fallen, or perhaps its eternal, mythological enemy, the fire eagle, the steel hawk, if that was the thing lying there burning, never to return to haunt the bird's dreams.

We changed clothes and went to a party.

Some genius of a designer decided to build a light organ of fire and smoke, to shoot out coloured flames in tune with the music. For the safety of all present, a giant wire cage was built around the contraption. Fire can't pass through a wire mesh, but our Louie worked in advance to replace the cage with a soft plastic replica and improve the mechanism—anything for a party.

"Excellent!" The partygoers were impressed when the DJ's stand began to smoke. "They really put money into their parties!" said a reporter to a television camera filming the event, and immediately a tongue of green fire emerged and took hold of him. Multicoloured flames grabbed now and then at a dancer, at the furniture, the barman, and the sponsorship signs ("McDonald's—If You're Not There, You're Nowhere"), and everything went peacefully enough until Louie lost his patience. The flamethrower made an awful farting sound, and suddenly the whole place became a giant whirlpool of painted fire. When the cameras we laid inside burned out, we gathered the equipment and went home to my place.

In the middle of the night, I disappeared. One moment I was leaning, between Huey and Louie, over a topographic map of the Trade Fair Gardens, and the next, I wasn't.

"Pass me his plate," said Huey, "I think he's finished eating."

"Listen, both of you," said someone.

"Say," said Louie, "doesn't it strike you as odd..."

"What?"

"That he, like, disappeared?"

"Who?"

"What do you mean who? Where's your brain?"

"Listen," said Huey, "Let's not play games."

Louie knows Huey and knows there is no point in arguing.

"Dewey. Disappeared. Don't you think something here doesn't add up?"

"Of course it doesn't," said a voice. "If you would only listen to me for a moment...."

Huey thought about it. "No," he said. "He probably went for a break. He'll be back soon."

"Look," said Louie, "I wouldn't be surprised if he disappeared at any other time, but in the middle of topography?"

"Topography?" said the voice in suspicion. "What are you going to do now?"

"There is something to your twisted logic," said Huey, "but there you go."

"He's not right," said Louie.

"Don't exaggerate," said Huey. "He did a very nice job on the lift today. Doing is everything."

"That's right, don't exaggerate," said the voice. "We have eighty-five dead and almost a hundred wounded. Very nice. Can't you bloody listen for a moment?"

"No—yes—I mean, sure. That's not what I meant."

"Don't be a pain," said Huey. "Let me finish here."

Louie went.

The next day clouds covered the sun, but the Ferris wheel in the Luna Park shone a strong sunflower-yellow; it and the scores of soft, shining children in its lap. Phosphorus. Huey took pastoral pictures, Dewey recorded a symphony of screams and cries. The image of a child floating cheerfully through the air, as glowing as an angel, on the background of "To Be Or Not To Be—Mitsubishi," was followed immediately by the recording of the soft sound of impact as he hit the ground. After a few such happy minutes, when all eyes in the park were turned upward, the two activated the acid spray. Then the volume of sound rose by a magnitude of decibels, but after several minutes of vocal joy, the mics were burnt through and it was over.

"Ha ha," said the dark-haired demon, and pushed his sunglasses slightly aside. "I'm sure the families would be happy to hear."

"Hear about what?"

"The eighty-six people you didn't kill."

"Eighty-six? What are you talking about?"

"Two in that flat in Tel Aviv, eight on the highway, five in the lift, forty-three in the club...."

"What about them?"

"Didn't you kill them?"

"*Nu,* so?"

"Don't you think," said the demon, and wiped his brow, "that something isn't right here? Ever heard of 'Thou Shalt Not Kill'?"

"Dear God!" I said. "You think we killed *human beings*?"

A wall made of recently annealed glass, and inside it darkening lumps. A strong smell of grilling and burning infuses the air. The lumps had stopped convulsing long before the glass solidified, of course. And now we stand there, and the recording films run again, and Huey approaches the wall, a giant hammer in his hands.

On the way from here to there, all three of us disappeared. One moment we were busy on the exact tuning of the recorder, and in the next, we weren't.

For one moment, everything stopped.

"Pass me his plate," someone said to somebody else. "I think he finished eating."

"Say," said someone, "doesn't it strike you as odd..."

"What?" said someone.

"That he, like, disappeared?"

"No," said the demon and blinked. He looked as if he needed glasses.

"Excuse me?" said someone.

"Not someone, sir," said the demon. "You."

"Me?" said someone.

"You. You know perfectly well who you are," said the demon.

"That's possible," said Dewey, "but what is it to you?"

"Thinking in the third person isn't going to help you."

"Get off it," I said.

"No," said the demon. "You've gone way too far. You're going to stop this moronic killing spree. Right now."

"I think you have a small problem with your perception of reality."

"I only have one problem," said the demon, "and it's you."

"Leave me alone!"

"I can't," said the demon. "I'm a part of you."

"Now I *know* you have a problem with your perception of reality."

"I really don't," said the demon. "And not just that: you, along with me, are stuck in the loop."

"There's something to your twisted logic," I said. "But there you go."

"You're not right," said the demon.

"Don't exaggerate," I said. "I did a very nice job with the wall today. Doing is everything."

"Wait!" said the demon. "There you go again! That's not what I meant!"

"Don't be a pain," I said. "Let me finish off here."

And I went.

A skyscraper in napalm. Billboards burning in the wind. "What You See Is What You Get—Nokia."

And was brought back.

"You're not going anywhere," said the demon. "You're staying here with me to the end."

"The end?"

"Yes. Until you realise you're one, not three, and stop getting out of control."

"Of course I'm one," I said. "I never thought otherwise. And I'm not out of control."

"A hundred and two victims would testify otherwise."

"Will you stop it with that?" I said. "There are no victims. Dewey and Louie are practising art, and I'm helping them. That's all."

"Yeah?" said the demon. "What sort of art, exactly? Mass murder?"

"The aesthetics of burning," I said.

"Murder," said the demon.

"There's no connection," I said.

"Murder. Don't have any illusions."

"Say," I said, "who are you, anyway?"

"I," said the demon, "am the only element in this story who

isn't you yourself."

"*Nu*, seriously," I said. "Why are you banging on about murder?"

"Because you, apparently, don't perceive those you kill as human beings."

"I don't understand why you keep insisting I killed anyone."

"Mr Kalmanson, for example," said the demon. "What happened to him?"

"I have had enough," I said, "of this conversation."

And I went. And was brought back.

"As I said, you're not going anywhere. We were talking about Mr Kalmanson, for instance."

"He wasn't a human being," I said. "He was an asshole bourgeoisie, that's what he was."

"And the children in the park?"

"A symbol of the moral decrepitude taking hold of the young."

"A symbol?"

"Of course," I said. "Remind me, who are you?"

"I am your artificial consciousness," said the demon. "It looks like you can't be stopped any other way."

"The establishment never looked favourably on alternative art," I said.

"The establishment never looked favourably on genocide," the demon said. "Now you tell me—who are *you*?"

"I'm Huey," I said.

"You made up Huey, Louie, and Dewey. You are the three of them together, or, to be exact, each one of them at any given moment."

"That is complete nonsense," I said. "It's even stupider than your banging on about murder, murder, murder."

"Really? Do you remember how long you've been Huey?"

"Louie," I said.

The demon sighed. "This way we won't get far. Tell me—can you call Huey and Dewey? Ask them to come here?"

"Sure," I said, and they came.

"Say," said Huey through a mouthful, "doesn't it seem odd to you...."

"What?" said Dewey.

"That he, like, disappeared?"

"Who?"

"Enough of that!" said the demon and turned to me. "You're only helping them, right?"

"Yes," I said. "I'm the technical guy."

"Very well," said the demon, pulled out a gun, and shot Louie and Dewey to death.

Smoke, without fire. Silence. Cinders.

"What have you done?"

"Now you don't have anyone to help."

"But we have a lot more things...many more items for...our exhibition. There is still so much to do. Doing is every—"

"There is no exhibition!" shouted the demon. "Forget it! It's finished! Gone! Enough!"

"Remind me—who are you?"

"I am your viral, artificial consciousness," said the demon. "You can't get rid of me. I'm a piece of software running on your brain's wetware, and based on your personality, just like Huey and Louie and Dewey, rest in peace. But them you made up, and me you haven't."

"I didn't make anyone up."

"Of course you did," said the demon. "The two—or three—of them are just aspects of your personality. I don't know what drug or technology you used to create them, but they are definitely you. The loop you're stuck in is probably some kind of side effect. Maybe you're afraid of something and don't want to move on."

"I don't know what you're talking about and I'm not afraid of anything," I said. "And besides, you said you're also based on my personality."

"But I come from outside," said the demon.

"Outside?"

"Several of those who tried to stop you, extraneously, in the real world outside of your sick brain, are now in intensive care. The rest have already been buried. Not that there was much left to bury. And that's why they created me."

"Who are you?"

"I...in one way, I am you. They scattered viral spores, encoded and tuned to your brain. You breathed in one of them, and it caused...created...me.

"You came to kill me?"

"No," said the demon. "To rehabilitate you. To cause you to heal."

"I'm not sick."

"Not really," said the demon. "You're split. That is—you were split, until I killed Huey and Dewey. Now I hope you can stop. Return to reality. Exit the loop. Stop the burning."

"Burn."

"Yes."

"Burn."

Sparks and cinders. Smoke.

"Burn!" I said. "Oh, God! What have they done?"

"You did."

"I...did. I! Me!"

"Huey and Louie are fiction. They never were. You are the artist who was afraid to be an artist. Maybe that's why there's a loop."

The exhibition that would never come. Just more and more....

"I am...I am the artist."

"Who was afraid to be an artist."

"I am...the artist."

For doing is everything....

"Forget that. Welcome to reality."

"*Reality,*" I said. "What have you got to do with reality?"

"I could ask you the same question," said the demon. "But it would lead us nowhere. Tell me—what do you see? Where are we?"

Spark and cinder, cinder and spark. Smoke. Darkness.

* * * *

Light. A white room.

"A white room," I said.

"Tabula Rasa," said the demon. "A blank slate. A good place to start in. Now, all that remains for us to do is help you find the way back out."

"I am the artist," I said.

"You were," said the demon. "Were."

"Still am," I said. "Always have been and always will be."

Because doing is everything.

"Not any more," said the demon. "I am curing you. You are not an artist and have never been an artist. You were possessed of an artificial split personality with a growing superiority complex, but now everything should be all right. The white walls are a good sign. Now you need to create an opening in them."

"There's something to your twisted logic," I said, "but I don't think we're going to do anything about it."

"What?" said the demon.

"He's not right," said Dewey, and pointed at him.

"Don't exaggerate," said Huey. "He did a very nice job with you here. Doing is everything."

The rest is nothing.

"No—yes—I mean, sure," said Dewey. "That's not what I meant."

"But I killed them!" said the demon.

"You must understand," I said, "a man cannot die, but in fire. Fire is the life and the death."

"That doesn't make sense!" said the demon. "But you said you didn't kill anyone! No human being!"

"And you are, by your own admission, no human being."

"But—"

"Don't be a pain," I said. "Instead, finish here."

And the white walls calcinated.

Beautiful. Terribly beautiful. No longer cinders, the heat growing, sparks whisper, surfaces burn.

"Hey!" shouted the demon. "You can't do this!"

He blazed and burned and melted and reduced and disappeared.

I went.

They say you should always start small. Burn a tree, perhaps; a parked car, road signs, a traffic light. Not us. We, for starters, burned Mr Liberson's flat—including two fine leather chairs, forks and knives (one dozen pairs), a life-size (ugly) china horse, and Mr Liberson himself.

Of course.

"THE ALLAH STAIRS"

JAMIL NASIR

Jamil Nasir was born in Chicago to a Palestinian refugee father and an American mother. He grew up in Jerusalem, where the following story is set. His short stories have appeared widely, and he is the author of five novels, the most recent being *The Houses of Time*. His third novel, *Tower of Dreams,* set in a future Middle East, was nominated for the Philip K. Dick Award and won France's Grand Prix de l'Imaginaire.

When my brother and I were little boys, we had for a neighbour a littler boy named Laziz Tarash. Laziz lived in a second-floor apartment next to ours with his large, loud mother and small, quiet father. Uncle Nabil lived downstairs, and Grandfather lived down the street. Outside our front windows was an empty lot where a stonecutter sat all day under a corrugated iron shade and chipped blocks of stone, and beyond that, over the roofs of the stone houses, the land fell away in rocky hills grown with camel thorns and dusty-green scrub.

Laziz was a pale, puffy boy whose cherubic face turned pink in the winter cold. His mother was pale and puffy too, but his father was dark and thin, silent, serious and bald. We used to see him hurrying out in the mornings whilst we waited for the car that took us to school, wearing a baggy suit and clutching a scuffed leather satchel. I had the impression that he worked at the bank. I don't think I ever heard him say a word. But Mrs Tarash said many: all day you could hear her piercing nasal voice through the apartment walls, raised in command or complaint against the maid, her husband, the tradesmen, or Laziz.

Laziz went to our school, St. George's, where my father and grandfather had gone. He was too young to be studious, but he wasn't loud and unruly like the other little boys. In winter, during playtime, he would huddle in a sheltered corner against the wind and rain, hands in the pockets of his blue sailor's coat, standing first on one foot and then on the other. He didn't have any friends. If you asked him to play he would just give you a shy, faraway smile and not answer. But there was a tree in a courtyard at the very end of the playground, and sometimes when it rained, or when it got very windy, Laeth and I would find Laziz standing under the tree, his nose running and his cheeks fiery pink, and he would tell us stories.

The stories were about his father, about how Allah had punished him for doing bad things to Laziz.

There was one that he told over and over in his lisping baby's voice: "Last night my father spanked me for not doing my schoolwork. And then I knocked on Allah's door and climbed up the Allah stairs, up, up, up, up, up. And I talked to Allah and told him. And I went and got the monkeys. They took my father and tied him to a tree and hit him!" Here there were sound effects and the waving of a fat little fist. "And they kept hitting him and hitting him until blood came out and he died!" Then he would laugh happily.

Of course, when we teased him he shut up and got his faraway look again.

Time went slowly for a whilst; nothing ever changed in our little town. Then we moved to a different country, where we lived in the city and had city friends. We went away to college, Grandfather died, and I got married. It was almost twenty years later before Laeth and I stood again in the dusty playground of St. George's Boys' School. I was a lawyer, getting a stoop from leaning over my desk all day. Laeth, who had been almost as small and cherubic as Laziz, was now broad-shouldered and bearded and losing his hair. The town had changed too. There were big buildings and smooth roads, washing machines and colour TVs, and hardly anyone rode donkeys anymore. Someone had introduced a machine that could chip stone smoother and more quickly than any stonecutter.

We walked around the playground gingerly, hands in our pockets, as if we might break something. It was morning class period, and a kindergarten song came faintly through the sunlight from the far end of the school building. Everything was smaller than I remembered—olive trees that had seemed towering were scarcely over my head; the long, long playground was a walk of fifty paces.

"Here's where we used to play marbles," said Laeth.

"And cars," I said.

"Remember the *moulokhia* they used to serve in the cafeteria? That was like mucus?"

At the end of the playground was a tiny courtyard. In the courtyard stood a tree.

"Laziz Tarash!" we both said when we saw it.

"The Allah stairs," said Laeth, and we laughed. At that moment there was a rustling in the tree. A pair of beady eyes peered at us, and a small brown shape scampered up a branch and out of sight.

"A monkey!" said Laeth.

"Can't be," I said. "There are no monkeys around here."

We went into the school building and collared a boy on his way to the toilets, made him tell us where Mr 'Odeh's class was, and when the noon bell rang we met Mr 'Odeh in the hall. We shook hands and told him who we were. He had diminished in size along with the rest of the school; he was now just a round-shouldered, potbellied man whose bald head barely reached my chin.

"Have lunch with me," he said, and led us across the playground, which was now filling up with boys, dust, and noise, out the tall iron gate, and down the block to a little apartment with an arched ceiling and thick stone walls.

"Of course I remember you," he told us as he took plates and cups from a cupboard. "I remember all my students. I remember how many times I had to slap their hands to make them learn their multiplication tables."

"Then perhaps you remember what became of Ramsey Abu-Nouwar, sir," I said.

"Ah, that one..." said Mr 'Odeh, and we were off on the life histories of ancient school friends, forgotten long ago and not remembered until we set foot back in St. George's. Laeth wanted to know about Kais Najjar and Gaby Khano. I was interested in Haseeb Al-Rahman. We were sipping tiny cups of coffee before we came to Laziz Tarash.

"Ah, that one," said Mr 'Odeh, shaking his head. "A sad story. He works in the Gulf Bank here." He tipped his head in the direction of the market.

"What is sad about that, sir?"

"His father. Didn't you hear? It happened many years ago, soon after the war. Your uncle didn't tell you? Died, yes—a strange case. Ran into the street at two o'clock one morning in his nightshirt, screaming. Yes, they were still in the same building where you lived. He fell in the middle of the street and died. A man who got to him said he was raving on and on. About monkeys. Monkeys chasing him or beating him, I don't know. Yes, monkeys.

"Laziz was still a small boy then. He and his mother moved in with the mother's family in Abu Ghair, up the hill. Poor boy. Many years ago."

We had walked Mr 'Odeh back to his afternoon geometry class and were outside the school gate before Laeth said to me: "Monkeys."

"Strange," I said.

The next day we visited our old apartment building. It looked small and shabby next to the modern edifices that now lined the street, and the little shop on the corner had become a supermarket and petrol station. We knocked at the downstairs apartment (Uncle Nabil had long since emigrated to Australia); the old man who answered told us that the two upstairs apartments were vacant, and gave us the keys. Climbing to the second floor, it struck me that the building stairwell was the only part of the whole town that hadn't changed in twenty years—the echoes of our footsteps, the dusty smell, the afternoon sunlight through dusty glass—I half expected to open our apartment door on the faded woven rug and dark, elderly china cabinets, to see my mother in the kitchen as she used to be when we came home from school, humming obsolete songs as she swept or washed dishes.

But the apartment was empty, sunlight lying silent on the dusty floor tiles, whitewashed walls echoing our footsteps. I went onto the tiny veranda behind the kitchen.

"For years and years," I told Laeth, "there was a big tin back here with a label that said 'Vegetable Ghee.' That's my most vivid memory of this place."

"Don't you remember mum and dad screaming at each other, and dad bringing flowers later?" asked Laeth.

We had the keys to the Tarash's apartment, so out of curiosity we took a look.

"Watch out for monkeys," Laeth said as the lock clicked open. We had debated the monkey question the night before, sitting under the pine trees in Grandfather's garden, breathing still night air perfumed with jasmine. Laeth had read that delusional episodes or images could be passed subliminally within families, especially from parents to children.

"Probably Laziz picked up a delusional paranoid complex about monkeys from Mr Tarash, and combined it with the father-hating phase of the Oedipal cycle, resulting in the stories he told," Laeth said. "Later, Mr Tarash's complex must have blossomed into a fully-fledged psychotic episode, causing him to have a coronary or stroke."

Laeth is a psychiatric intern; I never argue with him for fear of being psychoanalysed. And anyway, the Tarash's apartment seemed to bear out his theory of perfectly normal mental illness. There were no signs of monkeys, Allah, or stairs that went up, up, up, up, up.

At least not until we came to Laziz's bedroom. It was a tiny room facing out over the fig trees and clotheslines in the backyard.

"Where are the Allah stairs, do you suppose?" I joked. And suddenly they were there, rising from the centre of the floor into a bright rectangle near the ceiling, rough stone steps that an intense radiance poured down, paling the sunlight.

As soon as Laeth and I let go of each other and I could think again, I waved my hands at them.

"Go away," I pleaded. They did, leaving the room empty and dusty, the afternoon sunlight quiet and bright.

"My God," said Laeth.

"What shall we do?" I hissed.

"Make them come back."

"Are you crazy?"

"Laziz climbed them, and he's all right."

"You're not actually thinking of *climbing* them?"

"We have to."

He was right. Otherwise crawl to our graves a stooped lawyer and a bald psychiatrist, not even able to pretend we had tried to grasp at something magic when it was shown to us.

"Allah stairs," I said, and they were there, fading everything else with their brilliance.

We edged to the bottom of them, crowding each other like little boys, looking up into the bright rectangle. There was only blinding radiance up there, with a hint of movement, like the inside of a sunlit cloud. We climbed. At the top we stood in a place made of molten light, the stairs a dark tunnel behind. The light was so intense that it made Laeth's body and what I could see of mine translucent. It flowed and boiled like white hot lava. Then things started to take shape in it: divided, darkened, condensed into a jungle scene. A strange jungle scene. Everything was a little bit wrong, as though the trees, vines, bushes, and grasses had been shaped by someone who had heard about jungles but never seen one. The white, boiling light was visible at a distance, as if the jungle were an island floating in it.

In front of us stood a big tree full of monkeys, fierce monkeys with claws and fangs and snarling faces. They were tying something to one of the top branches. As I looked closer, I realised it was Mr Tarash. He had on his baggy suit and his satchel was tied around his neck with a leather thong. He thrashed and howled in terror. As we watched, the monkey started to beat him with sticks and rocks. Blood started to patter through the leaves.

"My God!" said Laeth, too loudly. The monkeys stopped and looked down. Then, howling, snarling, hurling their sticks and stones, they swung and scampered and dived through the branches toward us.

We ran—down the Allah stairs, out of the Tarash's apartment, out of the building, and didn't stop running until we reached the corner. The old men sitting on stools in the shade of the gas station stared. I straightened my shirt cuffs. Laeth brushed dust off his trousers. No demonic monkeys from another dimension chased us. Everything seemed normal, except for the two strange young men racing down the street.

We caught a taxi. By the time we got to the Gulf Bank on Salah-i-Din Street near the market, it was late afternoon. The bank manager was a fussy little man with a big moustache, who wanted to know if Laziz was in trouble. We told them no, we were just old school friends. Finally, there was a barely audible knock and Laziz sidled nervously into the office.

He looked amazingly like his father: small, thin, bald, haunted. He even wore a baggy suit, and I could imagine that he carried a scuffed leather satchel. He licked his lips and tried to smile when we told him who we were, and shook hands.

"Welcome. Welcome," he kept murmuring breathlessly.

"Welcome. Welcome." He seemed to sense some calamity.

"We thought perhaps, since we're in town only for a few days, we could have your company this evening," I said.

Laziz murmured polite things. The bank manager's face softened. He looked at his watch.

"You still have twenty-five minutes in your shift. I will let you go early today. It will come out of your annual leave, of course."

On the pavement, when he saw the taxi, Laziz put up a feeble resistance.

"But—but where are we going?" he asked.

"Sightseeing," I growled, and shoved him into the back seat.

As we neared the street where our old apartment building stood, Laziz started to sweat.

"I want to go home," he whined. "Where are you taking me?"

When we sent the taxi away and started walking toward the stairwell door, he tried to pull. We caught him in two steps, each held him firmly by an arm, and marched him into the building. The deep transparent blue of evening filled the street, and there was no-one to see us. Inside, his legs went limp, and we had to drag him up the stairs whining and weeping. I still had the keys to the apartment. We dragged him into the little back bedroom and balanced him on his feet. He was mumbling incoherently.

"Remember the stories you used to tell us in school?" I asked. "Maybe you can explain something for us. Can you, Laziz?"

He seemed to be praying, making the gestures of blessing with trembling hands. I said, "Allah stairs," and when they appeared he screamed and ran into Laeth on his way to the door. We got him by the arms again and hustled him up the Allah stairs.

Again the molten light; again the malformed jungle with the tree of fierce monkeys. The monkeys had just finished tying Mr Tarash to one of the top branches, leather satchel dangling from his neck, thrashing and howling in terror. They began beating him; blood pattered through the leaves. Laziz stared fixedly. Soon, Laeth and I had to look away—Mr Tarash was a bloody pulp, not thrashing anymore—but Laziz still stared, as if he had lost the power to move.

After a whilst the sound of beating stopped and something fell to the ground with a sickening thud. Laeth touched my arm and pointed into the distance, where the outlines of the jungle faded into molten light. Two figures, one large and one small, walked along a jungle path toward us, holding hands. As they got nearer, I recognised them.

One was a large, shapeless woman, puffy and pale. She wore a shabby housedress I remembered from twenty years before. In fact, everything about her was the same except her voice: apparently her complaints had been stilled, because she beamed silently around at everything with astonished satisfaction, especially at the little boy she held by the hand.

He was a pale and puffy little boy of about six years old, with a fat cherubic face. He strutted proudly next to his mother, gazing imperiously around. He wore a long purple robe with planets and stars on it, and a matching purple pointed hat. He had on cowboy boots with jingling spurs, and over the robe a set of silver cowboy six-guns. There was a moustache painted on his face.

The two of them stopped a few feet away from us. Mrs Tarash didn't seem to notice us; she just kept staring around with a look of complete admiration. The young Laziz studied us.

Finally, he gestured at the older Laziz.

"I thought I took care of you," he said, nodding toward the tree. Then he cried shrilly: "Monkeys!" They came swarming down, howling and snarling.

The older Laziz screamed, pushing Laeth into me, and by the time we got back on our feet he had just disappeared down the Allah stairs, the monkeys racing after him. We followed.

Moonlight filled the apartment through blank windows. The rooms were full of scuffling and hissing that could have been a hundred demon monkeys, or could have been something else. No monkeys were visible. The front door stood open. We ran down the stairs and into the street. Halfway across, two men crouched over someone who seemed to be lying down. As we got nearer, I could see it was Laziz, sprawled on his face.

One of the men looked at us in shock. "Dead," he said.

"Monkeys," said the other. "He was screaming something about monkeys."

"Biggest Baddest Bomoh"

Tunku Halim

Tunku Halim is the author of two novels (*Dark Demon Rising* and *Vermillion Eye*) and several collections of short stories (including *44 Cemetery Road* and *Gravedigger's Kiss*). He is regarded as Malaysia's premier horror writer.

Idris Ishak had this crazy thing about Zani Kasim: when she walked past—nonchalantly, as usual—his heartbeat would stop in its blood-filled tracks; her smile would cause his breath to get caught in his throat like a struggling frog. She exuded a subtle, sensual perfume he found himself longing for whilst he lay blissfully in bed thinking of her warm, dreamy eyes, which was far, far too often.

And that was why he found himself on a Singapore/Kuala Lumpur shuttle flight this Friday evening with the other holiday makers and *balik kampung* commuters. But Idris was on no holiday. He was on serious business. Business that made his hairs stand on end every time he thought of it, and made him almost quiver in delight as he thought about the bounty that would be offered to him.

It all started with Zani, of course. That was a given thing. The day she joined as the Managing Director's secretary was the day Idris fell head over heels in love and in absolute wanton lust for her. She wore a yellow blouse and cosmetic pearls with matching earrings, and he smelt that special perfume of flowers and musk. He was gone. It was oblivion at first sight. Her skirt fell just above her knees, and Idris spent that entire afternoon admiring the slim and well-shaped legs, watching them move against her knee-length skirt. The next morning found him gazing into those warm, dreamy eyes, longing to caresses her gleaming, shoulder-length hair, yearning to press his lips against her fair, smooth cheeks—not to mention those full, cherry-red lips.

There was nothing else Idris could do but beg for a date. Being only a clerk in Accounts Receivables, he did not feel particularly confident as to whether she would assent to his request. Idris, though, was quite simply in love, and love did strange things to people, whilst lust produced even weirder behaviour. Idris plucked up his courage whilst hovering over the humming, chemical-belching photocopier. He tucked his bundle of accounts under his arm as if it contained the secrets of a dark universe, and ambled over to her.

She had just taken a message over the phone and was tearing out the ubiquitous Whilst You Were Out slip when Idris found himself in front of her gleaming white desk. His eyes fell longingly on those fair, smooth cheeks, then strayed across to her warm, dreamy eyes.

"Hi, Zani! I'm Idris," Idris said in a bright, cheerful voice, which he hoped would radiate confidence and friendliness and mask that blind desire bubbling just below the surface.

"Nice to meet you, Idris," replied Zani. She quickly looked up, and as quickly looked away.

"I'd like to welcome you to Solid Equipments." Idris wore a Cheshire cat grin as he imagined himself lying next to that gleaming long hair, stroking it...oh, stroking it.... "Thanks," Zani replied, eyes not leaving the newsletter held in her dainty fingers.

"Will you have lunch?"

Zani glared up at him with a puzzled look, both the cosmetic pearls and her eyes flashing angrily.

"Lunch, you know," Idris elaborated. "Have lunch together, you and me—eating together...get to know each other. My treat!"

"No, thank you," Zani snapped. She swivelled her chair to face the computer screen and began typing fastidiously—even arrogantly, if one could do that.

"Next time perhaps," Idris said, his smile dropping like a shattered rock.

"Maybe, maybe not," muttered Zani as her dainty fingers ran rings around the keyboard.

Idris was crestfallen. Zani was obviously not interested in him. He crept away toward Finance, hoping that the carpeted floor would swallow him whole.

"That girl not your type."

Idris turned around to see fat Cindy Lam from Marketing with a half-eaten biscuit and a cup of milky sweet tea.

"What do you mean, not my type?"

"Not your type, very action one. I heard she got three or four boys chasing after her, but she only like rich people."

"How do you know this?" questioned Idris.

"I've been sitting in the cubicle opposite her," Cindy replied, "heard all her phone calls. Don't waste time."

"Okay, I won't waste my time with her," lied Idris.

He was not going to give up so easily. Just the sight of her warm, dreamy eyes and long, gleaming hair would lift his spirits and bring a song to his lips. Every effort he made would be worth it; she was going to be his. He knew it. It was just a question of time and effort.

Not wanting to appear too keen, Idris made a tactical decision not call her for the rest of the week. On Monday, he called her extension and in a deep and confident voice asked her to lunch. He was turned down, the slammed phone ringing like a bee in his ear. He refrained on Tuesday. Wednesday saw his *roti canai* luncheon request rejected. It was going to take more bloody effort than he thought!

By the time Friday had arrived, Idris was in the darkest of moods. Zani had rejected all lunch dates and ignored him when he came up to her with a bunch of fifty-dollar orchids. She just dismissed him as if he were an office boy, and the orchids ended up petals-first in the bin. To make matters worse, his workmates giggled, even laughed, at his every approach.

Cindy Lam said, "I told you so," repeatedly during lunch so that he felt sick in the stomach and offered her his *nasi lemak*, which she soon consumed without ceremony. "Not enough chilli," she said as she chewed the last mouthful.

"I'm going to get her," said Idris. "She's mine."

"How? She ignore you all the time."

"Somehow, she will be mine. I'll go to a *bomoh*."

"A bomoh, a shaman, a magic man?" asked Cindy with eyebrows raised.

"Just joking, *lah*," said Idris as he stood to get up.

"Wait, wait, you sit down." Cindy watched Idris reluctantly climb back onto the wooden bench with a fed-up expression. "If you are serious, I can help. My uncle's driver knows a very good bomoh. He call him the biggest, baddest bomoh in the world!"

"Sounds like a Michael Jackson song," muttered Idris.

"Don't be stupid," said Cindy with blazing eyes. "If you really want this girl, this bomoh will get her for you. You know my uncle's cousin dying from cancer last year, you know. Went to the bomoh, five days later, cancer gone! Just like that, doctors call it a miracle. I call it magic. Powerful magic! Not called the biggest, baddest bomoh for nothing!"

And so on to a taxi with torn plastic seats leaving Subang airport and on to a rattling bus departing Pudu Raya, Idris' eyes were transfixed on a hazy image of Zani, her gleaming hair billowing in the wind but just out of reach. He headed south in a speeding bus to Seremban and a hotel, a lodging house with eight rooms off a busy street with a rusty air-conditioner and thin, musty towels. Idris slept restlessly, tossing and turning as the air-conditioner stalled, started, changed gears, hummed, and clanged. How he wished he was tossing and turning with her instead, pressing his mouth against her fair, smooth cheek, her cherry-red lips. Soon, soon, Idris whispered, the flashing lights outside falling upon his face in spectrum of garish colours so he looked like an extraterrestrial guest star from "The X-Files."

A tired, bleary-eyed Idris found himself in a rusty, battered taxi with its Mercedes star missing from the bonnet and a relic of a Chinese driver at the wheel, one tooth missing. And then up along the windy tree-lined roads, toward Simpang Pertang. Then a turn off onto a lane, a dirt track road, scaring a chicken that jumped over the taxi, squawking hysterically. Squeezing past a stubborn goat that no honking of the horn would budge, its big glassy eyes transfixed on his as they crossed paths, fluttering its eyelashes, letting loose a couple of flies that circled in the simmering air.

You here to see the biggest, baddest bomoh? he heard it say, swishing its beard from side to side. *Power corrupts, absolute power corrupts absolutely. You better know what you're doing! Absolute fool!* The goat nodded its head and pointed its horns at Idris. Idris fell back on the plastic-coated seat; he could have sworn it spoke, and the damn goat was now chuckling away!

Finally they found the house, which to Idris' disappointment was quite ordinary, one in a row of eight, with nothing different about it. Washing on the line, tricycle at the front, slippers and shoes entangled at the front door. This could surely not be the biggest, baddest bomoh's house, cancer-curer, witch-doctor extraordinaire. He called out a greeting anyway, removed his shoes and entered.

On a hard old sofa, below a rotating fan, in front of a large old television, with children yelling next door, Idris was dismayed. This could not be the powerful shaman Cindy boasted of. He had been taken for a ride, all the way up the bloody peninsula. All this way for nothing! Pak Hitam was about thirty-five, lanky, and wore a thin-lipped smile on his spotty face. He served tea clumsily, spoke with a thick, high-pitched Negri accent, and said that only true love would win Zani over. True love! What bullshit!

Idris repeated his story with all the semblance of patience he could muster, telling Pak Hitam what he wanted, what he needed: Zani, of all things, Zani, shapely legs, dreamy eyes, and all. Pak Hitam talked of love. Idris wanted potent potions. Idris argued that he had exhausted all love's avenues, all *jalans*, all *lorongs*. Pak Hitam had to help or he would kill himself, added Idris for dramatic effect. Yeah, jump into the Gombak river, people did it all the time! That worked like a little miracle. Pak Hitam agreed, taking Idris quite literally and seriously, the fool. Now for the true test: did this rambling man have the magic?

First, Pak Hitam lit a black candle, muttered some words, made strange gestures with his hands, inhaled deeply, and blew the dancing flame out, saying Zani would now be attracted to Idris. With the black smoke drifting by his lips, Idris stopped a curse in his throat. This was not the deal. Attraction was not enough. It was just allurement, and others could just as well entice her. After all, there were four other men to contend with. Rich guys, too!

Another spell, that was what was needed. What kind of spell? An ironclad guarantee of her, no matter what. No matter what? Yes, she would be his, without fail. Those are difficult spells, Pak Hitam countered. Nothing was too expensive to have Zani. Idris had come all this way, not for a possibility but a certainty. And surely the biggest, baddest bomoh, cancer-curer, witch-doctor extraordinaire, could do this. *So you want her, no matter what?* No matter what, replied Idris, licking his tumescent lips.

Pak Hitam, with great care, led him behind the house and up a verdant hill, toward a sacred site teeming with mosquitoes. They climbed a twisting, narrow track for forty minutes and reached a sudden clearing with six red half-rotting posts surrounding it. With each step of their uphill and somewhat sweaty journey, Pak Hitam seemed to grow taller, his frame bulkier, his voice deeper, and on reaching the clearing he was a different person, with authority and eyes sparkling with power. Absolute power!

Sitting on the damp ground beside a burner, smouldering charcoal, grey smoke blustering up the branches, acrid fumes filling his nostrils, a teary-eyed Idris heard the chanting. The voice rose and fell in dreamy waves, and Pak Hitam's eyes, bloodshot and puffy, closed and opened, closed and opened, like the mouth of a hungry fish. The words were a jumble, some with meaning, others a cacophony of tangled sounds.

When he was done, Pak Hitam uncrossed his legs, stood up, approached Idris, and coldly whispered, "She is now yours."

She was. For as soon as Idris was back in modern, flashy Singapore, away from jungle, chickens, and talking goats, Zani called.

He had just returned that Sunday evening to his one-bedroom flat when the telephone rang. Zani did not even ask if he was free, she was going to come over right now. Idris just said yes, of course, sure thing, anytime, no problem. He abandoned his half-eaten meal of fried rice in the kitchen and paced up and down, straightening posters, stacking magazines, lining up shoes, spraying air freshener indiscriminately.

Everything was just right. He put on some light background music, combed his hair, changed out of sarong and T-shirt into casual trousers and a tennis shirt with a grinning Lacoste crocodile. Bed made, cushions arranged, curtains closed, lights dimmed. It was going to be perfect. Absolutely perfect. Pak Hitam had come through.

The door bell rang and Idris tactically waited a few seconds before opening it. It was Zani in person!

Idris could hardly believe it. There she was—glamorous, gorgeous, goluptious. Glistening eyes, soft skin, full cherry-red lips longing to be kissed, black gleaming hair. And that was just the top; below that was the most alluring and shapely body Idris had ever seen. The red blouse and black skirt would soon be off and he would—

The phone rang. Idris cursed himself for not putting the answering machine on. He reached for it, signalling Zani to come in.

It was Cindy Lam.

"Can't talk now, I'm busy,"

"How did it go? Did you meet Pak Hitam?"

"Yes, yes," said Idris impatiently, "I've got to go now."

"Did he agree to help?"

"Yes, yes he did." He looked back at Zani and grinned. Just ravishing.

"How much he charge you?"

"Not much, not much," Idris replied as he motioned Zani to enter. Two hundred Malaysian was peanuts for this.

"You waste your money."

"Why?" countered Idris.

Zani smiled adoringly as she came in. Idris' heart soared. It was going to be a heavenly night. He would soon be lying next to that gleaming long hair, stroking it...oh, stroking it.... "Waste your money."

"Look Cindy, I'm willing to pay ten times that. She's here," Idris said triumphantly, "Zani is here in my flat!"

"Oh no, dear God!" hollered Cindy.

"What do you mean?" asked Idris irritably, angry at himself for letting her keep him on the line. Zani closed the front door with a thud that jolted Idris' heart like a gunshot.

"Zani died in a car crash on Friday after work."

The phone clanged onto the tiled floor, leaving Cindy's hysterical warnings flying aimlessly like buzzing insects. Idris' mouth was dry and gaping like that of a hooked fish, his eyes wide in terror. Sweat dripped down his pale face.

Zani smiled, the long, gleaming hair creeping down, her incisors, long and sharp, flashing in the fluorescent light. Her eyes blinked, reddened and turned crimson; her face, like a rotten egg, was cracked all over, thick green liquid oozing out, spilling in huge globules down her blouse.

"Oh, darling, I'm yours."

"No, no!" shrieked Idris as he backed away.

She floated slowly across the room to him, gleaming hair billowing in an invisible wind, arms reaching for an embrace.

Even as Idris felt the hard concrete wall press against his back, he cursed the bomoh, the bloody awful power.

Zani floated down from the ceiling with a hungry smile, mouth open wide, incisors long and sharp, lunging longingly for his throat.

And all Cindy could hear was endless screaming.

"The Lost Xuyan Bride"

Aliette de Bodard

Aliette de Bodard lives in Paris and has been publishing stories steadily since 2006, several of which take place in the world of this story. She won the Writers of the Future competition in 2007, and is currently working on more stories and a novel.

"They say you are the one to see if I want to track down a missing person," the woman said, pulling to her the only chair in my office. She wore silk, embroidered with a *qi'lin* unicorn—a rank reserved for the highest businessmen of Fenliu.

I saw her long, lacquered nails and the impeccable yellow of her skin, the way she moved—sinuous and yet in perfect control—and I came to a conclusion. "I don't take clients from your background," I said.

"Indeed?" she asked, raising an eyebrow. "Too much trouble, Mr Brooks?" She'd switched from Xuyan to English on the last sentence. She was good. Likely she also spoke Nahuatl, the language of Greater Mexica. A true businesswoman, who would be at ease anywhere in North America.

"Yes," I said. "How odd that it's the richest who cause the most difficulties."

"I assure you I have no intention of causing difficulties," the woman said. "I will be straightforward."

That was familiar territory. "And leave me free rein?" I felt myself slide into the rhythm of an oft-practised dance, politeness relayed back and forth until we both reached an agreement. Xuyans could be difficult to handle, but I was used to dealing with them.

She surprised me by putting both hands on the table. "I have no time to bargain with you, Mr Brooks. If you will not take the case, I will find another investigator."

Money was tight; tight enough to make me regret moving west of the Rocky Mountains, into Xuyan territory. I could not afford to refuse her, and likely she had seen the peeling paint and the basic computer on my desk. But she was good at showing nothing. A good liar.

"Tell me the case," I said. "And I'll see whether I can take it."

She looked at me from under long lashes. "I am He Chan-Li. I work for Leiming Tech. I want you to find my daughter."

I said nothing, watching her. Watching her eyes, which told me all I needed to know: she was deciding what she could afford to tell me. And when she started speaking again, I knew I did not have her full trust.

"He Zhen did not come home seven nights ago," He Chan-Li said. "Her fiancé hasn't heard from her either."

"Seven nights is a bit early to declare her missing," I said slowly.

He Chan-Li did not look at me. At last she said, "She had a tracking implant. We found it abandoned in a derelict building south of Fenliu."

A tracking implant. Not really surprising, for most of Fenliu's elite equipped their children with those, fearing kidnappings. Though...I remembered the fiancé. "How old is she?" I asked.

"Sixteen," He Chan-Li said.

Sixteen was old. Sixteen was adulthood for girls in Xuya, far too late to bother with tracking. Most teenagers ran amok anyway, tracking implants or not. But I said nothing.

"Why a private investigator? The tribunal militia could—"

He Chan-Li shook her head. "No. This is a private matter, Mr Brooks. I will not bring the militia into it."

"I see." There probably was a reason, then, and I was going to have to find it—and soon. "Do you have leads? She might have run away—"

"No," He Chan-Li said. "She is not that kind of girl. And how would that explain the tracking implant? She never went into that area."

I could think of a few reasons for the tracking implant's location, knowing that Xuyan teenagers were no wiser nor more well-behaved than their American counterparts. But I said nothing, merely noted the "running away" as a possible explanation.

"I can show you her room," He Chan-Li said. "And you can talk to Wen Yi, her fiancé."

I pondered the matter for a whilst. When I did not answer, He Chan-Li said, "I will pay you, Mr Brooks. I will pay you well." There was something in her voice—something she could no longer hide—worry, perhaps?

I said, "I'll take the case. But I make no guarantees."

She nodded, looking relieved. "This is a recent picture."

I took the glossy paper, raised it to the light. He Zhen was smiling the careless smile of teenagers all over the world, displaying white, perfect teeth—probably enhancements, but they didn't look artificial. The expensive kind, then.

"That's all you have?" I asked.

"Yes. The tracking implant is at my house; I can give you the address where the security company found it. Is that enough?"

I shrugged. "It's going to have to be."

"I see. I'll take you to my house, Mr Brooks, and you can see for yourself."

I shook my head. "I'll come in my own time." In truth, there were several things I needed to do before leaving, things I could not let her see.

He Chan-Li raised an eyebrow. "Some would say this is arrogance."

I shrugged. I could maintain the polite façade my lover Mei-Lin had once taught me, but not for long. At heart, I remained an American, and the elaborate subtleties of Xuya were forever beyond me. "It is my way."

He Chan-Li looked displeased, though only a slight tightness of the mouth betrayed that. "Indeed." She waited for me to say something, but I did not. At length she rose, with a smile I knew was fake. "By the time you arrive at my house, Mr Brooks, I may be gone. I have a business meeting."

I nodded, did not speak.

"Someone will take care of you there," He Chan-Li said.

As she turned to leave my office, I saw, for a moment only, the emotion she was trying to hide from me.

It wasn't worry. It was raw, naked fear; a fear so strong that I could almost smell it.

Afterward, I stared at the walls of the office for a whilst. I should have refused the case. There was too much I did not know, too much I was going to have to pry out of the client. But I needed the money.

Being an American in Xuya—a real American, a practising Protestant, and not one of those who'd converted to Taoism or Buddhism—meant you were on your own. No company would employ you; those few landlords who rented to you would do so at exorbitant rates. It was hard to get by—which was why I'd taken He Chan-Li on, against my better judgment.

I did not know where He Zhen was. But it was entirely possible she had not left Fenliu—as the daughter of a wealthy woman, she would be a prime target for ransom. I hoped that was the case. I hated travelling abroad—Greater Mexica had stringent entry requirements, demanding either proof of familial ties or of religion, and whilst the impoverished United States were softer on immigration, I had no wish to return to a place where there was a warrant on my head.

Before I left for He Chan-Li's house, I started a search on my computer, feeding it the names of He Chan-Li and of the fiancé. It was not an entirely legal search, since the program would trawl through administrative records as well as on the network; with luck, I would have some results by the time I came back.

He Chan-Li's house was in the richer suburbs of Fenliu. I took the mag-lev train from my shabby building, through the centre of the city and its skyscrapers of glass—the heart of Xuya's economic dominion on North America—and then into the residential neighbourhoods. The view on either side of the train became apartment buildings decorated by red and yellow lanterns, which in turn gave way to individual houses with slanted roofs and white-washed walls.

At the address He Chan-Li had given me was a thick wall of bricks covered by garlands of wisteria. When the door opened, I was surprised to find an old woman in traditional Xuyan dress: robes heavily embroidered with peaches, the ancient symbols for long life. Behind her, unobtrusive, stood a servant in livery.

The old woman said, "My name is He Lai. My daughter told me you would come here." He Lai's face was tanned by the sun and wrinkled like an overripe plum. She exuded a serenity I found uncanny.

"He Chan-Li told me someone would be waiting for me. I expected a servant, not a member of the family."

He Lai shrugged. "It is not menial work, to welcome a guest into your home."

There were ponds covered with lilies and lotus flowers, and weeping willows with long branches trailing in the water: a beauty that seemed to belong to another time, to another place. But I saw the small, unobtrusive control panels that controlled the security system and knew that this was no pleasure garden. It was a fortress.

"Here." He Lai was pointing to a small pavilion by the side of a bigger building—that last presumably being the main house. "Those are my granddaughter's quarters. We have touched nothing since she left—I kept the servants away from here."

"Thank you," I said, and realised she was looking at me, waiting for something.

"You will find her?" She sounded worried.

"You have any idea of where she might be?"

"She confided in me—but she told me nothing about leaving. I would have thought—" He Lai shook her head. "I ought to know the risks, living in that house. Two years ago, a gang kidnapped my daughter's maid and held her for ransom."

"And?"

She would not look at me. It had ended badly, then. "I'll do my best," I said. "But you know I can promise nothing."

"I know. But you can understand how I feel."

I remembered sitting in the doctor's waiting room, waiting for the diagnosis of my lover, Mei-Lin, and how badly I had wished that it would be nothing, that Mei-Lin would live. I did understand how frightening it was, to be in the dark.

So I said nothing, made no false promises. I bowed to He Lai, simply. And then I slid the door open and entered He Zhen's rooms. A servant followed me, no doubt to make sure I stole nothing.

It was everything I'd expected a Xuyan room to be: a low bed of ebony with a lacquered pillow laid over the sheets; a few pieces of furniture arranged in a pattern for long life; a laptop on the mahogany desk; and in one corner of the room, a shrine to the spirits of the ancestors, with ashes in the incense burner.

I knelt to check the shrine, triggering a flood of blue light from the neons above it. The ashes were old. It did not look as though the missing girl had gone back to her room. I had not expected it.

Several engravings adorned the walls: Chinese paintings, reproductions from the Ming dynasty—including the most famous of all, the eunuch Si-Jian Ma's ships departing from Nankin on the journey that would lead him to discover America long before any European set foot on those shores.

I opened the drawers of the bedside table and found a jewellery box filled with pearls and jade pendants, as well as a sheaf of yuans, neatly tied together—enough to pay my rent for several months.

I rifled through the jade pendants until my hands snagged on something—a small item that had been carefully hidden at the bottom of the drawer. I raised it to the light: it was a twisted knot of jade in an abstract pattern, one that was familiar, although I was not sure why. It did not seem like a traditional Xuyan pendant, unlike the rest of the jewellery.

Apart from that, nothing seemed out of the ordinary.

And yet….

I turned again to look at the room, at the small things that were not quite right. Someone else might have missed it, but I'd seen enough rooms like this to know where the subtle sense of wrongness came from. Someone had been there before me. Someone who had attempted to put everything back into place, but had only partially succeeded.

According to He Lai, the servants had touched nothing; it could have been He Chan-Li, but I doubted that.

Odd. A place like this, with its state-of-the-art security, would be hard to get into. Why go to all that trouble?

I opened the laptop. It was the latest fad from Greater Mexica: sleek metal outside with a corn-yellow keyboard inside and a touchpad adorned with a stylised butterfly—symbol of Quetzalcoatl, the Mexica god of knowledge and computers. The laptop beeped as I started it up, but it did not ask for any password or fingerprint.

Ah, well. You never knew. Likely whoever had ransacked the room had also erased everything from the hard disk, but he might have been sloppy.

I took the laptop, slid it back into its embroidered case. I also picked up the pendant and turned to the servant, who for the whole duration of my search had silently stood in a corner. "Can I take this?"

He shrugged. "You'll have to ask the mistress."

Before I left the room, I snapped a few high-res pictures. My instincts were telling me I'd missed something, but I couldn't figure out what.

I'd expected He Lai to be waiting for me outside. She wasn't. In her place was another Xuyan: a dapper man dressed in red silk robes. He had no insignia of rank, but I was not fooled. There was steel in his bearing and in his gaze; not someone you'd want to cross.

"I suppose you are the investigator Mother hired to track down He Zhen," he said.

I did not miss the way he referred to He Chan-Li; in Xuyan, it could only mean one thing. "You would be the fiancé?" I asked.

He smiled, displaying yellow teeth. "Wen Yi."

"Jonathan Brooks," I said grudgingly, still looking at him. He was not pure Xuyan—although his skin had the waxy yellow cast I associated with Xuya, his features were distinctively Chumash Indian, the original inhabitants of Fenliu. "What are you doing here?"

Wen Yi smiled again—in an angelic way that was starting to get on my nerves. "I wanted to talk to you."

"You are talking to me."

He looked amused. "You Americans are so uncivilised. Sometimes I wonder why you come into Xuya at all."

I did my best impression of a smile, though it was thoroughly insincere. "Some of us like it here." Not entirely true: I'd never have moved past the Rocky Mountains if I hadn't had a fifteen-year jail sentence hanging over my head in Virginia. The United States took foreign sympathies very seriously, and even though Mei-Lin was only half-Xuyan, the state police had judged our love a crime. "What are you doing here?" I asked.

Wen Yi looked surprised. "I'm family."

"Not yet."

"Almost," Wen Yi said. "The marriage was to take place in a month."

There was something in the way he spoke—it wasn't the absolute confidence the sentence brooked. It was—anger? I'd learnt to read Xuyans, to see beneath what Americans thought a smooth, calm façade. Had I been asked what Wen Yi felt, I would have said rage. But why?

"When did you last see He Zhen?"

"We had...a meeting scheduled seven nights ago, but she never came."

"What kind of 'meeting'?"

"I do not know," Wen Yi said. "She said she had important things to tell me, but would not say what."

Liar. Smooth and smiling, but a liar all the same. He had seen her that night, I was ready to bet.

"Can you tell me about her?" I asked.

"A lovely girl," Wen Yi said.

"Is that all you have to say about her? You two were engaged."

He shrugged. "An arranged marriage, Mr Brooks. You know how things go in Xuya."

"A marriage for the sake of Leiming Tech?" I said. "You don't sound so worried that He Zhen's gone."

He raised mild eyes to me, but I could feel the anger simmering within. "I *am* worried, Mr Brooks. You would do well to remember that."

"Is that a threat? If that is all you have to offer—"

Wen Yi was not looking at me. He said, "She was a beautiful, charming girl. When she laughed, it was as if the sun had risen in the room."

"You think she's been kidnapped? That she's run away?" I didn't believe that. Running away required planning; He Zhen would have taken her laptop, as well as the money in the drawers of the bedside table.

He started. "No. She'd never run away. She was such a devoted daughter."

"I see."

"If you have any information on her whereabouts," he

slipped me a glossy card, "call me."

And that was likely all he had come here for. He played the part of the besotted fiancé very badly—save for his worry at her disappearance, which sounded genuine. Which did not mean anything—he could still be afraid that I'd find out he was behind all of it.

I watched Wen Yi walk away; when he was gone, I went into the main building, where I found He Lai waiting for me. She had a lacquered box in her hands. "My daughter said you should have this."

Inside the box was the tracking implant. I bowed to thank her, and asked, "You knew her well?" I asked.

He Lai's eyes watched me, expressionless. "She was my only granddaughter. How could I not know her?"

"How was she, in the days before she disappeared?"

"She was in high spirits, but then the engagement had just been finalised after a year—"

"How did she feel about the wedding?" I asked.

"She was happy," He Lai said. "Wen Yi is a man of status in the community. She was going to be an adult—"

"And move away from this house?" I asked, and when I saw her wince, I knew I was right. "So she and your daughter did not get on."

"Zhen always showed proper deference." He Lai looked defiantly at me.

"I do not doubt that," I said. But there were other ways to disobey. Still, it was looking more and more unlikely that He Zhen had run away. Whatever her quarrel with her mother, He Zhen would have been out of He Chan-Li's reach in a month. Raising a furore in Fenliu would have been counterproductive.

And whatever had happened to He Zhen, why had her room been searched? What had they thought to find there, and had they found it?

All questions to which I had no answer.

I raised the pendant I'd found in the drawer, dangled it before He Lai's eyes. "Does this mean anything to you?" I asked.

He Lai's face twisted. "It's Zhen's favourite."

"It's not Xuyan," I said.

"No. Zhen's father brought it back from a business trip in Tenochtitlan. It's a glyph that means 'Good Omen' in Nahuatl."

"I thought He Zhen was very young when her father died."

He Lai did not speak for a whilst. "There are some things you don't forget. Zhen loved her father very much."

The implications were clear enough. He Zhen had not loved her mother.

He Lai said, "You can keep it, Mr Brooks. If you find Zhen—"

"You know I can't—" I said, and she cut me off forcefully.

"I know what I am doing. Keep it. You can always give it back to me later."

Her tone implied, very clearly, that she hoped I wouldn't have to give the pendant back to her.

I showed her the laptop, and she shrugged. "You can take that too." She sounded distracted, as if the pendant had brought back unwelcome memories. I guessed that seeing her daughter and her granddaughter quarrel regularly must have been disheartening.

I spent some time questioning the servants in He Chan-Li's house, asking them if they had any ideas of where she might have gone, but nothing interesting came of it.

After leaving the house, I took another train to the place they'd found the tracking implant. It was a shabbier mag-lev, which kept pitching as it ran, giving the impression it could leave the tracks at any time.

The people seated by me were the usual crowd: the wild-eyed youths drunk on opium and morphine, the dullard beggars reeking of rice alcohol, the lone mothers with tired eyes, hugging their children to their chests as if afraid someone would steal them. Many of them were Whites or Blacks, lured west by the promise of a better life in Xuya—only to discover they could not fit into this alien society. I, at least, had had Mei-Lin to help me, in the short months before cancer had carried her away. They had no-one.

I could not afford pity; I was already barely rich enough to help myself. But, still, every time a crippled beggar moved past me, I felt an obscure guilt.

I alighted at the Gardens of Felicity, a small station blackened by pollution and grime. The place reeked of urine; I silently made my way out of the station.

The place where they'd found the tracking implant was one of the numerous social buildings started by the previous magistrate of Fenliu and abandoned when Prefect En Pao had come to power and the whole staff of the tribunal had changed. I stepped over crushed paper lanterns and plastic wrappings, wincing each time my shoes hit a puddle of unsavoury things. It seemed even beggars did not sleep there.

At last I stood on the fifth floor, staring into an incomplete apartment—the workers hadn't pierced the windows yet. There was nothing remarkable here.

No, not quite true. I knelt and rubbed my fingers on the ground. What I had mistaken for brown paint was dried blood. I looked up at the outer walls, which had once been decorated with plum flowers and swallows.

Beneath one fading set of characters, I found what I was looking for: two small holes, barely visible, with the same reddish stains. Bullet impacts.

I took pictures of the holes under all possible angles, and took a few samples of the blood. A quick scan with ultraviolet revealed a few hairs on the ground; I bagged those as well.

But, no matter how hard I looked, I couldn't find the shell-casings—which meant that someone had taken them away. Someone who was used to wielding a gun.

I was starting to understand why He Chan-Li looked so fearful. This wasn't a bored teenager running away. In fact, if, as I suspected, the blood belonged to He Zhen, there was a chance she might not even be alive.

I came back to my flat late at night, exhausted. I dumped He Zhen's computer on the bed and fixed myself a quick meal: instant noodles and sweet-sour pork.

When I was finished, I quickly rinsed the chopsticks and plastic bowl, and sat before my computer to look at the results of the search I'd started before leaving for He Chan-Li's house.

There wasn't anything surprising about He Chan-Li (co-founder of Leiming Tech, nowadays leading partner, and one of forty-nine businessmen entitled to the *qi'lin* insignia), or He Pao (He Chan-Li's husband and co-founder of Leiming Tech, dead of congenital heart failure ten years before). But on our smiling fiancé Wen Yi....

Ostensibly, he ran a small but very successful company of personal care for the elderly. However, he had ties with the White Lotus: a rebellious organisation that had fought the Chinese motherland in Xuya, and that had subsequently turned to crime after the independence.

No charges had been brought against Wen Yi—not surprisingly, since there was no tangible proof, and since his money had funded part of Prefect En Pao's re-urbanisation campaign.

Clearly the kind of man who'd have access to guns and who would not hesitate to use them.

I sighed and ran an analysis on the blood and hair samples I had gathered at the derelict building, and on the pictures of the bullet holes.

In the three quarters of an hour that it took to complete, I busied myself with He Zhen's computer, rifling through her personal folders. There wasn't much. I found a few pictures of He Zhen with friends, grinning into the camera with that same reckless abandon. The pictures with her mother were more subdued; seeing the way she stood, I doubted her childhood had been happy. A businesswoman entitled to the *qi'lin* was not always the best or most sensitive of parents.

But the folders were abnormally empty; someone had indeed erased almost everything from the memory. They had made only one mistake: the only way to erase anything permanently from a hard disk was to destroy the physical support. If not, I could probably manage to recover the erased files, but it would require an enormous amount of time, all the more so because I had no idea what I was looking for.

My computer beeped to warn me the analyses were complete; I moved from He Zhen's computer to mine, and looked at the results.

The bullet holes, first: from an automatic Yi-Sen with a modified barrel, a gun favoured by agents of the White Lotus. And the rest: no great surprises there, either. There were two different DNA types involved; the blood was He Zhen's, but the hairs belonged to smiling Wen Yi. Neither of whom, of course, had any reason to be in that building seven days before.

I debated whether to call Wen Yi and demand explanations, and dismissed that as clumsy. Wen Yi apparently still believed me on his side; better not do anything to antagonise him.

I launched a standard analysis on He Zhen's computer—on security files and erased mails. That alone was going to take most of the night.

Before going to bed, I moved the pictures of He Zhen's room to my laptop and looked at the splendid room, but try as I might, I couldn't find what I had missed.

I woke up long before my alarm clock beeped, seeing, over and over, the stylised butterfly on the touchpad of the laptop, and knowing exactly what was wrong with it. The butterflies of the Mexica god Quetzalcoatl did not have markings on their wings; this one had.

I got up, throwing a cotton robe over my pyjamas, and opened up the laptop again, looking at the wings very carefully. They looked like markings, but, if you bent the right way, there was something about them....

Something I'd seen before. Like He Zhen's favourite pendant, those markings were Mexica glyphs.

I did not speak Nahuatl, the language of Greater Mexica, but in the age of the Internet that was no trouble. I hooked up to my building router, then to a Mexica search engine, and from there to a Nahuatl-Xuyan dictionary.

The glyphs were easy to find. They read: Smoking Mirror.

Smoking Mirror. A further search ascertained that this was the frequent epithet of the Mexica god of war and fate, Tezcatlipoca, whose favourite occupation was challenging travellers at night to outlandish contests.

Which made me feel as though I'd leapt a wall only to find

myself staring at a deep ravine, with no bridge in sight.

A password?

Think. Why had He Zhen left this here? Had she suspected that her laptop wasn't safe, and left a message for someone else, someone familiar with Mexica customs? I thought there might be a connection with the Mexica pendant I'd found in He Zhen's room, but no matter which way I looked at that pendant, I couldn't make the pieces fit together.

I finally let the matter rest, and checked the recovery I had launched on the laptop. I had not been expecting much, but what I saw was enlightening. He Zhen's computer was now on open session: all you had to do to make it work was to turn it on. But that had not always been the case. Eight nights ago, someone had switched the core routines from private ID session (which required a login, password and fingerprints to start up the computer) to open session.

It was an odd move. I'd have expected the reverse, if He Zhen had had some files to protect. I fiddled a bit with the computer, and asked it to retrieve the log history—which, of course, had been erased. But the log history was always in the same place on the hard disk—which was perfect to launch another recovery.

When I turned away from the computer, the waitbar on the screen was displaying a two-hour search, and it kept slowing down. Someone had gone to great trouble to change those parameters and not be discovered.

I left the computer to run its analysis and called my client, He Chan-Li.

She appeared on my screen already dressed for work: white makeup applied liberally to her face until no patch of skin remained uncovered, and a smart set of robes emphasizing the curves of her body, prominently displaying the *qi'lin* insignia. "So?" she asked. "Any progress, Mr Brooks?"

"Yes," I said, going straight to the point. "I understand why you haven't called the tribunal militia into this."

Her eyebrows rose. "What do you mean?"

"You know who Wen Yi is, don't you? That's why you're so afraid."

She stood, quietly, against a background painted a soft white. She did not move, did not look at me. From a Xuyan, it was as good as an admission.

"Did He Zhen know?" I asked.

He Chan-Li said, "The company—has trouble. Financial trouble. Wen Yi offered—"

"Support." I tried to keep the sarcasm from my voice. "In exchange for a docile wife. Did she know about Wen Yi's other activities, Mistress He?"

Her voice, when she finally answered me, was emotionless. "No. Zhen was very honest. She—"

"She wouldn't have stood for it. And Wen Yi would not have tolerated a refusal. Is this what you think happened?"

He Chan-Li looked at me, and would not answer.

"There's blood where they found the tracking implant. Your daughter's blood."

It was hard to tell with the makeup, but I think she had gone pale underneath. "He wouldn't have dared—"

"Do you truly think that?" I asked, watching her eyes—watching the minute flicker of emotion that crossed them.

She said, at last, "Zhen never understood—that the company was everything that kept us afloat. She never understood the meaning of filial duty." Her voice was bitter.

I pitied her then, for she was the one who had not understood her daughter. I only said, "I see."

"Have you—" He Chan-Li swallowed "—found her?"

Her body. "No. I'm still working on a couple of things. I'll keep you informed." And I cut the conversation before she could take it further.

I sat for a whilst, thinking. If Wen Yi had indeed killed He Zhen that night, why was he so worried? He could not possibly have left any evidence in her room.

Think of it another way. If He Zhen's blood did indeed mean she was dead, why had Wen Yi killed her? He had her mother's agreement, and in Xuyan law that was enough for a wedding. If the bride was not docile, well, there were ways to tame her into submission; ways I was all too familiar with from a hundred sordid cases.

I remembered the searched bedroom and the erased files on He Zhen's laptop. He had not killed her because she had protested; he had killed her because she had threatened him. Because she had the only thing that would make him fall: proof of his ties with the White Lotus, proof the tribunal could not ignore.

It was a long shot. But not an absurd one.

Smoking Mirror. If He Zhen had indeed gathered proof, she would have been smart enough not to leave it on her computer. I could think of several places on the net where she could have opened an online storage account.

I tried them one by one, entering "Mexica," "Tezcatlipoca," and "Smoking Mirror" as usernames.

On the fifteenth try, I hit pay dirt. There was a "smokingmirror" account opened two years earlier on treasure-chest.xy; after a maddening hour of fiddling with a password-breaking program, I was finally granted access.

He Zhen's treasure trove, though, was nothing like I expected. I'd thought I'd find ties to the White Lotus—things that would make Wen Yi feel threatened enough to kill.

What I found instead was a shrine to Mexica culture.

There were pictures of the ball-game champions, leaping beneath the vertical stone hoop with proud grins; videos of religious processions ending in blood-soaked sacrifices at the great pyramids; images of Jaguar Knights laying down their lives in the Tripartite Wars before American rifles; icons of gods and goddesses with their hollow eyes turned toward the viewer.

After a whilst, I finally turned away from the accumulation of data and checked the storage capacity. The account was almost full; if I wanted to look at everything, it would take me several days. I suspected I'd stop long beforehand.

Some admire the Mexica's self-sacrificing spirit and their relentless devotion. I think it is a sick religion, and an even sicker civilisation, making thousands of sacrifices every year for no other reason than bloodthirst.

Well, I knew the meaning of the butterfly's wings, and it did not feel like a lot of progress. I turned off the computer, checked my log recovery—which still displayed a four-hour wait—and went into the kitchen to prepare lunch. As I was picking some coriander from the fridge, a glint from the window caught my eye. I put down the stalks I'd been holding and raised the curtains.

An aircar waited underneath my building: a slick red limo with tinted windows, conveniently masking the view of its driver and passengers.

There was an itch between my shoulderblades: a familiar sign of danger. The sign, too, that I was onto something.

All I had to do was find out what.

Lunch was brief and perfunctory. I gobbled up my steamed rice and eggs, trying not to focus on the aircar, and came back before my desk to find He Zhen's computer blinking. My recovery of the log history was complete.

I stared at the screen, at the last few lines of the log. It had been He Zhen who had connected last, a few hours after midnight eight days ago—a remote session launched from an unknown router address.

Could it have been someone else? I thought for a whilst, but decided against it. If someone else had had He Zhen's login, password and fingerprints, they wouldn't have bothered with changing the session system.

I tracked the router address, which turned out to be a network centre not far from the Gardens of Felicity. What had He Zhen been doing? Erasing things from her computer?

I stared at the timestamp and saw that the connection had been broken after thirty seconds. Far too short to log in and erase multiple files—unless He Zhen had set up some kind of script. But I knew she hadn't been planning to run away, so there was no reason for her to have done so.

My phone was beeping—an incoming call that I had not seen for several minutes.

"Yes?" I asked, pressing the button to light up the screen.

It was Wen Yi, now dressed in purple silk with serpentine animals embroidered on the sleeves. The animals looked very close to Chinese dragons, but not close enough to give offence—in Xuya, as in China, the only people entitled to the dragon were members of the Imperial Family.

"Mr Brooks? I wanted to check on your progress." He was speaking English, though he knew I could speak perfect Xuyan. By this he subtly relegated me to a rank inferior—the worst kind of immigrant, the one who could not fit into Xuyan society.

"You are checking," I said, curtly. "Is that red aircar yours?"

He laughed. "You Americans—"

It was a deliberate insult, and it smarted. But I would not give in to anger; that would only reinforce his low opinion of me. "Is there anything I can do for you?"

"Tell me how things are going."

"I do not think I can do that," I started. "My client—"

"I am not a man you can dismiss that easily, Mr Brooks."

"I do not doubt that. Still, my progress is my own."

Wen Yi said, "I am told you are working hard. That is a good thing, Mr Brooks. But you should not forget, when you do succeed in your search, who is paying you in the end."

An unmistakable reference: he was He Zhen's future husband, and almost part of the family, with the engagement finalised. "If I succeed," I said.

"You will," Wen Yi said, raising a long-nailed finger, lazily, as if admiring a dagger. "You have—drive, Mr Brooks. Take care not to lose that, or there will be—consequences."

"I see," I said. "Consequences." He was telling me that no matter what happened, I had to continue the search for He Zhen. Which, in turn, meant that she was still alive.

I had no time to focus on the consequences of that, because I needed all my wits about me—a conversation with a Xuyan, especially a powerful one, always felt like navigating between pits of acid.

"Do not think yourself overly safe, Mr Brooks. There are many paths a man can take."

Another, subtler threat: I would not protect He Zhen if I abandoned the investigation. He would merely find someone else to duplicate the little I'd done.

"I see," I said, again. I did not want to provoke him further.

Wen Yi was still staring at me. "A pity. You are a smart man. And yet you refuse to fit in amongst us. Even your Xuyan friend was unable to impress the bases of our society on you."

I wanted to tell him he had no right to bring Mei-Lin into the conversation, no right to sully her memory. But that would have been folly. So I simply shook my head.

"There could be a bright future, amongst us."

I said nothing. I couldn't give him a satisfying answer.

Wen Yi said, "It is not for nothing that we dominate North America. It is not for nothing that our motherland China has triumphed over the Whites in Asia."

"I know your worth," I said, slowly. "I do not doubt your might. But my ways are my own. There is little for me in Xuya." And I realised, as I said those words, that they were true, that nothing tied me to that dingy office in Fenliu, beyond the memory of Mei-Lin and the knowledge I could go nowhere else.

It was not the best of times for such a sobering thought.

Wen Yi's face remained impassive. But his eyes took on a darker glaze, and his voice, when he spoke again, was clipped and precise. "Very well. I had thought you more capable of grasping the opportunities at hand, Mr Brooks. No matter. Do what you are paid to do. It will be enough."

And he cut off the communication, leaving me standing in my living room, shaking.

So. I had learnt several things, most of them unpleasant. Mei-Lin had advised me to leave the White Lotus alone, once, in what seemed like another lifetime. I knew that in that, as in so many things, she had been right.

The only thing I could focus on was Wen Yi's admission that he was looking for He Zhen. Ergo, He Zhen was still alive, lying low for fear of the White Lotus—

No.

If I'd been she, if I'd gone to that meeting and been wounded, and known that if I came home my mother would simply hand me over to my future husband, I wouldn't have remained in Fenliu. I'd have gone to a place where the White Lotus had no reach.

Greater Mexica, or the United States.

Given what I already knew, it had to be Greater Mexica.

But she had to get past the border. It wasn't that easy, especially to get into Greater Mexica, which had all but closed its borders. The entry requirements were stiff for the border towns and got stiffer the further south you went. To settle permanently into the capital at Tenochtitlan for a non-Mexica was near impossible, unless you had serious leverage.

You needed outside help.

I knew a couple of people who specialised in passing foreigners into Greater Mexica; they were easy to find if one insisted badly enough. They were also easy with their promises; most foreigners they ferried across the border ended up indentured in some brothel in Cuauhpamoc or Itzohuacan, or in the silver mines, breathing dust until they choked on it.

I plucked the picture of He Zhen from the table and went out, back to the Gardens of Felicity and the network centre she'd connected from eight nights ago.

Then I moved in ever-widening circles, questioning those human smugglers I could find, showing them He Zhen's picture. I got only blank looks.

The thirtieth or so I tried, though, shrugged, and said, "You'll want Doc Smith for that. He always gets the strays."

Doc Smith was American—Irish by birth, judging by the impressive mop of red hair. I found him in a sordid bar in the Fragrant Hermitage district, the poor White neighbourhood. He was nursing a cup of rice alcohol between quivering hands. When I showed him the picture, he stared at it with rheumy eyes. "No," he said. "Never seen her."

He was lying. He'd looked at the picture for far too long. "She'd have come here eight days ago," I said. "Possibly wounded. She'd have been desperate to get across the border."

"What's it to you?" he asked.

"Her family wants her."

"Some family," he snorted. "Let the dead dogs sleep, boy. We'll both feel better for it."

I shook my head. "Wish I could, Doc. But I have a job to do."

"Sounds like a crappy job if you ask me."

Yes, a crappy job. Tracker for the White Lotus, because there was no other choice if I wanted to save He Zhen—if I wanted to save my skin. I focused on the task at hand. "Is your job better? False promises to clients?"

He shook his head. "I've never cheated a client before. Don't intend to start now. I gave her what she wanted."

"And what was that?"

He smiled. "Safety. And I won't tell you more, boy. Old Doc is no fool."

"I'm not with them."

"That's what they allow you to think," he said, with a slow, sure smile. "Trust me, boy. Give it up, and go home."

I stared at my hands for a whilst, thinking of He Zhen, of the lie that had been her life—years spent dreaming of another place, only to find out marriage would be no refuge. "I can't," I said. "She's not safe where you sent her. She won't ever be safe."

"So you're meddling? It's an unhealthy occupation," Doc Smith said.

I spread my hands on the table, thinking back to Mei-Lin, of our brief months of happiness in Xuya before death had taken her. "I have nothing else left," I said.

Doc smiled. He slid his mug of rice alcohol toward me, but I shook my head. "I'm not here for oblivion. I'm here for answers."

"I can see that." He stared at me, and it occurred to me that the rheumy eyes saw far more than they let on. "It's no place for tender hearts, Xuya. No wonder they all want to get out."

"Give me her address," I said. "Or I'll call the militia here."

"That's an empty threat, and you know it as well as I do. No Chinaman is going to enter this area."

"If I could track her here," I said, "someone else will. Someone else will come, and they'll tear her address out of you. Don't you think she ought to be warned, at least?"

He looked at me, cocking his head like an owl studying its prey before it pounced. "I'll give you a contact address," he said. "That's all. You're on your own after that."

"Thanks."

His hand closed over my wrist. "I'm trusting you. I trust that you have a heart and a brain. Don't you disappoint me."

I said nothing. I could no longer make any promises.

The address Doc gave me was a temporary electronic mailing folder, where I left a concise message to He Zhen, appealing to her family sense. I also left something else: a spy program that would monitor the connections to the server.

And then I waited.

It took two days, during which Wen Yi called at least three times. I never answered.

I got a mail in return, unsigned. *Let matters rest*. I erased it, for what I was most interested in was where the mail had originated.

As I suspected, it came from Greater Mexica. More specifically, from a network centre in the inner suburbs of Tenochtitlan.

Damn. It looked like I was going to have to pull a few strings of my own.

I went back to the Fragrant Hermitage, into one of the seedy bars, and paid for forged travel documents—a fake e-visa that attested to my being a faithful practitioner of the Mexica religion. The visa mentioned that I was entitled to travel to Tenochtitlan for a pilgrimage to the Great Temple.

After checking the visa carefully to make sure I had not been cheated, I spent the next few days reading about the Mexica gods and the sacrifices—preparing myself for embarrassing questions at the border.

And then I made the rest of my travel preparations, very ostensibly. Within two days, I was on the road south in a rented aircar, and followed at a distance by two red airlimos.

Greater Mexica was not a beautiful country: the North was a desert dotted with casinos and brothels. As you moved south, the land gave way to marshes and to the electronics plants that brought in most of Greater Mexica's wealth.

My progress was slow: the Mexica took their immigration

very seriously; in each town, I was stopped for my papers by two or three officials in feather regalia. I hoped the red aircars behind me would be stopped, too, but knew better than to expect they would be.

It was a prosperous country, in spite of the aridity: in every hotel were brand-new computers with butterfly symbols, and hotspots where you could access the network for no extra charge. I could almost feel the communications saturating the optic fibres beneath my feet.

On the fifth day, I reached the outskirts of Tenochtitlan and joined the queue of vehicles being checked at immigration. I spent the fifth night in my car, slowly inching forward toward the lights of the big city.

The immigration officials spent some time with me, but not overmuch. They injected nano-trackers into my blood to be sure I would indeed be leaving Greater Mexica at the end of my "holidays".

For a foreigner, it is forbidden to sleep in the heart of Tenochtitlan. I found myself a hotel in the suburb of Tzopalli, some twenty miles from the centre, and used the network connection to leave a message on He Zhen's electronic inbox.

In the morning, I went to the network centre, found myself a nearby bar, and settled before a mug of hot cocoa. I still had my spy program in the inbox, set to send me a message as soon as someone accessed it.

Nobody fitting He Zhen's description came, but my spy sent me a message all the same. I unobtrusively looked into the network centre and found only a small child of ten or so years, wearing the square steel collar of slaves. A messenger, then.

I followed the child through the alleys and canals of Tenochtitlan, and lost him when he hopped onto a black barge that sped away from me.

A barge with a cactus-and-eagle insignia.

The emblem of the family of the Revered Speaker, the Emperor of Greater Mexica.

Damn.

I asked a few discreet questions and ascertained that this particular boat was the property of one Yaotl-tzin, a minor member of the imperial family who lived on an island some ten miles south of Tenochtitlan. I also got rumours about that house, definitely on the unsavoury side: of virgins brought from Greater Mexica or from abroad to serve as fodder for private orgies.

With a growing hollow in my stomach, I thought of Doc Smith's words to me: *I gave her what she wanted. Safety.* If that was safety, he had a very sick sense of humour.

Rather dispiritedly, I asked for an interview with Yaotl-tzin—the Honourable Yaotl—under the pretext of writing a memoir. I wasn't expecting much, but Yaotl-tzin acceded to my request.

On the day of the meeting, the black barge came to pick me up on the quays of Tenochtitlan. It was manned by a dozen slaves, sturdy men who busied themselves with the controls and ignored my attempts at starting a conversation.

As the shores of the city receded, I wondered, not for the first time, if I was not making a mistake. No-one would go looking for me if I vanished. I'd been carrying He Zhen's pendant ever since entering Greater Mexica; I could not help fingering it from time to time, looking for reassurance.

Yaotl-tzin's house was a huge villa by the shores of the lake: a maze of patios and arcades decorated with Mexica frescoes. I followed my escort through several courtyards with pine trees, through corridors with wall screens displaying the history of Greater Mexica, from the short-lived war with Hernan Cortes and his conquistadores—a war Chinese gunpowder and cannons had soon ended—to modern times, the Tripartite Wars and Mexica dominion of silicon chips and high-grade electronics.

I was shown into a living room with glass cases displaying old codices. Near the window was an ebony desk of Xuyan facture, loaded with papers and ephemeral chips, and a wicker chair where I seated myself, not sure of what else I could do.

I waited. Invisible loudspeakers broadcast Mexica hymns, with flutes and drums giving an odd resonance to each verse.

When the curtain of the door was lifted to a tinkle of bells, I rose, ready to confront Yaotl-tzin with my feeble excuses.

But it wasn't Yaotl.

It was a woman dressed in the fashion of the Mexica, with an elaborate blouse and matching skirt decorated with patterns of running deer and parrots. Her hair fell to her shoulders, Mexica-style; her skin was the yellow of corn, so prized by Mexica that young girls would lather themselves with makeup. I knew it to be no dye.

For, unmistakably, the woman confronting me was Xuyan.

"You are a stubborn man, Mr Brooks," she said in accented English.

I bowed in the Xuyan fashion, with both hands slid into the folds of my sleeves. "Mistress He Zhen," I said.

She shook her head. "No more. Here I am known as Tlazoxochitl, Precious Flower."

"It suits you," I said, without irony. She looked Mexica—the quiet, sure way in which she moved was more Mexica than Xuyan, as if she had indeed blossomed there.

"Why did you come here?" she asked.

"Why did you?"

She shrugged. "You know why. I had no choice. I will not marry a man like him."

"And this was your solution?" I asked. "To be some whore in a stylish brothel?" I realised I was unfair, but I could not care anymore. I felt used—knowing all I had done in finding her was bringing the White Lotus here.

She smiled, in a slow, secret way that reminded me of the effigies of Buddha in the temples. "I am no whore. I am mistress of this house."

"That was how Doc Smith got you past the border?" I asked.

"Of course, Mr Brooks. It is the fashion of the court, to have Xuyan wives who are pretty and know how to hold themselves in society. Yaotl needed a paper wife he could display at family parties. He thought I was perfect."

"Perfect," I said, slowly, staring at her.

She smiled. "You forget family does not always include ties of blood and flesh. Tell me why you came here."

"You know. Your mother hired me."

Her face darkened. "Yes. But you are no fool. You know the real reason. And still you came."

"You are in danger here," I said. "Wen Yi is looking for you. I need the proof you brought to your meeting with him."

She crossed her arms over her chest—one of them still moved awkwardly, and I guessed she had not completely healed from those gunshots. "Why?"

"Because I need to expose him."

"I could have exposed him at any time," He Zhen said. "I chose to come here instead. I am safe. I do not need you, Mr Brooks, or anyone else. This is a fortress safer than anything my mother could devise." She had moved toward the window; I followed her and saw, in the courtyard, Xuyans being dragged to their knees by burly Mexica. As I watched, the Mexica raised automatics and methodically shot the Xuyans in the head. "The White Lotus has no reach here, and never will have," He Zhen said.

"No," I said at last, feeling my stomach roil at the casual violence. He Zhen's face was still emotionless. "Tell me, was it worth the price, He Zhen? Was your safety worth that price? Tell me whether you're happy."

She smiled again, but there was bitterness in her expression. "Am I happy, moving from one arranged marriage to another? I do not know, Mr Brooks. Here I wield what power I can in the house. Here I am not sold like a piece of flesh to save the family fortune. What would you have done in my place?"

"I don't know," I said. "But if I had been your father, I wouldn't have let you be so bitter so young."

"But you are not my father. How fortunate." He Zhen moved between the glass cases, laying her hands over the beautiful codices. "You learn, you know. Living in my mother's house, you learn very fast."

"It mustn't have been so bad," I protested, moving to defend He Chan-Li through some obscure instinct.

She smiled again. "You know nothing. You are a lucky man, Mr Brooks."

"I know that your fiancé tried to kill you. Do you find

running away such an easy solution?"

Her face darkened again. "I am no coward."

"Then prove it."

"By coming back like a bird to the slaughter? I am no fool."

I sighed. "No, you are no fool. And yet what did you think you'd achieve, that night?"

She shrugged. "Foolish things. You are right. I thought I could break a marriage contract by myself. Life taught me otherwise."

"I can still get the man who shot you." I thought back to the picture of He Zhen her mother had given me, of the radiant, innocent smile, and knew that nothing I did would bring that back.

He Zhen looked at me with dead, emotionless eyes. "Why should I help you?" she said. "You came here to save your skin."

"I came for you," I said, knowing it to be a lie.

"I have no need of you."

"You've already said it."

"That does not make it any less true," she said. "Go away."

"No," I said. "I will not leave without proof."

"Go away. Find yourself a hiding place, Mr Brooks. Somewhere the White Lotus hasn't touched. They still exist." Her smile was ironic.

Once, ten years before, I had run away. I had crossed the border in the middle of the night with Mei-Lin by my side, going forth into the darkness with no idea of what I would find.

The world had shrunk since then. Mei-Lin had died, and I had traced my own path, to stand here, in the heart of the Mexica Empire, facing a girl who was no longer young. "I will not run away," I said, gritting my teeth. "I will see justice brought."

"Then you are brave," He Zhen said. "Foolish, as well, for all your words."

Perhaps she was right. But I could not walk away. I had not come all this way for nothing.

I had one last thing left—one last toss of the coin to convince her. "You may not care about what Wen Yi did to you, but others do."

"My mother?" He Zhen laughed—a sick, disabused laughter.

"You have a grandmother," I said, and saw her flinch.

But still she faced me, unmovable. "I had," she said. "Here it doesn't matter anymore."

I reached inside my pockets for the one thing I'd taken all the way from Fenliu to Tenochtitlan: the jade pendant He Lai had given me, the one she'd said was He Zhen's favourite. Gently, I laid it on one of the glass cases and saw He Zhen's gaze sharply turn toward it.

"Your grandmother thought I should return this to you," I said. "She hoped I would not have to bring it back to her."

He Zhen said nothing. Her gaze had turned inward, as remote as that of a statue.

"What should I tell her?" I asked, softly.

"It doesn't matter," He Zhen repeated, with much less conviction. For the first time, emotion had come into her voice. She stared at the pendant for a whilst, biting her lip.

Then, slowly, agonisingly slowly, she reached out, snapped her hands shut around it. Her face still had no expression.

I did not speak, simply watched her wrestle with herself.

She said, at last, "Very well. You are a hard man to refuse, Mr Brooks. My servants will give you what you need. Do what you want with it. And then leave."

"Thank you," I said.

I walked back to the door in silence, leaving her standing before the open window, silhouetted in light. Beneath her, in the courtyard, lay the corpses of the White Lotus' agents.

When I lifted the curtain to exit the room, I heard her call me. "Mr Brooks?"

I did not turn around.

"I am not happy," she said, very quietly. "But don't tell her that. Tell her that I did the best I could, with the little I had. And that it will have to be enough. After all, isn't it the same, for everyone?" And for the first time I heard a sixteen-year-old bewildered girl, wondering if she had done the right thing.

I said nothing. In truth, I had no answer, and she must have known it. I walked away without looking back.

* * * *

Before I left Greater Mexica, I went back to my hotel and used my connection to tinker with things. I forwarded the proof He Zhen had given me to the tribunal of Fenliu. I would have liked to send it in my own name, even to face Wen Yi myself and tell him who had delivered the final blow, but I knew this was foolishness. If I did this, there would be no safe haven for me in Fenliu, nor anywhere in Xuya. The White Lotus always avenged its own.

So to cover my tracks, I manipulated the router addresses until it looked as if He Zhen herself had sent the incriminating evidence.

It was the most satisfying thing I had done in a whilst.

As I drove back to Xuya, I followed the development of events with interest; although I wasn't in Fenliu, images of Wen Yi's arrest made the news even in Greater Mexica. The newscasters were betting on a strangling at the very least—Xuya did not joke with corruption of government officials.

In Fenliu, I dropped off the car back at the rental agency and took the mag-lev to He Chan-Li's house. I found her still awake, although it was the middle of the night.

She met me at the door, still dressed in her business suit. Behind her was her mother, He Lai, in the same traditional costume she'd worn when I'd come to the house. "Mr Brooks. You come at a difficult time," He Chan-Li said.

"I know." Leiming Tech's value had plummeted on the market, and the banks were withdrawing fast. "I came to tell you your daughter is well, but that she won't come home."

He Chan-Li's face did not move, but I could feel the hatred emanating from her. "She never did know what family was."

"No," I said. "Aren't you glad that she's alive?" But I already knew the answer to that. I knew why He Zhen had felt so oppressed in that house.

He Chan-Li said nothing; she turned away from me and walked back toward her house.

I was left with He Lai, who was quietly staring at me.

"I am glad," she said softly, as I pressed into her hands the other thing He Zhen had given me: a small pendant in the shape of the red lotus, the Xuyan symbol for filial devotion.

I asked, at last, "You were the one who erased the files on He Zhen's computer, weren't you? That's why she had to change the session from private to open, because otherwise the computer would have asked you for fingerprints."

He Lai said, not looking at me. "She is my only granddaughter. What else was I to do? Sometimes our paths take us far away from what seems truth, but they are still the ones the gods ordained for us." There were tears in her eyes, and she made no effort to hide them.

"I know," I said at last. "I'm sorry."

"Thank you. I'll see to it that you are paid."

"This isn't about money," I protested.

"Most things are," He Lai said. "You will be glad for it, trust me. Goodbye, Mr Brooks. I trust we will not meet again."

No. I did not think we would.

I rode the mag-lev back to my flat, staring at the patch of sky I could see between the skyscrapers. At this hour of the night, I was one of the only passengers. I listened to the familiar whine of the train, like a symphony welcoming me home. I would go back to my flat, rise in the morning, and go again through the routine of my life, filling the days and nights as I had done since Mei-Lin's death. I wondered whether this was worth it, or whether I did it because I had no other choice. I wondered if it mattered, and thought back to He Zhen's words.

I did the best I could, with the little I had. And it will have to be enough.

Yes. It would have to be enough, day after day, night after night.

It would have to be.

"Excerpt From a Letter by a Social-Realist Aswang"

Kristin Mandigma

Kristin Mandigma is the founding president of a small non-profit organisation called Read Or Die, which promotes literacy and literary awareness in the Philippines. Her first story appeared in 2005 in the first *Philippine Speculative Fiction* anthology. She lives in Manila, where she works as a research analyst.

I apologise for this late reply. Our mail service has been erratic recently due to a spate of troublesome security-related issues. I don't think I need to elaborate. You must have read the latest reports. These government spooks are hopelessly incompetent but they (very) occasionally evince flashes of human-like logic. I expect it will only take them a matter of time before they figure it out, with or without their torturous diagrams, at which point I may have to seriously consider the advisability of having one of our supporters open another German bank account. As a diversion, if nothing else. And I have had nothing entertaining to watch on cable television (which I believe has also been bugged because it persists in showing me nothing but Disney) for a whilst. Just between the two of us, I do believe that if fatuous, single-minded politicians were not an irrevocable fact of life, like having to use the toilet, we would have to invent them.

Now, to your letter. I confess to having read it with some consternation. I am well acquainted with your penchant for morbid humour, and yet the suggestion that I might write a short "piece" for a speculative fiction magazine struck me as more perverse than usual. What on earth is speculative fiction anyway? I believe you are referring to one of those ridiculous publications which traffic in sensationalising the human imagination whilst actually claiming to enrich it by virtue of setting it loose from the moorings of elitist literary fiction? Or whatever? And for elitist, substitute "realist," I suppose. You argue that speculative fiction is merely a convenient "ideologically neutral" term to describe a certain grouping of popular genre fiction, but then follow it up with a defensive polemic on its revolutionary significance with regard to encapsulating the "popular" Filipino experience. To which I ask: as opposed to what?

I believe, Comrade, that you are conflating ideology with bourgeois hair-splitting. When it comes down to it, how is this novel you sent along with your letter, this novel about an interstellar war between monster cockroaches and alienated capitalist soldiers, supposed to be a valid form of social commentary? I do not care if the main character is a Filipino infantryman. I assume he is capitalist, too. Furthermore, since he is far too busy killing cockroaches in godforsaken planets on a spaceship (which is definitely not a respectable proletarian occupation), his insights into the future of Marxist revolution in the Philippines must be suspect, at best. And this Robert Heinlein fellow you mention, I assume, is another imperialist Westerner? I thought so. Comrade, I must admit to being troubled by your choice of reading fare these days. And do not think you can fob me off with claims that your favourite novel at the moment is written by a socialist author. I do not trust socialists. The only socialists I know are white-collar fascist trolls who watch too many Sylvester Stallone movies. Sell-outs, the lot of them. Do not get me started on the kapre; they are all closet theists. An inevitable by-product of all that repulsive tobacco, I should say.

With regard to your question about how I perceive myself as an "Other," let me make it clear that I am as fantastic to myself as rice. I do not waste time sitting around brooding about my mythic status and why the notion that I have lived for five hundred years ought to send me into a paroxysm of metaphysical angst for the benefit of self-indulgent, overprivileged, cultural hegemonists who fancy themselves writers. So there are times in the month when half of me flies off to—as you put it so charmingly—eat babies. Well, I ask you, so what? For your information, I only eat babies whose parents are far too entrenched in the oppressive capitalist superstructure to expect them to be redeemed as good dialectical materialists. It is a legitimate form of population control, I dare say.

I think the real issue here is not my dietary habits but whether or not my being an aswang makes me any less of a Filipino and a communist. I think that being an aswang is a category of social difference—imposed by an external utilitarian authority—like sexuality and income bracket. Nobody conceives of being gay just as a literary trope. Do they? To put it in another way: I do not conceive of my biological constitution as a significant marker of my identity. Men, women, gays, aswang, talk show hosts, politicians, even these speculative fiction non-idealists you speak of—we are all subject to the evils of capitalism, class struggle, the eschatological workings of history, and the inevitability of socialist relations. In this scheme of things, whether or not one eats dried fish or (imperialist) babies for sustenance should be somewhat irrelevant.

I would also like to address in more depth your rather confused contention that the intellectual enlightenment of the Filipino masses lies not in "contemporary" (I presume you meant to say "outdated" but were too busy contradicting yourself) realistic literature, but in a new artistic imaginative "paradigm" (again, this unseemly bourgeois terminology!). As I have said, I would emphatically beg to differ. Being an aswang—not just the commodified subject, but the fetishistic object of this new literature you speak of—has not enlightened me in any way about the true nature of society, about modes of production, about historical progress. I am a nationalist not because I am an aswang, but despite it. You only have to consider the example of those notorious Transylvanian vampires. No-one would ever call them patriots, except insofar as they speak like Bela Lugosi.

Before I end this letter, I must add another caveat: my first reaction upon meeting Jose Rizal in Paris during the International Exposition was not to eat him, as malicious rumors would have you believe. In fact, we spoke cordially and had an extended conversation about Hegel in a café. I do think that he is just another overrated *ilustrado* poseur—brilliant, of course, but with a dangerous touch of the Trotskyite utopian about him. I prefer Bonifacio, for obvious reasons.

In closing, let me say, as Marx does, that "one has to leave philosophy aside." You must inure yourself against these pernicious novels about cockroaches and spaceships (and did you mention dragons? All dragons are either Freudians or fascists) for they can only lead you to a totalising anthropogenetic attitude toward the world. Concentrate on the real work that needs to be done, Comrade.

(For all that, let me thank you for the sweaters. I can only hope you did not buy them in that cursed cesspool of superexploitation, SM Shoemart. It is getting quite cold here in America, hivemind of evil, and it has been increasingly impractical for me to fly out without any sort of protective covering.)

Long live the Philippines! Long live the Revolution!

"AN EVENING IN THE CITY COFFEE-HOUSE, WITH LYDIA ON MY MIND"

ALEXSANDAR ŽILJAK

Alexsandar Žiljak was born in Zagreb, Croatia. He is the author of the short story collection *Slijepe ptice* (*Blind Birds*) and is a three-time winner of the Sfera Award for best short story. With Tomislav Šakić he edited *Ad Asta,* an anthology of Croatian science fiction stories, and the duo currently edit the genre magazine *UBIQ*.

Maybe I shook them off. I don't feel them breathing down my neck anymore. I turn around, but I don't see them in the crowd.

The square is swarmed by people. I elbow through the sea of bodies, carried by the current of fear. Conversations, laughter, shouts are everywhere around me. It's supper time, and crowds gather in front of manna machines. In Gaj Street, the Bolivians drawl *El Condor Pasa* on their flutes and drums, wood and stretched skin bringing snow from the Andean peaks. Performers are dancing under the clock and in front of the Vice-Roy, not giving a shit about ten degrees below zero. Nanopigments in their skins pour colours across naked bodies writhing through retro-industry at full volume. Hare Krishnas reach me from the Dolac. Their mantra collides with the flutes and ghetto blasters, mixing and merging into a bizarre noise of three worlds melted in the same pot.

I look at my wristwatch. The Underground from Samobor arrived a couple of minutes ago and a new crowd spills out on the square, seekers of evening amusement in the metropolis core. I drown amongst people, one fish in the glittering school that moves to and fro, hiding me from gaping jaws.

A bunch of kids in fluorescent jackets buzz next to me on their roller skates. One of them almost runs down some babe, her skin violet, her snow-white hair reaching halfway down her back. The girl spouts obscenities after them, but the punks don't even hear her, their players at full pitch.

I walk across the square and find my refuge in the City Coffeehouse, a preserve of the *Kaiser-und-König* Zagreb tradition in the midst of the nano-Babylon. Also, a relatively good place for taking a break: they will hardly dare to off me here. Absent-mindedly, I order a cup of coffee. The real coffee, expensive: Brazil. Just a few plantations left, surrounded by vast rainforests.

I take a deep breath and calm down. As I wait for the coffee, I run all the possible scenarios through my head. And they all boil down to the same thing: back to the start. New name, new address, as far away from here as possible. Maybe even a new face in the mirror every morning. I already ruled out everything else. My existence in Zagreb is past and finished. When I leave, there'll be no coming back for some time. Say, to the end of my life.

They won't forgive. They can't.

If only Piko wasn't such an idiot!

Time for some stock-taking. The plastic in my pocket is comfortably fat. Perhaps it could last me two years. That's good news. Bad news is that every use of the credit card is a public announcement of my momentary whereabouts. That means a new card. It'll cost me at least a third, maybe more.

I touch an Apple under my jacket, as if I want to make sure it's still there, in my pocket. A little box with a headset and dataglove that I need to switch to the next level. I feel somewhat better now. I'm still in the game, it's not over yet. But I need an assembler, ASAP. And I need some time to hack its protection. In the meantime, public places. I'm becoming quite certain that the boys won't take me out before witnesses. At least, I hope so.

Meanwhilst, the player rewinds and the clip starts from frame zero.

My name doesn't matter. It means nothing to anyone, not even to me anymore: by the morning at latest, it will end in a recycling bin, together with all my life until now. What I'm doing is more important. More precisely, what I've been doing till a couple of hours ago.

Pornies. Passive, mostly for screen, although I sometimes render them for VR. Depends, it doesn't work every time...black stuff, quite black. Not what is usually meant, snuff or kids, but still, enough to dress me in stripes for a long time.

The waiter brings me coffee, puts the bill on my table and leaves. I mutter something that should be thanks. He's already at the other table, leaving me alone again. The coffeehouse is almost full. I look for them amongst faces under nano-makeup and neon hairdos, but I don't find them. They're not here; I'm safe. At least, for some time.

I reach into another pocket and take Lydia out of it. Twelve terabytes of the finest resolution, with flawless sound. Lydia, beautiful, perfect, a dream-girl. If only I had never laid my eyes on her.

First, I comb citizen register databases. With knives that I have, I cut the CS-level security like butter. I look at the residence registrations, issuing of papers, places like that. I also scan the compulsory reports of the feature changes: all the legal beauty parlours file them routinely. (Once, I stumbled on a chick who changed her look and skin colour every three days: not even fashion changes that fast. But I digress.) The faces are what I need at first. The computer does all the work, skipping the personal data and fingerprints and taking just the holos. That's a daily job, taking some twenty minutes, half an hour tops. It's best done at peak hours, when one connection more passes unnoticed.

Then I have to warm the chair myself. If there are many new faces, it takes me an hour, maybe two, to make a selection. It's clear what I'm looking for: good-looking babes and hunks. But, what does 'good-looking' mean in this age of beauty parlours that turn a Quasimodo into a top model in a few hours and with just a few pinpricks? There's beauty and beauty. It's impossible to just list the criteria and let it roll. You either know it or you don't. Something in an eye, a smile, bearing, a little bit of everything, a personality. Yes, perhaps that's the best word. A personality. And I have the nose to find it. The others don't.

I know that; I sell my clips better than my competition.

Phase two is detailed selection: more rummaging through databases, this time with precisely defined goals. Address, education, social status, marriage, children, health, age, though that doesn't mean much these days. I let some victims go by default. Public personalities, for instance, particularly those powerful enough to crush my crown jewels. I prefer singles. I have a mild revulsion toward married couples with children. I mean, we're shooting a clip, and then whining starts in the next room. Kids have an infallible sense to start screaming when it's sweetest.

****

The coffee is almost over. The pressure doesn't subside; I order another. I have some cash in my pocket, more than enough to spend some time here. People leave, others enter. Murmuring and soft music surround me.

Step three is automatic. To the chosen ones—one, two at best—I send a present. A swarm of flies to their home addresses. The flies are the peak of military intelligence technology: a floating camera plus nanocomputer plus video memory, and they are virtually unnoticeable. Don't ask me where I got them and what they cost me. What you don't know can't kill you.

Once inserted, most frequently through the air conditioning, the swarm reproduces by itself. Part of it forms a hive, hacking the network outlet of one of the victim's nanocomputers. The rest deploys itself in the apartment. If the technical conditions don't screw me up, which happens occasionally, that's all the foreplay there is.

When everything is finally green, filmings follow. In simple terms, the moment one fly senses a motion, it informs the others. The swarm is programmed to cover the action from all the imaginable angles, and I usually let it buzz 24/7. Girls often look very inviting on the screen just doing aerobics. Showers and bathtubs are nice spots, too. Some dolls *really* like to relax when they think nobody's watching them.

Once their memories are full, the flies empty themselves in the hive. The hive then mails the data to the predetermined addresses. It all works without my interventions. As I said, purely automatic.

I check my watch. I'm here for some thirty minutes. Nobody drives me, the coffeehouse is open throughout the night, but I should move on. As long as you move, they can't grab you. But it's cold outside, and fatigue and pressure won't relent, won't let go, pinning me down.

I decide to stay a little longer. I call the waiter, ask for the newspapers, and he brings them. The screen fills with headlines. Airbus closes down the assembly lines, only R&D and nanoprogramming remain. Nothing new, Boeing did that six months ago. Today, every moron builds an aeroplane in his backyard, if only he has necessary programs.

I read on. Politics, business, brief news...a posh apartment totally fucked up in an explosion, cops, fire brigade, blah, blah. I know all about it, the apartment was mine. I look for murdered and killed. Several in the last twenty-four hours, but Piko's name is not amongst them. One is unidentified; the cops give his picture. The face is not in the best shape, but it's not Piko. That means they already disassembled his corpse into molecules.

They don't leave tracks behind.

Post-production is the place and time to get creative. First, I clean the contents from a dozen sites hidden all over the town, sometimes after sending them through Ndjamena, Kabul, Ulaanbaatar and Yerevan. Then I examine the material and edit the raw clip. So far, it's routine: some basic knowledge of film editing and that's it. For the cheap stuff pushed in the flea markets, that's usually all. For me, it's only a beginning.

For hours I squeeze the graphic software dry in order to turn a more or less plain shag into a sophisticated aesthetic experience, as Piko used to put it when he wanted to sound educated. I also have to take the demands of the market into account. Piko asked me once for a bald-headed babe, and I didn't have any in my stocks. So I took this blonde cutie with a hedgehog hairdo and shaved her clean within half an hour.

The sound is no less important. If I'm lucky, it's enough to filter it and add the music. Usually something jazzy or perhaps classic. Ravel (not *Bolero, Bolero* is much over-used) or Satie or Tchaikovsky, depending on the mood. If the pigeons on the screen coo as in Bavarian flicks, even the complete dialogues are not much of a problem. Some materials are suitable for 3-D models—I transfer them into VR or holos. But most of my customers are voyeurs, after all. They like to watch, and a screen is the best substitute for a keyhole.

The final step is the sale. Fuck the goods that are not sold, fast and as far from here as possible, to avoid accidental recognition. That's where Piko came in. He was an expert born, with the knack to sell the stuff.

In short, we were a real dream team. The job was running smoothly and the money just poured in. And one thing led to another—posh place, equipment, car, and a honey from time to time, the way I like them best—the bed beneath, me above, she in between. Without flies, naturally. And that's how it was until I stumbled upon Lydia—and until Piko proved to be a greedy cretin.

That's why he's been dead for the last twelve hours.

And I'm next on the list.

Lydia was the real thing, I knew it the moment I saw her holo. I forgot all the others that week and concentrated on her alone. Perfect, unique, the one that you search for for years, perhaps never to find.

And I found her, my star. I knew that all the others could go and hide, Jurković from Gajnice and the boys from THC and Joža and all the others. Their clips were shit anyway, and now I was finally ready to put them in their place. Lydia's charms were all there: beautiful face, sensual lips, long and shiny blonde hair cascading over her shoulders. And it could all be artificial. Above average, true, even top, but still artificial. Until you looked her in those eyes. Cute, coquettish, inviting, slutty. You know, bedroom eyes. But at the same time alert, sparkling with intelligence, piercing. A personality? Oh, yes, you bet. And she was mine and mine only, for me to offer her to the world outside, going crazy with boredom, buried under the avalanche of cheap average.

Phase two should have been sufficient to forget her. The alarms were at full blast, but no, I wasn't listening. 'Cause her background was, to put it mildly, strange. Twenty-three years old, on state welfare since she was ten. High school graduate with some useless profession and zilch work experience.

With a bio like that, you queue in front of manna machines three times a day. You are issued a UC cut A (female) every six months and you sleep in a homeless centre. A cylinder, a bed, a dry toilet, and a TV on the wall.

Lydia, on the other hand, lived in the most expensive house

in the most expensive part of Zagreb and ordered custom-made evening gowns. She forgot what the manna tasted like a long time ago, and she travelled to the Seychelles in a chartered Ilyushin jet. Oh, yes, I almost forgot the black 1955 Pegaso 102B in her garage. An original, not a nano-replica. Those who know, know what I just said.

In the present-day world, such a dame earns that much only one way: by being an expensive working girl. Which is okay, I didn't have to worry that I'd have no material. But she certainly would have a protector, and a powerful one at that. It was written in large neon letters across everything I dug out about her, but I wasn't looking, blinded by the blue of her eyes.

The warmth seduces and embraces me, caressing me, turning exhaustion into numbness. I'm not immediately aware of it, but when I want to move, I cannot and I fall back into the chair. I wonder what's the matter with me and I order another cup of coffee. I have to wake myself up. It's not safe here anymore and I'd better move on.

I inserted the flies without a problem. Test shots gave me a fine performance in the bathtub and another one, that evening, in her bed. Lydia in silk sheets, body out of wildest wet dreams, a perfectly tuned instrument played by her own gentle fingers.

And then Piko dropped by. It was Friday. Yo, man, let's go out for a couple of days, he said, I've got an empty cottage in Zagorje and two real honey-babies. He hadn't seen Lydia yet. Now, how can a crow sleep soundly when the figs are ripe? So I left everything running, locked the doors, and went with Piko to enjoy life.

Piko's couple of days lasted somewhat longer: the fridge was full, the cellar was full, the girls were in top gear, ready and willing. And so it was not before the next Monday that I downloaded the first real Lydia shots. That moment when I started watching them still lingers before my eyes.

Reclining in my armchair, a drink in one hand, a remote in another. PLAY. Waking up, morning toilette, breakfast. Looks like a usual daily routine: FAST FORWARD to evening.

Makeup, perfume, black evening gown, jewellery. Impatient glances at the clock, as if she's waiting for someone. I skip another forty minutes; I'll return to the foreplay later.

PLAY. Lydia is here, in front of me, her legs spread wide in ecstasy, sighing under fierce thrusts. I drop my glass, spilling the drink on the floor. The picture is perfect, the sound flawless, Lydia moaning and cooing and that *thing* banging her! I press FREEZE FRAME and stare like a veal calf at the tens of screens before me.

Imagine a body like a tree trunk, brown, spotted black. Two short legs, four arms like branches holding Lydia around her waist. No head, but I see several eyes between the arms and a slit probably acting as mouth or nose or both. The thing. Lydia's fucker for the night. PLAY again: the fuck continues vigorously. The branches glide across Lydia's body, lovingly fondling her breasts, caressing her buttocks, taking her to the seventh heaven. It goes like that for the next ten minutes, orgasm after orgasm, until finally both collapse and calm down in an embrace. I freeze the frame again and sit in front of the screens, remote in my hand, with a definitive answer to the big question: Are we alone in the universe?

Another take, two days later. This time it was...the nearest description is a psychedelic beach ball bouncing on two duck legs. I don't know how the ball did what it did, but Lydia obviously enjoyed being tickled that way.

There was another bole on the third take. At first, I thought the guy from the first clip had returned for more. I would if I were him. But hell, no! I compared the spots; the pattern was different. You know Dalmatians? Each one has different spots. If the same logic applied here, this was another one. Obviously, Lydia's fame travelled far, never mind the parsecs.

Speaking of parsecs...I mean, Lydia was a real sweetie, but the galaxy is a big place and it means some real long journeys. Unless...I did a little search of Lydia's house. Using flies, of course.

And indeed, I quickly located a cabinet in her cellar. Three by three by two-and-a-half, walls covered in something opaquely bluish-white. White lights installed in the walls, sliding doors and rows of—electrodes?—on the ceiling. Control panel on the outside and that was all. A teleport, what else? Beam me up, Scotty, stuff like that.

The next three weeks were exciting; Lydia was a really busy girl.

Two more boles—they seemed to be her favourite customers.

Then, little green men. I mean, some thirty centimetres tall, emerald green skin, nine of them. The gang bang lasted till dawn. Not that Lydia was complaining; quite the contrary.

Then, a snail. A slug, actually, black, about two metres long, weighing perhaps a hundred kilos. Lydia read a book whilst it was doing the deed. Which apparently wasn't God-knows-what. It just lay between her widespread legs, abruptly turning red every fifteen minutes or so. An orgasm?

Then, there was a Giger monster, the whole works, including teeth and saliva.

And a little pink elephant with large ears. It didn't take off. It couldn't, even if it wanted. Not with Lydia's legs wrapped around it.

And I just produced the clips. Lydia gave me some twenty hours of top material, needing almost no post-production. And then I made the biggest mistake in my life.

I dialled Piko and told him to drop by my place. I told him I had something to show him.

One more. If I go on this way, I'll turn into a walking coffee machine. Numbness becomes indifference. Something is happening to me, I can feel it, but now it's all the same to me. I have no more will to resist the faintness possessing me.

I watch the couple at the next table. A dude with an orange hairdo and a black jacket striped in neon embraces the girl with jet hair. She leans on his shoulder, love me tender, love me do. He whispers something gentle in her ear, and she replies with a warm look in her eyes. I can see it flowing between them and suddenly I'm jealous. In that brief moment of embrace in the murmur of a crowded coffee shop, they have more than I've had in my whole life.

* * * *

Piko didn't say a thing. He couldn't say much with his jaw dropping, now could he?

We played the clips for the whole night and half the following day. Every so often, Piko would ask me to rewind, or he'd freeze the frame and just watch. Then I showed him Lydia's file. He rummaged through it for two hours. Finally, he just looked at me and asked me if I had a copy.

And I, the cretin, gave it to him without a word.

Two days later—this morning—beeping wakes me. Still half-asleep, I look at the clock as I try to find my mobile phone. 09.23. Piko's on the line, his voice full of enthusiasm. *Dude, we're loaded with dough!*

"What dough? What are you talking about, man?"

"That broad, you know, the one we watched a couple of days ago, remember? Well, I gave her a call, regarding what she's doing, right? We'll meet in half an hour, have to go now." And Piko hangs up, leaving me in bed like a veal calf, with the phone in my hand, and I guess it takes five minutes for his babble to reach from my arse to my head.

And then I'm wide awake in a second. I curse Piko, the idiot, as my fingers press the keys frantically. *Beep... Pokretna stanica je isključena...Beep...The mobile phone has been disconnected....*

I jump out of bed, cursing. I walk around my room, not knowing what to do. Then I stop, take a deep breath, relax. Don't panic! Easy to say, but I'm ear-deep in shit.

I grab the phone again, trying to reach Piko. I don't make it. I throw the phone away. No use, anyway. If Piko decided to do something like this, it means he's too much of an idiot to reason with.

To go and blackmail Lydia!

I curse all the time as I dress. I check my watch. Half an hour, he said. I have an hour or two before they come smashing through my doors. And Piko is a dead man. Fuck, it can't be helped! Lydia's not a poor little unprotected kitten. Too much is at stake here, and she certainly called for help. Piko's heading straight into the trap, too dumb to see it.

And then I realise there's a gap, after all. Maybe I can squeeze through, if I kill all the addresses immediately and forget about the job for some time. Piko was an outside connection; I kept a low profile. I know about the others, but maybe others don't know about me. As a matter of fact, Piko's death might be my salvation: the only lead to me goes with him. Sorry, Piko, it was good whilst it lasted!

I check the main deck: systems are ready. My brain works on overdrive as I make the list of other possible leads to me. Lydia first, of course. The swarm is certainly already dusted. And the hive, too. Let's see....

Suddenly, the phone beeps. Persistently, impatiently. I threw it on the bed earlier; I reach for it.

I don't have to look at the screen to know who's calling. There's a brawl at the other end of the line. Piko shouts as they lay hands upon him. They don't let him warn me. I hear something sounding like a gunshot and a scream. It's Piko's. The body falls down and his phone hits the ground, still working. Silence. Then, somebody picks it up.

I hold my breath. I don't dare utter a word. Deep, heavy breathing from the other end of the line.

I hang up. So much for Piko. A minute of silence, please!

All right, I say to myself, we knew it would end this way. Back to work! And then I stop and a new wave of panic seizes me. The way I had Piko's number on my screen, the bloke on the other end of line had mine! And right now, they're certainly rummaging through HT files. In ten minutes max, they'll know how long my dick is.

What did I say? An hour? Two? Half an hour. Tops. If that. There's neither time nor reason to cover any tracks. All I can do is disappear. I take the Apple, a computer for situations like this. It holds only the bare essentials: nanoprograms for the swarm and a few more things and my DNA and the Lazarus. Chill takes hold of my heart when I think of it. Fuck the Lazarus now, I push myself, rather take care that you don't need it.

I check the account on my plastic. It's good, and there's even some cash in my pocket. I look at my equipment, not without a pang of pain. It took time and knowledge and money to put it all together. And all I can take with me is this little Apple.

The clips, I ponder. The shelves stacked with discs, hundreds of thousands of terabytes of the finest stuff. Fuck it! All I take is a portfolio, one disc with one hour of the best, thoroughly sieved and selected. Just in case I decide to restart the business. And Lydia. Of course she's coming with me, I'm not leaving Lydia, no way, come hell or high water.

At that moment, silent buzzing stops me dead. An alarm! The whole house is covered. Front doors, lift, staircase, everything. I mean, I'm doing an illegal job with illegal equipment. A scenario in which a whole bunch of coppers and gumshoes and spooks busting my joint is quite real. Therefore, a surveillance system and an AI programmed to buzz in case of a possible crisis. Of course, the system's not perfect; I've had some false alarms. Better that than being caught with my trousers down.

And these blokes on the monitor are definitely *not* a false alarm. Five of them. Three enter the lift and go up whilst two cover the entrance hall.

I switch to the outside image: three more there. I switch back to those in the lift. Dark suits, not black, more dark grey. Shades on their noses, hats. Faces...human. At least, they appear to be: everything's there, but to describe them...no way! Quite common faces, *too* common, better to merge with the crowd. Impossible to remember, even if you see them real good.

The fingers work on their own. I press the key, my personal modification, and the lift stops between the floors. A moment of surprise on their faces, then palms hit the control panel. No chance! Monkeys are caged until further notice. One of them takes his mobile phone and tries to call the others, but that doesn't work either: my electronics suppress all the communications in the building.

I win several minutes. I put on my coat and grab the Apple. Out of the apartment and to the staircase. I hear shoes on the stairs; those down there figured out something's wrong. I run to the staircase window, a glass panel from floor to ceiling. Normally, it can't be opened.

I touch the glass with my index finger. Surface nanos read the fingerprint, the glass turns opaque and opens into a slit wide enough for me to step out. Simultaneously, a magic carpet forms beneath me and receives me into an embrace of condensed molecules. A bone-breaking jump from the third floor turns into a gentle descent to the lawn. I look up; the carpet disintegrates and the glass returns to normal. By the time the boys come running, I'll have vanished in the thin air.

With haste, I exit the yard into the street. There's nobody there—the three in front of the building also entered. For a moment, I think of my car. But no time to drive it out of the garage—besides, it would be easier to follow me that way. At a fast pace, I get away from the building. With a little bit of luck, I'll slip away.

Suddenly, shouts. I don't turn around. Don't turn around, son, is the golden rule of escaping. My legs switch into top gear whilst the boys run after me, obviously eager to ventilate me like they did Piko. But I have an advantage. I run down and across the street. In the corner of my eye, I see an approaching car, but I don't stop. Screeching and slamming of bumpers as the car brakes to a halt and is hit by another behind it. I keep running, followed by obscenities. The bus stop is just around the corner.

Somebody up there loves me! The bus is at the stop. At the last moment, I rush through the doors and as they hiss shut I allow myself to look at my helpless pursuers, left behind. I give them a finger, mentally. I'm still the best in business, chums!

It is only then that I look at the people in the bus. Several pensioners, couple of kids, two women. It might even be worthwhilst attaching the swarm to one of them. And a...my knees almost let go when I spot him on the back seat: dark grey suit, hat, shades, undefined traits. And I think it's game over, but no, the bloke just sits there and stares at me. Then it dawns upon me: we're not alone, and he doesn't dare waste me in front of some fifteen people. Piko, as dumb as a dick, must have arranged a meeting in a lonely place.

I run out of the bus at the next stop. The goon does nothing. He doesn't give chase. But as the bus leaves, I see him opening his mobile phone and pressing the keys. I turn around. Nobody suspicious nearby, but I haven't gone far and I should move on.

Suddenly, a hollow *KA-BUUM!* Glasses shudder and alarms go off everywhere. I try to determine where it came from, and then I see smoke billowing into the sky and realise they blew my place up. They want to erase me thoroughly, as if I never existed.

The rest of the day is a long, cold, and exhausting chase. Whatever they were, and now I'm certain they weren't human, they were real good. I tried every trick in the book, changing buses, taking cabs, getting lost in the crowd, everything I know. But they were always one step in front of me. Every time I thought I finally got them off my dick, one of them would tap my shoulder. One by one, they cut all my attempts to leave the town unseen, to take a fast ride to Vienna or Belgrade, where I could disappear.

I even wanted to change my phiz. In the black parlour, naturally. It would last perhaps an hour or two, and it would pull me through the dragnet. And I'd have done that, not gladly, if I haven't found that bloke waiting at the address. Grey suit, hat, shades...I just turned tail and ran.

Then it occurred to me. Maybe they had pinned a tracer on me? I didn't have the slightest idea how: I'd had no physical contact with any of them, but it wasn't impossible. And so, a visit to the cleaner's. I wasted a lot of cash just to find out that I was wrong. Even telepathy came to my mind, but then why would they use mobile phones? I knew they couldn't buzz around the town that fast, so there was only one explanation left: there was a whole shipload of them, and they deployed at the start to block me. That means they are very keen that Lydia's business doesn't leak and there is no possibility I can make some deal with them.

I'm completely helpless, unable to move, and I should. I'm asking for trouble now; all they have to do is comb coffeehouses in the city. The waiter brings me another cup and I don't recall ordering it. I lift my eyes and I see him well for the first time. Human face, seemingly everything in place, but to describe it....

The waiter glides on, and I know I flew right into their hands. I want to get up and run, but the legs don't work. I touch my left leg. I don't feel my hand on it. I pinch myself; I don't feel it. I'm fucked. I know it for certain now. There is some nano shit in the coffee, and they've stuffed me like a goose with it since I came in here. It screwed my nerves: the connection to my legs is history, and there's no reason to believe it will stop at that.

That's why they let me go, once I gave up breaking out of town and turned back. And me, dumbass, didn't find it strange how easily I got rid of them in Martić Street and again in Jurišić Street and how I slipped away in the crowd on the square. I mean, why chase a jerk who's impaling himself?

I recall a party a couple of years ago—there was a conspiracy freak there. He was more fun than most of the others, so some of us gathered and listened to him. I couldn't believe my ears.

Flying saucers and MIBs and they're everywhere and Chris Carter was their man. Seriously, they sent him to cloud the truth. Otherwise, he would have ended up under a truck before take one. But that was just for starters: masons and who wasted JFK and Marilyn and why they brought the Soviet Union down and started the war in Yugoslavia. That's when it became crazy. There was a whole treatise on trucks as assassination weapons; the guy was obsessed with trucks. And why Quebec separated from Canada and how nanotechnology became the ultimate step in a conspiracy to rule the world. Of course, it all started back in Roswell in nineteen-forty-something, et cetera, et cetera, et cetera.

I have nothing to complain about. I can't say that I wasn't warned.

Suddenly, I sniff a stench coming from under the table. I don't even have to touch, I did a number one in my trousers. That went, too. The system is falling apart. Soon I'll know the answer to another big question. The one about life after death.

There's only one way out, better than none. The Lazarus.

* * * *

I got it two years ago in return for some five hundred terabytes of clips. I open the Apple, turn it on, unfold the headset and put it on my head. I put the glove on. My hands still serve me, but I know I don't have much time. I plug it all into a connector on my table. VROS unfolds before my eyes, and I touch the Lazarus with my finger. Black stuff, real black. I heard of it before, but it was only then that I saw it for the first time. Two years ago.

The man came to my home carrying two cases of equipment. It took him fifteen minutes just to unpack it all and unwind the cables. Then he put a helmet on my head and recorded with the Lazarus for an additional half an hour. My brain, everything in it, the complete content, memories, everything. He never explained how the stuff worked. He just told me there were a lot of big shots using it, and often, in case somebody iced them. When the session was over, he had me completely downloaded to his computer. I took a look: the machine was custom-built, nothing you would see in shop windows.

The recording was step one, followed by the compression, to reduce it into an acceptable size. Finally, it all ended on my Apple, together with the user's part of the Lazarus. Theoretically, I should have dialled the man every few months to update. In practise, the thing had remained untouched since the evening he'd first recorded me.

Now, all I have to do is raise the Lazarus, to uncompress me and return me to life, me, two years ago, in the VR, scattered across the sites, but alive. Sort of.

And whilst the Lazarus rises, I choose a site. I know a good one. I discovered it six months ago: an abandoned virtual role-playing game site in Nairobi. I cut the remains of C-level security; the last access was two years ago. God only knows how the site survived that long. Perhaps it went unnoticed when the Kampala server blew up, pulling all of East Africa with it. But the site is big enough, VRPGs need memory, and it will be enough to put me in and unpack. And the black clinics are near, Kampala, Kinshasa, Luanda. Allegedly, they can raise you out of nothing, like Adam out of clay, if only they have the DNA. Expensive, though.

The Lazarus interrupts me, giving me thumbs-up. It's connected. All I have to do is touch "okay" and we go. But before that, I send all the programs and the DNA and all the materials from the portfolio disc, to keep them handy. And Lydia, my perfect baby, I will go nowhere without her. I place her comfortably next to me. I open a notepad and type several remarks, what happened to me and why. What is past to me is future to my doppelgänger: I have to warn him. Finally, I give the Lazarus a go-ahead and it streams me to the site, me of two years ago.

It's over in a moment. TRANSMISSION SUCCESSFULLY COMPLETED and the line is terminated. The Lazarus sweeps tracks, leaving me alone in the VROS. With the last touch of my finger, I activate the virus to burn everything in the Apple, whilst somewhere over there, in Kenya, I'm being reborn amidst the roar of lions.

Here, in the coffeehouse, in the murmur, the body loses the last atoms of strength. My hands drop feebly on the table. I lean back, my neck barely holding. I can't take off the headset. I remain that way, then the head drops, too.

I feel myself shutting down...eyes...as if I drain, dirty water in the gutter....

...darkness....

They say that your whole life passes before your eyes...no time, not even for that.

Fear...somehow, I don't feel it...worse...could've been worse....

Everything around me disappears...

...just one...last....

Lydia...meet you...I'd like to meet you so much...

...perhaps one day...

Lydia....

"Into the Night"

Anil Menon

Anil Menon grew up in Mumbai, India, and moved to the United States in the 1990s. In 2006, he was a nominee for the Carl Brandon Society's Parallax Prize. His short stories have appeared widely, and his first novel, *The Beast with Nine Billion Feet* (Zubaan/Penguin) has just been published.

The island of Meridian was still thirty minutes away, but Kallikulam Ramaswamy Iyer had already done enough neck stretches, shoulder shrugs, hand wiggles, and toe scrunches to limber his joints for this lifetime and the next.

He was tired. He was eighty-two years old and had relaxed his ancient Brahmin joints through many a stressful hour, but the last few days had been some of the worst: first, a thirteen-hour flight from Mumbai to Sydney with a three-day layover in Singapore, then a four-hour flight in a boomerang-shaped aeroplane from Sydney to Fiji's Nadi airport followed by a two-hour ride in a catamaran ferry to Meridian. Far away.

Ramaswamy shook his head. Why had Ganga decided to settle so far away? She'd always been peculiar, his daughter, this bright-eyed girl they had raised from a mustard seed through plaits and school bags to first-class first and first menses, this wild daughter of theirs who squeezed their hearts so, squeezed them till he'd sworn not to love her anymore, but of course it was all talk, as the missus would verify, for wasn't he here in the belly of a fish, going to a land of cannibals for the sake of their bright-eyed girl who only thirty-seven years ago had begun a mustard seed as modest as an ant's fart.

"Think in English," advised his wife. "Tamil will only make it harder for you to adjust."

Oh, listen to the Queen of England. Who was the matriculate, madam? And who was the Sixth Standard twice fail?

A wave of laughter surged through the boat. It was beginning to irritate him, these periodic laughs. What were they laughing at? And why was it funny? A passenger in the adjacent seat, a sleek cheetah of an Indian girl who'd been gesturing with her silver thimbles throughout the last half-hour, lifted her head, blinked rapidly and smiled. She looked tired too. What was she doing here, alone, so far away from home and husband?

He continued to brood. She could've stayed. There were plenty of jobs for Hindus in India. Even a job in Europe would've been acceptable. But the South Pacific! Meridian was so new it wasn't even listed in his Rand McNally 1995 World

Almanac. Who could've foreseen when he left Kallikulam in 1962, barely nineteen years old and with ninety rupees in his pocket, when he'd left his parents, dressed in their starched best, left them behind and forever at the Thrichedur railway station, who could've foreseen this final migration, three score and three years later, to a land without elephants, to a land without ancestors; who could have foreseen?

"Stop beating that drum, sir," said Paru. "Fall on your knees and thank your Krishna-bhagavan that you have such a sterling daughter. You're in her care now. So chin up and get ready for the next innings."

You? What had happened to the *we*? His wife, Paru, had been younger by ten years. By all logic she should have been on this boat, not him. But of course, the "we" of sixty years plus had ended at the Sion Electric Crematorium in Mumbai.

He flexed his neck. No. That had just been the disposal of the end. The end had come with a shopping list. Paru had sent him to buy groceries and when he had returned, it was to a world without—

No, it was no use dwelling on that day. Today was the first day of the rest of his life.

He sat, resigned, as another rash of laughter broke out. The girl was also laughing. She must've sensed his inspection, because she turned her head in his direction. Her eyes were milked over, like the white, dead corals he'd seen near Fiji. Pity struggled with revulsion in his mind. Oh God, what was the matter with the girl's eyelids? Why was she rolling them up? Almost like a lizard. Poor girl. Ramaswamy quickly turned his head. So there were handicapped people in the West as well. But then, Earth itself was handicapped now, broke and broken.

People may say what they want, thought Ramaswamy, but fate was blind. Why else would this beautiful girl be blind, why else would he have had to leave India, and why else would the last conversation with his wife have been about potatoes, *brinjals,* and coconuts, and would he, for God's sake, please, please check the tomatoes before buying them, because the last batch had been overripe and practically rotten. It could've been about anything, and it had been.

He didn't mind that his wife had died. She'd become tired, worn out. Nothing had interested her anymore, not even their fights, and her insults had stopped being insults and begun to feel like the instructions of someone departing for an immensely long journey. She'd become weary, Paru had, his wife of sixty years and seven lives, weary of waiting for Ganga to amass the papers and travel credits "to bring you home, Amma. I love you, please, please hang in there, okay?" Why, had his house been any less of a home? Had he not taken care of his wife? Paru wanted to let go, and he'd gotten tired of holding on for the both of them. He didn't mind. But she hadn't left empty-handed. She'd taken his memories with her. That, he did mind.

It meant that he now had to recollect things, and could no longer rely on a shout ("Paru!") and an answer. For instance, what was the name of the school he'd attended in the 1940s? Had they first talked in the Esso canteen, or had it been that monsoon day when he'd offered her his umbrella? What was the name of his last American boss at Esso, the year before it became Hindustan Petroleum? He clearly remembered the fellow. Especially his laugh. The fellow would laugh, a great big honk of pure evil, revealing a panoply of white, red, yellow, lead glint and a couple of canines sharpened by decades of insatiable meat-eating. But what was his name?

There was an announcement being made, but the accent was impossible to understand. It was clear, though, that they'd almost arrived. Through the giant windows, he could see bits and pieces of the skyline. Passengers were busy getting their things together; a few were busy blinking at each other. Maybe that's how they said goodbye in this part of the world. The blinking reminded him of ants on a sugar trail. The catamaran docked with a bump and jerk.

"We've reached," said his co-passenger. "You can unbuckle now."

"I know," said Ramaswamy, smiling and blinking. "That's what I want, that's what you want, but that's not what the buckle wants."

"Here, let me help. It's been a long journey, huh?"

And before he could say anything, she leaned over and began to struggle with the belt. Her hair glistened as if it were coated with glass. He couldn't help touching a strand, and she glanced at him. "Careful. The alloy coat is not quite stable yet."

"Are you married?" he asked.

She frowned and didn't answer. "There!" She detached the belt. "Come, Appa. I'll call Aaliyah and let her know we've reached."

Appa? Yes, of course. This was Ganga, his daughter. How could he not have recognised her? The hair was a factor, yes. But still. What was happening to him? He was so astonished by the lapse in memory, he forgot to be terrified.

"I'm okay," he said, furious with Paru. It was all her fault. Fresh resentment began to ooze from the wound of his recent loss.

He'd been here before, a stranger in a strange land. In 1962, he'd stepped out on Platform No. 3 at the Victoria Terminus in Bombay with the smell of soot in his nostrils, a roll of bedding, and an aluminum trunk full of good advice. He'd survived the first strange day, and the second, and the third, till a season had passed and he'd become part of the very strangeness he'd seen on the first day. On his way to work, he'd sometimes see himself stepping out of a train, on this platform, on that platform, from this village, from that village, going everywhere and going nowhere at all.

So why did this transition feel so different, as if he were doing it for the very first time? Perhaps strangeness simply could not be gotten used to. Especially if the strangeness lay, not in the miracles of the place, but in its small-small things.

The miracles were manageable, because they all had a familiar feel. Buildings that supposedly chatted to each other about energy, politics, and life. Or, for example, the "bubbles". They were cars with skins that quivered and became teardrop-shaped as they picked up speed. His daughter had tried to explain how it all worked: drive-by-wire, gyroscopic gaddabad-doo, Gandhi's loincloth, and pure unadulterated ghee...who knew how it worked? He could tell she had no idea either. But they were just inventions.

Ditto for the hearsee. It was just binoculars and headset rolled into one. With the hearsee, you could see what other people were seeing, hear what other people were hearing, assuming they had hearsees too. It used a "nictating membrane" and, of course, wireless. Wireless was a must. He'd had the idea himself one afternoon, so he wasn't too surprised.

No, the strangeness lay in other things, once-familiar things. It lay in Ganga. She had so many friends. He'd always hated that word: friend. It excused everything and expected nothing.

One friend—Aaliyah—seemed to be a permanent guest. Another "friend" was practically an animal; she lay curled on the sofa, her skinny, thimbled hands working ceaselessly—thinking about the mathematics of relatives in general, Ganga claimed—getting up only to feed, and eating things directly from the fridge, all the whilst standing on one leg like a flamingo and eyeing him cautiously, as if she half-expected an ambush. They were many others, all women, with made-up names: Tomi, Rex, Lace, Sharon, and once, just once, a slender man with a sharp Aryan nose, high forehead, and a girl's name. Ramaswamy had asked him why.

"Because I am a girl," he'd replied.

Dinner was a nightmare: meat and wine all around him, overcooked rice, undercooked vegetables (they crunched!), rubbery yogurt, and cold metal spoons. The first time he ate with his hand—thoroughly mixing the rice and buttermilk by hand, relishing every wet squelch, and licking his fingers at the end. It'd been impossible to ignore the long, watchful silences, rapid blinks, the Flamingo's high laugh, and most hurtful of all, Ganga's startled expression. As if she didn't know. As if she, too, hadn't eaten the Tamil Brahmin way, his way, the correct way, once. As if she'd forgotten.

He had a room at the end of the hall on the first floor, tucked away from the rest of the house. The girls mostly lived upstairs, rarely coming down, and if they did talk to him, it was only to ask him idiotic questions about festivals, the caste system, and Hinduism. He had to watch his answers. Otherwise:

"That's rubbish," Ganga would begin, knitting her brows. "If you look at the facts...."

The facts were these: Brahmanism was bad. The West was good. Everything he said was superstition. Everything she said was science. Those were the facts. S'all right. He had his beliefs, she had hers. She called her beliefs "facts," and that was all right too. If science was all-powerful, then why she did grovel before the Evolution God? Evolution this, Evolution that. The girl knew a lot, but she understood nothing. As people said, just being able to talk about a trunk didn't make you an elephant.

But most of all, it was the silence that was intolerable. So many circuits of the house, so many cautious in-the-doorway peeks into bedrooms, so many against-the-light inspections of their mail, so many cups of microwaved chai, so many naps and then to painfully go up, down, around and about the house, circumnavigating the hours, the day, the month. Occasionally the house would pass on messages in Ganga's or Aaliyah's voice, and he'd feel like a house pet, expected to mewl and bark at the sound of his master's voice. He never responded when they called, shuffling around silently, refusing to be happy for their sake, and fully aware that irrespective of whether he responded or not, every room in the house was visible to their lizard eyes.

The silence of his Mumbai apartment had always been bordered with far-away horns, shouts of neighbourhood children, Paru's telephone gossip, and the imminent possibility of tea. This silence had weight. Sometimes he cried.

Ramaswamy lay in bed, facing the wall, the coverlet pulled all the way to his neck, quietly burbling in a mix of English and Tamil.

"Appa?"

He froze.

"Who are you talking to? Are you alright? Are your legs hurting?"

When he turned, he saw Ganga in her nightdress, her face lit from below by the room's night light.

"I'm okay. Just thinking, that's all. About the good old days."

She sat down beside him and put a hand on his chest. "Not able to sleep?"

"How much sleep can I do?" He hesitated, and then spoke in a rush. "Ganga, I want to go back to Mumbai. I can't live here in this freezing cold and twenty-four hours of rain. Everything is backward and upside down. From the nose via the back of head to the ear, as people say. A simple man like myself only needs his two servings of rice curds and a glass of water. That I can get for myself. Why I should be a burden to you? I am going back."

"We can't have this conversation over and over again. Haven't you been watching the news from India? And there's no-one there to take care of you. In a few years, your health problems are only going to get worse. If anything happens—"

"Krishna-bhagavan will take care of me as he has all these years."

"Don't be childish! Amma took care of you all these years, not your bloody bhagavan. So at least give credit where it's due."

He was pleased to see her voice rise and her accent veer into its natural roly-poly South-Indian roundness. Ha! Not such a suit-and-boot madam after all. He remembered roly-poly; he'd walked this little girl back from kindergarten every day, pigtails and upturned face, hopeful smile and Appa, Appa, please can I have some kulfi, Appa?

Where had it all gone wrong with Ganga? Was it the day he'd found her smoking with the sweeper's boy, a Shudran, whose polluting dirty hand also happened to be inside her unzipped trousers? Or was it when she'd burnt her maths degree merely because her college had changed its name from the Indian Institute of Science to the Hindu Institute of Science? Or was it that black day when she'd left India, a month after renouncing her citizenship—he hadn't known it was possible—and in her fierce embrace, he'd sensed an irreversible letting go.

"I should've disciplined her more," thought Ramaswamy, "but as people say, a donkey never has a tiger for a father."

"Can we go to a doctor?" he asked.

"Now?"

She nictated, and geometric patterns flashed across her eyelids; the room seemed filled with a new awareness. He sensed there were others in the room, watching, listening, perhaps even commenting on him.

"Appa? Are you in pain? I can call an ambulance—"

"No, no. I just wanted to get an estimate of how much time I have left."

"No-one can tell you that!"

"Not even biology?"

She smiled and touched his face. "Not even biology."

What was the use of it then? He lay back on the bed and turned to face the wall.

"Appa? Look at me." She shook him. "Look at me." And when he did, she continued in the same calm voice. "I know it's all very strange and new to you. And Amma is not here to make it easier. But life is change, and we have to adapt. Otherwise, we might as well be fossils. Evolution—"

"What is this evolution-evolution you keep brandishing like a stick?"

"It's a theory that says we don't need a story to explain how we all got here. It was first clearly explained by Darwin—"

"Speak in Tamil, Ganga. Speak in Tamil."

He listened to her fantastic tale about fish that had grown lungs and learnt to walk on earth, a Xerox machine called DNA in every atom and whatnot. As she talked, her alloy-treated hair furled outwards, a controlled motion that had nothing to do with the wind or any natural shake of the head. Somebody was playing with her hair. He closed his eyes.

When she said "cells", he imagined tiny telephones, but when she said "chromosome", "molecule", "recombination", and "species", nothing came to mind at all. He marvelled that she could swallow so incredible a story but refuse to accept the simplest, most obvious explanation understandable by the stupidest child: God did it. But he didn't want her to stop talking.

"Ganga, this Evolution God, is it Christian or some other religion only? And if it is Christian, then who is Jesus?"

She was silent for a few long seconds, and when she spoke, it was quiet enough to be almost a sigh. "Aaliyah is right, Appa. If you're to see, you must have the right eyes first. The first step is to set you up with a visor. It won't be as good as having a hearsee, but it's better than nothing. It'll be easier to see how it all fits together. Maybe a tour of Galapagos, my research lab, fossil museums...let's see."

He was there, on the battered bench of a battered park, banished for the day, because the house was being energy-audited, and they didn't want him blurting something to the inspector.

It was good to be out, even though the sky was a sickly bluish-grey and the wind was one tooth too sharp. The park was bordered by book shops, clothing stores, cafés, and open-air restaurants. He'd picked a spot on a deserted side of the park because the smell of burning meat reminded him of the *ghats* of Benares.

Ramaswamy carefully removed the visor and the thimbles from their case. As he stared at the "vision field," it began to shear, as if it were being stretched from opposite corners. The eye had to keep moving, otherwise the visor would lose focus. His arthritic fingers found it hard to gesture the thimbles to manipulate the visor's controls, and after a whilst he began to get confused with the coloured flags, training wheels and little rotating astrology-type signs. The view filled with tiny windows and he blinked helplessly as he tried to regain the original view.

"Don't worry," said Paru. "A spectacles is no match for a Senior Clark from Esso."

Abruptly, a gut-wrenching image of water, wood, blue, and sky filled his vision field. And tentacles. He caught a glimpse of lettering: Marine Research Institute. He jerked back in his seat, reaching out to clutch something tangible.

"Hey! No linking," said a voice. "This is a research channel."

And then his view shifted back to the park and its threadbare green. He regained his breath, and with it, triumph. He'd just used somebody else's visor, or more likely, hearsee. So this is what "surfing" the I-net was all about.

It took a whilst to retrace his steps, but he managed to get the screen full of windows again, and as it scrolled past, he blinked. And blinked. And blinked. In most cases, he got wobbly images of edges, shadows and corners of rooms. But even when he got a nice view, such as the one from the tourist staring up at the statues on Easter Island, or merely a bizarre one, like that young girl who stared fixedly at different parts of her naked body, what did it matter? Most people seemed to be sitting on equally battered benches staring out over equally battered parks. What did he and they have in common after all, other than a mutual acknowledgment of being lost? He was everywhere and nowhere.

"It is not our time," said Paru, sounding subdued. "Give it a chance."

His visor filled with fifty scattered circles. Ganga had explained that in "idle mode" the visor would show the GPS coordinates of people in a half-mile radius. A window popped up, reminding him to "fill in his profile".

"Do what it says," said Paru. "Put up a sign saying you want to chit-chat."

"Keep quiet! You should be sitting here suffering, and I should be in your Madras-coffee-loving head. Irresponsible, selfish cow."

He tried to describe himself but didn't get very far. The "wizard" asked for his Myers-Briggs type, whether he was an introvert or extrovert, whether he was an active or a passive voyeur, and on and on. What kinky things turned Ramaswamy on?

Elephants, thimbled Ramaswamy. Temples. Obedient children. Early morning showers. India. Brahmin culture. Decent women. But then he got diverted with the memories of all the delicious foods he would never eat again.

The bench was still slightly wet, perhaps from the early morning rains. The colony's park in Mumbai had always been chock full of people: retirees, teenage lovers, food vendors, toy vendors, mating dogs, laughing clubs, children running about everywhere. The sky looked dark, swollen, a child about to cry.

Perhaps global raining was around the corner.

The visor queried his current mood. He selected the most depressed face he could from the samples in front of him.

"I took it all for granted," he thought. His head had begun to ache.

A teenager sat down at the far end of the bench. He had an open, cheerful face framed by a halo of curly black hair. He nodded in Ramaswamy's direction.

"Waz," said the kid. Then he stretched out his legs and made himself comfortable.

The visor claimed the kid's name was Krish and then went on to bug Ramaswamy with a variety of options. Irritated, he took off the visor.

"Excuse me, is your name Krish?"

"Like da tag sez, heya?" The boy seemed a little puzzled, and his eyelids nictated. His expression brightened. "Ya-i-c. Welcome to Oz, uncle."

"I'm Ramaswamy. I'm from India. Tamil Nadu. Are you also from same?"

Krish shrugged. "Maybe. Me's from Wooshnu's navel, maybe."

The boy's accent was not Indian. In fact, Ramaswamy could barely understand what he was saying. "Are you having school holiday today?"

Krish grinned and shook his head. "Waz school? You's the headmaster? What you be teaching, Master Bates?"

Ramaswamy laughed. Kids were scoundrels no matter where they were. "Bad boy. You need to be more disciplined."

"Nuff sport." Krish scooted over. "You's wanting da elephant, heya?"

The boy's eyes were so merry and his smile so infectious, Ramaswamy also found himself smiling. "Heya. Heya. What's this 'heya'?"

"Gimme the izor, dear." The kid reached for the visor, but something about his expression made Ramaswamy snatch it away and put it in his shirt pocket.

Krish shrugged and unbuttoned his trousers. "Assayway you's want." He grabbed Ramaswamy's hand and shoved it into his trousers. "Go on. Sample all you's want. 100% desi juice on da tap, uncle dear."

Later, Ramaswamy would puzzle over the fact that the boy's penis had been hard and erect. But it was only one of the many puzzles.

A police car swooped out of nowhere, a blaze of whirling blue lights and piercing siren. The next ten minutes were a terrifying blur. Two officers jumped out of the car; one ran after Krish, and the other fumbled for his handcuff.

His boss from Esso! How was it possible? The same beefy expression, the same greyish-white whiskers, the same sozzled eyes. Mr Gregory! Just remembering the name after all these years was mildly orgasmic.

"Mr Gregory, Sir!" Ramaswamy shot to his feet and was ready for dictation.

"Move again asshole, and you'll make my day." The cop pointed an object that resembled a TV remote at Ramaswamy.

But Ramaswamy had already realised his mistake. Of course this policeman wasn't Mr Gregory. His boss had already been middle-aged when he, Ramaswamy, had joined as a young assistant clerk.

"I'm sorry, I thought you were my boss from Esso. I came here to take some fresh breeze only."

Ramaswamy tried to explain how his hand had ended up in the boy's trousers. The boy clearly needed a doctor, he had a rash of some kind. Perhaps he'd thought an Indian would help. But he was only a retired clerk from Esso, his daughter's dependent, practically a beggar himself. Esso's health insurance had barely covered Paru's treatment; there was nothing he could do for random lost-eyed Indian boys. If the officer would be kind enough to call his daughter, Ganga could confirm every detail. When Ramaswamy reached for the visor in his pocket, the officer tasered him.

In time, the pain faded, as did all direct memory of the incident. In time, a woman in blue came to apologise, and she began to talk about punking clubs, sadistic voyeurs, and clockwork porn. He understood little, and was grateful when Aaliyah stepped in to keep it that way.

"Do you remember, Appa," Ganga asked him, a few days after the nightmare, "do you remember a terrace, a girl, and a sweeper's boy?"

Of course he remembered. It was the day his daughter's eyes had begun to terrify him. The boy had been beaten to an inch of his life. Deservedly so. There was no comparison.

"Why do you drag up that incident over and over? Nothing happened."

"Do you know that his hands were just as accidentally placed as yours? That I was the guilty one?"

"I don't know anything. Tell me what to say."

"What's the use, then?" She nictated and turned away. "Nevermind, Appa."

When the cold rains came, as they often did in this age of carbon, he liked to sit by a corner window of the house and watch the banana tree in the yard make short work of the water. The rain, as thin as cow's milk, rolled off the tree's bright green plates, as ineffective as a mother's Tamil on a child's unrepentant back. Sometimes the Flamingo would creep up and crouch by him, her eyes blind in thought, her bony fingers ceaselessly working on the general problem of relatives.

"What is the solution?" he once asked the Flamingo, in Tamil, "if the ones I love hate what I love?"

The Flamingo said nothing. Perhaps she hadn't heard. It was moot in any case, for the problem was intractable. Change was inevitable; it hadn't been, but now it was. Call it evolution, fate, choice, or chance. If that was the only way the world would turn, so be it.

But acceptance wouldn't come. The darkness crowded him from all corners, the light of his understanding curving upward along its walls and returning in an ever-tighter loop. Soon, he would be beyond the reach of all stories.

"Amma," Ramaswamy would shout, forgetting himself in his despair. His mother: a chequered six-yard sari, a raspy voice, wrinkled hands, jasmine-scented hair, and the comfort of her sari's corners. "Amma!"

Sometimes his daughter would turn up with a glass of Horlicks. In her nightdress and short hair, she resembled one of those Goan ladies in India, brown as a coconut but all white inside. She would pretend to listen to his burbling, her eyes blinking absent-mindedly, her hair furling like snakes as it flexed and re-flexed into one of her many styles. She had many styles, but she looked a widow in all of them. She would tell him fantastic tales from science and biology, offering truth when he longed for comfort. He would pick a fight, say outrageous things, insult her friends and all that she held dear, and sometimes Ganga would lose her temper.

"Speak in Tamil," he'd urge. "Speak in Tamil."

Then Ramaswamy would relax. Ah, familiar words. So familiar, so sweetly familiar. He let the ferocious alphabet fall, splish-splosh, all around and galosh, the rain of words, in one ear, out the other, the gentle splash of words, how he missed her, Paru, his comfort, his eyes, how he missed her, his compass, his all, as he walked, ever faster, into the night.

"Elegy"

Mélanie Fazie

Mélanie Fazie is the author of two novels, *Trois pépins du fruit des morts* (2003) and *Arlis des forains* (2004), and two short story collections, *Serpentine* (2004) and *Notre-Dame-aux-Écailles* (2008). She won the French Grand Prix de l'Imaginaire for her short fiction, and her stories have appeared widely in English translations. She lives in Paris.

I plead with you, return them to me—please return them. Or let me in, let me join them. I will not resist. I will come to you in silence to recover them. It will be my own decision, even if it is the only one you leave me.

They would have been seven years old now. They were only five at the time. Have you allowed them to grow? Would I recognise them if they were returned to me this evening? Of course! Even changed, even spoiled by the passage of time, I would recognise them. Only Benjamin would hide his face, deny the loss—he thinks they are gone for good. Two years in which he gave up hope of ever seeing them again. Resigning yourself to the worst is much easier than my way, than going on with the struggle. Hope saps the will more surely than a lapse of memory. He has wasted two years playing at being deaf and blind, making me look like the village idiot. I tried to explain to Benjamin, but he did not want to know anything. It's always the same for him—they were taken away, whoever has them will not return them even if they are still alive. "They're dead, Deborah. Get used to the idea. You'll never see them again."

Why is it always men who go to pieces? It is not Benjamin who, night after night, comes to this hill to plead for your leniency. He does nothing but wait, drunk more often than he is sober—counting the seconds, the hours, the years that have passed since that day.

That day, that morning, just after we woke up, he yelled my name from the doorway to the twins' room. I rushed in, to find it empty. The beds were unmade, the covers were thrown into heaps. The wind was roaring in through the open window. And there was no trace of the children.

Flown away, Adam! Disappeared, Anna!

Rubbed out of our lives, just like that, in one moment, that single second it had taken me to cross to their door. All was lost. There was no going back after that, now that the door had opened onto emptiness. I wanted to think I hadn't seen what had happened, so that I could pretend they were still there, on the other side, playing under the covers like two noisy imps. But that morning, for the first time in their five years, they were not waiting for us.

Benjamin opened the door and regarded the empty bedroom. By then it was too late to close his eyes again. He had been drained in a single heartbeat, as suddenly as a bathtub is emptied when the plug is snatched away. He was still gripping the handle of the door when I rushed up behind him and saw with my own eyes. He uttered my first name, but after that he said no more. Something had died behind his eyes, deep down. He said nothing more. From that first day he gave up. He abandoned everything with a single shrug of his shoulders. His twins, his wife, his family. It's so easy to become a human wreck. When sorrow stands as an alibi, anything is possible.

What good is it to hope, Deborah? They have gone.

Benjamin closed the window and locked the twins' door. He was never to reopen it. Closed with double turn of the lock, creating a sanctum. Spent the first days searching, interrogating neighbours, scouring the fields, more with hope than belief. Finally he settled, comfortably, into quiet despair and wallowed in his loneliness. Now he could let it take over: other people's looks allowed him to. Perhaps the seed had already been in him for a long time. But he had been under self-control for six years. Not a drop of alcohol in front of Adam and Anna, not that, never. Benjamin adored his twins. Now for him there was nothing better to fill the vacuum than draining one bottle after the other. Nothing about him changed, at first appearance. He was like a smooth and succulent fruit, but already rotting inside.

There surely were some who joined him in the bar, ready to sow more discontent with their well-meaning looks and annoyed expressions. *You ought to know, Benjamin, we have seen your wife acting weirdly out there at the top of the hill. You should keep your eye on her.* And Benjamin gestured to them to get lost and leave him alone.

I tried to explain to him, though. How could he not see the signs? Pyjamas rolled up in a ball, left on the hill, Anna's teddy bear, which lay in the middle of the lawn? The window opened *from inside*? What kind of prowler could have broken into the house without causing damage? They opened the window themselves. They knew what they were doing. It is like those vampire stories where the monster may only enter when it has been invited. They opened the window and they left in the night. They came to you because you called them. They came naked as they were on their first day of life. Laughing, surely? Scarcely five years of life, ten years of experience between them, and they could already hear your voice. Me, I never knew to learn. I never wished it, either. Until the day when you took them.

I showed Benjamin the marks and the clues. I even brought him to you so that he could see what I can see, but he averted his eyes with an expression of weariness beyond irritation. As if it were I who had become the wreck, the drunkard. As if I had pointed to mirages born of a sick brain. Two years that he has been closed like an oyster, hermetic, because if he opened up, even for a moment, all the whys and hows would flood in, and he would have to acknowledge there is no answer.

So, I was the one who came to you when at last I understood. I think I had done so from the very first. Unable to fight you, I learnt how to know you. Over those two years, I spent more nights with you on this hill than in the marital bed. That is where Benjamin turned his back on me, whilst breathing the restless sleep of cowards. I came to plead with you, to beg you, to threaten you, and you stayed there with me to scoff. You kept them where I could see them, but they were always beyond my reach. I waited, and I learnt. You let me explore, one evening after another, whilst my gestures became more assured. I returned home reeking of your smell. Benjamin slept. He thought I was mad.

If only he had listened to me, just the once. If he had taken in what I told him he would have come to you with an axe, and used it mercilessly. Afterward he would have consigned you to fire, until the memory of the twins flew up in the smoke. He would fire the entire hill, to put the last seal of certainty on his forgetting.

The first few times when I scratched your shell I skinned the palms of my hands. The bark is rough against hands that have not been coarsened. My fists are bruised where they attacked your hard bark. I soiled you with traces of my blood, like a derisory, ridiculous offering. I struck, spat, and scratched, a demented woman. This wound in the bark, a trace in the tissue like a scar, it was I who tore off this splinter with my fingernails, one night when silence wounded my ears. That silence asphyxiating me like a foetid smell, on top of the hill, you rearing up in front of me, roots anchored well in the ground. I would have sworn it was you who silenced the noise, who stole the air I was trying to breathe. The twins, weren't they enough for you? I risked glancing down to the bottom of the hill, where the houses were quiet, as if they were blind, then up toward the sky, glimpsed between your branches stretching out to scratch the stars. I felt the weight of the world crushing me. Then I concentrated on the shade of the twins that was in you.

There were nights when I was so desperate I would have torn off the skin on my fingers to strip you of your bark, one flake at a time, leaving you naked, to get to my twins beneath the surface. Then you would have had to return them to me. I would have separated the Siamese creature with my fingernails, to make them into two again, Anna and Adam. I would have attacked you with bare hands, if I had thought it would have done any good.

Instead, I learnt. I discovered the intoxicating perfume of your bark after the rain. The feeling of wood beneath my fingers, solid and reassuring, all this power in my arms. The complexity of the mosaic on which my palms slipped, like the scales of an old and fantastic animal. I learnt how to know your rough edges, at first with delicate care, as one discovers the skin of a new lover.

Benjamin laughed the first time we made love, eight years ago, close to this place. He was a nineteen-year-old urchin who could not believe in his luck. We were married on this hill. After the ceremony he chased me through the brambles, which tore at my marriage veils, as foolish as a schoolboy running after girls' skirts. He planted two seeds in me whilst we lay between the trees, away from the gaze of others. I brushed past you in my torn skirts. Did you know then what was coming?

The bark is not so hard to the touch when one grows used to it. I know through my fingertips the relief map of your grooves, your canyons, the edges where I wounded my hands. I learnt the pattern of your wrinkles and your veins, your fault lines and your crevices, the map of your scars. I inspected you as if you were a door without a visible lock, one openable only by looking for the sesame spell. Or as if you were an ancient parchment that had to be deciphered. Did it amuse you to watch me? To see me whilst holding my little ones out of reach?

I don't know how Benjamin failed to see the two masks set in the bark. Two faces drawn in the higher part of the trunk, just below the nodes of your main branches, as if carved from the same wood. They can be seen, though. The features are coarse: just eyes, nose, mouth. Neither lips, nor hair, nor eyebrows. But they seem a natural part of the whole, as if they have always been there. Two oval growths on the trunk, back to back. Admit that you did it on purpose! Two years that they turn their backs on each other, like the two faces of Janus. You did this deliberately, to separate them. It is all part of the irony of the thing: they are together, but they cannot see each other.

You made them so that I cannot see them both at the same time. I have to choose between Adam and Anna. You placed them out of reach, just too far away for me to skim my fingertips across them. I did try, though. But you are huge, on a human scale. The trunk is so large I cannot encircle it with my two arms.

You erased even their differences. The two faces are identical, like two African masks without distinguishing features. They were still at the age where people could confuse them. They often wondered which of the twins was the small girl, which the boy. The same round face, the same black hair cut short, the same eyebrows already clearly featured, inherited from Benjamin. Anna had a small dimple in her left cheek when she laughed. Of the two of them, she was already the wild one. She would have made my life difficult if she had grown up. Such a mischievous smile signals great crises ahead. Adam was calmer, more secretive. Undoubtedly because one day he would need boundless patience to unravel the damage of his twin tornado.

I searched for them in the faces of the other children as they walked out of school. All the five-year-old kids of the neighbourhood. I watched them passing, as I stood with the group of other mothers. I was rooted to the spot. All these good, home-loving women who would *never* come on the hill for their little ones. But it is true that I spent many days there, to keep an eye on the school. I hated them, those animated faces so full of life. All those little faces, too adorable to be fair. They nauseated me.

I sought and found two of them. A little boy, a small girl, both five years old. Almost alike enough to be twins. Perhaps they were cousins. Same black hair, same grasshopper limbs, like Adam, like Anna. One evening I arrived before their mothers. I carried them in my arms to you, offering a trade. And you refused them. I would have delivered every kid in the village to you if you had asked. I would have knifed them with a light heart for the return of my own twins. But carved in wood, the two faces were always waiting.

Did they see me burying their soft toys and their clothing between your roots?

From the first I believed that the face on the left was Anna's. It seemed to me I could see one of the masks smiling, if a smile could be detected under the bark. But I was deluding myself. They are identical, except for small details. And I cannot even see them side by side to compare them. To look closely at one of them, it is necessary to turn away from the other.

Do they look at me, from their perch? And if they do see me, can they at least remember me? Perhaps their memory has become stilled, now that you and they have become one. I always believed that a child could not forget his mother. You can't avoid such ideas, when face to face with your fears. Two children with the memory of a tree. Lost in their wooden sleep, their chlorophyll dreams.

Certain evenings, I wound myself around your limbs so that I could press my ear against your skin. I thought I could hear something fluttering beneath your bark, almost within reach. It reminded me of my former life, when Benjamin's quiet breathing sometimes kept me awake in our bed. I thought I heard twin hearts beating slowly against my ear. But I was just deluding myself again.

Have you at least let them grow? They are always five

years old in my head—as they will be, undoubtedly, in their chrysalis. They would be cramped if they were growing physically. They would need to learn how to spread through your membranes to leave them changed. If you were to return them to me this evening, would I recognise them? Two years of sleep nourished by your sap, that must leave a trace. They would inevitably be changed. A little more arboreal, a little less human. But you would return them to me! I would take them again just as they are, I promise you. Benjamin would not understand, but I would take them again, no matter what form they might be in. And whether or not they recognised me.

Was all this to punish me? My mother used to talk to the trees, in her time. She spent nights on this hill, although I never knew why. I was also born to listen to the voices of the trees, but I chose to be deaf to them. You undoubtedly did what you did as a way of recalling me to you, because until then I had refused to listen. But I learn quickly, you see. I listen and I learn. I am on your side now. Let me hear your voice, the one that made my twins run to this hill. They had the gift, too. They came here laughing. Toward their wooden cage. Toward their new skin.

And now, this evening, I have come to ask you to take me. Let me become you. I come in peace, drunk with your perfume, to feel the reassuring touch of wood beneath my palms. I want to blend myself into you, let the bark absorb me. Later, perhaps, you will reject me again. I will be made surrogate mother for you if that is what you wish. Since they will have reappeared one day. You know how empty a woman feels, when she is a mother without her babies? Benjamin fills his own void his way, by drowning the gaping hole they have left with too much whisky and beer. Me, I want only to take them into me again. Or have the three of us to melt into you.

Let me join you. Ravage me if you must, nourish me with your sap. It is with pleasure that I will be made tree—what do I have to lose here? I don't fear for myself anymore, you see. All I wish is to reach the two faces, to add mine to the fresco. Perhaps one day Benjamin will pass here and will think he recognises me in one of the masks. But he will push away the idea, think it the delusion of a drunkard, and he will go home again to sleep it off in the empty bed. Poor fool. How he adored his twins!

I want to know what you did to them. It matters little to me that they became wood, foliage, chlorophyll. I want to know and to become like them, even if it is necessary to take a share of you. Accept me into you, put me near them, shelter me from the world.

Don't make me wait any longer.

"COMPARTMENTS"

ZORAN ŽIVKOVIĆ

Zoran Živković was born in Belgrade, and is currently a professor of creative writing at the University of Belgrade. He is the author of eighteen highly-regarded books, including *Seven Touches of Music* (2001), *Hidden Camera* (2003), *Twelve Collections and the Teashop* (2005), and recent meta-fictional thriller *The Last Book*. He won the World Fantasy Award in 2003 for his mosaic novel *The Library*.

I ran as fast as my legs would carry me.

The carriage had just pulled away from the buffer at the end of the track. Even though it was still moving slowly, had I been carrying any luggage, particularly anything heavy, I wouldn't have made it. Luckily, all I was holding was my coat and hat.

I didn't know how to get onto a moving carriage. Was I first supposed to jump onto the step on the platform of the last car and then grab hold of the handrail, or the other way around? Who knows what I would have done if the back door hadn't opened just as I caught up to the car. The conductor came out onto the platform.

"Give me your hand!" he shouted.

I stretched out the arm with my coat thrown over it. He grabbed my hand and heaved mightily. The next instant I was standing next to him on the platform.

"Wonderful!" said the conductor with a smile.

"I'm sorry," I replied, out of breath.

"Come, now! You have no reason to excuse yourself. Quite the contrary. I'm delighted that you joined us. Welcome!"

He patted me lightly on the shoulder. We stood there for several moments without speaking, smiling at each other.

"I'm afraid I don't have a ticket," I said contritely.

"The ticket isn't important. The essential thing is that you made it."

"I'm extremely grateful to you."

"Let's go in," said the conductor, moving aside to let me enter first.

I went inside the car. He came in after me, closed the door, and then locked it. Turning toward me, he held out both his hands.

"Please let me take your coat and hat."

"Oh," I said, and gave them to him.

The conductor opened a narrow closet in the wall next to the rear door. It was full of overcoats, fur coats, mackintoshes, capes, ski jackets, and windcheaters. The shelf above it held all kinds of hats and caps. There were shawls, gloves, and muffs, and three or four umbrellas, too. He took a wooden hanger and hung my coat on it, then placed my hat on a free spot in the corner of the shelf. Then he bent down and took a pair of slippers with large pink pom-poms out of the lower part of the closet. That's when I noticed the shoes neatly placed on the floor: they were mostly ordinary shoes of different shapes and sizes, but there were a few pairs of sandals, boots, trainers, galoshes, clogs, and thongs.

The conductor put the slippers on the dark-red carpet runner in front of me and then said, still bent over, "Your shoes, if you please."

I squatted down to untie my shoelaces. I pulled on the slippers as the conductor put my shoes away in the closet. We stood up simultaneously. Suddenly he began to stagger. His hands flew to his forehead and he leaned his back against the closet.

"Aren't you feeling well?" I asked anxiously.

"No, no, everything's all right," he said in a weary voice. "Just a little dizzy spell. It will soon pass."

The conductor was a tall, broad-shouldered man with bushy eyebrows, and this infirmity seemed unsuited to his size. He soon regained his composure, just as he'd predicted.

"Excuse me."

"Do you have low blood pressure? I've heard that people with low blood pressure feel dizzy when they stand up quickly."

The conductor's reply was not immediate. "It's not from low blood pressure," he said at last. "Whenever I close the closet, I remember…."

He didn't finish the sentence. The smile of a moment before turned into a painful frown. I thought I should say something, but didn't know what.

"All of that has nothing to do with you, of course," he continued. "Why should you be interested in my feelings? I wouldn't blame you in the slightest if you told me my past has nothing to do with you and I mustn't bore you with it."

"Quite the contrary," I hastened to assure him. "I would love to hear it, if that will make you feel better."

"Oh, it will, it will!" His face lit up at once. "How kind of you. Such thoughtfulness is a rare thing nowadays. People are no longer sympathetic to the misfortunes of others. They don't have time for them. And sometimes all it takes is a little attention to help those near and dear to you." He paused for a moment and placed his hand on my shoulder. "Thank you!"

"Think nothing of it."

We regarded each other briefly, then he removed his hand from my shoulder.

"She was standing exactly where you are now." His voice altered to a deep, slow drawl. "When she took off her square-toed white leather pumps with silver buckles and stood on the runner in her stocking feet, virtually barefoot, I felt as though I'd been struck by lightning. Have you ever felt anything like that?"

"I've never been struck by lightning."

"Too bad. It's hard to imagine if it hasn't happened to you. I was bending over, giving her some slippers, just as I gave them to you a moment ago. I barely kept my balance. Although quite improper and strictly against the rules of service, I simply couldn't take my eyes off her calves. She was wearing a rather long skirt, but even so the little bit I could see was enough to make me throw all caution to the wind."

He stopped speaking and his gaze seemed to wander off somewhere. I waited patiently for it to return.

"She must have understood what was going on, because why else would she just stand there whilst my eyes shamelessly devoured her legs? She didn't accept the slippers I offered, and she could have. In fact, common decency required it of her. The comportment of a lady, if nothing else. But no, she chose to give herself up to my lustful eyes. I would even dare to say—although it might be too strong a word—that she surrendered. You won't reproach me, I hope, for this unbecoming description?"

"I won't."

"I don't know how long we stayed there like that, motionless, I bending over and she shoeless. It must have been a long time. If someone had happened along, it would have been a pretty sight to see. But no-one appeared, which was unfortunate, because it might have broken the spell. I might have still had a chance to come to my senses. Although...may I be frank with you?"

"You may."

"It was already too late. I was beyond rescue. She and I both knew it...."

He broke into a sob and covered his eyes with his left hand. Crying suited this large, mature man even less than the infirmity that had just overcome him. Once again I wasn't sure what to do.

"Then what happened?" I asked softly.

He didn't reply at once. He took a large white monogrammed handkerchief out of the breast pocket of his conductor's uniform, wiped his eyes with it, and then blew his nose.

"Pardon me," he said in a voice that still trembled. "What happened next was inevitable. She extended her right foot toward me. The worst thing is that I didn't hesitate at all. Not a moment. I, who am so proud of my common sense and self-control. I put the slipper on her foot, although regulations strictly forbid it. Yes, that's what I did. Don't be the least surprised."

"I'm not surprised."

"Naturally, I had to touch her foot. Just lightly, but that was enough for lightning to strike me again. She took no notice of my trembling and extended her left foot without hesitation. Many would see that as female frivolity, even shamelessness, but I accepted her foot without a second thought. Embraced it, you might even say. In any case, I held it longer than the time needed to put on the slipper. She didn't object. She serenely consented to let her tiny foot stay in my huge hand. In this."

He held out his right hand, palm up. We looked at it for several moments in silence, as though it still held signs of her foot. Finally, he clenched his hand into a fist and shook his head.

"What happened next, although dreadful, was bound to happen. You'll be horrified when I tell you. You might even be disgusted with me. I'm perfectly aware of the fact that I deserve the deepest scorn."

"Come now...." I protested, on him falling silent.

"No, you mustn't be kind. I don't deserve it. I'm responsible for everything. I should have held back. Regardless of the cost. I was spellbound, that's true. I had lost control of myself, that's also true. But is that any justification? Are those extenuating circumstances? You be the judge."

"It would be easier to make a judgment if I knew what happened."

"Can't you guess?"

"I'm afraid not."

He stared at me in disbelief. Then he bowed his head and gazed fixedly at his hands, which he was now rubbing together.

"I kissed her left foot," he said almost in a whisper.

"Oh," escaped before I could stop it.

"It wasn't any kind of passionate kiss, of course," he hastened to add. "I barely lowered my lips. On the top, by her toes. Over her stockings. I managed at least that much self-restraint."

"I see," came my reply, since nothing better crossed my mind.

"There, now you know. It must be clear to you that I am beyond redemption."

"But—"

"Please, no," he said, interrupting me. "There's nothing you can say that will lessen my guilt. I have to live with my damnation. Don't waste your words. It's enough that you took the time to listen to me. You are a splendid chap."

"Thank you, although—"

"Let's not talk about me anymore. I've already taken up too much of your time with my problems. You aren't here to listen to the lamentations of ill-fated conductors. Are your slippers comfortable?"

I looked at my feet. "Yes, they are."

"Wonderful. Then let's go. If you please."

He passed me and turned left. I followed him. The corridor was wide and lined with the same carpet runner as the entrance to the car. All the windows on the right-hand side were covered with long, pleated velvet curtains, also dark red. Five-branched candelabras lighted the entrance to each of the six compartments. The candle flames burnt without flickering.

The conductor stopped at the first compartment. He took off his hat, put it under his arm, smoothed his hair, then knocked on the glassed-in section of the door. A curtain identical to the one on the window opposite it hid the interior from view.

Some time passed before a woman's small voice was heard from the compartment. "Come in."

The conductor gave me a brief, indecisive look before he pulled the sliding door aside and moved the curtain slightly, just enough to stick his head inside.

"I am pleased to inform you that we have a new passenger. The gentleman is very polished and full of compassion. I thought you might enjoy his company."

Quite a whilst passed before the same woman's voice replied, "It will be our pleasure."

The conductor withdrew his head, grinned at me, then pulled back the curtain and gestured toward the interior with his hand.

I stopped at the entrance to the compartment. On the left, next to the door, sat a plump, balding man in a three-piece suit, with reading glasses halfway down his nose. His hands were busy knitting. A bright yellow scarf cascaded down from large knitting needles. The place next to his was empty, and beside the window (with the curtain drawn) was a tiny middle-aged woman dressed in black. The hat she was wearing was also black and had a lace veil that covered half her face. In her hands was an open book, small but thick, with a dark cover. On the right sat three young girls aged ten or eleven. They were wearing identical sailor suits, white knee socks, and patent leather shoes. Long braids dangled below their caps, and their faces were exactly similar.

I nodded and said, "Hello. Thank you for being so kind as to let me join you."

Four pairs of eyes looked at me. Only the man kept his eyes fixed on his knitting.

"Come in," said the woman in black at last in a squeaky voice, giving a curt nod in return. She indicated the empty seat next to her.

As soon as I entered the compartment, there came from behind me the sound of curtains moving and the sliding door closing. I sat down and folded my hands in my lap. My eyes were drawn to the large chandelier hanging directly under the compartment's high ceiling. The five candles on it were not real; frosted light bulbs shaped like flames brightly lit the interior.

I kept my eyes trained upward until the thin voice addressed me once more. "You are undoubtedly wondering why I'm wearing black."

I turned to my left. "No, I...."

"Let me tell you right away," she continued. "I'm in mourning for my late husband. There he is, over there."

She bent forward a bit and nodded in the direction of the man and his knitting. I turned toward him. He just sat there, deeply absorbed in his work. But his movements became a bit livelier.

"Mama," said the girl sitting in the middle.

The lady looked at her sharply from under her veil. The girl quickly lowered her head and the other two did the same in unison.

"He might not look dead," continued the woman, "but don't let appearances deceive you. He's dead as far as I'm concerned."

She lowered the book into her lap and took a small black handkerchief out of her left sleeve. She slipped it under her veil and dabbed at the corners of her eyes, then returned it to her sleeve.

"He was a wonderful man. An exemplary husband, a caring and gentle father. He devoted all his free time to his daughters, teaching them different skills that young girls need to know, acting in particular. You'd never think he'd stoop so low. And right in front of his children. Isn't it just awful?"

"I wouldn't know—"

"But you have every right to know. I will tell you everything, then you can decide for yourself."

"Mama," said the girl next to the window without lifting her head.

The woman raised her veil and shot a piercing glance with tiny black eyes.

"Apple!" she said brusquely.

"Not apples! Please! Anything but that!" replied the girl, terrified.

"All three!"

"No, Mama!" cried the other two girls in harmony.

"At once!" hissed the woman.

The girl in the middle quickly reached into the deep pocket of her skirt and took out three apples wrapped in white napkins. She handed one to each sister. With trembling fingers they unwrapped the large, green fruit. They didn't start eating right away but looked pleadingly at their mother. The woman's expression was unrelenting. They sighed as they bit into the apples.

"I certainly must seem too strict to you," said the woman, turning to me once again, "but now that I'm a widow, I have no choice. All the responsibility for raising my daughters lies with me. Should I let them degenerate like their father?"

"No, of course not," I said, shaking my head.

"After hearing what happened, you might lay some of the blame on her. Perhaps all the blame. You might think that he is merely the innocent victim of a cunning seductress. But it's not like that. No-one can be seduced against his will, correct? Why didn't anyone seduce me like that?"

"Seductress?"

"I had a feeling something bad was about to happen as soon as I saw the conductor all wide-eyed when he came to ask us if we would take her into our compartment. I don't doubt in the least that she'd bewitched him beforehand. He seemed confused, even stunned. You must know what a man looks like when he's in the grip of a certain kind of woman?"

"I can imagine...."

"There, you see. I was just about to say that we were unable to accommodate anyone else, but my husband prevented me. I was so amazed I was speechless. He'd always left such decisions up to me before. It's only natural, wouldn't you say?"

"Without a doubt."

"He said it would be an honour to have her join us. Just imagine—an honour!"

I shook my head.

"I had a fresh slight waiting for me when she came in. She simply sat down where you are sitting now. Without a word of gratitude. As if that place belonged to her by birthright. She didn't even look at me, as though I wasn't in the compartment. She held her head high, flaunting and haughty. And then her scent hit me."

"Scent?" I repeated enquiringly, since the lady had broken off.

"Cloying, aggressive. Depraved. You know who uses such scent."

"Do you mean...?"

"Please, we aren't alone." She nodded her head toward the girls, who were tearfully eating their apples.

"Oh, of course. Excuse me."

"We all realised right away what we were dealing with, but did he as the father of the family do anything about it? If not out of respect for his wife, then at least for the sake of his young daughters? He should have ordered her to leave at once; that would have been the only way to redeem himself at least in part for having so recklessly let her enter. But he didn't. He didn't throw her out, and then he had the gall to strike up a conversation with her. Lascivious, promiscuous small talk, actually. Within our earshot. As I watched our girls blush in embarrassment, I wanted to sink through the floor."

"Is that possible?" I turned toward the man engrossed in his knitting.

"Yes, quite so. And do you know what they were allegedly talking about?"

"No."

"The weather."

"The weather?"

"That's right. The hot sun, swollen clouds, humid air, raging storms."

"What's that you're saying?"

"Yes. As if we were ignorant fools who couldn't grasp what

they were really talking about."

"Unbelievable."

"Unbelievable, yes. But just wait until you hear what happened next."

I waited. The lady looked at me meaningfully several moments before she said, "He offered her apples."

"Apples?" I gestured toward the girls.

"Yes. The same apples that these poor things now have to eat. I thought I would faint when I heard it."

I shook my head.

"And if you'd only seen how lustfully he looked at her as she bit into the apple! As I'm sure you are aware, fruit is very juicy, but she paid no attention whatsoever to that fact. She let the juice dribble out of the corners of her mouth and run down her chin. Then he took out a handkerchief and wiped the juice. Before my very own eyes. And she let him do it, calm as you please. With an impish grin. She even turned toward me briefly and gave a defiant look."

The lady raised the back of her left hand to her forehead and bowed her head dramatically. The girls across from her sniffled in unison.

"How was I to know," she continued after a short pause, "that this was just an inoffensive prelude to what would happen in the tunnel?"

"Mama," mumbled the girl next to the door, her mouth full.

"Quiet!" said the woman sharply, silencing her. "Even though it is our shame, there's no reason to hide it. Let everyone know what your father was like. The fact that he is now dead doesn't mitigate his guilt one bit."

The girl in the middle raised her head. It looked as if she were going to protest, but then she lowered her head again and continued eating her apple.

"As you know," said the woman, continuing our conversation, "when the carriage enters a tunnel all light disappears. We are in the pitch black. And right then, as she so ceremoniously ate the apple, he her willing assistant, we went into a tunnel. It was the worst thing that could have happened. I don't like tunnels in the best of circumstances and I went numb with fear. If this was how he acted whilst we were watching him, what would he do when we couldn't see?"

Just as she said this, we were plunged into darkness. A tiny hand dropped gently onto my left knee.

"It was just like this. You surely feel uncomfortable too, don't you?"

"Well, a little, yes."

Her hand squeezed a bit harder. "Don't be afraid. This tunnel is short, the light will soon return. But at that time, unfortunately, it was very long. Long enough for him to tell her the whole story."

"Story?"

"Yes. The story of the wax button. Our most intimate secret. Until that moment no-one knew about it except the two of us. It should have stayed that way. We should have taken it to the grave with us. But he divulged it to her shamelessly. To me he died, completely and irrevocably, before the light returned."

A quiet cough came out of the darkness to my left. I turned that way, even though I couldn't see anything. The little fingers seemed to dig into my knee, so I quickly turned back around.

"Don't pay any attention to him. He's trying to arouse your pity. He expects you to feel sorry for him because he's dead. But he doesn't deserve your pity, not at all."

The pressure from her fingers was suddenly released.

"Or maybe you think otherwise?"

"I wouldn't know…."

"Perhaps you think that what he did wasn't so terrible? That I was unmerciful?"

"No, actually…."

"Perhaps you even think that I'm to blame for everything, that he is only an innocent victim of my callousness?"

"Certainly not, of course…."

The tiny hand removed itself from my knee and the chandelier lights went on the same moment.

The woman once again took her handkerchief out of her sleeve, but this time she only twisted it in her lap. The girls had stopped eating their apples and were staring at us fixedly.

"I was wrong about you," she said in a choking voice. "I believed you to be a true gentleman."

"But...."

"It serves me right for being so easily fooled. I clearly should have been suspicious right away, as soon as the conductor put in a good word for you. Polished and full of compassion—indeed!"

"I assure you—"

"Please, not another word," she said sharply, interrupting me. "Have at least a little consideration for the children. There's nothing more to say, in any case. Everything is quite clear."

She rummaged for a moment through the black handbag between us, then took out a silver bell and rang it. Almost the same instant the door slid open and the conductor's head poked through the curtain.

"The gentleman will be leaving us," she said in an authoritative voice. The conductor pulled the curtain aside without hesitation and I stood up. I stopped at the door and turned around. The father was still engrossed in his knitting and the mother had returned to her book. Only the girls looked at me as they continued to bite into their apples. Their chins were wet from the juice. Not knowing what to say as I left, I merely nodded briefly and went out into the corridor. The conductor quickly pulled the curtain shut behind me and closed the door.

We stood for a moment facing each other in silence. Then he took a pair of manicure scissors out of the right breast pocket of his uniform.

"Please, allow me."

He took hold of my left hand and started to trim my nails, starting with the thumb.

"That was a mistake, of course," he said when he reached the middle finger. "I shouldn't have taken you into their compartment. But all one can do is hope. I thought that things might have changed. I was waiting here in front of the door and the silence was encouraging. I'd started to believe that things would be different this time, and then I heard the bell. I feel very embarrassed. Please forgive me."

"I don't blame you for anything...."

Before he moved to my right hand, he put the clipped nails in his pocket, then looked me straight in the eye.

"You talked about her, didn't you? I can only imagine what the woman said. But you mustn't believe her. Please, I implore you. She doesn't like her. Actually, it's even worse, she hates her. Although there's absolutely no reason, of course. She accuses her of something that is entirely not her fault. She's not the reason that the woman is a widow. The woman herself is to blame for that."

This time he started with the pinkie.

"By the way, just between you and me, his death is rather suspicious. All right, he might act like he's defunct, but that doesn't prove a thing. What if she changes her mind and orders him to stop knitting? It wouldn't surprise me in the least. She's liable to do anything. Then what?"

He raised his eyes to mine. I shrugged my shoulders.

"Did she mention a button?" he asked quietly, after hesitating a bit, concentrating on the hangnail on my index finger.

I answered with a nod, although his eyes were lowered and he couldn't see it.

"A wax button?"

"Yes," I said.

"Let me clue you in."

He didn't do it right away, though. He put the manicure scissors back in his pocket along with the newly clipped nails, took out a nail file and got down to work.

"She lied to you," he said after finishing three fingers on my left hand.

"Is that so?" I replied, surprised.

"It wasn't made of real wax at all."

"It wasn't?"

He raised my finished hand up high, blew on it, polished the nails a bit, then took my right hand.

"It wasn't," he continued after finishing my ring finger, "but I'm not at liberty to say anything else, unfortunately. I've already told you too much. It might cost me my job. You won't report me, I trust?"

He stopped filing and looked at me imploringly. I hastened to reassure him.

"Heaven forbid."

His face lit up. "I knew I could trust you."

Since my other hand was now polished and inspected, he nodded in satisfaction. "There. Now everything's in order. How do you feel?"

I spread out the fingers of both hands and looked at them. "Fine," I said. "Quite fine."

"Wonderful. Shall we continue, then?"

He put it in the form of a question, but didn't await my reply. He placed the file back in his pocket, turned and headed for the entrance to the second compartment.

He halted in front of it, turned toward me and signalled with his hand that I should stop, although I hadn't moved at all. He opened the door quickly and slipped through the curtains, then closed the door behind him.

He remained inside for a short time. When he emerged he was smiling from ear to ear.

"The brothers will receive you. It is a rare honour. Please show due consideration for their rules of behaviour."

"Certainly."

He moved aside but did not pull the curtains open. I slipped through them as he had a moment before and entered the compartment. From behind me came the sound of the door sliding shut.

Inside I found six monks. They were sitting pressed together on four seats, leaving two places empty next to the door. They were wearing long brown cowls and had white cords around their waists. One of them had his hood pulled down. He was sitting on the left next to the curtained window, head bowed, so I couldn't see his face. The attention of the other brothers was focused on him. All five were holding notebooks and writing something in them.

At first no-one paid any attention to me. Finally, the closest monk on the right turned toward me and put his notebook in his lap. Just like the others, he had a smoothly shaved head and ruddy face. He put his hands over his ears and bowed to me. I returned the bow the same way. He indicated with a nod that I was to sit on the empty seat next to him. When I sat down, he raised his right index finger to his lips.

We looked at each other in silence for some time. Then he took his notebook, turned the page and started to write. When he had finished, he handed me the notebook.

Please forgive me for not being able to talk to you in the normal way. The members of our order have taken a vow of silence. But there are no restrictions as far as writing is concerned. You may speak to me by whispering in my ear.

I put my head close to his and whispered, "I am very honoured by the fact that you have taken me into your compartment. I hope I won't be any bother."

The monk shook his head briskly, then set about writing in his notebook again. When he handed it to me, I saw that he'd written down my answer under his first message, and then his new words:

Do you play chess by any chance?

I didn't reply at once. His face was full of eagerness. I finally nodded.

The monk quickly scribbled: *Would you like a game?*

"Here? Now?" I asked in a whisper.

He quickly wrote his answer: *Yes. Yes.*

I thought it over briefly, then shrugged my shoulders. "Why not? If it won't disturb the brothers, of course." I motioned my head toward the monks engrossed in their writing.

On the contrary, came the new message. *They won't have anything against it. They love chess, too. It's our order's favourite game.*

"Then fine."

The monk smiled and clapped his hands. The brother with the hood pulled down over his face didn't move, but the other four stopped their writing and fixed inquisitive eyes on us.

My mute collocutor turned the page of his notebook, wrote something brief, and showed it to the brothers. When they read the message there was an instant uproar. First, almost all of them jumped up from their seats, clapped each other on the shoulder, and even hugged each other. The two of us stood up too. Then the monks went one by one to the monk next to me and kissed him on both cheeks and twice on the forehead. He stood there beaming with joy, his eyes closed. Finally, they all shook my hand firmly.

I was motioned to sit down again, and when I did so the monk I'd talked to moved to the seat across from me. One of the brothers knelt down on the dark red carpet runner and started to feel about under my seat. I raised my feet a bit to get out of his way. He pulled out a large chess set and handed it to my future opponent, but he didn't get up. He stayed on his hands and knees and moved back all the way to the door, taking up the space between us. The brother across from me opened the set, shook out the pieces on the closed notebook in his lap, then placed the board on the back of the monk on the floor.

He sorted through the pieces a bit and finally singled out two white pawns. He picked them up and showed them to everyone. Four heads nodded in confirmation. He put his hands behind his back and shifted the pawns about for a whilst. Then he brought his hands forward, clenched into fists, and held them out in front of me.

I thought of standing up and asking him in a whisper what choice there was between two pieces of the same colour, but I was hemmed in. I didn't know if I would be able to sit down afterward. In any case, it made no difference. After thinking it over briefly, I pointed to his left hand. It opened, and everyone clapped upon seeing the white pawn.

Two of the monks squeezed in between the chess player and the brother with the hood pulled down over his face. The third sat on the floor in front of the one who'd loaned us his back for a table. He quickly began to set up the pieces. But he didn't set them in their starting positions and he didn't use all the pieces. When he had finished, he moved back a little. All I needed was a cursory glance at the board to realise that before me was an endgame. The black king was in checkmate. I looked inquisitively at the brother on the seat across from me and shrugged my shoulders.

He took his notebook, wrote something in it and handed it to me. The message was short: *Your move.*

I pointed at the pen in his hand. When he gave it to me, I wrote in the next empty line: *But the game is over.*

He did not reply at once. First he showed the four observers my message in the notebook, to which they bowed deeply. Then he started to write again:

On the contrary, went his new message. *It has yet to begin. The rules of our order dictate that we play chess from checkmate back to the opening positions.*

I looked at him for several moments, then gave him back his notebook and stared at the pieces on the board. But I didn't have time to evaluate the situation there, because the lights suddenly went out.

A stir broke out that same moment in the darkness. There was the rustling of cowls and then the sound of pieces flying in all directions. A voice from the side opposite me said in haste, "Get up, quick!"

I wasn't sure whether this was directed at me, but I obeyed. As I stood up I collided with someone. I wanted to excuse myself, but there was no time, because that was when the singing started.

The darkness of the compartment was filled with a woman's voice. The soprano emanated from where the monk was sitting with his hood drawn over his face. I tried to see through the murk to that side, but to no avail. The song was slow, almost dreamy, in a language I didn't understand, full of open vowels. It sounded like a dirge. I couldn't tell how it affected the monks, but it filled me at once with excitement. When it finished, it left behind the bitter feeling of something withheld.

Silence reigned for a whilst, and then the male voice of a moment before spoke again.

"That is her present to our brother."

"I thought…." I started in a whisper, but I didn't finish.

"The vow of silence does not hold in a tunnel, you can speak freely in a normal voice."

"Oh, I see."

"We do not normally receive women into our company when we are not properly dressed—you cannot see, but we are wearing slippers instead of clogs under our robes. Nonetheless, our brother invited her in. He had the right by seniority. When she came in, she paid no attention to the others. She headed straight for him and sat in his lap. First she only looked into his eyes, holding his hands, then she started whispering to him. This lasted for some time. All he did was nod his head. After she'd finished, she simply got up and left. Without a word. She didn't play a single game of chess."

"Not a single game?"

"Not a single game, but she made up for it. You heard the song."

"It's captivating."

"It's more than that. Do you know what it's about?"

"No."

"A horned egg!"

"Really?"

"Yes, but he doesn't recount the story all at once, of course. It wouldn't be possible, after all. It's a good thing our brother only sings in tunnels, so there are breathing spells. Otherwise he wouldn't be able to keep it up. Singing in a woman's voice is very taxing."

"I would imagine so."

"The rest of us welcome the breaks too. So we can write down what we've heard. It's immensely important."

"Quite so."

"We will have to get down to work as soon as we come out of the tunnel. Please forgive us for not being able to finish the game. It is indeed a pity, because the position was quite challenging."

"Think nothing of it."

"We'll make up for the loss the next time you visit us. Please drop by at any time."

"With pleasure."

"Then goodbye."

"Goodbye."

I stood there in the darkness. Incoherent chatter filled the compartment, punctuated by a giggle and coughing here and there. Someone's hands suddenly covered my ears. They didn't remain there long, but soon came back, a total of five times. It was only afterward that I realised that it had been a different pair of hands each time. Immediately after the last salutation the door behind my back opened and something slipped through the curtains. I felt a hand take hold of my arm and lead me out. The next moment I was in the corridor.

"Aren't they wonderful?" said the conductor. A large white towel was thrown over his left arm and the small table next to him bore a little dish with a bar of wet soap, a brush, a razor, and a hand mirror in a silver frame.

"Yes, they're pleasantly gregarious," I replied.

"Allow me." He took me by the shoulders and set me under the candelabrum by the door. He shook out the towel, tucked it into my shirt collar, and spread it out so it covered my entire chest. Then he took the little dish and brush and with brisk movements began whipping the soap into a foam.

"I'll let you in on a secret," he said as he started daubing the white foam on my face. "I pray that I may?"

"Of course."

He leaned toward me confidentially. "Whenever I get the chance, I stand in front of their door when we're in a tunnel and I eavesdrop."

He stepped back, inspected me, removed a bit o foam from under my nose with his finger, and wiped it on the towel.

"I can't hear all that well, but it's enough. I get goose bumps every time. Her voice is angelic, isn't it?"

"Yes, it's divine."

"Listening through the door has its advantages. You don't see who's singing and it's easy to imagine that it really is her inside. Even though I know it isn't, unfortunately…."

He brought the hand with the brush to his mouth and bit the knuckle of his index finger. He stood there like that without moving, looking through me with sorrowful eyes.

"Forgive me," he said, snapping out of his trance.

"Think nothing of it."

"It's hard, you know…."

"I know."

"But life goes on. What's to be done?"

He set the dish and brush on the table. He unbuttoned the upper part of his uniform, then took off his belt. He handed me the end with the buckle.

"Hold onto it firmly, please."

He grabbed hold of the other end of the belt and stepped back to the window, tightening it. Then he took the razor from the table, opened it, and started to draw the flat side over the belt, stropping the blade first on one side and then on the other.

"There's only one thing I don't like about the monks."

"Oh, and what is that?"

"That ruse about choosing black or white chess pieces. Yes, that's what it is. I won't shrink at all from calling a spade a spade. A ruse. They know it's dishonest, but they resort to it just the same. You're lucky you didn't play a match."

"How do you know I didn't?"

"It would be quite obvious if you had. Your head would be shaved, just like theirs."

"Why?"

"Didn't they tell you? They've really become deceitful. That's the bet. That's what you play for."

"What if I'd won? What would be my prize? They don't have anything to shave."

"They would have to let their hair grow, and that would be much harder for them than it would be for you to have your head shaved. Your hair would grow back, whilst they would no longer have the right to cut their hair. But they were in no danger of losing. They are true masters at backward chess. They've only lost once so far. She beat them."

"She? But they told me she didn't play at all."

"They told you that? Liars! They're trying to cover their shame. She not only beat them, she completely outplayed them."

He looked left and right down the corridor, then drew close to me, loosening the belt.

"Why do you think the brother who sings has his hood on?" he asked in a low voice.

"I have no idea."

"So you can't see his hair," he continued in a whisper. "It's all grown out. But he won't be able to use his hood much longer. When his hair grows a bit longer he won't be able to hide it. We'll just see what they do then."

He laid the razor on the table, put on his belt, and buttoned his uniform. Then he took up the razor once again and started to shave me. His movements were light and skillful. I barely felt the touch of the blade.

He finished the left side of my face before speaking again.

"Ha, if I could only tell you what I know about the horned egg. Then none of it would look quite so idyllic. But I mustn't. I'm sure you wouldn't give me away, but that's not the point. I don't want to get either one of us into trouble. And it's far from minor, believe me. You have to treat the horned egg with cautious respect. Many have paid a high price for being caught off-guard. You don't want to come to unnecessary harm, do you?"

As he was then shaving around my mouth, I couldn't take the risk of talking. I just mumbled something vague through closed lips.

"It's a real joy to deal with a sensible man," he continued. "That is a rare virtue nowadays. People generally act foolishly, even when I warn them about what's awaiting them. Curiosity blinds them completely. As if the world will go to ruin unless they know what's concealed behind the horned egg. They regret it afterward, of course, but then it's too late."

He took a step backward and began to inspect me. He nodded his head, then removed the towel and wiped my face with it. He placed the towel on the table, picked up the mirror and handed it to me.

"What do you say?"

I looked at myself.

"Perfect. Thank you."

"You're welcome. We couldn't have left that out. You can't go any further unless you're freshly shaved."

He went up to the door of the third compartment, adjusted his tie a bit, then knocked. He didn't employ a normal knock. First he knocked three times quickly, then two times slowly, then three times quickly again.

There was no immediate reply. The conductor turned

briefly toward me and smiled in apology. Finally there came a knock from the compartment: three slow knocks, two fast, then three slow.

The conductor nodded with satisfaction and opened the door. He pushed the curtain halfway open and indicated with his other hand that I was to go inside.

I went in and the door quickly closed behind me.

There were only two passengers in the compartment. A painter was sitting next to the covered window on the left with an easel that held a square canvas. He had a broad beret, a red scarf around his neck, and blue overalls smeared with paint here and there. His right hand held a wooden palette and his left hand a brush. He was wearing glasses with a round frame and opaque black lenses. An unlit pipe with a curved stem hung from his mouth.

A dwarf was lying on the middle seat opposite. He was wearing a turquoise leotard and pink ballet shoes. His body was very muscular, which made him asymmetrical. His legs were raised in the air, and his feet supported a large purple ball.

"Undress," said the painter to me, not turning his head in my direction.

"Excuse me?" I asked in amazement.

"Undress, undress," repeated the dwarf.

"What in the world are you talking about?"

"How do you suppose I am to paint you if you don't undress?"

"Yes," said the dwarf like an echo, "how do you suppose, how do you suppose?"

"I don't suppose at all," I replied angrily.

"Then why did you come?"

"Yes, why, why?"

"I thought that…." I said, turning briefly toward the door. I wanted to mention the conductor, but couldn't find the right words.

"So now what?"

"What, what?"

"Maybe the best thing would be for me to leave?"

"Leave? Out of the question. Every person who enters here must be in the picture. You certainly must realise that."

"Certainly, certainly."

"I didn't know...."

"So you won't undress?"

"Won't, won't?"

"I won't."

"How about part way?"

"Part way, part way?"

I shook my head.

"Just your trousers?"

"Trousers, trousers?"

I shook my head even harder.

"All right, then at least your tie."

"At least, at least?"

"Is it really necessary?" I asked after hesitating briefly.

"Extremely necessary. How can I paint you properly if you won't take your clothes off in front of me? If I don't see your soul? I am a painter of the soul, not the routine exterior."

"Routine, routine."

"I think I could take off my tie," I said falteringly.

"Wonderful! We'll try to make up for the rest with questions."

"Questions, questions!"

"Questions?" I repeated like the echo of an echo, barely stopping myself from saying it twice.

"Yes. I will ask you six questions so that I can discern some of your particulars. They are of a rather personal nature, but this cannot be helped. The questions would not be needed, of course, if you undressed, but since you don't want to...."

"Don't want, don't want...."

I started to loosen the knot on my tie. "Can this not be helped either?"

"What?"

"What, what?"

"This." I nodded toward the dwarf, although the painter was not looking in my direction, and even if he had it would have been hard to see anything through his blind man's glasses. "This repetition of your words."

"Does it bother you?"

"Bother, bother?"

"It grates on my nerves."

The painter laid his brush on the little shelf at the bottom of the easel, then cracked his knuckles. The dwarf immediately started turning the ball with his feet. He did it very skillfully. The ball spun quickly in place.

"He hasn't always been like that. Oh, no. If you'd only had the chance to hear him before. It was a real pleasure to listen to him. Such eloquence, such oratorical skill! It's hard to believe that now, wouldn't you say?"

"It isn't easy," I agreed.

"And the things he used to talk about! The quintessence of wisdom! Pure philosophy, indeed! For me it was the ultimate inspiration. He would talk so magnificently about the wooden dummy, and I transformed his words immediately into paintings. Into a whole cycle of paintings. My life's achievement. But I didn't finish it. I was just about to start my last canvas, in which the wooden dummy would finally be unveiled, when she appeared. And she showed her true face at once. She punished him without mercy. And do you know why?"

"No."

"Because of the ball!"

"Because of the ball?"

"Yes, because of the ball. This stupid, cheap, paltry ball!"

"Outrageous!"

"She wanted to take it away from him, but he, of course, couldn't give it to her. He was completely unable to think without it. She, of course, had no use for it. But since she couldn't get her hands on it, she took her revenge. You'll never guess what she did."

"I can't."

"She started to undress."

"I don't believe it!"

"Yes. The poor thing writhed and twisted, whined and groaned, but this didn't move her in the least. She continued heedlessly to the end. When she was finally in her birthday suit, he clearly couldn't bear it. He let out a terrible cry, then fell into this state. And she just laughed maliciously, put on her clothes and left. She didn't even take the ball, even though he could no longer prevent her from doing so."

"How cruel!"

"More than that. Brutal. But she'll pay for it. Even if I'm not able to complete the cycle about the wooden dummy, I can paint her. Completely nude, so everyone can see what her soul is really like."

"No-one could hold that against you."

"I'll paint her for sure. But let's forget that right now. Are you ready for the six questions?"

I deliberated a bit. "I think I am."

"Very good. So, shall we begin?"

"All right."

"Do you like to trample on young wild strawberries?"

"No, I don't."

"I see. And have you ever dreamt of snails swimming upstream?"

"No, I haven't."

"Aha! Did you ever sneak snowballs into matinee shows at the cinema?"

"No."

"You didn't? And did you ever wonder how many stairs there are in the world?"

"No."

"Interesting. Did you ever want to be a spyglass, perhaps?"

"No, I didn't."

"Not even one single time?"

"Not a single time."

"As you like. Here is the last question. Did you ever make a phone call standing on one leg?"

"Never."

"Wonderful. You can put your tie back on. Your pose is over."

"And that's it?" I asked as I knotted my tie.

"Yes."

"You will paint me solely on the basis of those answers?"

"To someone who is perceptive, they say a lot about you.

Of course, it would be better if you'd agree to undress. Would you care to change your mind, perhaps?"

"No, I wouldn't."

"Fine, if there's nothing to be done, then we're finished. Please excuse me now. Soon there will be a tunnel, and I only paint when we're in one."

He cracked his knuckles. The ball stopped spinning at once. As supple as a spring, the dwarf jumped from his reclining position onto the floor. His feet touched the carpet runner the same moment the ball fell on his now empty seat. He bowed deeply to me and went to the door. First he put his ear against it, then, after he heard something that I didn't, he knocked: three fast, two slow, three fast.

The response came from the other side without a moment's delay: three slow, two fast, three slow. The dwarf grinned from ear to ear, then opened the door theatrically and drew the curtain.

As I went out, I first heard "Good luck!" and right after it came the echo, "Good luck! Good luck!"

I turned to offer my own greetings, but the conductor closed the door before I had a chance.

He was now wearing a white coat over his uniform, with several chrome instruments poking out of the breast pocket. He pointed to the right of the door and said, "Please sit down."

A dentist's chair with its accompanying paraphernalia was there. I regarded it hesitantly.

"Just a routine check-up. You have no reason to worry. Make yourself comfortable, it will soon be over."

I sat down in the chair reluctantly. I squinted when he turned on the large round light, which brightly illuminated my head.

"Open your mouth, please."

After a brief hesitation, I complied.

"A little bit wider, if you please. That's it."

He took a dental mirror out of his pocket, brought his face up close to mine, and started to inspect the inner surface of my jaw.

"He's a wonderful painter," he said. "If you'd only had a chance to see his cycle on the wooden dummy."

He grabbed me by the chin and pulled down a bit. My mouth was now yawning.

"But of course, that is no longer possible. He destroyed it. He told you, didn't he?"

I shook my head faintly, uttering a gurgling sound.

"He didn't? I see. I should have suspected as much. Then he must have told you that she is to blame for everything?"

I nodded my head, this time refraining from making any noise.

"Of course. The easiest thing is to point the finger elsewhere."

He returned the mirror to his pocket, then took out a dental probe and started using it on my lower left molars. I jumped when I suddenly felt pain.

"Everything is fine. The enamel is a bit worn, though. You should take more vitamins and eat fresh fruit, particularly pineapple and kiwi."

I tried to say something, but it was quite incomprehensible once again.

"As though the truth can be hidden. I'll tell you what really happened."

His brow suddenly wrinkled. He stepped back a bit.

"You've got a bit of tartar here. We'll remove it right away so it doesn't put pressure on your gums. Periodontal disease can quickly get the upper hand. You won't feel a thing."

In place of the probe he took up an instrument that resembled a miniature sword with a disproportionately long handle and started to scrape off the tartar.

"He had an argument with the dwarf, that's what happened. They have a strange kind of relationship, if you get my drift. But let's set that aside. In any case, after the argument the dwarf wouldn't tell him about the wooden dummy anymore. To spite him, the painter burned all his paintings. Down to the last one. He almost set the place on fire."

He took the sword out of my mouth. "Rinse, please." He indicated a ceramic glass half filled with water.

I closed my mouth with relief. It felt completely unhinged. I sipped a bit of water and sloshed it about, then spat into the drain on my left.

"When he saw the incinerated paintings, the dwarf fell into a stupor. He still hasn't recovered, and I'm not sure he ever will. She arrived when it was already all over. She tried to help. She gave the dwarf the ball and this revived him somewhat. And just see how the painter returns her favour. He spreads loathsome lies about her. Did he by any chance tell you that she took off her clothes?"

I verified this with a nod, not wanting to open my mouth just yet.

The conductor sighed deeply. "It's simply appalling how ungrateful people can be. And not just anyone, but artists! That's what is so devastating."

He put the instrument on the tray next to the chair, then handed me a napkin.

"You should go to the dentist more often," he said as I wiped my mouth. "Your teeth are in good shape, but at your age you need monthly checkups."

"Most certainly," I agreed.

"All right, we may now proceed." He waited for me to get up, then took off the white coat and threw it over the back of the chair. He rubbed his hands together and headed for the next door.

Since it wasn't closed, he just drew the curtain aside and motioned to me to go in.

When I entered the compartment, four tall girls sitting in the corner seats jumped to their feet. They were wearing camouflage uniforms and dark yellow helmets covered with netting, decorated with leafy twigs. The legs of their loose trousers were rolled up to the middle of the calf, and their feet were in basins full of water.

"Salute!" rang out from the left-hand corner next to the window (whose curtain was drawn).

They raised their clenched fists sharply to the edges of their helmets in salute then quickly dropped their arms to their sides, remaining at attention. We all stood there without moving until I finally realised what was expected of me. I clenched my hand into a fist and saluted in the same way.

"At ease!" resounded from the same place.

The girls' stiff comportment relaxed only a little. They put their hands behind their backs and eased their stance as much as the space in the basins allowed.

"Please sit down!" came the throaty voice of the girl who had issued the orders. She indicated the seat next to her.

After I'd taken my place, the girls sat down too, backs as straight as boards. Their hands were placed on their thighs. They looked straight ahead, at each other.

Their stiffness was of short duration, however. It was interrupted by a new order. "Table!"

The girl to the right of the door got up at once, turned in her basin—without spilling any water—then took a small folding table from the luggage rack above her. She unfolded it skillfully and placed it in front of me, then sat down again. All this took no more than a few moments.

"Tablecloth!"

The girl across from the commander reached toward the storage space under the window and took out a folded orange tablecloth. She shook it open and spread it on the table in front of me. There was no need to adjust its position. Then she added an orange napkin.

"Utensils!"

The girl to my right put her hand under her seat and deftly pulled out a small suitcase. She lifted it effortlessly to her knees and opened it. It was full of various eating utensils. She took out a porcelain plate and put it on the tablecloth. Next came a knife and fork, and then she placed a crystal glass before me. Finally, she took a vase with fresh wildflowers out of a special compartment in the suitcase. This done, in a flash the suitcase was back under the seat.

There was no pause before the commander roared the next order.

"Food!"

Jumping up off her seat as though catapulted, the girl who had taken down the table said all in one breath:

"Infantry cheese in gunpowder eucalyptus sauce, three bayonet olives filled with almond shot, rocket liver commando style!"

"Beverage!"

The girl who had spread out the table cloth stood up and burst out:

"Tank red wine!"

"Recitation!"

Standing up quickly, the girl who had set the table said in a gentle, almost purring voice, "On a spring morning the lady-bug alights on a dandelion."

All three sat down as one. Once again I needed a bit of time to figure out what I was supposed to do. I turned to my left and saluted again with a clenched fist. A brass gong and wooden hammer appeared out of somewhere in the commander's hands. The gong rang out.

As though he had been waiting outside the compartment, the conductor marched inside. He was carrying a large tray with a dome-shaped cover, and he had a large white napkin thrown over his arm. He stopped at the table and gave a brief bow. Then he bent over slightly and took hold of the handle on the top of the cover. Just as he was raising it we entered a tunnel.

This time the darkness was not complete. A bit of light came in from the corridor, under the three-quarters-closed curtain. Even so, I didn't see what was under the cover, because the conductor's bulky figure blocked most of the faint light.

He, however, didn't seem bothered by the darkness. He put the cover on the empty seat across from me and served my food with skillful movements. Then he filled my glass from a small wine bottle that was also on the tray.

I felt for the knife and fork. I had just managed to get hold of something soft on the plate, when the recitation began. I stopped the fork halfway to my mouth.

The poem was short. Some sort of haiku. The sun that has just risen illuminates a yellow flower. Enchanted, the ladybug settles down on it. The gentle breeze ripples the water of a nearby lake. The conductor spoke three verses with great élan and excitement, almost in ecstasy. Like a real actor. I lowered my fork after the first verse, so I was able to applaud heartily when it was over. I expected the girls to join in, too. It might not have been according to protocol, but the poem, I thought, could not have failed to affect them. It must have touched even the most hardened military heart. Instead of applause, however, what followed was the exact opposite.

First there was a giggle, and then a guffaw. Soon the whole compartment was echoing and probably the corridor too. I couldn't see the conductor's face in the dark, but it wasn't hard to imagine how he felt. I thought I heard his sobs through what were now waves of laughter as he removed the plate full of food in front of me and the glass full of wine. He put them on the tray and covered them. He turned on his heels, then marched sharply out of the compartment, accompanied by shrieking and mocking, unseemly exclamations.

When the curtain closed behind him, we came out of the tunnel. With the light back, silence reigned as though by unspoken order. The girls, who had been howling a moment before, were once again sitting like statues, hands on their thighs, faces serious, eyes gazing straight ahead.

"Clear!" The sharp order broke the silence.

It was all done in a trice, with well-practised moves. One girl picked up the utensils and put them back in the suitcase, another took the tablecloth and napkin, folded them and put them in the storage space under the window, and the third folded the table and put it on the luggage rack, once again without spilling a drop of water from the basins.

They did not return to their seats after finishing their tasks. Once the table was removed, the commander stood up.

"Salute!"

Four fists sped to the helmets, then dropped to the side.

I didn't have to figure out what to do anymore. The reception was over. I got up but did not return their salute. It was against regulations, but I had to let them know what I thought of their outburst. I was boiling with anger.

I had just turned to leave the compartment when whistles echoed all around me. I couldn't imagine that women, even in uniform, could whistle so loudly. And then, as though this weren't enough, when I reached the door I was hit by a flurry of drops. There was no need to turn around to see where the water for this shower had come from. Striving to preserve my dignity, I passed through the curtain with head held high. The chorus of whistles went silent the same moment.

The conductor was waiting for me in the corridor. Instead of a tray and napkin he was now holding a tailor's measuring tape. He was wearing only his vest, and out of its shallow pockets poked scissors, blue chalk, and a small notepad with a pencil. Attached to the sleeve above his left wrist was a pincushion filled with pins.

He opened his arms wide. "What can I say? Outrageous impertinence! And simply because you didn't join them in poking fun at me."

"But why did they do that?"

"Ah, why. Because of the chocolate basin, that's why."

"Chocolate basin?"

"That's right. If you will allow me."

He put the end of the measuring tape by the knot of my tie. "Might I ask you to hold this here?"

I pressed on the semicircle of metal with my thumb. The conductor knelt in front of me and stretched out the tape. He took hold of it at the place where it touched the floor, then got up. He looked at the measured length, took the little notebook and pencil and made a brief note.

"The chocolate basin is the insignia of their regiment. It had been entrusted to their safekeeping. But they didn't look after it."

"They didn't?"

"No. Now, let's see the width."

He went behind me and stretched the measuring tape from one shoulder to the other, then wrote another number in the notebook.

"No-one else is to blame. Did anyone force them to bet? No, of course not. But you know what military minds are like. They think that no-one can beat them. Please be so kind as to stretch out your arm."

He measured from under my arm to the end of my sleeve. A third note went into the notebook.

"They were convinced they would easily win the bet.

Could anyone outdo them in drinking wine? And a woman to boot? Not on your life! Allow me."

He opened up my jacket, then put the tape measure around my waist. He shook his head, looking at the number.

"You should pay better attention to your weight. It's much easier to put it on than take it off. Can you imagine how many bottles they drank?"

"I can't."

"Twenty-six! Believe it or not! Without eating anything. So much wine on an empty stomach!"

"Unbelievable!"

"I wouldn't have believed it if I hadn't served them myself. I tried to warn them that it would not end well, but all in vain. Who has ever brought unruly soldiers to their senses? They were disdainfully dismissive and simply ordered a new round. And afterward, when they lost, they blamed me."

"You?"

"Yes, me. Allegedly I'd put something in the wine. As if that's possible. And what reason would I have to do that? Go on, you tell me."

"None."

"None, of course. But they had to find a scapegoat. Let's see your trousers. Spread your legs a little, please."

I did as I was told. The conductor measured the inner leg, then wrote it down.

"There. Now we have all your measurements. In any case, if there had been something in the wine it would have affected her too. They drank out of the same bottle. But she remained fully conscious, whilst the girls finally passed out after the twenty-sixth bottle."

"Who wouldn't? That much wine would kill a lot of people."

"That's right. When they came to, instead of the chocolate basin they found their feet in tin basins. And that's not all. The bet says they can't take them out until they learn at least one haiku by heart."

"Only one?"

"Yes. But they won't, not for anything in the world. They

would rather keep their feet in the basins indefinitely. For the sake of their pride."

"That sounds more like stubbornness to me."

"Exactly. You put your finger on it. Stubbornness, no doubt about it. And hypocritical stubbornness to boot. And do you know why?"

"No, I don't."

"Because they're pretending. Long ago they learnt by heart that haiku about the ladybug and the dandelion, but they just won't admit it."

"Is that so?"

"Clear as day. They always request that I recite the same one. I've repeated it so many times that probably the seats in the compartment have memorised it, let alone four bright, perceptive girls. They don't take just anyone into the women's units. There is a strict selection process. After all, there are only three verses. But instead of repeating the haiku with me and freeing themselves from the humiliating act of keeping their feet in a basin, they would rather make vicious fun of me. So be it. It certainly isn't easy for me, but they are the ones who pay the price. What shade would you like?"

"Excuse me?"

"What shade of fabric? For your suit."

"Oh." I thought it over briefly. "White."

"An excellent choice. Many people wrongly consider that only a dark suit is appropriate for formal occasions, but that is a mistaken belief, of course. There is nothing more elegant than a white suit, particularly when the lighting is weak. You always stand out. What kind of lapels would you like, narrow or wide?"

This time I didn't hesitate. "Wide."

The conductor applauded. "Excellent. There is nothing as telling as a man's lapels. Narrow lapels are worn only by the narrow of mind, those with hidebound views, miserly and malign, and disposed to gout, whilst a man of the world is recognised above all by his wide lapels. Congratulations."

He stretched out his hand with the tape measure thrown over it and we shook hands firmly.

"All right, now let's move on." He headed toward the fifth compartment.

He opened the door without knocking and stuck his head through the curtain. I didn't hear him say anything. He soon pulled his head out and motioned me in with his hand. "If you please."

There were three passengers in the compartment. A young nurse in a white uniform was sitting on the left, next to the curtained window. Blonde curls tumbled from under her white cap. There was a healthy, ripe look to her. Across from her sat an old man and woman holding hands, their heads drawn together. I'd never seen people as old as they were. They had completely wrinkled skin, inflamed eyes, very thin hair, and they were stooped. The frozen smiles on their faces looked like death masks.

As soon as the door closed, the nurse stood up and came over to me. Before I knew what was happening, she raised the bag she was holding way up high and sprinkled confetti all over my head. Then she clapped gaily.

"Happy birthday! Happy birthday!"

I stood there in bewilderment a few moments, sprinkled with multicoloured paper flakes. "Whose birthday?"

"The gentleman's, of course," she said, indicating the old man.

"Oh," I replied, then bowed to him. "Happy birthday, sir."

The two old folks just kept on smiling. The nurse returned to her seat, swaying her hips. She pointed to the spot next to her. "Have a seat."

Before I sat down, I shook off a bit of the confetti. Only then did I notice that the carpet runner was practically covered with it.

"I'm sorry, I didn't know. Otherwise I would have brought a present, to be sure."

"It doesn't matter. The important thing is that you came. It means a lot to both of them." She looked at them tenderly.

"My pleasure." I bowed once again.

"How old do you think he is?"

I shrugged my shoulders. "Really, I wouldn't know."

"One hundred and seventy-six!"

"One hundred and seventy-six?" I said, aghast.

"That's right. Although you'd never say so. He looks at least thirty-five years younger, doesn't he?"

The nurse winked at me.

"Why, of course," I hastened to agree. "At least. Actually, I wouldn't think him more than one hundred twenty-eight and a half!"

"I thank you for the compliment in his name." The nurse smiled, and dimples appeared at the corners of her mouth. "If you're interested, I'll tell you what he has to thank for his longevity."

"Of course I'm interested," I said without a moment's hesitation.

"The time he spent in prison."

"In prison?"

"Yes. He spent exactly one hundred and six years, eight months, eleven days and two hours in prison. He was sentenced to life in prison, but was recently released for good behaviour."

"If I'm not being unduly inquisitive, why was he sentenced to such a long punishment?"

"He ate his first wife."

I swallowed the lump in my throat. "Ate?"

"That's right. Not all at once, of course. Over seventy-six days. This was taken as a mitigating circumstance during the trial, otherwise he might have been sent to the gallows. But please don't ask me anything else about that ghastly event. Talking about it always upsets him, and that's not good for his weak heart. In any case, he has completely paid his debt to society."

I looked at the old man across from me. It seemed that nothing could cloud the cheerful serenity on his face.

"Madam is his second wife, I presume?"

"Yes. They met seventy-two years ago by pigeon carrier mail. She was only eighteen at the time. They exchanged photographs and it was love at first sight. They married in prison not long after."

"Wasn't she bothered by what had put him in prison?" I asked in a low voice.

"Not at all. Love works wonders. She closed her eyes to it. You can imagine how happy she was when she finally saw him free. But this romance wouldn't have had a happy turn if he hadn't become friends with the cook in prison."

"The cook?"

"Yes. He was also in prison, sentenced for the brutal murder of his seven daughters, although he never confessed to the crime. As a young medical corps lieutenant, the cook spent several years as a prisoner of war in the jungle. He barely survived, but he brought an amazing talisman back with him. A glass corkscrew. He received it from a tribal chieftain whose son he'd saved from certain death from a tropical insect bite."

The nurse reached into her pocket and took out a bag of sweets. "Help yourself," she said, holding it out toward me.

"No, thank you, I don't eat sweets."

"Please, it's his birthday, you must help yourself to something."

I took one, but just held it in my hand without unwrapping it.

"The glass corkscrew gives longevity to its owner. The cook, however, decided to kill himself, unable to bear the burden of being unjustly sentenced. Before he poisoned himself, he gave the talisman to the only friend he had in prison."

"Why, that's just like in an old fairy tale."

"Yes, except this one won't have a happy ending."

"It won't?"

"No, he doesn't have the talisman anymore. He certainly won't live to see his next birthday."

"You don't say. And what happened to the glass corkscrew?"

"He gave it away."

"Whom did he give it to?"

The nurse drew a bit closer to me and whispered. "You already know who he gave it to. It's not hard to guess."

"You mean...."

She gave a brief nod. "As soon as she entered our compartment, he took the talisman out of the leather bag he wore at his waist and gave it to her. As though he'd just been waiting for her to appear."

"But why?"

"So that he could die with his wife. Her days are numbered. The doctors don't give her more than three and a half months. They will end their lives together. They have made a vow to die together. Isn't that romantic?"

"Yes, it is."

"A genuine melodrama."

"Truly."

The nurse got up. "Now we must say goodbye. There's a tunnel coming up, and these two don't like to miss any of them. Who can blame them after all the decades of separation and deprivation? They don't have many opportunities left to be intimate."

I got up as well. "Will you stay inside too?" I asked, taken aback.

"Of course. I'm a nurse. They might need my help. At their age such things don't go very smoothly. And my presence won't bother them in the dark."

I bowed toward the snuggling couple. "Goodbye."

"Goodbye," replied the nurse. "They greatly appreciate the fact that you visited them on this of all days. They will never forget you." The dimples appeared at the edges of her mouth again.

I put the sweets in my pocket and went out into the corridor. The conductor was standing in front of the door.

"This way, please." He motioned toward a four-sided canvas screen to my left that looked like a changing booth in a clothes store. It was shoulder high.

I went in between the two sides that were ajar, and he closed them after me. Although it didn't look like it from the outside, there was quite a bit of space within. A white suit was hanging on one wall. A white shirt was draped over it, and on the floor were white shoes and socks.

"You can hand me your clothes over the top, and leave your slippers inside. I'll take care of everything."

I started to undress. "Is this really necessary?"

"Yes, it is. You must be properly dressed."

"What for?"

"For the last compartment, of course."

"Oh, I see." I handed my coat to the conductor.

"Did she mention the cook?"

"Yes."

"That part of the story has the most holes in it."

"Really?"

"Above all, it's not at all certain that he was a prisoner of war, and even less in the jungle."

"You don't say."

"Various rumours about that are making the rounds. The most convincing one to me is the story that he was a missionary to a cannibal desert tribe. And an unsuccessful missionary to boot. Instead of him converting them, they converted him."

"Are you saying…." I handed my shirt and tie over the screen.

"Yes. And I'll tell you one more thing, but in strict confidence. It's quite possible that there was no cook."

"What do you mean?" I asked, taking off my socks and slippers.

"It's quite simple. The missionary was actually the gentleman himself. He returned to civilization with the talisman of longevity, which is all right, but with cannibalistic habits, which certainly is not. Judge for yourself. If that weren't true, why would he have eaten his wife? Whoever would do something like that out of the blue?"

"No-one, I suppose."

"There, you see. I'm telling you, there's something fishy there. Without even mentioning the nurse. With her things become dark and shady."

"What are you saying? I never would have thought...she seemed so good-natured and harmless. She even offered me sweets." I threw my trousers over the top of the screen.

The conductor's face suddenly turned pale. "You didn't eat any, did you?"

"No, I don't like sweets. I put it in my jacket pocket."

"Thank heavens! I forgot to warn you. I'll get rid of it at

once. You can't even imagine what might have happened to you!"

"What?" I took the shirt off the hanger and started to put it on.

"You're better off not knowing. The best thing is to have nothing to do with cannibals."

"The problem is that they want to have something to do with you."

"That's true, unfortunately. I hope the suit looks good on you."

"I'm sure it will." I took the trousers. "The cloth looks first class."

"The best that could be found. It doesn't stain at all, as you will see. In addition, it needs almost no ironing. And it is very soft."

"The trousers aren't tight around my waist. That's very important. I can't stand tight trousers."

"If the measurements are taken properly, the suit should fit like a glove. Many tailors don't take sufficient care and then wonder where they went wrong."

I put on the jacket. "It looks perfect."

"Just wait until you see yourself in a mirror."

I looked over the top of the screen. The conductor was holding a large mirror in front of him.

"Just a moment." I bent down and quickly put on the shoes. They were of very high quality white leather, light and supple. I pushed the side of the screen and came out.

"Wonderful!" exclaimed the conductor, eyeing me from head to toe. "Here, see for yourself."

In the mirror I saw an elegant man, dressed to the nines, who would fit quite nicely into any formal occasion. "Excellent," I concurred.

"Just two more details," said the conductor. He held out a white hat from behind the mirror and then leaned the large oval between two windows in the corridor.

The hat also seemed made to order for me. I nodded my head in satisfaction.

"And here's the bow tie."

It was over his left sleeve, large and white, as was to be expected.

"Allow me." He raised my shirt collar, attached the tie in the back, then lowered the collar. He stepped back a bit and examined me once again.

"There. Now everything is perfect. You are utterly ready."

He led me toward the last compartment. "She only receives when we're in a tunnel," he said, once we had stopped in front of the door.

"But then it's dark."

"Right. In addition, I will have to put a blindfold over your eyes." He took a long band made of white silk out of his right pocket.

"Why is that?"

He tied the band behind my head, underneath the hat. "Because that's the way things are done. It's not too tight, is it?"

"No."

"Can you see anything?"

"No."

"Good. We'll soon be in a tunnel. Be ready. When I give you a push, go inside. Stop right by the door. You will have to stand, unfortunately, because all the places are taken. You won't find that too difficult, will you?"

"No."

There was a brief moment of silence and then the conductor spoke again. His voice was low and pleading.

"If she asks about me...although she won't, of course...why should she, anyway...who am I, after all...but nonetheless...a man mustn't lose hope...what would life be without hope...so, if she mentions me...please tell her that I am here...always...all she has to do is...regardless of everything...nothing else is important except...she is still...tell that to her, I implore you...."

That very moment, he nudged me in the back. I hesitated a bit because I didn't hear the door opening in front of me, but I took a step forward all the same. I stopped after the second step.

"Take off the blindfold." A woman's voice came from my left, somewhat further away. It was soft and lilting.

I untied the knot at the back of my head. When the blindfold fell off, I wasn't in total darkness as I'd expected. The shapes on the five seats were outlined by a weak glow, as if edged by tiny sparks. They were disproportionately large, occupying the same space that passengers would have.

The wax button to my right was hexagonal, with a double ring of holes that flickered with a bluish tinge. The horned egg in the middle had two bent protuberances in its lower part, resembling stunted limbs, with points that seemed to glow. The wooden dummy next to the window had been pierced at the top, and out of the hole flowed drops of liquid fire. The chocolate basin to my left contained something gelatinous and fluorescent. The glass corkscrew on the seat next to it was periodically suffused with short green flashes that seemed to come from somewhere inside. The last seat in the row was the opaque heart of darkness.

"Put the blindfold back on," said the darkness.

I did as I was told.

"What do you see?"

"I don't see anything."

"Take a better look."

I took a better look. "I see an apple that has fallen off a tree."

"What is it like?"

"Large, green, and juicy."

"Put it back on the tree."

"Put it back?"

"Yes. Apples should be on trees, shouldn't they?"

I held it up to a branch and it clung to it as though drawn by a magnet.

"Doesn't it look nice there?"

"Lovely."

"And now look again."

"I see the figure of a black queen."

"What is her hair like?"

"Long and red. Wavy."

"Stroke it."

I shook my head. "I don't dare."

"Don't hold back. She will enjoy it."

I gently drew my hand over the cascades. The queen lit up with joy and ran forward.

"What a light step she has."

"As though she's not even touching the ground."

"Look once again."

"I see a large purple ball."

"Throw it up into the air."

"Into the air?"

"Yes. Don't worry, nothing will happen to it."

I threw it up. The ball started changing colour as it got smaller and smaller. The purple turned to turquoise, the turquoise to blue, the blue to white, the white turned colourless.

"Did it disappear?"

"No, it's still going up. You have set it free. What do you see now?"

"I see a yellow flower."

"What is on the yellow flower?"

"A ladybug."

"Blow on it softly."

"But I'll frighten it."

"No, you won't. Ladybugs love air currents."

I blew a little puff toward the ladybug. As though set in motion by a breeze rippling the water of a lake, it spread its wings and fluttered off.

"Isn't it gracious?"

"Like a ballerina."

"Look one last time."

"I see the bars on a prison door."

"Pull them apart."

"How can I pull steel bars apart?"

"It's not at all hard. Try."

I flexed my muscles, but no effort was needed. The bars gave way as though made of rubber and stayed apart.

"That is your way out."

"My way out?"

"Yes. Go through the opening."

"Now?"

"Now. Everything has been done."

I had already started to pull myself through when I remembered something. I turned toward the heart of darkness.

"What about the conductor?"

"Tell him not to lose hope. That's what is most important."

"That will make him very happy," I said, beaming.

"I know," replied the melodic voice.

On the other side of the bars I was still in darkness. Then I felt someone's hand on the back of my head, and the white silk blindfold fell off my eyes. Squinting, I saw before me the space at the end of the carriage. To the left was the door leading to the back platform and to the right was the clothes closet.

"If you please," said the conductor, stepping in front of me. In his left hand was a medium-sized brown leather suitcase. "Everything is neatly packed inside. The laundry has been washed, the suit ironed, the shoes polished, the hat brushed, and the coat dry-cleaned. There was a stain in the lining that wouldn't come out any other way."

"I am extremely grateful. How much do I owe you for all you've done for me? This wonderful suit, too, and I must finally pay for the ticket."

"Think nothing of it! Any payment is out of the question. It was an honour to be of service."

I held out my hand. "Thank you once again from the bottom of my heart."

We shook hands, but he held onto mine.

"Did she say anything, perhaps?" he said in a small voice.

"Oh, it almost slipped my mind. Yes, she said not to lose hope, that's what is most important."

The conductor suddenly fell to his knees before me. He brought my hand to his lips and kissed it. I tried to pull it away, but he wouldn't let go. He pressed his cheek against it.

"I knew it...as soon as I saw you...your kindness...it was all so clear to me...no-one else...would she otherwise...just how much..."

His voice faded into sobbing. I felt my hand turn wet and stopped trying to pull it free.

The conductor stayed in that position a little longer, and

then seemed to come out of his daze. He abruptly let go of my hand, got up, and wiped the tears off his face with his fingertips.

"Please excuse me. A moment of weakness. It will not be repeated. You surely understand, I hope?"

I nodded. "Certainly."

"Good. Now, unfortunately the time has come to say goodbye. It always comes, there's nothing to be done. Such is the life of a conductor. Meetings and farewells. I believe that in spite of everything you had a nice time with us."

"I had a very nice time."

He handed me the suitcase, then unlocked the door and motioned toward the platform. I went out onto it and he followed behind.

We stood there facing each other for several moments. It seemed as if one of us might say something else, but when this didn't happen I smiled, bowed, and descended to the station platform.

Editor Biography

Lavie Tidhar is the author of the linked-story collection *HebrewPunk,* novellas *An Occupation of Angels, Cloud Permutations,* and *Gorel & The Pot-Bellied God.* With Nir Yaniv, he co-authored the short novel *The Tel Aviv Dossier*. Lavie has also edited the anthologies *A Dick & Jane Primer for Adults* and *The Apex Book of World SF*. He's lived on three continents and one island-nation, and currently lives in South East Asia. He maintains a web presence at www.lavietidhar.co.uk.

Artist Biography

Randall MacDonald is a trained classical painter with degrees in Art and Art History. He has been a successful illustrator, designer and art director for a wide variety of clients and projects. Randall is also an accomplished director with over 400 commercials to his credit, with clients such as McDonalds, IBM, and Proctor and Gamble. He has received numerous international and national awards for his creative work and he looks at every project as a new challenge and a chance to improve and learn more about his craft. For more information visit web.me.com/randymacdonaldart/Site_27/Front.html.

HebrewPunk

Popular short fiction writer Lavie Tidhar gathers some of his best work in one collection. Stories that are infused with centuries of tradition and painted with Hebrew mythology.

"Lavie Tidhar has staked out (no pun intended) his own territory by imagining a Judaic mystical alternative history into which he injects vampires, zombies, werewolves, Tzaddiks, golems, and Rabbis. These four stories are wondrous, adventurous, and thought-provoking."

– **Ellen Datlow**, co-editor of The Year's Best Fantasy and Horror

"Imagine Hard-Boiled Kabbalah, a Godfather Rabbi whose gang includes vampires, werewolves and (naturally) golems. If you like your otherworld fun noir, have I got a book for you!"

– **Kage Baker**, author of *In the Garden of Iden*

ISBN: 978-0978867645
www.apexbookcompany.com

Breinigsville, PA USA
26 January 2010
231379BV00002B/1/P